MW00778494

Crss my heart ♡

xo-

Cambria

SOME MEMORIES ARE
BETTER OFF FORGOTTEN.

AMNESIA

Hebert

CAMBRIA HEBERT

ISBN: 978-1-946836-03-8

This is a work of fiction. Names, characters, places, and incidents either are the product of the author's imagination or are used fictitiously, and any resemblance to actual persons, living or dead, business establishments, events, or locales, is entirely coincidental.

Cover design by Cover Me Darling
Edited by Cassie McCown
Interior Design by Cover Me Darling
Formatting by Athena Interior Book Design

Published by: Cambria Hebert
http://www.cambriahebert.com

AMNESIA

CAMBRIA HEBERT

I washed ashore in a little lake town.

A place where everyone knows everyone, yet...

No one knows me.

I don't know me.

If a woman doesn't know her own name, does she really exist?

I don't know my natural hair color, my birthdate, or where I live.

I am invisible.

To everyone, to everything, even to myself.

Except to him.

I see the recognition deep in his stare, the way it lingers on my face as if I'm a puzzle he's desperate to put together.

I just want answers, the truth... knowledge.

His lips are sealed. Still, his eyes beguile me.

I can't trust anyone, not even myself. Someone wants me dead, the same someone who tried to bury me in a watery grave.

They'll come for me again... I won't know their face.

I don't even know mine.

I am amnesia.

for Kaydence
You inspire me.

CHAPTER ONE

EDWARD

The water called. Like a siren on a foggy night, singing beautifully to lonely boaters, luring them closer. Promising companionship but ultimately dragging them deep into the dark depths until life faded away and the onyx, cavernous water swallowed them completely.

The lake at night was an eerie place. The sound of the water lapping softly against the pebbly shores, the damp scent of the air, and how the sky seemed so much closer to man because of the way thick fog hung low, skimming over the ever-bobbing surface. Those things weren't necessarily eerie to some, but they evoked a darkness within me. A mood always lurking beneath the surface, beneath the ready smile I wore for people on the street or members of my own family.

Though the mood was unpleasant, I couldn't stay away. It was a strange sort of addiction, at times an intense craving. They say those with a dependence are only addicted because they get something out of it.

Whatever it is they crave fills a need, satisfies some kind of void in their lives.

It was true. At least for me.

Besides the sound of swaying water and a steady breeze, it was quiet down here, save for the occasional call of a bird or the repetitious croaks of frogs. The shoreline was usually vacant when I walked along because usually it was dark, well past the hours of socialization. The side of the lake I was drawn to most was less populated. Night parties and bonfires, parking and necking took place on the other side, where there was more of a beach.

I preferred the seclusion of this shore, the way my thoughts went undisturbed in solitude. Thoughts and memories to be exact. How something so long ago could be so innately ingrained in my mind was sort of eerie in itself. Details that should have faded over time, feelings people said would dull to the point they would merely be background noise.

Lies.

People were ignorant, talking about things they knew nothing about. I let them entertain their obliviousness. After all, it was easier. For them and for me.

The bottoms of my feet were almost desensitized to the uneven, sometimes jagged pebbles. I never walked with shoes down here. I preferred the cold, boney fingers of the water, when it washed up over my foot, momentarily swallowing my skin. I felt a sort of kinship with the rocks underfoot, the way they sat haphazardly, always keeping me slightly off balance… But oddly, the unbalance made me feel more stable.

The end of summer was drawing close. Soon, this small, touristy lake town would grow quieter. The autumn breeze would bring in a crisp chill, and the year-long residents would close in ranks around one another, creating a community so tight it was almost suffocating.

A wind colder than those before wrapped around me, ruffling the hair around my ears and whipping it into my eye. Instead of pushing it out, I turned my face, gazing out at the wide expanse of the lake. The still-blowing wind tugged the hair out of my eyes and pulled it back off my face completely.

Fingertips beginning to sting a bit against the cold as the water lapped over my bare toes, I shoved both hands deep into my white jeans. My fingers curled into my palms. I stood stock still, water soaking into my ankles, wind pushing and pulling at my hair and clothes. It was dark, fog hanging low, and the stars and moon were lost in the night. Even still, I could make out the shape of the island that seemed to always float on the surface of the lake about a mile from shore.

I didn't know how big the island really was. No one did. No one ever went there; no one was ever invited. All I knew was the way it appeared to float was an illusion, because if it had truly been floating, it would have drifted off years ago… but it remained.

Chained in place by roots and earth that likely reached far down into the bed of the water, creating an anchor only Mother Nature herself could provide.

The island and the house built upon it was a mystery. And so was the person who lived there.

Everyone here in Loch liked to speculate about that island. Rumors and theories swirled. Whispers floated through the streets, especially when the woman who lived out there came to town on a rare supply run.

I heard all the speculation but kept my own to myself. If I did speak up, I wouldn't be able to explain how my eyes always wandered to that unsettling mound of land shrouded by fully mature trees and distance.

Another gust of strong wind blew in from the side, pushing in even thicker fog, creating an opaque shroud and blocking what small view I had of the island's outline. It felt as if someone had drawn a curtain over a window I'd been trying to peer into.

Water splashed up my calves, drenching my jeans, weighing down the fabric. Ignoring it, I turned, hands still tucked deep in my pants, and half walked, half waded through the shallow water farther down the shore.

I should go. The sliver of time I allowed myself to spend down here each night was over, yet the pull tonight was even stronger, almost painful, and it kept my feet anchored on the coast. Tucking my head toward my chest, I settled into a slow, wandering gait.

I felt as though the wind pushed me along, and though I had muscle, I was powerless against its insistence. As I walked, I noted the way my pants seemed to glow in the dark, no less bright even at the bottom where they were drenched.

Memories washed up the back of my throat, or maybe it was what would have been. Whatever it was tasted slightly salty even though the lake water was fresh. I told myself (only because it took years of conditioning to form the argument) I had no way of knowing what might have been because it was ripped away... or rather buried somewhere out there in thirty-five miles of water.

Wallowing in the water but also in thought, I moved along, not noticing how the fog wrapped around me like a sick hug. An odd feeling crawled up the back of my neck, tightening the muscles and creating a rippling chill. My feet stopped, but the movement of the wind and water made me feel as if I were still moving.

Not far in front of me but a little farther from shore, something bobbed in the waves. Blinking, thinking it was only a trick of the mind or maybe of the lake itself, I gazed that way again.

A light swell brought the pale-colored shape forward, then gently pulled it back as if it weren't sure whether the water wanted to keep the object or give it up.

Starting forward, my eyes remained trained on the object, still expecting it to fade away or break apart in the water, but it never did.

The closer I splashed, the harder my heart thumped in my chest. A sick feeling unfurled in my lower belly, sloshing around like two-day-old alcohol, and threatened to reappear at a moment's notice.

The saliva in my throat was thick and oddly dry as I forced it down. What appeared to be a strand of hair, light enough in color it contrasted with the dark water, seemed to reach out toward me, as if it were reaching out for help.

I started running. The silence of the night completely disrupted by the sounds of heavy splashing and the ominous way the water sucked at my pants, trying to hold me back.

"Hello!" I called out, half bent now, using my arms to cut through the water.

It was farther out than I first suspected. Another trick of the lake.

An intense sense of urgency hurled in my veins, causing me to drop into the water in a swimming position.

I was oblivious to the chilled temperature of the lake, the way in which the black water tried to swallow me whole. My arms and legs cut through like a hot knife in butter, and in just moments that seemed to feel like a lifetime, I had reached where the body floated.

There was a body floating in the lake. Drifting ashore like a piece of lifeless garbage.

Closing my hand around a thin and too-cold arm, I used all the adrenaline coiled inside me to yank the body close.

Pale skin collided with mine as I forced myself to my feet, slipping a little on the uneven, muddy floor of the lake. When I was fully upright, the water came only to my waist. Hefting the body above the surface, my limbs shook with cold and fear as I fumbled to cradle it in my arms.

It was so very dark, the fog like a shield, and I was focused on getting ashore. I barely glanced down at the unresponsive body. It was a woman. The knowledge threatened to thrust me back in time, but I fought it even though part of me wanted to go back there.

"It could be a child," I told myself out loud, hoping the sound of my own voice would anchor me.

No. I didn't want it to be a child. Not because I was some stellar guy with a hero complex and children were the most innocent victims of all. It was because I wanted it to be someone else.

Someone I knew it couldn't possibly be. Someone who was long gone and was never coming back.

My feet stumbled when I bolted out of the water and into the too-long grass, but I didn't fall. Instead, I dropped to my knees and laid the body before me.

Long strands of hair stuck to her face, concealing all her features. Sediment from the lake clung to her skin, and her clothing was ripped and practically see-through.

"Can you hear me!" I yelled. "Hey!"

Her face was turned away, something I couldn't bear. Water ran down my face, dripped off my lashes, and clung to my clothes. Wiping the offending drops out of my line of sight, I made a muffled sound, grasping her chin between my long fingers.

I turned her face toward mine, holding on firmly, and brushed all the wet strands from her face.

Emotion so raw slammed into me I nearly fell back. The only thing that held me upright was the grip I still had on her chin.

Not even a hit that had my stomach roiling and vomit splashing up into the back of my throat was strong enough to make my fingers let go.

Hungrily I stared at her face until I saw the blue tint to her lips.

"No!" The word ripped out of me as if I were being tortured. Moving fast, I tilted her chin back, swept the inside of her mouth with my finger, and began CPR. I lost count of how many compressions I applied to her chest. My mind was scrambled, and the more I looked into her prone face, the more frantic I became.

Giving up, I grasped her face and blew a breath into her waiting airways. When she did nothing, I blew into her again.

It took immense mental power to rip away and begin chest compressions a second time. Just when I was about to really lose my shit, the sound of water bubbling up inside her brought me back.

Thinking fast, I turned the woman to her side as lake water spewed from her mouth and her back worked extraneously to expel it all.

When I was sure she was empty, I laid her flat. Her breathing was extremely shallow, her eyes still closed. Oxygen seemed to scrape like broken glass down her throat, making me fearsome. Tilting her head back, I gave her two more strong breaths.

They seemed to force some much-needed air into her system, and then the ragged inhalations she took seemed not quite as dire.

Practically climbing on top of her, I palmed her face. "Can you hear me?" I yelled. "Wake up! Are you okay?"

Nothing.

Her body was so limp I began to shake again.

"Shit!" I growled, scrambling up and lifting her into my arms. Her body was frail and her skin still almost translucent. My heart nearly stopped when she fell into my chest, and I gazed down at her face.

"It couldn't be." I reminded myself. Then, as I turned toward where I parked my truck, I repeated, "It's not."

A ragged, painful-sounding gasp scraped by her lips. I stiffened as her body moved just slightly. Her eyelids fluttered, struggling to open.

"Can you hear me?" I asked, desperate.

Her eyes collided with mine. I gasped, nearly falling. A name I hadn't spoken in so long it sounded foreign to my own ears cut through the sound of my pounding heart and uneven breathing.

Her eyes drifted once more, refusing to open again.

I started to run, using my familiarity with this place as a GPS. Sight wouldn't be useful right now because my eyes were incapable of looking at anything but her face.

It wasn't her.

But oh my God, what if it was?

CHAPTER TWO

AMNESIA

Slivers of light pricked my eyelids, which up until this moment seemed far too heavy to lift. As I lay against something soft at my back, thought and awareness barely registered.

The gritty feeling as I struggled to raise my eyelids scraped and burned over my eyeballs as if warning me it wasn't a good idea. Swallowing past the sandpaper in my throat, I stopped working and lay still. Cognizance slowly came forward in the form of something weighing me down and the echo of footsteps nearby.

Adrenaline jackknifed through me, and my body arched upward with the force of my gasp. The weight of whatever held me caused severe panic to fill me, and I began to fight against it.

"No!" I screamed, flailing about, trying to escape the binds. "Let me go!"

High-pitched beeping filled my ears, and the footsteps I'd heard grew more insistent and much closer.

He was coming!

"No!" I screamed.

Strong hands grabbed my arms and pinned me down. I tried to fight back, but they were much stronger than me. Kicking my legs, I tried to free them, but even more weight came down, holding them still until I was gasping for breath and ready to beg.

"Please!" I pleaded as wetness coated my cheeks. It made me realize the grittiness under my lids was rinsed away, and my eyes sprang open.

A man was leaning over me. He had graying hair and wore some kind of white shirt. The scream that ripped right out of me scared us both.

More hands and voices came out of nowhere, and I thrashed around again.

"Miss!" the man yelled. "Miss, calm down."

"Get away from me!" I screamed again.

"Miss!" another voice yelled, a woman this time. Turning in her direction, I saw a pair of kind brown eyes staring at me. "We aren't trying to hurt you."

I calmed some, but the thundering of my heart made me feel as if I might spiral out of control. "You aren't?"

"No." The woman, who was also dressed in white, spoke. "You're at a hospital. You were in an accident."

"W-what?" I stammered, collapsing back against the bed, no longer straining against the binds.

"You're at a hospital."

"You're trying to hold me down!" I accused.

"We don't want you to hurt yourself." the woman explained. The hands, even the man's, remained.

"I don't like it," I admitted, recoiling.

The man straightened, stepping back. The nurse was slower to withdraw, but she did so after a few seconds.

"My legs," I rasped. Suddenly, my throat hurt.

"It's just the blankets."

A quick glance down proved I was covered with blankets. Between suspicious glances at the people crowding my room (there were four), I gazed around, concluding I was in fact in a hospital.

"I don't understand," I admitted, all my weight pressing into the bed.

"It's okay," the man replied. He was a doctor, with a name badge and a stethoscope. "It's completely normal and expected to be confused after the ordeal you've been through."

"What ordeal?" I asked instantly, anxiety pressing in on my ribcage.

"We were hoping you could tell us," the doctor said.

"What?" My brows furrowed.

The nurse leaned close, over the side of the bed. I noticed the railings were pulled up on each side. It made me feel as if I were in jail. Instantly, I hated it and began shoving at the bars, trying to push them down.

"Okay, hang on," the nurse said and put the rails down. Once it was done, she pinned me with an insistent stare. "You have to stay still. You can't thrash around. You'll rip out your IV and reinjure yourself."

"What happened to me?" I asked for what felt like the fifteenth time. I looked around at the four people in the room, hoping one of them would just spit it out.

The doctor motioned to two of the nurses and then quietly left the room.

I glanced back at the nurse. "Can you tell us your name?" she asked.

"My name?" I nodded once, then opened my mouth... only nothing came out.

Anxiety spiked in me again; I started to become agitated. "I... don't know."

"Calm down." The nurse reminded me.

How dare she tell me to calm down? I couldn't even remember my name.

Oh my God, I didn't know my own name!

"I don't remember!" I gasped, jerking up into a sitting position. "Why can't I remember?"

Before I could fling the covers off and jump out of bed, the doctor was there, pinning me back down. "If you don't calm down, we'll have to sedate you. I don't want to do that. You've been out long enough."

I stilled. "How long?"

"A while." The nurse hedged.

I ignored her. She was terrible with questions. "How long?" I demanded.

"A little over two months," the doctor replied.

I gasped. "What's my name?" I yelled.

I'd been here for two months and they were asking for my name? Shouldn't they know it?

The doctor wasn't looking at me; he was looking at the nurse, giving her a curt nod. She rushed out of the room.

"No!" I shouted. "No drugs! Please! Tell me my name. I just want to know my name."

"You need to calm down. You've had a great deal of trauma, miss."

I dropped back against the pillow, boneless. He called me miss. "You don't know my name, do you?" I asked, meek.

Sensing all my energy was drained away, he moved back. A frown pulled at his lips. "You were brought in with no identification." He began.

Fear unlike anything I'd ever felt wrapped around my heart and squeezed. I searched every corner of my mind for something. Anything.

There was nothing.

"I don't remember…" I whispered.

The doctor seemed to soften. "I know this must be very scary, to wake up and be so disoriented."

I laughed, but it wasn't a humorous sound. I wished I were disoriented right then.

"You've been through a lot. Give it a few days. Now that you're awake, your mind will catch up and you will remember."

"I will?" I asked.

"There's a good chance."

Disappointment speared me. "If I don't?"

"Let's take it one day at a time." He placated me.

"Easy for you to say. You know your name."

A ghost of a smile appeared on his face. "Time." He reminded me.

The nurse came through the door, holding a syringe, and I cringed away.

"I don't think we're going to need that," the doctor told her.

I let out an audible sigh.

He glanced around again. "Now that you're awake, I'll get you down for testing."

"What kind of testing?" I asked.

"Routine stuff for someone who's been in a coma."

Nothing about this was routine. I was in coma… for *two* months. And I didn't even know my name.

When both the nurse and doctor were gone and I was alone, my eyes overflowed with tears and a formidable feeling of dread crowded inside me. The doctor said there was "a good chance" I would remember my name very soon.

The problem was it wasn't just my name I needed to remember…

It was everything.

CHAPTER THREE

EDWARD

Lake living was slow paced, especially small-town lake living. I didn't mind it much. In fact, I liked it. It was one of the reasons I never left as I'd planned to all those years ago.

Lately, things hadn't been just slow; they'd pretty much halted. The days were endless, the nights even worse. Inside, I paced all the time, even when my body stood still. It was amazing how exhausting waiting could be.

The store was in top shape, though. Without anything left to do, I put my agitation into organizing and updating the place.

The familiar scent of a brown paper bag wafted up toward my nostrils when I lifted it off the stack and shook it out. The sound it made was also very familiar. After packing the contents from the counter into the bag, I ripped off the receipt and slipped it inside with the purchases.

"Have a good day, Mrs. Grady," I told the woman as she picked up her stuff.

"Thank you, Eddie. See you next week."

The second the bell sounded and the door closed behind her, I leaned back against the long counter and rubbed the back of my neck. Just a couple more hours 'til closing time. By experience, I knew there would likely be a last-minute "rush" of people who were hurrying to get what they needed before I closed for the night and maybe a few travelers getting supplies before heading back to wherever they came from.

After I locked up, I would hit the gym and then swing by the hospital, even though it probably would be the same as the day before.

Against my upper thigh, my cell began to vibrate. Reaching beneath my apron, I fished out the phone, recognizing the number of the hospital. My pulse and breath quickened.

"Yeah?" I said into the phone, sounding as if I'd just left the gym, not just been standing here behind a register.

"It's Mary Beth," the woman on the other end said. Her voice was hushed and her words quick.

"What's happened?" I asked, straightening and glancing at the door. I didn't bother to tell her she didn't need to tell me her name when she called.

"She's awake," the nurse whispered.

The hand not holding the phone slammed down on the wooden countertop, making a sharp slapping sound. "When?"

"Just a few minutes ago. The doctor's still with her. She'll be going for tests if she stays awake."

"Is something wrong?" I demanded, the words harsh. "Why wouldn't she?"

"I don't know. I'm not a doctor."

"What aren't you saying?" I ground out anxiously.

"She was very agitated. Screaming her head off."

Without another word, I leapt over the counter to land on the other side. "I'll be there in a few."

"No!" Mary Beth whisper-yelled.

"Why are you even whispering?" I said, moving with intent through one of the aisles toward the back of the store. "You know damn well everyone who heard her screaming is on the phone, loose tongues wagging."

"They won't let you back to see her, even if she is awake. The tests and—"

"Thanks for the info, Mary B." I cut her off. "You're my favorite nurse at that old stitch shack."

I heard her begin to laugh, but I cut the connection before she could say anything else. I didn't care. The door banged against the wall when I shoved into the back room. My apron hit the table, and I snatched my keys off the hook on the wall.

I still had two hours 'til closing time. I'd already let Brian go home early, something I was regretting right about now.

She's awake. Finally. It seemed like forever since I'd barged into the ER with her that night, yelling for a doctor and reluctantly surrendering her to a gurney.

At first, they kept me out of her room, claiming I had no right to be there. I wasn't a relative or next of kin, so it was against policy to allow my admittance.

After a few days of obeying, I stopped. I'd wait until no one was around and sneak into her room undetected. For a few nights at least. One night, I fell asleep in the chair I'd pulled right beside her bed, and the nurse found me.

I'd gotten a stern lecture out in the hall after she dragged me out by my ear, and they told me if I did it again, they'd call the cops.

The cops didn't scare me. It was pretty much a laughable threat. Hell, I'd gone to school with half the force. Still, I heeded their warnings and instead set up camp in the waiting room down the hall.

After a couple more weeks, the nurses began to soften, as did the doctors. I didn't know if it was me they softened toward or her. I didn't care. All I knew was one night, Mary Beth came into the waiting room and motioned me back down the hall.

"She should have somebody," Mary Beth told me right outside her door. "And you're the only one…"

I grabbed the handle to let myself inside. Mary Beth grabbed my arm. Her words were gentle. "Eddie. It's just not possible," she'd said, not wanting to be cruel, but also trying yet again to talk sense into me.

I paused mere moments longer, allowing her words to sink in before I started forward again and slipped into the room.

After that night, I visited her every day. Mostly in the evening, but sometimes earlier. I always came when it rained. Always.

The moments I spent in her room were the only ones that didn't drag since I'd pulled her out of the water. Those were the minutes that ticked by incredibly too fast, speeding toward the time I had to peel myself out of the chair at her bedside and go back to waiting for the next time I was beside her again.

More time passed. She remained unchanged. I went anyway, waiting for this day to come. Waiting for her eyes to open. Waiting for answers.

Back out in the store, I jogged toward the wide, wooden entrance doors and flipped the open sign to closed. We were just going to have to close early tonight. Some of the townies were going to be good and mad, like Scarlet Welding, one of the oldest residents here and definitely one of the spunkiest.

She came in every day before closing to buy herself a fresh green apple. It was her nightly snack with a cup of hot tea. She refused to buy a sack of apples, instead walking to the store each evening to get just one.

With a curse, I raced back inside, grabbed a small paper sack, plucked a plump, shiny green apple off the top of the pile, and dropped it in the bag. On the way past, I snagged a single white rose out of the case and slid it into the sack, a few leaves and the white petals sticking out of the top.

After I closed and locked the doors, I hung the package on the handle. I didn't worry the apple wouldn't still be there when she arrived. I knew it would. That's the way the town of Lake Lochlain was; everyone knew everyone and no one wanted to get in the way of Ms. Scarlet's nightly apple.

I hurried down the brick sidewalk, past the shops, potted plants, and freestanding chalkboard signs. I didn't stop to talk to anyone, but remained focused on getting to the small gravel lot at the end of the block where a lot of us town employees parked for the day.

I had no idea what to expect when I got to the hospital. All I knew was finally she was awake.

CHAPTER FOUR

AMNESIA

Silence.

My mind was filled with the kind I found intensely unnerving. Not the kind of silence from the present, but of the past. Currently, my thoughts churned with questions of course.

Why can't I remember? Who am I? What happened to me? Where is my family? Did I have a family?

Every waking second I had was consumed with trying to understand how I ended up here—wherever that was.

But that was all. There was absolutely no background music in my head. No memories to fall back on when the answers didn't come. No general wandering of the mind about my favorite color, what kind of food I craved, or even meanderings about my favorite song or the last movie I saw.

It was sort of like staring at a stark-white wall (which this room had plenty of) and waiting for it to mutter a reply.

There was nothing.

I was frightened, but I didn't know of what exactly. I supposed it would be everything. If I knew nothing, then didn't I have to fear everything?

I didn't even know myself to know how I should act right now. What would my "normal" response be to this kind of situation? Was there one?

I had no idea.

The doctors and nurses said my brain just needed time. Time to heal from the injuries, which I was still unclear on, and then everything would come flooding back.

It had been two days since I woke up and couldn't tell anyone my name. It might not seem like that long in terms of waiting, but when you're in the middle of a drought, a flood is your savior.

The longer I waited, the more alert I became, the more anxious I grew.

I wanted answers. From the inside of my head and from those around me. I got the distinct impression I was being handled with care, like a piece of fissured glass showing signs of shattering. I didn't like that feeling, the first actual tangible sense of truth.

Having the staff tiptoe in and out of my room, the hallways going silent when I was wheeled for testing, and receiving sweet smiles of pity—not my thing.

I embraced those surly feelings. Being grumpy was better than being scared. How was I supposed to ever get better if everyone was acting as if I wouldn't?

I would.

Something became abundantly clear: I was strong. I was a fighter. I didn't know the full extent of my condition when I was brought in, but to have been in a comma for almost three months and basically had my mind completely wiped *and* still survive? That made me strong.

So although the stillness in my mind as I searched for something, anything at all, about myself was most certainly unnerving—and so was being in the hospital all alone (why was I alone?)—I would figure it out. Somehow.

The door to my room opened, and the doctor walked in wearing his signature white coat over a set of green scrubs. His gray hair was combed back, his stethoscope around his neck, and he carried a clipboard.

I groaned. "Please tell me I don't have to look at more flashcards."

He smiled. "Not a fan of the cards?"

"Maybe if I was in kindergarten," I said grudgingly.

The doctor laughed. "Ah, should we add sense of humor to your list of traits?" he asked as he pulled up a rolling stool near the bed. He was in here so much (along with a slew of other doctors), they actually just kept the stool in the room.

"I think it's too soon to tell," I muttered.

I wouldn't call what I said humor; it was more like angry sarcasm with a hint of prayer. Since I'd woken, I'd been subjected to test after test and a ginormous pile of flashcards. We spent quite a bit of time holding up cards with pictures on them and me saying what I saw. They weren't pretty pictures either. It was images of things like a cow, a hamburger, a car, a man, a woman, etc. Basically, the doctors had to figure out the level at which my brain dumped all its info.

So far, I knew everything except any single thing about myself or how I got here.

And my name?

Still didn't have a clue.

I started telling everyone to call me Amnesia. It's what I was. *Who* I was. They all thought I was joking (ah, maybe that was also why the doc wanted to write down sense of humor), but I wasn't. They had to call me something.

"No flashcards today. I think it's pretty safe to say you know about the general world around you."

"So then…?" I asked, wondering what fun new things were waiting.

"I was hoping you could tell me about yesterday," he said as if we were having a friendly conversation.

"Yesterday?"

He nodded. "What you did, what you ate, who you spoke to. That sort of thing."

"It should all be there in my chart." I frowned. "Everything I do here is written down."

He smiled briefly. "Yes, I'm well aware. I want to hear it from you. It's so I can ascertain some details about your memory loss. See if you can recall things that have happened since you woke."

I went through my extremely exciting day yesterday, even adding in the part about not liking bananas. The nurse said they were good, but she lied. Those things were mushy and nasty. I wouldn't be taking food advice from her again.

For extra bonus points, I added in the details I remembered about right after I woke from my coma. As he listened, he jotted down notes on the top sheet of paper. It was a little strange to realize everything I knew about myself was literally right there in a stack of papers.

How could I have so little sense of self?

"Miss?" the doctor said, and I jerked my head up.

"Amnesia." I reminded him.

He frowned. "I don't think that's a good name. I'll have one of the nurses bring you a book of baby names and you can choose something for yourself."

"I like Amnesia," I rebutted, stubborn.

"Why?" he inquired. He sounded like the head shrink that also came to see me.

Shrugging one shoulder, I replied, "Because it describes who I am. A total loss of memory."

"You don't think you're more than that?"

"Sure, but I haven't figured out what yet."

"Do you have the desire to figure out who you are? What your likes and dislikes are?"

Slowly I nodded. It was a daunting task it seemed, but really, what choice did I have? My nose wrinkled. "Why wouldn't I?"

"Your current condition is very rare and can be accompanied by a great sense of loss, depression, and overall hopelessness."

"What *is* my current condition?"

"Have you had any memories or recollections at all today? Any sort of flashbacks or thoughts that felt more like memories? Dreams when you sleep?" the doctor asked, sidestepping my question.

"No, and when I try, there's just... nothing." I spread out my hands as if I were just as confused as he probably was.

"What do you think about?"

"Mostly I wonder what happened to me and how badly I got hurt."

"Do you think about the future?"

"It's hard to think about the future when I have no idea where I came from. And also when I have very little idea of what my present is."

"Do you feel anything at all—anything, no matter how small an inkling it might be—when you turn into your own thoughts? Or even when you try to remember? Pain? Fear? Sadness?"

I opened my mouth to reply, then snapped it shut. I felt an inkling of something, but I wasn't sure I was ready to say it out loud. I couldn't say nothing, though, because Dr. Beck already picked up on the fact I'd been about to say something. "I am scared," I whispered. "But I don't think it's to remember... Well, maybe it is. I don't know."

He nodded slowly. Then he seemed to make up his mind. Adjusting the clipboard in his lap, he glanced up. "I believe you have what most refer to as fugue or dissociative amnesia. As I mentioned, this is a very rare condition, and admittedly, I've never treated anyone with it."

"Why?" I asked simply. It didn't bother me I was his first patient like this. It was my first time, too.

Well, uh, I thought it was.

"Patients with fugue amnesia forget their entire past but also their identity. They have no idea who they are. Even reminding them who they are, showing pictures, etc. doesn't jog their memory."

"Why does it happen?"

"Well, in most cases, it's because the person has suffered something severely traumatic. So much so their mind wipes out everything as a protective measure."

"Well, that seems a little overboard," I muttered.

He paused, scribbled something, and then glanced up. I got the feeling my less-than-freaked-out attitude wasn't something to be proud of. I didn't know how else to be, though.

"When you were brought in, you were completely unresponsive. There was a large gash in the back of your head and another lump on your temple. Your body temperature was low, breathing very shallow, and you had quite a bit of water in your lungs. Frankly, I was surprised you were alive."

My belly twisted at his description. Even though I had no memory of it, I still felt for that girl. "Water in my lungs?" I asked.

Dr. Beck nodded. "You were found in the lake. Nearly washed up on shore. You were lucky he was there to find you. That side of the lake is much less populated."

I grasped at the information like a carrot dangling before a rabbit. "Why was I in the water?" I wondered, trying to clench onto more detail.

"We don't know. What little clothing you had on was ripped and bloody. It was clear you were in some sort of accident."

"No one saw anything? Reported something?"

His face darkened. "No."

"How is that even possible?"

"You suffered a severe concussion and had twelve stitches in the back of your head."

Immediately, I reached around, my fingers probing into the thick strands of hair as I explored, feeling for the stitches.

"They aren't there anymore. They were removed about a week after. The wound is healed, but you probably feel a raised area forming into a scar."

Just as he said it, my fingers slid over a long bump. It was smooth and raised. I hadn't even known it was there.

"What else?" I asked, folding my hands in my lap. I ignored the fact my fingers were shaking.

"There were several lacerations on your body. Most of them appeared to be from rocks in the lake. You had an infection in a cut on the bottom of your foot, one that didn't appear as fresh as the others. You also contracted pneumonia."

I didn't know what to say. It was like he was reading off someone else's chart. Why did I feel so detached? "Is that all?" I asked, wanting to know all of it.

"Your body was badly bruised and…" He paused, hesitating.

"I want to know. I have a right to know," I said, firm.

"You have some scarring on your body. On your back and legs, some on your chest. The kind of scars that are consistent with regular abuse." My stomach dropped, and he cleared his throat. "You were also very malnourished and dehydrated."

I took a moment, focusing on my breathing. I admit it was a technique the head shrinker mentioned when I met with her that morning. *When things get hard or seem impossible, take a deep breath.*

"And now?" My voice was shaky.

He smiled as if he were relieved to say something positive. "Clean bill of health. Your body healed very well while you were in the coma. I don't see anything to indicate you won't make a full physical recovery."

"And my memory?" I pushed.

He sighed. "The brain is a very complex thing. There is still so much we don't know. The data on patients with fugue amnesia states that your memory could come rushing back all at once or piece by piece over time. There is also a chance you may not ever remember everything, more specifically, whatever it is that traumatized you."

I wouldn't ever know if I remembered everything. I would always wonder. Always in the back of my head would be the thought, *What did I permanently forget?*

"Where is my family?" I asked abruptly.

"I think you should get some rest, take things slow." He stood from the rolling stool.

"I want to know," I intoned.

"We haven't been able to find your family. No one has come forward to say they know you."

Tears sprang to my eyes. "What?"

"I know this must be very hard—"

I cut him off, slicing my hand through the air in front of me. "You don't know," I growled. "How could you possibly?"

"You're right." His voice was contrite. "I couldn't."

"Not one person in nearly three months has come looking for me? No one?"

His eyes slid toward the floor. He didn't want me to see the pity they held. "The police are still working on it. They haven't given up."

Had I been a horrible person? Was that why no one came for me? Was everyone glad to see me go?

"I don't understand." I sank back against the pillows, defeated.

"Get some rest," Dr. Beck said gently. "I'll ask Dr. Kline to stop by before she leaves for the day."

I turned away, looking at the blank wall. Another visit from the shrink. Should I be glad someone wanted to see me?

"Not one person," I murmured, kind of shell-shocked. A real sting of pain sliced through my middle. It was the first intense feeling I'd had. I felt abandoned and not as strong as I'd convinced myself I was.

I had no one. No name, no thoughts, no people.

"There is someone," the doctor said, almost as if he knew he shouldn't, but couldn't help himself.

I turned to look at him. "Who?"

"The man who pulled you out of the lake. He comes every day to see you. He sat by your bed when you were in your coma. Sometimes he read to you."

"He knows me?" Hope bloomed.

"No. He just..." The doctor's words fell away. I could practically hear him picking and choosing his words. What was he not saying? Who was this man who sat by a stranger's bedside on a daily basis?

"He came every day?" I asked, wanting to actually be sure.

"Every single day. We wouldn't let him in here at first, so he sat in the waiting room."

"Why?" I questioned, so incredibly curious.

"Because he's the one who pulled you out of the lake." The doctor opened the door, ready to leave.

"He didn't come today." I hurried to call out. "Or yesterday."

The doctor glanced around, half out of the room. "He was here. He's here now."

Fear shot through me. How quickly the curiosity turned to something more sinister. Why would he come here every single day? He claimed to not even know me.

But he still came.

"I want to see him," I announced.

My words were met with a swift shake of the head. "It's best you wait."

"Wait for what? Memories that might be gone forever?"

"Until you've had time to process everything I just told you." He paused. "Perhaps tomorrow." With those words, he shut the door behind him, leaving me alone.

I was tired of being alone. Apparently, I'd been this way for months... And before that? Well, the picture Dr. Beck painted wasn't exactly of some idyllic life.

He'd asked me about the future, if I thought about it. I hadn't, but I was now. I didn't have the past, but I was damn sure going to have a future. The silence in my head was going to be replaced with thoughts, faces... knowledge.

Starting with the man who came every day but didn't know me.

Gripping the covers on the bed, I threw them back, revealing my pasty, thin legs. My body was wobbly and weak when I stood, but I did it anyway. I was getting stronger. I'd walked more today than yesterday.

If the staff wouldn't bring this mystery man to me, then I was going to have to find him.

CHAPTER FIVE

EDWARD

I was being kept away again. Mary Beth met me practically at the elevator; she knew I'd be coming. I recognized the look on her face the minute I saw her.

"Hell no," I snapped and tried to move around her.

"Eddie, you can't go in there," she said, following closely behind.

"I've been going in there for months, Mary B.," I argued, swinging around to face her. A few of the other nurses and staff gave us a wide berth. They likely knew this was coming, too.

Everyone liked me; no one wanted to tell me no. Not about this. Not about her.

"She was in a coma then. You know this is different."

"How is she?" I asked.

"So far, she seems okay, all things considered. It's only been a couple hours."

I wanted to ask, yet I didn't. In the end, the words rasped out of my throat like two rocks scraping together. "Did she ask for me?"

Mary Beth just looked at me for long moments. Her palm slid over my forearm, and I glanced down to where she touched me. "Why don't we sit down?"

Allowing her to lead me to the row of nearby chairs, we sat at the end. Mary Beth perched on the end of her seat, angling her knees toward me, leaning her torso close. Her fingers were still wrapped around my arm, but I barely noticed. I just wanted in that room.

"She has no memory, Eddie."

My head lifted swiftly. "What?"

"She doesn't remember anything."

I sat forward, the movement so abrupt her hand fell off my arm. "Like nothing at all?" I asked, trying to understand.

"Not even her own name."

"But she remembers her past, though."

Mary Beth shook her head sadly. "Nothing."

"Is that normal?"

"It's rare." She hedged. "But considering her condition the night you brought her in, it's not unheard of."

Shoving up out of the chair, I paced, pushing my hands into the back pockets of my jeans. "She must be terrified."

"The doctor said her memory could come back in a few days."

"I'm going back there," I insisted, starting back down the hall.

"No." Mary Beth sprang up. "Doctor's orders, Eddie. She's already dealing with enough. She doesn't need you—" Her words cut off abruptly.

I swung around, my eyes glittering with anger. "I wouldn't do anything to make her upset."

Mary Beth's brown hair was pulled up into a ponytail and the ends slid over her shoulder when she sighed and stepped closer. "I know that. We all know that. But this is best for her."

A few curse words slipped out when I paced away, stacking my hands at the back of my neck and staring out the small window nearby.

Seconds later, Mary Beth was at my side again. Tentatively, she touched my side, and I stiffened. "If she asks for you, I'll come get you."

She didn't ask for me.

Not yesterday and not today. She hadn't remembered anything, and everyone in the hospital— hell, the entire town—was talking about her. This was the juiciest gossip in Lake Loch in over ten years.

Everyone loved our quaint little town, the quiet, the way it was sort of untouched by modern day. We were a little retro here, a little backward. Even still, the people loved drama. Something to spice up the monotony of this charming place. There was a new buzz in the air, a charge not usually found. I knew I was also part of the speculation. People were watching me, waiting to see what I would do.

All I wanted was to see her.

When I arrived earlier, I got the head shakes and finger points to the waiting room. I trudged in glumly, thinking maybe I could snag Mary Beth and talk her into letting me back. It seemed eventful today, as everyone was moving around busily and had no time to talk. Not that I minded... but I did wonder if maybe they were all just looking busy so they could avoid me.

After hanging out for about two hours, my impatience got the better of me. I waited so long... so incredibly long. I just wanted to see her. To talk to her. Then I would know.

I had to know.

At the nurses' station just down the hall from her room, I rested my forearms on the counter and leaned toward one of the older nurses on staff. "Hey, Ellen. Is Mary Beth around?"

Ellen glanced up from her paperwork. With a sigh, she shook her head slightly but then smiled. "You are a persistent one, Eddie."

I smiled, making sure to show my teeth. I had dimples. Everyone loved dimples.

Ellen chuckled, getting up from her chair. "Mary Beth isn't here. Her shift doesn't begin until seven. So you'll have to sweet-talk someone else."

"Like you?" I smiled a little bigger.

Ellen reached out and pinched my cheeks. "I'd love for you to try, but I have to get this paperwork downstairs. It's a nice day out there. You should go enjoy it."

I didn't reply, and she went off to deliver her paperwork, leaving me alone at the counter. One of the other nurses walked past me and down the hall, turned the corner, and disappeared out of sight.

My stare wandered down to the room where I spent so much time. I could slip right in. No one was around to notice. Before she woke up, I never hesitated. I just went. Now, though, it seemed I needed to think about things first. Suddenly, I was nervous.

What would she be like with no memory? Would she know me if she saw me? What if it wasn't her? What if it was?

With a heavy sigh, I backed up, moving away from the counter until my back hit the wall. Slouching in a little, I tucked my hands in my jeans and bowed my head to think.

For all the bustling going on around here today, things seemed to hush, to settle down, as if everything held its breath.

A low creaking filled my ears, a noise so low I wouldn't have heard it if it weren't so quiet. Lifting my chin toward the sound, my eyes went right to the figure that seemed to appear in the hallway out of thin air. Shock and anticipation battled in my chest, rumbling down to my stomach, making it flip over.

It was her.

Paralyzed, I couldn't move at all. I stayed there in my position against the wall, my eyes clinging to her every move. Her every detail.

She didn't see me. All her focus was on putting one foot in front of the other, moving cautiously over the tile.

I couldn't tear my eyes away to see if someone was coming to help her or if maybe she was out here because she was supposed to be. As soon as the thought drifted through my mind, I knew she was out here rebelliously.

There was no way the staff would let a girl with no memory wander the halls alone.

The white-and-blue-checked hospital gown was all I'd seen her in since I brought her that night. It hung off her thin frame like curtains on an open window on a breezy summer day. The scratchy fabric floated around her, swaying slightly as she walked.

Her movements were slow. She leaned on the IV pole, which was what made the low squeaking sound. The one wheel probably needed tightened.

She was medium height, shorter than me, but not what I would consider short. I was just tall. Her feet were bare, and she had long fingers. Her skin was pale, and there was a spattering of light freckles over her nose. As I watched, her teeth sank into her lower lip in concentration, and something in me melted a little.

I was so weak when it came to her. I didn't even know why.

Well, yes, I did. I'd always been weak to this girl, but looking at her now, it seemed in more ways than I even realized.

Slowly, I slid up the wall so I was standing straight, my eyes not leaving her once.

Thick, wavy strands of wheat-colored hair fell around her face when she looked down at her feet. They were uneven, some long and some oddly short. But it looked soft, regardless of how uncombed and unequal it was.

As she drew closer, fatigue seemed to cloak her. Her feet paused, and she practically sagged against the unstable pole. I pushed off the wall, thinking to help her, but my movements startled her.

Her head snapped up so quick it unbalanced her. Her feet went back, trying to keep her upright, but the IV slid forward. She was left in this awkward fall/tug-of-war between her body and the pole.

I surged forward as the wheels began to teeter and lift off the ground. "Careful!" I said, shooting over just in time to catch her before she fell.

I couldn't help but notice the way a few of my fingertips brushed against the smooth skin at the small of her back. The damn hospital gown wasn't enough coverage if she was going to be wandering the halls.

Her hand wrapped around my forearm, gripping as if her life depended on it.

We stood there for a few prolonged moments, almost as if we'd been dancing and ended with me dipping her toward the floor. I glanced down. She glanced up. Our stares collided.

It was unsettling to realize how infinitely drawn to her I was.

I searched the depths of her round brown eyes the way I'd longed to do for so long. I wasn't even sure what I was looking for. Something. Anything. A spark of recognition from either of us.

Her lips parted on a breathless gasp, her eyes the first to pull away. Long, thick lashes swept down, closing off the honey-brown irises and disappointing me.

When they reopened, refocused on my face, I felt as if I'd won an award.

"I almost fell," she told me.

I shook my head slowly. She wouldn't have fallen. "I got you."

She tried to scramble up, but her body didn't move as fast as she wanted. So I helped her, keeping my palms at her waist and nearly lifting her back onto both feet. Reluctantly, I let go, sliding the IV pole close beside her in case she needed it again.

"I'm pretty sure patients aren't supposed to be wandering the halls," I said, resisting the urge to reach out and fix the neckline of her gown.

"I'm pretty sure most patients have visitors," she murmured.

I tilted my head, but then she realized what she'd said and straightened. "I'm not wandering. I have somewhere to be."

Amused, I folded my arms over my chest. "Oh? Where's that?"

"I'm, ah, looking for someone."

A stab of jealousy pierced me. Who could she possibly be looking for? Her doctor! What if she was in pain, had called for the nurse who wasn't around, and decided to get help herself?

My hands shot out. She flinched and stepped back. Immediately, I felt like an ass. "I won't hurt you," I vowed, hoping she heard the truth in my words. "I'm sorry I scared you."

She laughed nervously. "I'm not scared."

Oh, but she was.

"Are you hurt?" I asked, forcing my hands back. "Can I get you a doctor?"

She rolled her eyes. "No way. All those doctors want is to write down my every move on that damn clipboard."

I chuckled. Immediately, I felt her eyes. Letting the laughter fade away, I glanced up.

"I'm Amnesia," she said.

My chest tightened. "The girl with no memory,"

"You heard about me?" She seemed surprised.

"Something like that," I murmured.

"I'm looking for someone. Maybe you know him?" Her head tilted to the side, a chunk of uneven hair falling against her chin. I noted the way she was leaning on the pole a little more with every passing moment. "The man who pulled me out of the lake."

Me. She was out here teetering on her bare feet in search of me. The thought made me slightly giddy.

I felt my Adam's apple bob. Suddenly, my mouth was very dry. "I know him."

Her eyes lit up like the sun came out from behind a cloud and shined its golden rays upon her.

She was beautiful. So beautiful.

"You do!" She perked up, glancing past me down the hall. "Can you take me to him?"

"No," I said, drawing her eyes back to me. *Where they belong.*

"Why not?" she demanded, putting a fist on her hip.

This time, I did reach out to fix the neckline of her gown. The second I smoothed the fabric, her fist slid from her hip and her chin tipped back so her face could fully study mine.

48

"You already found him," I murmured, pulling back.

Her lips parted. They were a pale peach. I wanted to count the freckles on her nose. "You're him?"

Shifting so I could push my hand out between us, I said, "I'm Eddie."

Amnesia said nothing, but slid her palm against mine so we could be formally introduced. "You saved my life."

"No," I replied instantly. "I didn't."

"You really come here every day?" she asked, slightly awed. Her eyes took in my face more thoroughly now. I wondered how I looked to her, if I was familiar at all.

"They told you that, huh?" I smiled.

"I think the doctor felt sorry for me." She admitted and leaned farther into the pole. The wheel squeaked under the weight.

"You need to sit down." My arm hovered close in case she fell again. This time she didn't flinch away.

"Will you come with me?" she asked.

In that moment, with that single innocent question, I realized I would do anything, be anything... go anywhere she asked.

I didn't say that, though. All I did was shake my head.

The short walk back to her room took a long time. The entire way, I fought the urge to sweep her into my arms like the night I'd found her floating in the water. At the door, I shoved it open, holding it wide, and placed my palm at the small of her back, gesturing for her to go ahead of me.

Her eyes glanced up, then away before she moved past.

"Eddie Donovan!" A booming voice sounded from down the hall. I winced. "I told you she was to have no visitors!"

From inside the room, Amnesia groaned. "Not him again."

Before I could reply, she poked her head out and spoke. "Really, Dr. Beck. What's he going to do to me? Steal all my memories and thoughts?"

"I'm writing down your sense of humor," he told her, almost fondly. "It's very dry by the way."

She tossed her head to the side to glance up at me. "He writes everything down. It's insufferable."

My lips tugged in a smile.

Dr. Beck stopped nearby adjacent to where we stood. "Why are you out of bed?"

"I told you I wanted to see Eddie."

Dr. Beck looked at me, a veiled warning in his gaze.

"I found her in the hall." I agreed.

"It's just a visit," Amnesia said. "Please. I *cannot* sit in this room with practically empty thoughts for another minute."

Those words would ensure I kept coming back. Nothing, not even a team of doctors and sassy nurses, could force me out of here. She needed me.

I needed her.

"Fine. But I need a moment with Eddie." He gestured toward her. "Back to bed."

"Thank you," she said genuinely. Then her gaze returned to me.

It was hard to describe how I felt when she looked at me. It didn't matter if it was a lingering gaze or just a swift glance. I'd only been with her mere moments, but already her stare was as essential to me as air.

"You'll stay?" she asked, her voice unsure and shy.

Always. "I'll be right there."

The second the door latched behind her, putting a barrier between us, I levelled my eyes on the doctor. "I won't stay away from her."

"Yes. You've made that abundantly clear."

"I won't hurt her."

He sighed, defeated. "I know that, Eddie. You and your family are good people. This isn't about you."

"It is." I lashed out quietly. "I'm part of this, too."

The doctor pinched the bridge of his nose. "She has a severe case of amnesia. The kind that's brought on by trauma."

"Will her memory come back?" I had to know.

"I have no way of predicting that."

I stepped closer, lowering my voice. "Do you think it's her?"

"You know it's not," he said sadly.

"But is it possible?" I pressed. I was probably the last person in this town, on this planet, who refused to give up hope.

He didn't want to say it, but he couldn't lie. Not to me. Not to himself. Hell, the entire town was speculating. "There are several similarities, and the age does seem to be about right."

"And the fact no one has come to claim her."

I'll claim her. I'll claim her right now.

"Don't get your hopes up, son." Dr. Beck put his hand on my shoulder. "Even if by some slim chance this is her, she isn't the same. She never will be."

I couldn't hear that. I didn't want to.

I turned to go into the room, but Dr. Beck stopped me. "You can't tell her, not yet. She's fragile. Her mind is still coming to terms with her new reality. Too much, too soon will only hurt her further."

Frustration welled within me. I wanted to march in there and pour it all out. Tell her everything and then hope recognition brimmed in her eyes.

I couldn't.

Actions like that, words like the ones bubbling inside me were pollution to her. She needed a friend. Someone to be there. No pressure to be anything other than who she was in that moment.

I didn't know how to do that, but I also couldn't stay away.

My head bobbed. "I can do that. I won't say anything."

"Keep her calm. Be her friend. *Take it slow.* Any signs of memory recovery, call me *immediately.*"

I nodded.

Dr. Beck moved to walk away. I grabbed his wrist. "How, um... how bad was it for her?"

His eyes darkened and his mouth pulled into a taut line. "You mean whatever it was that caused the complete dissociation?"

I nodded.

"Severe. So severe…" He stopped and shook his head.

"What?" I cajoled.

"So severe it may be better if she never gets her memory back."

CHAPTER SIX

AMNESIA

The last thing I expected was to fall into the arms of a dark-haired, blue-eyed man with dimples for days.

Not that I really expected anything. I mean, that's all there was for me. Nothing.

I thought maybe the man who found me was a fisherman or someone older... less attractive.

I guess there was something else I could add to my ever-growing list of character traits. I liked men. Or rather, I found one in particular attractive.

Eddie was attractive; I couldn't deny it. So handsome it filled in some of that stark silence in my mind. His face was exactly what I needed to mull over when nothing else was there. The blue of his eyes was almost startling, reminding of what the sky looked like on a summer day. The blue was accentuated by dark, long lashes and a head of hair so dark it made me think of midnight. It was thick and curly, kind of unruly in the sense it flopped over his forehead and ears. I liked his jawline, too, the strength in it, the clean line. I bet when he got angry and it flexed, it would make my stomach flip.

And he was tall, too. So tall. I had to crane my neck back to study him. When I almost fell and he was there, I noted the warmth of his skin, how alive he felt, even the erratic beating of his heart.

Settling back into the bed, I marveled at my own thoughts. It amazed me how effectively my mind was whirling, how noticing mere details on someone sprang alive parts of me that I thought were gone, too. It gave me hope. Hope that maybe I wasn't as lost as everyone assumed.

Surely if I suspected the flexing of a man's jaw would cause my tummy to quiver and understood a summer sky was blue and the midnight sky was black, then there was so much more buried inside me.

Right?

I had no idea. The things I was thinking could just be common knowledge, things my brain didn't feel necessary to dump. I was overwhelmed, and it embarrassed me. I'd walked a few feet down the hall for crying out loud. I saw one person. One. Yet here I was trembling in my bed as if I'd seen a ghost, trying to figure out the meaning of life.

The door opened slowly. Eddie poked his dark, curly head inside. A little bit of my anxiety melted away. Enough so I was able to breathe.

"Still okay if I come in?" he asked.

I nodded.

I liked the way he didn't stride right in, allowing the heavy door to slam behind him. Instead, he slid in, turned around, and guided the door shut softly. My eyes couldn't depart from him even when he was turned away. Eddie was lean and long. His shoulders were broad, but they would have to be to support his height. He was dressed in a pair of faded jeans that were frayed at the hems, like he'd owned them a long time and barely wore shoes so they dragged the ground.

His shirt was navy blue and written on the back in white were the words "Loch General." I had no idea what that was. There was also what looked like a picture of the Loch Ness Monster. The shoes on his feet were plain sneakers, all white with some blue stripes down the sides.

He ignored the rolling stool all the doctors used, instead reaching for the chair against the wall, and dragged it over beside the bed. It was like he planned to stay a while. The chair was more permanent than the stool. With a heavy sigh, he sat down, leaned back, and propped his shoes on the side of my bed.

"Your shoes are dirty," I said, glancing down at the soles.

He made a small laughing sound and grinned. He had an ornery grin, the kind that said he got away with basically everything. Eddie pulled his feet off the blankets and made a show of kicking off the shoes. The sound they made on the tile was distinct. When it was done, his feet reappeared on my bed, this time covered in white socks.

"Better?" he asked, not bothered in the least.

I nodded once. "Much."

He smiled again, and even though I barely knew anything, I understood the twinkle in his eyes was something rare. Something pure.

"So how are they treating you in here? How's the food?"

I had a severe case of amnesia. He'd pulled me out of a lake, half dead. He'd obviously been waiting almost three months for me to wake up. And now his first question was about the food?

"Don't really have anything to compare it to." I tapped on the side of my head and shrugged. "'Course I would think there has to be something out there better than soup and Jell-O."

"Depends," he remarked casually, tucking his arms against his middle. "Is it red or blue Jell-O?"

My lips curved upward. I wasn't really used to the action. But I went with it. It was kind of nice. "Green."

"That's just unacceptable!" he said in mock outrage. When he sat forward, his sock-covered feet dropped off the bed. "How dare they serve something so foul!"

A sound came out of me. It was a laugh. I was laughing. *Now I know what that sounds like.*

Covering my mouth as if I were embarrassed to be happy, I added, "But nothing is worse than the banana they tried to make me eat."

Eddie's eyes lit up with amusement, but he shook his head and scowled. "Green Jell-O *and* fruit? I'm gonna give the first nurse I see a piece of my mind."

I stuck out my tongue. Just thinking about that mushy yellow thing made me recoil.

Eddie chuckled, and thoughts of food faded from my mind. We stared at each other for long moments. The air around us seemed to shrink, or maybe my skin just felt momentarily tight. Reality crashed into the humor we shared, and a lot of the questions in my mind came to the surface.

Quietly I asked, "Where am I, like what state?"

His eyebrows shot up his forehead. "No one told you?"

I made a face. "They haven't told me much of anything. They think I'm too delicate."

His feet returned to the mattress when he lounged backward. "You've been through a lot."

"None of it I can remember." Was I allowed to be upset over things I couldn't remember? I knew I wasn't unaffected... But it was hard to feel like I was.

"You really don't remember anything?" He regarded me closely. I didn't know why, but every time he looked at me, I felt he was looking for something. Besides, how could I be upset when I really had no idea what was going on? All I had were bits and pieces... pieces of a not-so-pretty picture, but it seemed I needed more before it all sank in.

Once again, I turned inward, toward my blank mind and hollow world, and tried to recall even the slightest detail about myself. Anything. But I couldn't. "Nothing."

"Not even me?" he asked, his voice less relaxed than it had been up to this point. It was almost as if he knew he shouldn't ask, but he couldn't help himself.

"Why would I remember you? Should I?"

A momentary look of disappointment flashed deep in his eyes, but then he shook his head. "No. When I pulled you out of the water, you opened your eyes for a moment. I thought maybe you saw me…"

"Oh. I'm sorry. All I remember is waking up here."

"It's okay. It's understandable."

"They told you not to tell me anything, didn't they?" I sat back against the pillow and sighed. Earlier today, during my alone time between doctor visits, I'd adjusted the bed so I could sit upright. Since I woke up from the coma, lying down was something I found I didn't like.

In fact, it made me sort of uncomfortable. I didn't tell anyone that. The doctor would have written it down with a constipated look on his face and then called the head shrinker. It wasn't that big of a deal anyway. I mean obviously, I should be feeling some sort of discomfort after waking from an extended coma. I'd been lying prone in a bed for too long; of course my body combatted against doing it more.

"They also told me I couldn't come in here and see you," he said with a wink.

"But you came anyway," I said, remembering what Dr. Beck told me. "Why did you come every day?"

"I couldn't stay away." His eyes roamed over my features, and for the first time since waking up, I thought about the way I looked.

"But why?" I urged, unable to look away from the intensity of his stare. I could be swallowed up in those deep blue depths.

"Because I pulled you out of the water. You were so… unresponsive. It was scary, and after bringing you here, I sort of felt invested. I wanted to make sure you were okay."

"You felt sorry for me." I pointed out.

"Actually," he whispered, and in his voice was something raw and utterly truthful, "I feel sorry for the people you left behind, the people who could be missing you."

"About that…" I blinked, trying to tear my attention from his face. "The doctors said no one has come here to identify me."

He shook his head. "No, no one has come."

Tears burned the backs of my eyes. Sometimes it was easy to push away, to feel detached, but then other times, it smacked me right in the face. No one came for me. I was utterly alone, and I didn't even have a name.

"The police have been looking?" I asked, repeating something else the doctor said.

"Yeah, from what I know. It was a hot news story for a while. It was in the papers and on the radio. They've been looking into missing persons' reports, but so far, nothing matches anything like your story."

"I don't even know my story!" I burst out. "How could they?"

Eddie cleared his throat. "I meant no one matching your description or general age has been reported missing since you've been here or a few months prior to that."

I felt bad for snapping at him. He was the only person here, and I was taking out my frustration on him. "I'm sorry."

"No." He sat forward, elbows hitting his knees and his torso leaning over the edge of the bed. "Don't apologize, not ever. Not to me."

"I shouldn't have yelled at you."

The storm in his eyes quelled. "I can take it." The confidence in his tone was oddly calming. I liked his sense of assurance; it was solid when everything else was pretty much in crumbs.

"So…" I urged, tucking my legs beneath me and ruffling the crappy blankets on the bed. "Are you going to give me some information or what?"

He mock gasped. "I feel used. You only want me for my mind."

"So far, your mind has been pretty un-useful." I pointed out.

His teeth flashed in a quick smile. "We're in Maine. A very small town up north."

"Maine," I murmured to myself, mulling it over, deciding if it felt familiar to me or not.

It didn't.

"That's on the East Coast, right? It's cold here?" I asked, wondering where that information came from and why all the other more important details weren't so easily reached.

"Yeah, but it's not cold right now. It's August. End of summer is coming, and it will start to get chilly soon."

"And there's a lake here?" I asked.

Eddie bobbed his head and pushed at the unruly hair on his forehead. "Lake Lochlain. Everyone calls it Lake Loch, though."

"Is it a big lake?"

"Yeah, it's big, bigger than the town actually. It's a quiet kind of place, kind of off the map, not as modern as most places nowadays."

"So women washing up onshore isn't an everyday occurrence?" I joked, attempting to lighten my troubled thoughts.

"No," Eddie replied, averting his gaze. His body shifted farther into the chair, though, and I couldn't help but feel a pang of relief that he wasn't about to leave.

I guess I could add something else to the list about me. I liked company. *Or maybe it's just Eddie.*

"What about your shirt?" I gestured to the blue fabric covering his chest. "What's Loch General?"

As if to remind himself of what he was wearing, Eddie looked down. "Loch General Store. We don't have a big chain grocery store or anything for about twenty-five miles. We just have Loch Gen. It's the town grocery store." Plucking at the fabric of his shirt, he added, "I work there."

"What do you do?" I said, curious.

"Bag groceries, run the register, handle payroll, stock shelves, inventory..." He laughed. "I pretty much do it all."

My cheeks grew warm as I listened to him speak. He had a way of keeping my attention. Everything about him was interesting.

"Do you live nearby?" I blurted out, wanting him to keep talking.

"Yeah, I have a tiny cabin on the lake."

"I'm sure it's beautiful," I murmured, my thoughts turning inward. I didn't have a place to live. Or a job.

"Actually, it's not."

I blinked, surprised. Eddie laughed. "It was half falling down when I bought it. That's how I could afford it. I've been slowly fixing it up."

"That sounds kinda fun."

He smirked. "It wouldn't seem so fun after about eight hours of sanding wood and painting walls."

"It's better than this hospital bed." I sighed.

Eddie sat forward. I thought he was reaching for my hand but changed his mind and pulled back. "Can I bring you anything? Anything at all?"

My life. "I think saving my life was more than enough. I'm the one who owes you."

"No." He spoke quickly and emphatically. "You don't owe me a thing."

"Did you see anything that night, Eddie?" I whispered. "At the lake? Was anyone else there?"

He didn't answer at first. Instead, his forearm rested on the side of the bed and on it, his forehead. He stared down at the floor, and I just waited, thinking maybe he needed time to gather his memory. When he lifted his head, the azure shade of his irises was bleak.

"Sometimes I walk along the lake at night. It's just something I like to do, to think." I nodded, encouraging him to continue. "It was foggy that night, like it sometimes is. The wind was stronger than usual and the water seemed choppier. You weren't on the shore."

"But the doctor said…" I rebutted.

"I know. You would have ended up on the shore if I hadn't seen you. You were a short distance out, about waist deep for me." He held his hand up to his waist. "I saw you floating there, and I swam out and dragged you in."

"Was I breathing?" I asked. It was odd. I knew this story was about me, but it didn't feel like it. It felt I was being told about someone I didn't know.

"No," he murmured. "I did CPR."

Without thought, I lifted the pads of my fingers to my lips, imagining his there, the breath from his body surging into mine.

"The second you started breathing, I drove you here to the hospital myself. Figured it would be faster than waiting for an ambulance."

"Dr. Beck said I was in pretty bad shape," I told him.

Eddie nodded. "Yeah, it was touch and go for a while. But I knew you would make it."

"How did you know?" How could he know something more about me than I did?

"Because this is where you belong." The intensity in his gaze was unnerving.

But instead of alienating me, it had the opposite effect. My deepest fear at the moment ripped right out of me as if it were magnetized and he was a giant lodestone. "What if I never remember?"

"Well," Eddie mused, glancing up at the ceiling while he mulled it over. Our eyes met and held when his lowered and he finished his reply. "You'll just have more space in that beautiful head of yours for new memories."

They were hopeful words. Almost a promise of something better in the days ahead. A second ago, I would have clung to that positivity like a lifeline. And maybe I would later, when I lay in bed and tried to sleep.

But right now, I didn't think about that. Instead, all I could think about was that Eddie just called me beautiful.

CHAPTER SEVEN

EDWARD

The lake was powerful. So formidable it took her away... Maybe the only thing able to bring her back. I asked it to bring her back every day at first. Then as I grew older, less and less. But I still went down there at night. My toes still sank into the pebbly shore. The icy water still pricked at my skin. I stopped asking the lake to give her back to me, but my heart never quit hoping it would.

Then one night, it did.

CHAPTER EIGHT

AMNESIA

I was floating, my body completely supported by the buoyancy of the water surrounding me. For a moment, I knew true peace. For a moment, it was just me and no thoughts, just blissful silence as the water muffled everything.

The water felt like silk caressing my skin, moving fluidly, bending around my form, all too willing to do the work and come to me. I didn't even have to try. Opening my eyes, everything was blurry, as if I suddenly needed glasses, the world around me no longer clear. My eyes followed a small trail of bubbles floating up right in front of my face. Tipping my chin back to follow the rapidly ascending orbs, long strands of flowing hair moved before of me. I watched it for a long moment, waving around like a flag in the wind. The strands appeared soft, the color not as blond as it usually looked, but a deeper shade.

A shadow moved around me, and reality came crushing back.

Adrenaline surged through me, making my body go rigid and struggle against the water I previously thought of as silk. But it wasn't silk. It was a chain, and it was so malleable it didn't matter how I moved and fought because it wrapped around me.

My limbs began clawing through the heavy water, pushing so I could get to the surface. It was dark down here, so dark I barely saw anything at all. Glancing around frantically, all I saw was the way my fair skin stood out against the water that now appeared dirty.

This wasn't peace. This was death.

I fought upward, hoping I was swimming in the right direction. The surface grew lighter. I swam furiously, my lungs burning.

Just as I was about to breach the top, a large, dark figure loomed above, blocking out the light I'd been using as a guide. The figure bent down, staring straight into the waves, looking at me... daring me to rise.

My heart beat so hard it hurt. My chest squeezed from lack of air, and my head grew woozy as the edges of my vision darkened. I couldn't give in, and with one last defiant shove, my head broke the surface. I gulped down air greedily.

An ominous presence tinged the air as I sucked in the precious oxygen, my eyes working to rid the water from my sight.

With still-blurry vision, I saw the large shape reach for me. I tried desperately to make out their face, but it was obscured by shadows. All I knew was I was scared, beyond scared... terrified.

"No!" I gasped, trying to swim backward, away from the hand.

With a grunt, the hand fell away, agitation making them move in quick, jerky actions. The water was dark and endless looking, but not as scary as the person trying to grasp me.

I swam back, my arms screaming with exhaustion, but I moved anyway, taking any amount of distance I could muster.

Suddenly, the shrouded person grew larger, as if he stood and was portentously trying to reach me. He couldn't; I was just out of reach of his dire grip. He hunched around, still concealed in darkness, and rose, something extending above his head. Something long and thick...

Water pushed against me, and I fought against the waves. The lake betrayed me, though, a sudden current shoving me nearer the person.

"No!" I screamed as the long, thick weapon was brought crashing down over me. I stopped treading water and threw my hands up to protect my head, the movement causing me to slip a little under the surface.

The heavy sound of wood slapping against water echoed, and the numbing pain sent me downward.

I was floating again, once more supported by the water as if the lake couldn't decide if it was friend or foe.

Arms wide, legs bent, I stared out at the darkness claiming me and slowly drifted away.

My gasp was so forceful it lifted my back off the mattress. Gripping the sides of the bed, I pushed up, sucking in air as if I hadn't breathed in days and trembling like a leaf ready to fall from a tree.

The clammy feeling of my skin was uncomfortable, but the way the dream lingered inside me was worse. Was that what death felt like?

Heaving a shaky sigh and noticing how my fingers ached from gripping the bed, I released them and shoved the blankets off my overheated skin. Cool air brushed over them and goose bumps raced along my skin.

I reached for the water at the bedside, only to find the cup empty. Being in bed was massively unappealing at the moment, so I pushed out, my bare feet slapping against the cold floor. Shivering, I carried the cup into the bathroom to fill it up.

It was pitch black, something that frankly creeped me out, so I flicked on the harsh overhead light and recoiled from the intrusive brightness. Still squinting, I drank from the cup, some of the tepid water dribbling down my chin as if my mouth forgot how to work.

What managed to get in me burned as it went down, as if the water stretched the constricted muscles in my throat. The cup made no sound when I set it on the porcelain sink and wiped at my chin with the back of my hand.

More accustomed to the light now, I caught my reflection in the mirror. I'd barely looked at myself since I woke up here. I didn't like looking in the mirror much because I didn't recognize the person I saw.

It was scary to know you saw yourself but also know if no one had told me this was me, I wouldn't have realized.

My hair was thick and wavy, a dark blond that hung unevenly around my face and over my shoulders. It was something else I found incredibly curious when I did dare a glimpse. Why was it so uneven with chunks missing here and there? My eyes were light brown, plain... and to me, mysterious. These eyes had to have seen so much, yet they kept it secret.

My skin was pale, nearly colorless. I'd likely look dead if it weren't for the light-colored freckles that spattered my face. My teeth were slightly crooked, and upon closer glance, the front right one was chipped.

A sound out in the bedroom drew me up short, the heavy wooden door closing. Nervous energy crackled through me. My fingers, still shaking from the nightmare, trembled even more. Quickly, I hit the light switch, plunging the room back into total darkness. I stood there trying to hear over my own erratic breathing for any other unusual sounds.

Muffled footfalls moved nearby.

I bit down on my lower lip, blindly reaching out for the cup of water.

I waited what seemed like forever, but no other sound came. Just as I was beginning to think I was being overly paranoid, the sound of the latching door echoed through the room once more.

I jerked as if shot, my back coming into contact with the cold bathroom wall.

Someone had been in there!

I knew instinctively it wasn't a nurse. They rarely came into my room in the middle of the night, and if they did, they most certainly didn't creep around like ghosts and not check the bathroom to make sure I was okay.

Who was that?

The looming figure from my nightmare flashed into my head. It was more a moving of shadow, darkening my thoughts because I hadn't actually seen anyone in the dream.

Without thinking, I took a sip of the sink water, my heart still near to beating out of my chest. Down in the cup, the liquid sloshed around because of the way I quaked.

"You're being ridiculous," I told myself. "You had a bad dream, and it freaked you out."

Just another reason I hated lying in bed. I'd had enough sleep to last me a lifetime.

The bathroom door swung out when I pushed it open and shuffled back into the room. Light from under my door spilled in from the hallway as well as from the small rectangular window.

I saw a nurse hustle by and on down the hall, and I let out a sigh of relief.

See? Everything is fine.

My knees were shaking on the way back to the bed, holding the cup in one hand and leaning on the pole of the IV stand with the other. I couldn't wait to get this thing out of my hand. They said it would be soon.

At the bedside, I set down the cup and glanced at the blankets with derision. Another person moved down the hallway, dimming some of the light filtering in from beneath the door.

With one knee on the mattress, one hand balancing on the IV pole, I prepared to heft myself the rest of the way into the clammy, damp-feeling sheets.

I never made it.

A hand clamped around my ankle as it lifted off the ground, and I shrieked, instinctively pulling to get away. The grip tightened, and I felt the pressure from strong fingers molding around my bones.

"No!" I gasped, but it was too late. The arm pulled me with so much force I fell backward off the bed.

The IV pole came with me, lifting off the ground and hitting the tile beside me.

Pain echoed in my back and shoulders as well as a dull ache in the back of my head. As I tried to scramble up, another hand shot out from beneath the bed and latched onto my other ankle.

I began kicking and opened my mouth to scream.

Instantly, the body catapulted out from beneath the bed, releasing my ankles, and I turned to rush away. The figure tackled me. My fingers griped the dark, thick fabric of the hoodie concealing their body and face.

A gloved hand covered my mouth, pressing down so hard the back of my head hurt where it rested on the floor.

I tried to scream, but the sound was muffled. The attacker outweighed me as I struggled to get free, and the line of the IV in my hand tugged as I fought, causing my hand to scream in pain.

I couldn't see the face; it was completely shrouded by fabric, but hate rolled off them. The more I fought, the calmer the person became, until they shifted, sat up, and brought down the second hand to pinch my nose closed.

My eyes shot open. They were suffocating me!

This was murder!

Opening my mouth, I did the only thing I could and bit down into the hand as hard as possible.

The person gave a muffled, low cry and wrenched away. I twisted from beneath them, kicking them in the chest as I went. The person fell back against the bed, and I rushed forward, literally dragging the IV stand behind me as I wrenched open the door and collapsed into the hallway.

"Help me!" I screamed.

The hallway was no longer lit up. The nurses I saw before were missing. It was oddly still and oddly quiet now.

I was alone. With a killer.

"Help!" I screamed again. The way the plea echoed down the long, lonely corridor was not hopeful.

I turned when I heard the assailant behind me. They stood hunched over in the doorway. Without saying a single word, they lifted their finger and pointed at me... just pointed and said nothing at all.

"No!" I screamed, back-crawling farther down the hallway.

The sound of squeaking sneakers around the corner made me openly weep. "Help," I called weakly as I prepared to defend myself again.

The attacker heard, too, and suddenly burst forward. I fell back, but they were done with me. The cloaked figure disappeared just as fast as he'd materialized, leaving me a hurting, trembling mess on the hallway floor.

"Amnesia!" one of the nurses exclaimed.

I began to cry harder.

The nurse crouched beside me, yelling for help. As she issued orders to those bustling around her, I took solace in the fact the hallway was no longer so bare. Even lights came back on.

I barely said two words the entire time they fussed. The dream replayed in my head over and over... and so did the feeling of being almost suffocated. I barely registered the smear of red on the back of my hand and someone yelling about my IV being yanked out of my skin.

I shut it all down and just sat there, a catatonic sensation weighing me down like a heavy blanket. Like the weight of the lake at night.

What haunted me most was the parallel the dream had with my sudden reality. I couldn't help but question if it was really only just a dream now.

The dark, shrouded figure was the same in my sleep as it was coming out from beneath my bed. It appeared chillingly identical hovering over me with obvious nefarious intent.

I thought of Eddie in the middle of my internal shutdown. It was his blue eyes and black hair I imagined when trying to push away the worst of my fear. I wanted to ask for him.

I didn't.

My thoughts continued to go back to him when the worst of the night would tug me into its clutches. How just a few hours ago I'd whispered to him my biggest fear... What if I never remembered?

That terror was now overcome, so obsolete it was almost invalid.

Now my biggest fear wasn't what if I never remembered...

It was what if I did.

CHAPTER NINE

EDWARD

Loch General opened at eight a.m. It wasn't so early it was unbearable, but it was early enough because this lake town was sleepy, a little slower to wake up than, say, a city or even a larger town.

Visiting hours at the hospital didn't begin until ten, but I didn't care. I was blind to the rules of that place, almost as if they applied to everyone except me. I was there for her, for the girl who told me her name was Amnesia. Being there for her made me exempt from their limiting rules.

I felt unbounded when I was near her. As if anything were possible.

The bakery just a few doors down from Loch Gen opened at six, the owners being the earliest waking couple at the lake. Joline and Jeremy had been married since before I was born. They always said a couple who baked together stayed together.

I had no evidence to prove them wrong.

About thirty minutes after their closed sign flipped to open, I pushed through the turquoise front door, the bell obnoxiously loud at this early hour. Even though it was summer, there was a chill in the air. And a fog that twisted along the streets, hovering just above the brick sidewalks and clinging to the quaint streetlamps lining the road.

Joline poked her head around the wall separating the kitchen from the front with a surprised look lifting her flour-covered eyebrows.

"Eddie!" she exclaimed, sounding way more awake than I felt, then disappearing for only a second before stepping out from behind the wall as she wiped her flour-laden hands on a white towel. "What brings you by so early this morning?"

Mustering up the smile I always had ready for everyone, my hands rested on the counter near the old-fashioned cash register (yeah, it still worked, and Joline still used it). "Tell me you already pulled some of those monkey bread muffins out of the oven this morning."

The sweet, rich scent lacing the air gave me hope while my stomach grumbled with greed.

"It's the first thing we made!" She confirmed. "Today's batch has a little something special, early apples from Severil's Orchard and some plump, warm raisins."

"I'll take four," I said, my mouth watering.

"Four!" She laughed. "You have an appetite this morning."

"I'm going to share." I grinned quickly.

Her eyes turned curious, and I knew it would be easier to just tell her where I was going than to have her ask every other person who walked through the door if they knew what Eddie Donovan was up to.

"I'm taking them to the hospital. Thought Amnesia would like something other than green Jell-O."

How easily her name rolled off my tongue. I'd been afraid I would slip up and call her by a different one.

"They're calling that poor girl Amnesia?" Joline asked, leaning on the other side of the counter. She was good and interested now.

Pushing my hands into the pockets of my zip-up hoodie, I said, "She insists it's her name now... since, you know, she can't remember her real one."

"So it's true? She really can't remember a thing?"

"Nothing."

"Such a tragedy. And to have no one at all come for her... She must be terrified."

"She has me," I said, my voice lowering.

Joline smiled, her dusty hand reaching out, and I surrendered mine from my pocket. Her hand was warm and dry giving mine a squeeze. "She's a lucky girl to have someone like you looking out for her."

My lips curled upward. "I'll be sure to tell her you said so."

Swatting at me before pulling back, she made a tsking sound. "You want coffee with those buns, hon?"

"Of course," I replied instantly. "My regular, but maybe make hers a hot chocolate. Not really sure if she likes coffee."

"Jeremy, get out here!" Joline called around the wall. Then she went over to the register and pressed a bunch of buttons.

Jeremy appeared with an apron tied around his front, wiping his hands on a towel just like the one his wife had used. "Eddie!" he said jovially, extending a hand for us to shake over the counter. "What can we do for ya?"

"I need a coffee and a hot chocolate, Jeremy, STAT. Eddie has places to be."

"Coming up!" He retreated to the coffee bar behind the large glass pastry counter and began filling the order.

"The buns are in the back still. We were just drizzling the glaze on them. They're still warm. I'll just grab them for you."

Joline and Jeremy worked like a fine-tuned machine. No sooner than she appeared with a pastry box with a clear window on top did her husband set the two beverages in tall paper cups on the counter beside it.

After handing over the money and adding a couple singles to the tip jar beside the register, I picked up the coffees and smiled. "Thanks, guys. I'm sure these are going to be great."

"Bring her by when they spring her. I'll let her sample everything in the case!" Joline offered, and I knew it wasn't just a polite invitation. It was genuine. "And tell your mother I said hello!"

"I will." I promised, then stepped back out into the dewy, foggy morning, balancing the breakfast in my hands as I walked to the truck.

I stepped onto Amnesia's floor before the clock even hit seven. It was quieter in here this time morning, but a couple nurses were sitting at the nurses' station. The second they saw me, the older one shot out of her chair and rushed around the counter.

"Morning, ladies," I said, smiling. "Just bringing Amnesia something from Joline's."

She didn't smile. "It's not visiting hours, Eddie." She moved in front of me.

"I won't tell if you won't." I winked and started past.

Her hand hit the center of my chest, gently pushing backward. "You can't go in there. Not right now."

Whatever I heard in her voice put me on high alert. Drawing back, I pinned her with a hard stare. "Why?" My mouth suddenly felt dry and my heart was no longer beating at its resting rate.

The nurse hedged, and I gave her a stony stare. "She had a rough night."

"Poor thing." The other nurse, still sitting behind the counter, chimed in.

I didn't know what that meant, but I was too far gone to even ask. It didn't matter. Stepping swiftly around the nurse, I strode right down the hall.

"No visitors!" the nurse exclaimed, rushing after me. She grabbed my arm and tried to restrain me.

My feet slowed but didn't stop. I looked pointedly at where she held my bicep, then flashed my stare up to her face. "I'm going in."

She drew back instantly, shock on her face. I brushed her off and strode away. People knew me as easygoing, ready to smile, never far from a laugh. Charm wasn't something I worked at; it just was, like my dimples. What people didn't often see was the steel at my core. When I wanted something, no one would get in my way.

I didn't pause at Amnesia's door. I walked right in. My eyes went straight toward the bed. I used my foot to make sure it didn't slam behind me.

She was huddled on her side, curled in on herself, eyes on the door. There was a flash of stark fear on her face when I first stepped in, but then recognition replaced it and with it I was sure came a look of relief.

"Eddie?" Amnesia asked, pushing up into a sitting position. She looked rumpled and tired, dark circles beneath her eyes. "What are you doing here?"

"Brought you some breakfast," I answered off hand. "What's wrong?"

Her eyes drifted toward the items in my hands. "The nurses didn't try and stop you?"

"They tried," I said, hooking my foot around the leg of the chair and dragging it across the room beside her bed.

"They're going to be mad." She frowned.

I paused. "Do you want me to go?"

Her reply was instantaneous. "No."

Warmth suffused my chest. "Then don't worry about it. I'll make sure no one's mad."

Her eyes seemed like saucers in her face. "Everything's okay out there? In the hall?"

Resisting the urge to frown, I set the box and cups on her bedside table. "Everything is fine. You gonna tell me what's wrong?"

"What did you bring me?" she asked, peeking at the treats.

I went with it because her voice sounded more like it did yesterday, and the color in her cheeks seemed to be getting warmer. I'd get my answers even if I had to sit here all day.

"Bananas." I teased her because I wanted to see her smile.

It worked. "I think I've changed my mind. You should leave." She teased.

"You would dismiss me so effortlessly?" I asked, feigning sadness.

"Bananas are no joking matter."

Chuckling, I held out the cup. "Hot chocolate. Extra whipped cream."

Taking it, she wrapped her hands around the heated cup and sighed a little. I noticed the goose bumps along her bare arms.

Her brown eyes shifted up to mine. "I don't know if I like hot chocolate."

"Give it a go." I gestured, my heart squeezing just a little.

Tenderness swelled within me as Amnesia tentatively tilted the cup to her lips, allowing the warm, rich liquid to coat her tongue.

Her eyes shot to mine the second she tasted the concoction. She went back for a second sip. Then she smiled. "Yes."

I sat down, pleased. "I would've had serious doubts about you if you didn't like it."

"What else you got?"

"Fresh from the bakery… monkey bread muffins."

She shrugged. "I have no idea what that is."

Flipping the lid over, I reached in and snatched a pastry out of the box, holding it out to her. She studied it cautiously, as if she really thought I was trying to somehow turn it into a banana. When she finally reached out for it, I snatched my hand back and took a huge bite right off the top.

"Hey!" she demanded.

"You snooze, ya lose," I said, chewing obnoxiously. With a sound of extreme pleasure, I took another huge bite. Then I retrieved a second muffin and handed it over.

She took it, studying the lumpy top that glistened with glaze and was dotted with cinnamon and raisins. It looked huge in her hand.

As I finished off my breakfast, I watched her. The hot chocolate was tucked into her lap. Then she plucked a chunk off the muffin top and stuffed it into her mouth.

Her eyes rolled back in her head, and a low moan filled the room. My lower belly tightened, and desire filled my limbs.

"This is so good." Her voice was excited, like she'd found a treasure.

I didn't say anything, just staring at her, completely taken in. She seemed different now from the first moment I walked in. Livelier, less stoic. It was almost as if she'd been lying in bed, trembling with fear.

I didn't bring it up just then, though I sorely wanted to. I waited, watching, bemused as she devoured her muffin between sips of hot chocolate.

"Thank you for this," she said after several minutes of us just sitting in the same room. "This is literally the best thing I've eaten since I woke up."

"You're welcome," I replied simply.

"I didn't think you'd come by until tonight," she said, almost shy.

There was no way I could have gone the entire day without seeing her. "What happened? Why did the nurse try and keep me out? And why did you look that way when I walked in?"

"What way?" she asked, self-conscious.

"Terrified."

Both her hands wrapped around the drink, as if she drew strength from the warm liquid. Once again, I noted the goose bumps racing along her bare arms and even over the exposed part of her shoulder.

I didn't bother pointing out the obvious. She was cold. Me saying so wouldn't change that. Instead, I rose out of the chair, unzipping the hoodie I'd thrown on this morning before I left the house.

"What are you doing?" Her voice was leery.

Moving slow, I wrapped the jacket around her back, tucking it beneath her chin. Her automatic reaction was to sigh perceptively and push her chin against the softness of the hood.

"Do you have anything to wear except that hospital gown?" I asked once I was back in the chair. My skin hummed, wanting to be closer to her.

"Not yet." She glanced down, lightly fingering the edge of the forest-green fabric. It was just like the T-shirt she'd commented on when I saw her the day before, except in sweatshirt form. The back had the logo for Loch Gen.

"What happened?" I asked again.

Her eyes lifted, that wide-eyed, shocked expression she wore when I'd walked in accosted me. Her throat bobbed as she swallowed, her body shrinking into the jacket.

"Someone tried to kill me."

CHAPTER TEN

AMNESIA

"You remembered?" Eddie's voice was part awestruck, part wary as he gaped at the words I'd just dropped into our casual breakfast like a bomb.

"I think so." I shook my head. "Actually, I-I'm not sure," I answered, confused. I barely had time to sort out how I was feeling or what I knew. I was too busy being overwhelmed by it all. I was beginning to think an empty mind might be a better one. It was cleaner, a whole lot less messy.

What a reprieve Eddie was. The second he walked in, it became clear why my thoughts continued to drift to him since what happened just hours ago. He was a safe place for my over-exhausted, blank-yet-incredibly-full brain to rest.

"So you aren't sure if someone tried to kill you?" Eddie said, sitting forward in the chair, nearly balancing his tall frame on the edge of the seat. His voice was patient, but his body language was anything but.

"Oh, someone definitely tried to kill me. They were here. In this hospital."

"When?" he demanded, glancing around as if suddenly compelled to check every last crevice and corner in this room.

It made me feel better, but he forgot the most important place. A place I would likely fear for the rest of my life. I pointed down at the bed. "Under the bed."

Eddie frowned. "What?"

"You didn't check under the bed."

Indulgently, without an ounce of disdain on his handsome face, Eddie crouched out of the chair, planted his hands on the floor, and actually searched under the bed.

Seconds later, he reappeared. "All clear."

I sighed with relief. I knew no one was under there, but the lingering feeling of being spied on was very difficult to shake.

"Tell me what happened," he urged softly.

I nodded, my eyes finding his and latching on. We didn't touch at all, but I still felt him just through the blue focus of his gaze. He made me feel stronger. I didn't know why.

"I've been having trouble sleeping." I began, still leaving my eyes trained on his. "Since I woke up from the coma. Lying in this bed just feels so overdone, you know? I lay here for months without moving or thinking... just being here. I'm tired of lying here. It's just all so unsettling."

"You've lost a lot of time." He spoke emphatically, sorrow deep in his tone.

It was as if he truly understood. I didn't know how he did, but it wasn't an act or even just sympathy. Eddie genuinely sensed the loss I'd experienced. Not just of the time either, but the loss of my mind.

"Last night I had a nightmare." I pushed on, wanting to spill it all. I wanted someone to believe me. "I dreamt of floating, sinking in the lake. The water was so dark it was like an entire universe all on its own. And I was there alone. At first, I remember feeling relieved, like a soul-crushing weight was finally being lifted."

"But?"

"But then I realized I was drowning, and my body began to fight. There was a dark figure, a person, lurking at the surface of the water." I shivered as I recalled the vision.

Eddie gently reached out and took the nearly empty hot chocolate from my hands. I surrendered it to him, then tucked both hands inside his sweatshirt.

It was the softest thing I could remember touching.

"When I broke the surface, he raised something above his head and brought it crashing down over me. He wanted me back beneath the water… He wanted me to drown."

"It was a man?" Eddie asked, his eyes sharpening on my face. There was a slight tick in the width of his jaw as the back of his teeth ground together.

My stomach fluttered a little, watching that muscle work.

"I don't know. I couldn't see them. It was too dark."

"You said someone was here, in this room. Was that part of the dream?" He pressed.

Against the warm, plush fabric, my fingers flexed. I shook my head. "No. He was here."

Eddie leaned forward, placing his hand on the bed between us. His palm lay open and exposed, inviting me in.

I stayed where I was, and he didn't seem the least offended. He didn't even pull away. Instead, he stayed there, offering his hand should I change my mind.

"I went into the bathroom to get a drink. I was upset from the dream. I couldn't tell if it was just something my mind made up or if it was some kind of sick memory. I thought I heard someone out here in the room. But after a while, I figured I was just being paranoid. When I left the bathroom and climbed back into bed, someone grabbed my ankle from beneath the bed."

Eddie's open hand flexed. His chin lowered so I could only see the top of his dark head. "Then what?"

"We fought. I fell, and they climbed on top of me, covered my mouth and my nose—" I stopped talking, recalling how I felt in the exact moment I realized this person wanted me dead. Blindly, my hand found his, slipping against his inviting palm.

Instantly, his warm fingers folded around mine, clasping them in a reassuring hold. He was much warmer than me, as if he were the sun and I a glacier.

"I managed to get away and into the hall. The person ran away when I started to scream." I finished.

The pad of his thumb brushed lightly over the back of my hand, just grazing over the thick bandage covering the spot where the IV had been.

"Is that why this is out?" he questioned, again lightly stroking the bandage.

I nodded. "It pulled out when I was fighting."

Still with his head bowed, Eddie said nothing for long, silent moments. Paranoia ate at me, making my stomach knot. He didn't believe me. He thought I was crazy, too.

When he pulled back slightly, disappointment crowded inside me. But he wasn't pulling away. As he moved, he brought my hand up, lifting it so he could press a gentle kiss to the back just at the edge of the bandage. Warm tingles spread across the surface of my skin from the softness of his lips. The sensation seeped into my pores, creating a certain, quiet peace that spread like a tree rooting in the ground.

My heart skipped a beat, and an overwhelming emotion welled inside me.

True blue eyes finally lifted, meeting mine. "Why aren't the police here, Am?"

"Am?" I tilted my head.

"Amnesia is a bit of a mouthful." He shrugged, the side of his mouth lifting, a rakish appearance transforming his face.

"The staff didn't believe me."

His boyish expression was replaced with anger and disbelief. "What?"

"No one saw anyone enter my room or run out. Apparently, no one saw the person anywhere. When they found me, security searched the whole building."

"They think you made it up?" he growled.

"They think I dreamed it all, and when I woke up, I was so scared I stumbled into the hallway. The shrink is probably on her way to see me now," I muttered.

"Tell me what you're thinking," Eddie urged, scooting the chair even closer to the bed.

My hand was still in his. The way his fingers flexed around mine in such a protective nature stirred something in me. Some emotion I didn't understand. It was a feeling I was scared of but at the same time craved.

"My mind hasn't shut off," I confided.

"Yeah, I know." Again, he seemed to truly understand.

"It sounds crazy." I warned.

The double dimples in his cheeks appeared, and just looking at them made me feel lighter. "I'd say this entire situation is a little crazy."

"They were here," I whispered forcefully, almost angrily. I'd cried when the nurses told me no one had been found. And nothing in the room or anywhere could prove I hadn't just been dreaming. They tried to give me some pills to help me "rest," they said. I took them like a good patient and then spit them out and put them under my pillow.

I didn't want to be drugged. My head was confused enough as it was. I didn't want muffled thoughts and a hazy cloud hanging over me when I was trying to make sense of my new reality.

"I did have a bad dream, but when I woke up, someone was *in this room*. I wasn't imagining it. I wasn't. It was too real... They wanted me dead."

"Okay," Eddie said, trying to soothe me. "I believe you. It's okay."

"You believe me?" I was surprised.

His eyes met mine, stoic and nearly intrusive. "I'm on your side. No matter what. I'll always back you up."

"Why?" I said, my voice trembling and wet. "Why would you be here for me, a complete stranger?"

His eyes saddened, the hold on my stare lost. "I don't want to be a stranger to you, Am."

My chest squeezed a little. I realized beneath his oozing personality, Eddie carried his own sorrow.

The door to my room swung in, and the clip-clap of the head shrinker's high heels was like a hammer in my brain. "The staff told me you—" Her voice cut off when she saw I wasn't alone. "You have a visitor."

Gently, Eddie tugged his hand from mine and stood, offering it to the doctor to shake. "Eddie Donovan."

"Ah, yes. I've heard a lot about you, Mr. Donovan."

"Eddie." He corrected. Then he glanced around at me with a wicked smile. "Talking about me, are you?"

"No," I retorted.

The look on his face made the doctor laugh, and I admit I thought about smiling, too. "From the staff." The doctor corrected. "They don't talk about the patients, but you, sir, are not a patient, and from what I hear, you're at this hospital quite often."

"I pulled Amnesia out of the lake," he explained. He didn't seem surprised at all the hospital staff would be talking about him.

I thought it was rude.

And slightly amusing. He definitely was a guy worth mentioning.

"It's nice to meet you," the doctor said formally. "I'm sorry to interrupt. However, I have an appointment with Amnesia."

"We can do it later," I said, in no hurry to see Eddie leave.

"My schedule is full today, and given the earlier events, I think we should talk."

I opened my mouth to argue, suddenly ready to do just that.

"It's okay, Am. I have to get to work anyway. The place can't open without me." His eyes met mine, his lips offering a reassuring smile.

I pleaded with my stare for him to not to leave me here.

His body language changed from relaxed and soothing to nearly formidable. Turning his back, he spoke to the doctor. "Can you give us a minute? I'd like to say bye."

The doctor seemed mildly surprised, but she inclined her head. "I'll be just outside," she stated before the door latched behind her.

I fell back against the pillows.

Eddie sat on the edge of the chair again, positioning himself toward me. Lifting his eyebrows, he asked, "How long do you think it will take her to get tired of waiting?"

I laughed. "Two seconds."

Eddie snickered.

"I thought you were leaving."

His reply was so simple. "You want me to stay."

A feeling of selfishness came over me. "I do." I admitted. "But I know you can't."

"If it's what you want, it will happen."

I tilted my head, a chunk of hair hitting my chin. "Didn't you say the store wouldn't open without you?"

"I do have the key." His voice was entirely ornery.

I giggled. "Go to work, Eddie."

"What about you, Am?" he asked, searching my face with his stare.

"I'll be fine," I said, but I must not have been too convincing, because he called me out.

"Liar."

"I just… They don't believe me."

Eddie thought about my words, sat forward, and held out his hand for mine. I surrendered almost immediately. His touch made me feel connected to something. To someone. "Do you believe someone tried to kill you last night?"

I didn't even have to think about it. "I really do."

"Then don't let them change your mind."

"Eddie?" I whispered.

He whispered back, "Am?"

"I can't help but think…"

His fingers tightened around mine. "You can tell me anything."

I believed him. With every part of me.

"The figure in my dream and the one here at the hospital... What if they were the same? What if whoever threw me in the lake is back to finish what they started?"

He sucked in a breath. Anger glimmered in his eyes. "I won't let them hurt you..."

It was almost as if he wanted to say more but didn't.

"What if that dream wasn't a memory? What if I really dreamt everything?" I just didn't know. I couldn't remember.

The worst thing about all of this was not being able to trust even myself.

Eddie stood, leaning in close, and cupped the back of my head with his palm. The fullness of his lips pressed against my hairline, lingering for a gentle kiss.

"One day at a time, Am." His lips brushed over my skin as he murmured, then pulled back.

Lifting my eyes, I watched him stay close, lean down, and tug the sweatshirt closer around me. "Hang on to this for me, 'kay?"

I nodded.

Our stares bounced between each other. He tucked a strand of hair behind my ear. "We're going to figure this out. Someday you'll remember."

I couldn't help but feel there was something specific he wanted me to recall.

"I'll bring you dinner tonight." Eddie promised, pulling away from the bed.

"Wait," I called out.

He returned instantly.

Delving my hand beneath the pillow, I fished around until I found the two pills I'd pretended to swallow earlier. "Throw these away for me?" I asked, dumping them into his hand.

He laughed when he saw them. "Refusing medication? You bad, bad girl."

I smirked. "I don't want anything that's going to make it harder to remember."

"These aren't pain meds, are they?" he asked, frowning at the tablets.

"No. I swear."

Eddie tucked them into his pocket and smiled. "I'll see you tonight."

The second he was gone, I pushed my arms through his sweatshirt and took a deep breath. It smelled like him.

How easily I could grow attached to him.

The thought was a beautiful one but one I couldn't allow to take root within me. In a world where I knew nothing, could trust no one, and might very well be the target of a faceless murderer, growing attached was the most foolish thing I could do.

But oh, if I were able to trust anyone... that someone would be him.

CHAPTER ELEVEN

EDWARD

I was a punctual guy. Not today, though. Today, I was late for work. It was the first day in what had to be at least ten years that Loch Gen didn't open at precisely nine a.m. Not that I could claim perfection for those last ten years. I wasn't quite old enough for that.

A lot of those years and the honor of always opening on time went to my father, the owner of the general store. Loch Gen was the family business. Before my father, my grandfather had run the place and his father before him. Even though Dad was still the official owner, over the past few years, I'd been doing more and more. I knew all the work, and he was basically grooming me to take over completely.

He was ready to retire, and most days, I thought I was ready to own my own store. Hell, most days, it already felt I owned it.

After parking in the gravel lot down the street, I walked quickly toward the store that sat at the prime location at the end of the block. The front of the building faced the street, so no matter where you stood in the "business district," this building was in sight.

Business district = all the shops everyone in town used.

As I approached, a tingly feeling climbed up the back of my neck. My gaze sharpened, bouncing around on various points of interest, looking for anything that might be out of order. Everything seemed fine, until I got close enough to see the door was ajar. Not all the way either, just slightly, as if someone thought they latched it behind them but didn't.

Alarm bells sounded in my head. My fingers flew to the front pocket of my jeans, diving inside to make sure I still had the key. It jangled when I yanked it free, further fueling my panic.

What the fuck?

A noise from inside pushed me forward, a heavy thud. Without hesitation, I plunged onward, hitting open the door so it swung in all the way.

"Who's in here?" I demanded in a half growl, half yell.

There was another muffled sound toward the back. Caution shot along my nerve endings, but I wasn't about to walk away.

Silently, I crept back toward the sound, which was coming from the large stockroom. They were probably trying to rob the place, doing it right under my nose. As I sulked along, I drew my cell out of my back pocket and called up the number for the local police station. They would have someone here in under five minutes.

The stockroom door was open all the way. Light spilled out across the floor, and whoever was in there made no attempt at being stealthy. Sucking in a breath, my heart pounding violently, I charged into the back.

"Drop the shit, scumbag!" I roared.

A deep yell and a flurry of movement drew me around to the side. "Edward!" a familiar voice exclaimed. "What on earth…?"

All the breath whooshed out of me. "Dad! What are you doing here? I thought you were robbing the place."

"This is my store, you know." He glowered, not realizing I'd nearly clobbered him.

"Yes, I'm well aware, Dad. But you don't come here very often," I replied, holding on to my patience by a thin thread.

"Well, when I get the call my store isn't opening on time, I come. I do have a key."

"I'm only a few minutes late," I grumbled. I should have known someone in town would have called him up and tattled on me.

"It's nine thirty, son," he said stiffly.

Fuck. Was it really?

"Sorry, Dad. It won't happen again." Actually, it might. If Amnesia needed me, then this store would sit closed until she was okay. I didn't bother announcing that, though. It probably wouldn't go over well, and I was already in a foul mood.

I wanted to be at the hospital with her. I wanted to make sure she was okay. It worried me no one believed someone had been in her room. What if they came back?

I wasn't confident she could protect herself. She was frail, just recovering from something terrible.

"I was getting worried. Thought I was going to have to call your mother and tell her you didn't show up to work," Dad remarked, turning back to the box he was hefting.

"Didn't the person who called also tell you where I was?" I muttered.

"You've been spending a lot of time with her." He observed, stacking the box and then reaching for another one.

I laughed, a humorless sound. Of course he already knew where I was. Town gossips for the win.

"You here because you're mad I opened late or because you and Mom don't approve of me seeing Amnesia?"

"I opened at nine on the dot. So technically, your record is still spotless."

"I appreciate that," I said, and I did. I liked this store. It was important to the town, and it was a place I'd spent a lot of time. As odd as it sounded, I'd put a lot of work into this place, but it had put a lot of work into me. In many ways, Loch Gen was the reason I was still sane.

Dad glanced inside the box he'd just moved and frowned. "This isn't the napkins. Where the hell are the napkins?"

Stifling a smile, I replied, "I reorganized everything back here. Paper goods are over there now, more accessible because they need restocked faster." I gestured, then walked over to show him. Then I went on about a few other changes I'd made.

He gazed around as if he were just noticing all the modifications. "Looks good," he said, gruff. "Very streamlined."

I didn't show it, but his praise meant something to me. "What do you need napkins for?" I asked, going to the box and pulling out some packages.

"You need some on the shelf out there, and we're almost out at home."

I loaded up my arms and went out into the store. It was a large place, and it fit in with the lake charm of the entire town. Loch Gen sort of looked like a big log cabin. The walls were all wood, the type that looked weathered. The ceilings were pitched, also covered with wood, and there were log beams that crossed the width of it. In between them, ceiling fans hung down, which I always kept on (set on low) for better air circulation.

The walls were decorated with old boat oars, the Maine flag, and some old Maine license plates. There was also a big, red metal lobster, but the paint was chipping. A few windows were scattered throughout the building. They didn't look commercial; instead, they looked like windows you might find in a house.

My favorite part of the large store was the upstairs loft. It stretched just half the length of the building, and the wooden railings were open so from up there, you could look down over the entire place.

The narrow staircase to get up there was against the wall toward the back, and tucked beneath them was a small bathroom. Up in the loft area was my office of sorts. There was a desk, an updated desktop computer, and everything else I needed to essentially run the place.

The back of the store was lined with coolers where we kept a lot of the dairy and cold items. Near it was also the frozen section. The produce section was toward the front of the store, the aisles for most everything else in the middle. Toward the back, near the bathroom and stairs, we had a section of clothing and other Lake Loch merchandise. T-shirts, hoodies, hats, etc.

I was hoping to expand on the place over the next five years, bring in some new groceries and goods, but it was something that took time.

After stocking up the napkins, I went to the front and closed the front door that was still wide open. The watchful eye of my father followed when I stepped behind the long counter and checked the register (which was not old like Joline's. I used an updated electronic one that took credit cards).

"I already booted it up and checked the drawer," he told me.

"Thanks," I said, still making sure it was all in order. Mostly, I was just avoiding him. I knew he was going to bring it up.

As much as I thought about Amnesia (she occupied about eighty percent of my thoughts these days), I wasn't so keen on talking about her. I felt defensive. Protective. Wary.

"How's she doing?" Dad asked. "Any memories yet?"

I thought of the dream she told me about, a conversation she shared with me in confidence, and how haunted and unsure of herself she seemed about the whole thing.

"No memories. None at all," I said. "But physically, she's doing better."

Abandoning the register, I propped my elbows on the counter and looked at Dad.

I looked a lot like him—dark hair, square jaw. I got my height from him and also my work ethic. My blue eyes, though, those I got from Mom.

"You're worried about her. Involved."

"I'm not involved with her, Dad. I'm being her friend, something she needs right now."

He sighed. "I didn't mean romantically. But I think we both know you want it to be more than friendship. I meant you're involved with her life, invested in her."

"Of course I am."

"You still think it's her? After spending time with her, talking to her. You think she's her?"

I looked up, meeting his eyes. "I know she is."

Dad came forward, stopping just on the other side of the wide counter and resting his hands on the top. "Just because you *want* something to be true, son, doesn't mean it is."

I knew he wasn't trying to be unkind. Or even pessimistic. He was worried. I saw it in the lines around his eyes and the set of his lips. I was sorry he was concerned. My mom, too. But it wouldn't change anything.

"You haven't seen her. No one has come to see her," I said, angry.

Just because I knew where he was coming from didn't mean I liked it.

"People are wary, son. You can't blame them. This is an odd situation. People are afraid to get involved."

"So in the meantime, Amnesia suffers for it. She's already suffered, Dad, more than any of us know. Someone tried to kill her. She was abused."

My father swallowed thickly, his eyes downcast. "Everyone feels really bad about what happened to that girl."

"Amnesia," I said, my voice rumbling with stone. "She asked to be called Amnesia. You know why?" I fumed, suddenly dumping out all the shit I'd been holding inside. "Because she thinks that's all she is. A total memory wipe. She literally has nothing. I gave her my hoodie this morning because all she has for clothes is that goddamn hospital gown."

"You better watch your mouth." He warned, sounding fatherly. "We're at your place of business. Anyone can hear."

"Maybe more people should hear!" I went on. "She's one of us! One of Lake Loch's own. This town takes care of its own; that's what this small town is about. But not right now. Right now, everyone's tongues are wagging and everyone is curious, but no one wants to do anything."

"I can see you're upset." Dad tried to reason.

I laughed. "I won't turn my back on her. If I had been there before, she wouldn't be sitting in a hospital room with nothing at all." Guilt threatened to crush me. "Things would be so different."

"Edward," Dad said, his voice stern. "This wasn't your fault. Your mother and I thought you understood that. We thought you'd finally begun to let go. But now she's here, and you're sucked back down. We don't want to see you give up everything for someone who probably isn't even who you want her to be."

"Even if she's not... doesn't she deserve help?" I asked, my chest tight. I felt I was grappling at thin air, trying to find something to hold on to. Something solid and real.

Dad's expression went soft and guilt flooded his face. "Yes. Yes, she does."

"I want it to be her," I whispered.

Dad covered my hand with his. "I know that, Eddie. But you have to know it probably isn't her, and if it is, she's not the girl you used to know."

The doctor basically said the same thing. I knew it, too. But it didn't stop me from being drawn to her anyway.

"I can't even ask her. Or bring it up. The doctor said her mind needs time." I confided.

"Your mother and I will stop by the hospital, visit her," Dad said. "If she's that important to you, then she's important to us."

"Really?" I was mildly surprised he was coming around.

"Of course. But you have to promise me something." He met my stare. "Do not let this consume you. Focus on your work, your friends, your house. Don't spiral down and let everything you've built crumble to nothing."

"I won't." I vowed. I was stronger than he gave me credit for. Maybe that was just a parent thing. I didn't know, and truly, I didn't care.

He nodded. "All right then. I'll go home and talk to your mother. I'm sure she'll be in to get flowers or something for your... for, ah, Amnesia."

"Thank you, Dad."

"And if you need some extra time off from the store, call me. I may be getting older, but I can still hold down this fort."

"Of that I have no doubt." I grinned.

The bell on the door chimed, and a customer walked in. Beneath the counter, the phone rang.

"Better get to work," Dad said, grabbed the pack of napkins, and headed toward the door.

I waved as I answered the phone and watched him go.

After I hung up the call, I noticed someone hovering near the end of an aisle not too far from the counter.

"Good morning, Maggie." I called her out and smiled widely. "I didn't see you come in. How are you?"

She moved forward, carrying a shopping basket filled with things. "I think you were in the back with your father when I came in. The door was open."

She was here the whole time when Dad and I were talking. She must have heard. We certainly hadn't been quiet.

"You heard," I said, not bothering to pretend. Gossip made this town go 'round.

Besides, Margaret Foster had a right to her curiosity.

Maggie set the basket on the counter between us, peering over the top of a head of leafy lettuce. "You really think it's her?" she asked, her voice quiet.

This time I knew there were other shoppers in here, so I was quieter as well. "Yes, I do."

Maggie's eyes filled with unshed tears and her lower lip wobbled. Margaret always looked put together, her face "always on," and her brown hair was always styled. But not in an overly done way, just in a way that said she cared about her appearance. Her clothes were casual, just a pair of jeans and a T-shirt bearing the name of our lake.

"Everything you said is true? She still hasn't recovered any memory?" Then she leaned over the counter to whisper, "And someone tried to kill her?"

I nodded. "Tried to drown her."

Her voice was hushed. "I'm so ashamed."

"Why?" I asked, frowning.

"I haven't been to the hospital. I was afraid it would bring up too many memories. But I was selfish. She's lost way more than I have."

"It's a difficult situation. Besides, up until a couple days ago, she was in a coma."

"But she's awake now."

"Yes, she is." I smiled. "She's got some spunk to her. She's a real fighter."

Maggie's eyes lit up. "You really care about her."

"Yes, I do."

"I want to help. What can I do?"

First my parents; now Maggie. People were coming around, and I knew once they actually met Amnesia, they would welcome her back.

"Well," I said, thoughtful, "she needs some clothes. Nothing fancy, not even a lot. All she has is the hospital gown."

"Poor thing." Maggie tsked. "I'll make some calls, get some donations and a few necessities."

"That would be great." I smiled. "I'll take them to her when I go visit."

"Actually, I'll take it. I need to visit. It's time."

Concern darkened my face, and Maggie saw it instantly.

"I won't say anything. I understand the situation."

"Thank you, Maggie. This will mean so much to her."

"It's like you said. People in Lake Loch take care of each other. I don't know where I'd be today if I hadn't had everyone's support after my Chris passed."

I rang up her groceries, and she rushed off to gather clothes for Amnesia, a spark of determination in her eyes.

Despite the fact no one else seemed to believe this was who I believed, they couldn't prove I was wrong. For now, she was just a victim of something horrible, and she needed help. People were starting to see this, and they would reach out.

It was good enough.

For now.

CHAPTER TWELVE

AMNESIA

It seemed more important than ever that I remember. No matter the significance, my brain just wouldn't cooperate. I turned inward so much sometimes it felt I was losing the present to try and catch up with the past. I bargained with myself, pleaded even, but to no avail.

My mind just wouldn't give up its secrets. I wondered more than once how bad those hidden memories were if my own mind wouldn't give them up.

The doctors all said it was a defense mechanism, my own body and mind protecting me from further pain. Part of me was grateful for the protection, but the other part of me was beyond frustrated.

How could I move on if I didn't know where I'd already been? What if there was a life out there, a life that belonged to me that had been sitting on pause all this time? What if people were waiting for me, wondering where I'd gone?

But those people never came looking. Those people must not care very much.

It was a constant tug-of-war. A constant struggle between knowing and not knowing. Which was better?

It seemed they were both hell.

The thing that bothered me most about not knowing was I couldn't prove someone was trying to kill me. They still didn't believe me about the attack, and the more time that went on without another one, the less and less likely it was I would ever convince them.

Hell, some days they almost had *me* convinced I'd dreamed it all. When that happened, I would think back on what Eddie told me the morning after. *Don't let them change your mind.*

True, there was a lot of stuff I didn't know, but I did know the difference between a dream and reality. I'd dreamed many nights since that first nightmare. All of them were the same: me drowning, floating in an underwater world of quiet and peace. But it wasn't the kind of peace I liked; it was eerie. Creepy even. And there was always the figure, sometimes a mere shadow— waiting, lurking, trying to claim me with total darkness.

The person never had a face. Their identity was never revealed to me.

Yet I knew, without a doubt, they were real.

The doctors said it was likely a memory trying to surface. A memory of the night someone tried to kill me. I wasn't sure how I got away. No one was. My only guess would be whatever it was the person hit me with shoved me down deep, and I got lost. They couldn't find me. The current was strong that night, and it likely saved my life. It pulled me away from the killer to where Eddie eventually found me.

Even though no one believed someone tried to kill me at the hospital (besides Eddie), no one disputed the fact I was almost a victim of murder. It had also been brought up—very gently, of course—I was the recipient of long-term abuse before I ended up in the lake. The condition I was in and a lot of the injuries (healed over and fresh) all pointed toward abuse.

Again, maybe I was better off not knowing. It seemed learning about it all might be more crippling than starting over.

But what about the murderer?

Who were they? What did they want from me and where are they now?

Maybe there wasn't a murderer at all. Maybe that night I'd just been a victim of circumstance, some random violent act.

It was exhausting to think about. Round and round my mind would go. Between doctor visit after visit, test after test.

I'd been in this hospital for three weeks since I'd woken up, and I was no closer to answers than I was that first day.

I was afraid but also oddly relieved.

Perhaps the relief came from no more attempts to attack me, though I still believed someone was out to get me. I just wished I knew why.

Eddie walked in, and the worst of my fears slipped into the background. They never went away, but Eddie was powerful enough to make me forget them for at least a little while.

He'd been here to visit me every single day since I woke up. For three weeks now, I saw him at least once a day, sometimes twice. He pretty much came and went as he pleased, the nursing staff finally accepting the fact he was going to be here.

My head shrinker (aka Dr. Kline) often warned me about getting too close or too attached to him. It annoyed me. I felt she was trying to take away the only thing I really felt was real in my life. I needed him.

And yeah, I guess I saw Dr. Kline's point. But didn't everyone need someone? Being alone wasn't easy, especially when you were alone and scared.

'Course, I wasn't as alone as I was three weeks ago. Not really. Things had been changing.

Wasn't that the saying? The more things changed, the more they stayed the same. My same was my mind. Its blank pages never filled in.

"You ready?" Eddie asked, bestowing upon me a grin that literally lit up my insides. His dimples always made my stomach flutter, and the way his eyes always looked at me as if he'd known me forever gave me some sort of peace.

"They said it was okay?" I asked.

"Who would say no to this face?" He scoffed, pointing at himself.

I laughed and slid off the bed toward him and the door.

"Grab your jacket. It's chilly out there."

I backtracked to grab the Loch Gen hoodie Eddie gave me weeks ago and tugged it on. It was too big, which was why I liked it. That and the fact he'd given it to me off his own back. Plus, it had the Loch Ness Monster on it. Who wouldn't want to wear that?

"You look good today," Eddie said, looking me over but ultimately settling on my eyes. "Healthy."

"That's the goal," I said, proud he'd noticed. It had been a long three weeks, but even I saw the difference when I looked in the mirror.

We walked past the nurses' station, down the hall, and stepped into the elevator. About a week ago, Eddie found me gazing out the window of my room, and he somehow knew I wanted to be outside. To feel the sun on my cheeks, the breeze in my hair. It was fall now, and the leaves were all turning these beautiful colors. It seemed the more I looked out my window, the more caged up I felt.

That day he got permission for us to walk outside in the garden. I hadn't even known there was one, but it was gorgeous.

When the elevator slid open, I bounded off with exuberance I'd only just started to feel recently. Sun filtered through the large glass sliding doors ahead, and I practically ran to get outside.

Eddie laughed, following closely behind.

A few minutes later, we stepped into the thick green grass on the side of the property that was bordered by tall, well-manicured shrubs. The entire garden was shaped like a rectangle, but there were different sections with flower gardens, bushes, and even trees inside. There was also a round stone fountain in the center.

Eddie and I fell into step beside each other, walking our normal route around the garden. Lifting my face toward the blue autumn sky, I breathed in deep and smiled. The air was crisp, the temperature definitely chilly. But I enjoyed it; it made me feel alive.

"Good day today?" Eddie asked.

I could feel his gaze. He looked at me a lot. His stare had a way of making a girl feel as if she were the most desired thing in the room.

"It was fine," I murmured, gazing at some of the leaves twirling in the wind just above the sidewalk. "Just like every other day."

"Any visitors?"

"Not today. But Maggie came yesterday." Several people who lived at Lake Loch came to visit from time to time. I could sense their curiosity, their fascination. But they were kind, and I could understand the interest.

Maggie Foster came more than anyone else (except Eddie). Sometimes we'd play cards or talk about what was going on in the world. She brought me magazines and books. She also pulled the town together and gifted me all the clothes I had to my name. Most of it was simple, like jeans and T-shirts and a pair of sneakers, but I was so grateful.

When she first came with it all, I cried. She cried, too.

Everyone here seemed so sympathetic about what happened to me. So horrified. They also seemed... reserved in a way.

I saw some of the looks I got when no one thought I did. I noticed how sometimes people would whisper when I walked by. I didn't understand it, but honestly, I didn't think much about it. I had enough to worry about as it was.

"I brought you something." Eddie beamed.

"Better not be a banana." I teased as he reached into the kangaroo pocket on the gray hoodie he wore.

Laughing, Eddie produced a red apple, then another. I took the one he offered, noting how perfectly shaped it was.

"From the local orchard. Fall around here always means good apples."

"Thank you," I said and rubbed it on my shirt.

Eddie took a huge bite out of his and smacked his lips as he chewed. "So I was thinking maybe I could sweet talk your doctor into letting me spring you for a while sometime. I could show you around town."

"Really!" I said, pulling back from the apple. "That would be amazing."

I glanced up at him, thinking to return his smile, only he wasn't looking at me. He was looking down at the apple as he devoured it.

A funny feeling wormed around inside me. I glanced around, suddenly very nervous. I felt like someone was watching me, as if I were the center of someone's attention.

"Am?" Eddie questioned, touching my elbow lightly.

I jumped and jerked back.

"Whoa," he said, holding up his hand in surrender. "I didn't mean to scare you."

"I'm sorry. I…" I glanced around again. All I saw was plants and shrubs. There was no one here. *I am losing what little I have left of my mind.*

"What's wrong?" His voice changed, grew deeper, and his body seemed to grow even taller.

"Nothing," I said, brushing off the feeling. "I just thought I saw something out of the corner of my eye." I lied.

Eddie's eyes narrowed.

To distract him, I hooked my arm through his and started strolling toward the fountain. "So tell me about the Loch Ness."

It took a moment to register what I said because he seemed a little lost in focus the minute I entwined our arms. I admit the momentary hum of electricity between us had been distracting.

"What?" he said, amused.

"There has to be a legend here, right? I mean why else the Loch Ness on the back of the shirts? And the lake is called Lochlain… which everyone just calls Loch."

"You want to know about the Loch Ness Monster." He cackled.

I shrugged. "It's a mystery of the lake. Just like me."

Eddie stopped walking, gently tugging me around so we were facing one another. "Amnesia," he said, regret in his eyes.

"It's okay," I said. "Maybe I'm better off."

His eyes darkened. I could tell he didn't agree. His lips parted, and I waited to hear what he would say. But from the entrance of the garden, someone called his name.

Both of us turned to see Mary Beth waving her arms, signaling for him to come over.

Eddie sighed. "Let's see what she wants."

"You go," I said, "I'll meet you by the fountain."

His eyes swept over my face in what felt like a caress. It made me long for more. I just wasn't sure of what. "I'll be right back."

I nodded and took another bite of my apple. He walked backward, eyes still on me until I laughed and turned away, toward the fountain.

A cool breeze kicked up the trees and fallen leaves. The scent of earth rose around me. Looking beyond the fountain toward the edge of the garden where fully mature trees were giving up their multicolored sprinkles to the air and grass beneath them, something moved.

I blinked and stared again. Someone was definitely there, just on the other side of the hedge between the trees and the hospital grounds.

I started toward them, sure the feeling I had of being watched wasn't just a feeling. I kept my eyes glued to the spot, hoping the person would reveal themselves. The wind picked up again, my hair blew into my eyes, and I struggled to push it away. Something touched the top of my foot, and I screeched, jumping back.

I laughed when I saw it was just leaves being blown over my shoe by the wind.

"Get a grip, Amnesia," I muttered and then started forward again.

Just as soon as I started walking again, I halted.

Maybe my low scream had drawn attention, or maybe they'd just gotten careless, but I saw them.

Someone crouched just on the other side of the thick shrub. I could see a pair of gloved hands reaching through the branches, parting them for just enough space to glance through.

I was being watched. Stalked.

"Hey!" I yelled impulsively and dashed forward. The branches snapped closed and the bush jiggled with movement. "Stop!" I yelled again, picking up my pace.

When I got to the shrub, there was no one behind it, but lying on the ground were a few snapped branches.

Spinning around, I looked toward the trees, hoping to see a retreating figure. Someone dressed in dark clothing darted behind a tree.

I took off running again, right into the trees, the leaves making a racket underfoot. They were damper here because the thick coverage of branches overhead didn't allow much sunlight through. I slipped once but managed to stay upright.

"Why are you following me?" I yelled, stopping in the center of a cluster of trees. Gasping for breath as my heart hammered relentlessly, I spun in a three-sixty, looking for the lurker.

Pounding feet and rustling leaves made my body stiffen and whirl again. A figure was running toward me, and without thought, I blindly ran toward it, not even sure what I was going to do.

"Whoa!" Eddie yelled, catching me before I collided with him completely. "Amnesia! What the hell are you doing?" he demanded.

Blinking, I glanced up. He was worried, his face frantic with alarm.

"I saw someone!" I said, tugging free of his grip. "Someone is out here. Someone was watching me!"

"Where?" he asked, lowering his voice. He too began scanning the trees.

"They're gone," I said, forlorn. "They ran away."

He snatched me by the shoulders again, staring hard into my eyes. "You're sure you saw someone?"

"I swear!" I burst out, still trying to look around. "What do you want from me?" I screamed.

"Shh, shh," Eddie said, pulling me into his chest.

The impact of my body against his was abrupt and unexpected.

It was the first time he'd ever pulled me into his arms. I'd wondered time and again what it would feel like to be held.

Now I knew.

He was amazing. His body was… enveloping. As if I'd just been folded into a blanket, a thick, comforting quilt. The fear and anger I'd experienced just seconds ago was muted. Wiped away as my cheek pillowed against his solid chest. He was warm. So warm it made me realize I was cold. The sound of his heart was rhythmic and slightly faster than I anticipated.

I pressed a little closer, wanting to commit all of this—all of him—to memory.

This was one thing about total memory loss. There were so many firsts to experience. Some not so great, but *oh*, the others… I needed more firsts. I needed Eddie to show me what else I was missing.

His hand was enormous when he delved it into the thick strands of my hair to cup the back of my head, holding me to him. I clutched at his shirt, no longer because I was scared, but because this physical contact made me feel lonely.

Strange how physical contact evoked loneliness, but suddenly, I knew what I'd been missing all this time.

"Hey," Eddie murmured, "I got you." He hunched closer around me.

I sighed deeply.

"Amnesia." My name slipped out, floating on the breeze, dancing around my ears like the leaves in the wind.

Reluctantly, I pulled back, tipping my chin up so I could stare up into his eyes. His latched onto mine instantly, and even though I was right against him, I felt tugged even closer. Up close, his eyes were even more beautiful. The blue was deep around the edges, which faded into a bright, sapphire shade. They were so blue the white around the irises actually appeared slightly blue as well. The lashes lining his eyes were thick and velvety. My fingers itched to explore his features, trace the strong lines of his jaw, and smooth out his ruffled brows.

He'd originally just grabbed me to stop me from falling, then to comfort me because I was frightened... but it changed. We forgot we were among the trees, out of bounds of the hospital garden. The sunlight here was dim, the air a few degrees cooler.

All I saw was his stare, how I was the center of his world. All I felt were his hands, which slowly slid to cradle the sides of my face. The pads of his thumbs stroked over my cheeks, and his full lips parted just enough for me to hear the intake of his breath.

"You are so very beautiful," he purred.

I pressed my cheek into one of his hands, my eyes sliding closed. I didn't know why, but an intense yearning erupted inside me, almost as if a sinkhole opened and threatened to drag me down.

I knew I basically only had three weeks of life to go on, but oh my God, it felt like I'd wanted something like this—someone like Eddie—forever.

It almost left me gasping in desperation. Against his chest, my hands trembled. And then my knees quaked. Concern started to divide his attention, but I wasn't ready to let this feeling go.

"Eddie," I beckoned.

A soft groan filled his throat, and I stretched up on unsteady feet toward him. His eyes darkened, chin lowered.

A loud crack filled the area around us.

I jerked so far, so fast I would have tumbled onto my ass, but Eddie held on, keeping me upright.

"What was that?" I feared.

Wrapping his arms around me, holding me fiercely, his eyes search over my head, and his upper body swiveled as he took in our surroundings.

"Must have been a branch falling off a tree," he said after a moment.

Slowly, he eased back. I didn't want him to go.

"You're sure you saw someone?" he questioned.

"I swear."

He nodded. "Well, whoever it was is gone now."

I bowed my head. Just when I thought things were getting better… that maybe that night in my room had been a one-time thing…

"C'mon. Mary Beth said they need us inside." He nudged me softly.

I bunched up my nose. "For what?"

"Let's go see."

My shoulders slumped. For more than one reason. He was going to kiss me just then. I wanted him to. I wasn't ready to go back in the hospital. I would drive myself crazy thinking about what just happened, and I'd never sleep tonight.

"Wanna hold my hand?" His words snapped me out of my inner pout.

He held out his hand between us, wiggling his fingers as if to entice me. Giggling a little, I surrendered my hand, and he pushed his fingers between mine, gripping them firmly.

On the way back through the garden, I couldn't help but linger on the edges of the area, peer into the darker bushes, and glance behind us every few steps.

Someone was out there. Watching me. Probably wanting me dead.

Why?

Another important thought then followed…

Someone knew who I was.

CHAPTER THIRTEEN

EDWARD

I resisted the urge to touch her often. It was one of the most difficult challenges I'd ever known. And now, after those few minutes beneath the trees, it would be infinitely more so.

She was thin, too thin really, but still she filled my arms. The gentle way she pushed close and the sound of her indrawn breaths were like steel shackles around me. There were so many unanswered questions, but there was also one endless answer.

I belonged to her.

I almost felt as if I couldn't exist without her. That if she somehow vanished tomorrow, most of who I was would also disappear.

It's why I believed her when she said someone was out there watching her. Watching us. I felt a threat, too. Someone wanted to take her. I didn't know why. Hell, I knew barely anything.

I just knew I wouldn't lose her. Never again.

We held hands the entire silent ride up to her floor, stepped out into the hall as one unit, and walked a few steps. Amnesia halted abruptly, and my torso rotated to see what was wrong.

Her brown eyes were focused on where our hands were clasped. Slowly, her eyes lifted to meet mine.

"I like holding your hand like this," she confided.

My chest tightened. "Me, too."

"I have to let go now," she told me, sadness in her gaze. "I'm afraid if the doctors think we're getting too close, they won't let you see me."

Determination swelled within me. "No one is going to keep me away."

He lips lifted, her face wistful. "Sometimes I wish I was a normal girl, but then I realize I don't even know what normal is."

"Normal is whatever you want it to be."

I felt her hand slowly slip from mine. I didn't grab it back, though I wanted to.

"They're waiting," she said, and we continued into the hall toward her room.

She walked in first. I saw the change come over her body. "What's wrong?" Quickly, I moved forward, rushing into the room and angling slightly in front of her.

"Sorry to interrupt your fresh air," Dr. Beck said, "but we want to talk."

The room was full. Dr. Beck, Dr. Kline, a few nurses, and a couple other doctors who had been working on Amnesia's case. The police officer who was working her case also stood by. There was another man I didn't really know. He was dressed in a suit, tie included. He oozed authority.

My stance in front of her didn't relax. In fact, I felt even more protective. "What's going on?"

"Doctor-patient confidentiality. If you could step out in the hall—" Dr. Beck began.

My laugh cut him off. "No."

"Mr. Donovan." The man in the suit spoke up. "I hear the staff here have been very... shall we say, *accommodating* regarding your coming and going in this hospital—"

"Who are you?" I cut him off, too.

"I'm the hospital director."

"It's fine." Amnesia spoke up. "I want him here."

Dr. Beck and Mr. Director backed off. I smiled at them.

"As you know, you've been with us about four months now." Dr. Beck began. Beside me, Am nodded. "I realize your memory is not recovered, but all your other injuries have healed. For all intents and purposes, you have a clean bill of health."

"You're kicking me out," Am said, her voice oddly void.

"Of course not," the director said. "But rules and regulations... Hospital policy states we cannot house a person who no longer requires care."

"She has no memory. No home, money, or means to support herself," I said, angry.

"What will I do?" Amnesia worried. Despite her words in the hallway about not holding my hand, I felt her fingers seek mine. Instantly, my hand flexed, inviting her in, closing around hers possessively.

She was afraid. I couldn't even tell her not to be.

"Given the uniqueness of this situation—"

Amnesia made a sound, cutting off the doctor, then turned toward the police officer. "Has someone come forward claiming to know me? Did you find out who I am? Is that why you're here?"

Regret shone in his face. "No, ma'am. I'm sorry to say we haven't had any new leads in the last couple weeks. Have you remembered anything more?"

Her shoulders fell. "No."

"Then why are you here?" I asked.

The officer's eyes moved to me. "I want to assure you"—he looked back at Am—"we haven't given up. This town is behind you one hundred percent."

"No one wants you to feel alone, honey," Nurse Ellen spoke.

"This is a very rare situation. We're working on some paperwork to try and get you on disability, which will support you until you can decide what you'll do," the director said.

My jaw clenched. He acted as if she were going to leave. I wouldn't let her. She had to stay.

"It's difficult because you are not physically disabled, and the fact that you have no birth certificate, social security number, identification… or even a name, well… it's very cumbersome."

"But I still can't stay here?" Her voice was shaky.

"It's going to be okay," I told her. "You can come home with me."

"I would advise against that," Dr. Kline was quick to say.

"So living on the streets is a better idea?" I snapped.

"We actually have worked out an arrangement, somewhere for you to stay for the time being," Dr. Kline told Am, ignoring me completely.

She didn't like me. The feeling was mutual.

The tall woman walked across the room. As she passed by Am, my hand tightened around hers. Dr. Kline stuck her head out the door and spoke quietly to someone. Seconds later, she came back in, holding the door open.

Maggie Foster stepped into the room. She was dressed in a pair of khaki pants and a blouse with flowers on it. Over it was a pink cardigan.

"Hi, Amnesia," she said, smiling. Am smiled back. I knew she liked Maggie a lot. "I was wondering if perhaps you'd like to come and stay with me?"

"With you?" Am said, surprised. "But why?"

"I think we've become friends over the last couple weeks. I've enjoy playing cards with you. You don't have anywhere to go, and I'm in a position to help. It's what the people here at Lake Loch do."

"That's a very generous offer, but me living with you is a lot different than playing cards."

"I live alone, with plenty of room in my house. Besides, Elmo would like the company. He's bored of me."

Elmo was Maggie's beloved Shih Tzu.

Am looked up at me, her eyes asking me what she should do. I loved the feeling, the weight of her eyes, the way she looked to me for an opinion.

Personally, I wanted her at my place. To have her around every day. That was what was best for me, though, not her.

"Maggie is a really good cook," I admitted, then grinned. "She's pretty good company, too."

Maggie chuckled.

Am debated, glancing around the room. Everyone watched her, waiting to see what she would do. Dr. Kline nodded, as if encouraging her.

"Thank you, Maggie. If you're sure it will be okay…"

Maggie smiled wildly and nodded. "Of course! I'm thrilled to have you."

All the doctors in the room appeared very relieved. "Wonderful," Dr. Beck concluded, glancing down at his clipboard. "I will have all your discharge papers ready for the morning."

"Outpatient care will continue with me," Dr. Kline said. "I will print out all your upcoming appointments, but if anything happens, such as a memory resurfacing or anything at all, please come to my office immediately."

Am hesitated, then said, "Okay."

Dr. Kline was very perceptive. "Amnesia? Is there something you haven't told me? Have you remembered something?"

"No. I haven't had any memories." She hedged. I knew she was thinking about what just happened outside and how she was convinced someone wanted to finish what they'd started.

"Then something else?"

I looked at her, her eyes meeting mine then skirting away.

"No, nothing," she said finally, pasting on a smile. "I'm just nervous about leaving."

"Leaving the hospital can be very scary." The doctor empathized. "This has been your safe place since you woke. But moving forward will help you feel stronger. Building some kind of life after the one you lost is crucial to your healing."

"What about my memories?" Am worried.

"Perhaps leaving will help bring some forward. I really can't say. I don't know if you will get them back." After gazing at Am a few silent moments, she seemed to feel bad, as if she wanted to make her feel more secure. "I do know this town is very safe and supportive. You couldn't ask for a better place to recover."

The doctors, nurses, and even the police officer all took their leave. Maggie and Amnesia made some plans for the morning, but I butted in and volunteered to drive Am over to her new place.

Once everyone was gone, she looked at me, her eyes unsettled. "How safe is Lake Loch really, Eddie?"

I didn't say anything. I couldn't give her the answer she needed, and I couldn't bring myself to voice what I knew she was already thinking.

I also knew, even better than her, that Lake Loch had some mysteries in its depths.

CHAPTER FOURTEEN

AMNESIA

Nothing can stay paused forever. Eventually, you have to hit play. Sometimes the only way to take a step is if someone pushes you forward. The hospital was definitely pushing me forward—more like shoving—but hey, it was basically the same thing.

Maybe not. But the result was still the same.

No more hospital. No more crappy sheets, crappy food, and doctors writing down every move I made. I kind of liked the idea really.

But it was also very scary.

I didn't know what awaited me outside the hospital walls. The farthest I'd ventured so far was the garden just steps from the building. And the last time I was out there, well, that hadn't gone so well.

Eddie almost kissed you... Hmm, now that an enticing thought. Maybe if I broke out of here, I'd get one of his kisses after all. That alone was enough to get me looking forward to stepping out into the unknown just a little bit more.

Kisses aside, I didn't know what I was going to do. No one, not one person had come forward to say they knew me. How could someone live as long as I had (seriously… how old was I?) and know no one. It was impossible. Actually impossible.

Knowing that only brought me back to my previous thoughts. Someone knew who I was. Out there was someone who knew exactly where I came from. The fact no one spoke up led me to believe maybe I didn't want to know them.

Well, that and the fact someone tried to strangle me in this room and was just recently lurking around outside like a ninja spy about to pull out some Kung-Fu moves on me.

Ninja spy? Kung-Fu moves? Where the hell do I come up with this stuff?

I had to move on. I couldn't stay in this limbo anymore. What happened if I never figured out my past? I couldn't spend all my present waiting. I had to build a new life so I could have a future.

I had no idea where to begin. It was all so very overwhelming.

A brisk knock on the door before it opened was my only warning of a visitor. Dr. Beck strolled in with the clipboard I was beginning to think he never put down. "Do you sleep with that thing?" I asked, only half joking.

"There you go again with your sense of humor," he mused.

Seriously, though.

"I have all your discharge papers here. You will just need to sign them." He went on. "We have your billing address down as Maggie's house for right now. If you end up moving, then please don't forget to let us know your forwarding address."

My billing address. I wondered just how much this long-term stay at the hospital was going to cost and where I was going to get the money. I didn't have a job. Or even a bank account…

"One thing at a time," Dr. Beck said, as if he knew where my thoughts travelled. "The hospital is well aware of your situation. A payment plan can be arranged, but nothing is due until you get some sort of, ah, arrangements made."

"You mean until I get a job."

"Take it slow." He cautioned. "Too much too soon will only cause harm."

"Right," I said. It seemed kind of stupid to tell me to take it slow after the meeting yesterday, when they basically said it was time to start a life.

After I signed the papers, Dr. Beck went over a few medical instructions with me and checked my vitals for the millionth time since I woke.

"There is one more thing." He began, almost as if he didn't want to bring it up.

"Yes?" I said, leaning back against the bed.

"When you arrived here, we did a full workup on you. X-rays, MRI, etc."

"Yes, that's what you said."

He nodded once. "And I told you about the signs of abuse and the fact that some of your old injuries were still evident."

"Yes," I answered, my belly tightening.

Dr. Beck pulled out an X-ray film from a large envelope he'd been holding in his clipboard. He clipped it onto a small light-up box against the wall. "I didn't want to overload you with so much at once," he explained as I looked at the image. "But I need to let you know."

He pointed to a place in what looked like my arm bone. It wasn't straight like I imagined it should be. It was slightly crooked, as if it had been broken and then the bone fused back together, but not quite right.

"At one point, your arm just below your elbow had been broken. It's obvious no medical attention was given because of the way it healed." He pointed to the part I'd been looking at. "The proper term for this is a malunion, meaning the bone healed, but not correctly."

"Okay, so what do I need to do?" I asked, staring at the X-ray, trying to imagine what could have happened.

"Well, to fix something like this, we would need to re-break the bone and then set it properly."

"No!" I said, surging up. "No more hospitals." *No more pain.*

He didn't seem at all surprised and nodded. "I figured you would say that, which is why I haven't brought it up. The arm still works just fine. It may be a little weaker than the other. Does the left arm cause you pain at all?"

"No," I said, glancing down at it. Again, I marveled at how so much was wrong inside my body that no one could see.

"I would advise just leaving it, then. It's not ideal, but given the situation, I think it's best."

If they said "given the situation" one more time, I might scream. "Well, *given the situation*," I said sarcastically, "I agree."

He ignored my annoyance. "I just wanted to make you aware and let you know if it ever becomes a problem or you notice increased weakening of the arm to come in and see me."

"I will." I promised. "Thank you."

Dr. Beck took down the film and put it away. Before leaving, he said, "I have to tell you, you have by far been my most intriguing patient. What's happened to you is extremely rare, and I just wanted you to know I've done everything I can to help you. Although I admit sometimes I felt I was just flying by the seat of my pants."

"Ah, so you know how it feels to be me, then," I cracked. Then I smiled warmly and slipped off the bed. "For the record, you're the best doctor I've ever had."

"You can't remember the others," he reminded me.

I laughed. "Not true. Dr. Kline might be very hurt over my declaration."

He chuckled. "Yes. Well, I'll be sure not to tell her."

"Thank you." My voice was sincere. "I truly do appreciate everything this hospital has done to help me."

"I'll see you at your follow-up in a few weeks," he said, offering his hand.

I slipped mine in and we shook.

When he was gone, a little bit of sadness washed over me. I knew I didn't really know these people; they weren't my friends or anything. I was just their job. But it still felt as if I were leaving behind the only people I knew.

I went to the window and stared out for a while, watching the clouds move through the sky and wondering what was behind the trees and parking lot.

So many unknowns…

"You ready to blow this joint?" Eddie sang, bursting into my room as if he lived here.

Swinging around from the window, I smiled. It was hard not to when Eddie was around. "Hey."

Blue eyes swept me from head to toe. When they finally settled on my face, his dimples deepened. "You look good today."

I glanced down at myself. I was wearing a pair of jeans that felt worn in and soft. Likely because they were secondhand and tattered. I wasn't sure where Maggie found the clothes she brought me; I just knew they'd come from people in town. With the jeans, I'd put on a white T-shirt that was loose, and over, I was wearing Eddie's zip-up hoodie because it was cool outside.

I had one pair of shoes, sneakers. They actually looked just like Eddie's (all white with blue stripes down the side). They were Adidas. At least that's what the label said. The shoes were new, a gift I suspected were from him (that would explain why they were the same), even though he never told me he bought them.

It felt a little strange that nothing I owned I picked out myself. Like I was piecing myself together with things other people said and gave me. The thought created sorrow inside me, I wanted to know myself. Be myself. Discover the things I liked.

You can do that now. Starting today.

Eddie cleared his throat, reminding me of the compliment. "Thank you," I said, nervously running my hand through my hair. My uneven, choppy hair. Something else that reminded me I had no idea about myself.

Surely I hadn't done this to myself. No one could think it looked good.

A mental picture of a huge chunk of dark, golden hair falling to a bare floor struck me. Woozy with the force of the image, I swayed a little.

"Hey," Eddie said, rushing forward, wrapping an arm around my waist from the side. "You okay?"

I blinked, leaned against him just one moment longer, then stood. "Oh yeah, I'm fine. Just got a little dizzy."

He frowned. "Is that because of the concussion?"

"I think it's just because I'm a little overwhelmed."

He nodded, understanding in his gaze. "Wanna hold my hand?"

I laughed and nodded. I always wanted to hold his hand.

"This all your stuff?" he asked, pointing to a bag on the bed. It was an LL Bean backpack, dark blue with brown straps.

"That's all of it," I said. Everything I owned fit in just one bag.

Pulling me along, Eddie snatched up the bag and slung it over his shoulder. "You ready? Maggie's probably waiting."

I glanced around the room, an odd feeling coming over me. This wasn't home. I wasn't leaving some place I'd grown up or even had fond memories of.

Still, this place was all I had.

"Yeah," I echoed, forcing my eyes back to him. "Let's go."

Eddie led me to the door, held it open, and gestured for me to go ahead. In the hall, I didn't go far because we were still connected. I stared into my room as the door slowly swung closed, watching it disappear inch by inch.

"It's gonna be okay, Am," Eddie murmured, leaning close and kissing the top of my head.

Briefly, my eyes closed. I sighed. When he pulled back, our stares connected. "You got this," he told me.

I smiled.

The hall was quiet as we walked down. Actually, it was bare. It gave me an odd sense of déjà vu from the night I was almost strangled. Where were the nurses? Dr. Kline? The fact that no one was here to even wave goodbye hit me hard. It reminded me that just because these people had literally been my entire life, it didn't make me the same to them.

These people all had families and friends. Others they looked forward to seeing. People who weren't just their job.

I stumbled a bit as I walked, and Eddie's hand tightened around mine.

"C'mon, slowpoke," he urged, pulling me around the corner toward the elevator.

"SURPRISE!" a group of people yelled.

As I jerked to a stop, my eyes went wide, and I took in the group of people standing there in the wide archway of the waiting room. Everyone was smiling, some were holding colorful balloons, pink streamers hung from the ceiling, and nurse Ellen stood in the center with a big square cake decorated with a pile of icing.

"What is all this?" I asked, slightly out of breath.

"You didn't think we'd just let you walk out of here without a proper good-bye, did you?" Ellen said.

Yes. That's exactly what I thought.

"You, girl, are a miracle!" Maggie exclaimed, materializing out of the crowd. In her hands was a bunch of colorful flowers. "The strongest fighter this town has ever seen."

Mary Beth nodded sagely. "You've been here so long it almost feels as if family is leaving."

I started to cry.

It was totally embarrassing, but I couldn't stop. I went from feeling completely overwhelmed by loneliness to suddenly being overwhelmed with people who cared. I wiped at my tears as they fell, sniffling and looking around at all the people.

There was some other sniffling going on around the room, but I wasn't sure who it was. My vision was too blurred to tell.

Eddie's arm wrapped around me, and I leaned into his side. "You have lots of people who care about you, Am," he said quietly. "Leaving this hospital won't change that."

I cried harder. Geez, I was a baby! "Better write this down, Dr. Beck," I announced. "I'm a big fat crybaby!"

"Showing emotion is nothing to be ashamed of," Dr. Kline announced.

"Let's have cake!" Ellen announced.

Eddie led me into the waiting room, where music played, balloons bobbed around, and cake was passed around the room. Joline and Jeremy from the town bakery had brought it, along with a bag of the monkey bread muffins I so loved. Even Eddie's parents were here. I liked them, even though I got the opinion they came to visit just so they could keep an eye on me. They were worried about their son and how much time he spent with the girl with no memory. Sometimes they stared at me as if they were trying to see something no one else could, but other times, it seemed they wanted to genuinely get to know me.

A few people brought me gifts, which made me cry again. I don't know if anyone knew just how much it truly meant to me just to have people care. I was a bit taken aback by how deeply this little going away party touched me, but it did. I felt their kindness and generosity deep, so deep it nearly stirred something inside me. But just as it started to rise to the surface, it was shoved back down again, out of reach.

The party didn't last too long because most of the guests were staff, but it was enough to make me feel as if maybe I wasn't leaving everything behind, instead just moving it all to another location. After promising to come back to visit and making a couple lunch dates, Eddie pulled me into the elevator.

"I was so not expecting that," I told him, partially breathless. Feeling his stare, I turned to look at him.

He was smiling, gazing at me once again as if I were all he saw. "You deserve it. That and so much more."

Outside, there was a black truck parked at the curb. I had no idea what kind or if it was old or new. It was just a black vehicle with big tires.

Eddie took my hand, tugging me near it. "This is us."

"You parked at the curb?" I asked, amused.

"Would you rather I parked in the flowerbed?" he asked, gesturing toward a big patch of mulch with bushes.

The plastic wrapped around the bouquet of flowers I held crinkled as I laughed. "Um, isn't there a parking lot for guests? I thought this was a no parking zone." I pointed to the sign that clearly read: NO PARKING ZONE.

"That sign is just a suggestion."

That sign was *not* just a suggestion. Eddie just didn't think the rules applied to him.

"So this is your truck?" I asked.

"Yep, this is her," he replied, slapping a hand on the hood. "Isn't she pretty?"

Pursing my lips, I asked, "Do you have a crush on your truck?"

"Jealous?" He smiled swiftly, then wagged his eyebrows.

A funny feeling flipped around inside me. "Can I drive?"

He frowned. "Do you know how to drive?"

I shrugged. "I don't know."

Eddie sputtered. "I think we'll save that little test for later. You're just getting out of the hospital. It's a little too soon to come back."

"Fine." I sighed.

Eddie opened the passenger door and beckoned for me to get in. Handing him my flowers and other gift bags loading down my arms, I jumped in and sat on the bench seat stretching across the interior. He put all the stuff on the floor near my feet.

Still holding the flowers, he glanced up. "Better scooch over. Make room for the flowers." I held my hands out for them, but he shook his head. "Scooch."

I slid over, and he dropped them beside me. Clearly, he was very concerned with their delicacy.

"Be right back," he said before slamming the door and jogging around the front. Inside the cab, he started it up and smiled. "Hi."

I was right beside him. You know, because the flowers took up *so much* room on the other side. "Hi," I said back.

"Ready?"

I shrugged.

I'm pretty sure he drove like a maniac. Or maybe he was just a terrible driver. Either way, I was forced to cling to him in fear of my life.

After taking a wide turn onto a tree-lined street with beautiful houses set back on green lawns and fall leaves dotting the landscape, I sat up and gaped at him.

He laughed.

I smacked him in the ribs. "You are the worst driver ever!"

"How do you know?" he teased.

"I think I'm going to vomit." I leaned forward.

He slammed on the brakes, his arm shooting out to block me from sliding forward. The second the truck bounced to a stop, he turned to me, immediately regretful. "Shit," he muttered. "It's okay. I'm sorry, I—"

My laughter bubbled up from my hunched over position.

He was silent for a heartbeat. "Are you laughing?"

Gleefully, I sat up and beamed at him. "Made you feel bad, didn't I?"

His jaw dropped. "Are you playing me right now?"

My smile grew.

"Holy shit," he swore. "You are totally playing me."

"You asked for it!" I burst out. "You drove like a madman just because you wanted me to hold on to you for dear life."

A sly smile broke over his features. "It worked."

"We could have been in an accident!" I demanded, even though I really didn't think he'd been driving that erratically. Especially in a town where we'd literally passed one car along the way.

Eddie shook his head adamantly. "No way. Never. I would never do anything to hurt you like that."

My head tilted at his deep sincerity.

He held up his finger and made an X over his heart. "Cross my heart."

"Hope to die," I echoed.

His whole face changed. It was almost as if I'd said something sacred. "What did you say?" he whispered.

"Nothing," I sputtered. "I mean, I don't know. It just came out."

The panic I felt must have shown on my face because he turned his body toward mine. "Hey, it's okay. It's just a silly saying."

"What is it?"

"Cross my heart; hope to die," he repeated. "We used to say that stuff when we were kids."

"We?" I asked, my heart stalling.

"Me and my friends," he explained. "Everyone at school really."

"Oh," I said, feeling a little crestfallen.

He smiled. "Whenever we'd say something that was like, you know, sacred, we'd say cross my heart; hope to die; stick a needle in my eye."

I laughed at the last part. "That's serious business."

"Yeah," he said, relaxing his side into the back of the seat. His eyes caressed my face, and it made me tingle, made me long to have his fingers touch me the way his stare did.

Eddie tucked a strand of hair behind my ear. "I didn't mean to scare you."

"You didn't," I answered.

An ornery look glinted on his face, his lips curving up sardonically. "I guess I did want you to have to hold on." He winked.

I was charmed.

"Next time, just ask," I whispered, reaching for his hand.

The look fell from his face, pure desire smoothing out his features. Inside the cab, the air around us changed, became alive.

Eddie stared down to where our hands were linked and resting on the seat between us. He was silent for a while, and I was content. Who needed words when the atmosphere was buzzing?

When his low voice cut through the energy, my blood spiked. "I want to kiss you,"

"No one's ever kissed me before," I whispered.

His head jerked up, his fingers tightening around mine.

"You'd be my first." Oh, wow, my stomach was flopping around and making me feel totally unbalanced. I didn't know what possessed me to say that, to basically entice him to put his lips on mine. I didn't even know how to kiss, but oh man, I really wanted to.

"First kisses shouldn't be had in the middle of the street, inside a running truck," he murmured, stroking the side of my face with his free hand.

"Seems like *the where* shouldn't matter as long as *the who* is right."

He made a groaning sound, sliding closer, so close our knees bumped. "Well then," he mumbled, leaning close, tilting his head sideways as if he were lining up our lips. "This must be the absolute perfect place."

My lids flickered as the distance between us closed.

He kissed a whole lot better than he drove. Eddie's lips smoothed over mine expertly, almost as if he glided against air. I felt the brush all the way to my core. Heat surged inside me like lava bubbling from a volcano.

He moved slowly, methodically, with just enough pressure I couldn't move away. Not that I wanted to. I was so ensnared by him, totally engrossed in every move he made. It was amazing to touch him like this, to be connected to someone in such a physical way. Our lips lapped at each other, melting together until I practically hummed.

He smiled against my mouth, pulled back slightly, tilted his head, and kissed me from a completely new angle. My hand went to his knee while his wrapped around my waist, tugging me just a little closer.

I kissed him back, following his lead, letting my emotions guide me. The soft slip of his tongue made me pause, but I didn't pull away. Eddie licked me again, and my lips parted. Tentatively, his tongue slipped inside just a little, and I allowed my own to do the same. Eddie groaned on first contact and then slid his fingers into my hair.

His tongue slipped all the way into my mouth, coaxing mine to play.

Oh my.

I couldn't breathe, but air wasn't even important. I couldn't think, but words didn't compare. Not even memories mattered because this moment eclipsed them all.

Easing back, Eddie withdrew from my mouth slowly. With one last brush of his lips against mine, his head lifted. Dazed, I watched him swipe at his lower lip with his thumb. Then he reached out and did the same to mine.

"What do you think, Am?" His voice was thick. "Still a perfect place for a first kiss?"

I sucked my lower lip into my mouth, then released it. I couldn't speak so I just nodded.

A car pulled around the truck and continued on down the street. Eddie chuckled, lifted my hand, kissed the back of it, then went back to driving.

How could he drive after that? Wasn't he completely woozy inside? I could barely see straight, let alone steer a car. But he did it expertly, so well, in fact, I was convinced he really had just been driving crazy so I would stick close against his side.

After that kiss, though, he wouldn't even have to try. There was nowhere else I'd rather be.

CHAPTER FIFTEEN

EDWARD

Just breathe and drive.

I repeated the mantra over and over in my head. I had to say it constantly, because if I didn't, I would forget. I'd probably run my truck right off the road and land in a ditch.

Her first kiss. Not really, but really. It wasn't the lake that was a siren. It was her. Something in Amnesia beckoned me like nothing else. I couldn't explain. Fuck, I barely understood it. Yet I sure as hell felt it.

I'd wanted to do that so long. So fucking long.

And now I wanted to do it again.

I saw my future spelled out for me now, plain as day. I would live between our kisses and die every time her lips met mine. Death and resuscitation all at once, that was Amnesia, the girl who forgot everything, a girl I would always know by heart.

When Maggie's house came into view, I wished I'd driven a hell of a lot slower. I wasn't ready to let her go yet, but really, I probably never would be. Amnesia brought out an intense greediness in me. I didn't want to share her. Not with anyone.

Obviously, I knew that was impossible and also sort of creepy. If you held on too tight to a butterfly, you crushed its wings.

I pulled straight into the driveway, parking directly in front of the garage door. I figured Maggie was probably already home and parked inside so it didn't matter if I blocked it.

"This is Maggie's place?" Amnesia asked, gazing out the window.

Well, shit. Guess I should have been less consumed with her on the way over here and given her a mini tour of the neighborhood. That made me a shitty guide.

But an excellent kisser.

"Yep, this is it. It's one of the nicest streets in Lake Loch." I looked at the two-story white home through the windshield. It was pretty traditional with black shutters, a black front door with a gold knocker, and planter beds full of colorful mums along the front. "She's lived here since I was a kid."

"With Elmo?" Am asked, glancing at me.

I smiled. "Yeah, her dog. He's a little fluff ball. Her husband used to live here with her, but he passed a few years ago. Sudden heart attack."

"Oh no. That's terrible."

"It was unexpected. It was hard. Maggie's had a lot of loss in her life."

"Maybe that's why she's been so kind to me," Am murmured. "She's very compassionate."

"Maybe," I echoed, a lump in my throat.

"Are you sure it's okay I stay here?" She worried, her hands wringing in her lap.

My hand settled over her clasped ones. "You're going to like it here. Maggie's great."

"It's hard to just…" Her voice trailed off.

"Hard to what?" I pressed.

"Hard to walk into a strange place and call it home."

"Maybe it's not home," I told her. "Maybe it's just a safe place to stay until you figure out where home is."

Brown eyes shifted to me and softened. "Think it will be hard to figure out where home is?"

"I think you'll find exactly where you belong."

Her smile was big and bright, the freckles on her nose and cheeks bunching up, and my heart turned over.

"I'll get your stuff," I said and catapulted out of the truck. At her side, I hefted the bag over my shoulder and gathered a few of the gift bags from the party. She had the flowers in her arms already, looking so fucking adorable I shifted all the shit I was holding into one arm so I could slip the other around her waist and lift her out of the truck.

Her body slid down mine when I stood her in the driveway, but I was remiss in moving away. I just wasn't ready yet. The autumn breeze ruffled her hair and a strand blew into her eyes. I grasped it, rolling it between my fingers.

"I don't know why it's like that," she said suddenly, almost as if the words just burst out without thought.

My fingers paused and my eyes shifted over to hers. "What is?"

"My hair," she said, ducking her face. "It's all uneven and chopped up."

"It doesn't make you any less beautiful." I promised. I did wonder about her hair, the way it was almost butchered in some places. The color was beautiful, dark blond, almost golden beneath the sun. I couldn't imagine why anyone would hack it up that way.

"Really?" she whispered.

"Duh," I said and rolled my eyes.

She giggled. "I don't like it."

"Change it then," I said, dropping the strand and moving back a step. "You can do whatever you want, Am."

Her eyes lit up as if her own independence wasn't something that occurred to her. "Maybe I will."

Catching her hand, we walked across the driveway and down the sidewalk toward the front door. The street itself was a quiet one, with sidewalks and large trees whose branches shaded the road. All the lawns were well taken care of, and many of the neighbors had plants and flowers dotting their property.

"You still have my number, right?" I asked when we stopped at the front door.

She nodded.

"Use it anytime you want, okay? Doesn't matter what time it is."

"I'm nervous," she rushed out.

I dropped everything I held near the door and pulled her into my arms. "It's going to be okay," I spoke against her hair. I felt her nod against my chest, her arms clutched at my back. After a few moments, I pulled back.

"How about I come get you tomorrow and give you a tour of the town? Show you around."

"Can I see your store?" she asked, interested.

"First stop." I promised.

"I'd love that."

"I'll come by late morning, just before lunch. I'll take you out." Like a date.

She nodded enthusiastically.

I smiled fast. I liked knowing when I would see her again. "You know," I said, taking her hand, "I'm used to seeing you every single day."

"Me, too." Her lips curved up.

Behind us, the front door opened. Maggie poked her head out the glass storm door. "Amnesia!" she said. "Just in time. Your room is all ready."

I nodded at Am, encouraging her. "I'll see you tomorrow."

"Tomorrow." She agreed softly.

After I put all her bags inside, I came back out, hesitating in front of her. I didn't want to leave. I hated walking away from her.

"Thanks for the ride," she said, smiling up at me.

I pressed a kiss to the top of her head. "I'll see you tomorrow, baby."

Her breath caught a little, which was very satisfying. "Bye."

"Go inside, Am," I ordered quietly, reaching around her to hold open the door. "I'm not leaving 'til you're in the house safe."

She went in, the glass door closing between us.

The second I pulled out of the driveway, I started looking forward to tomorrow.

CHAPTER SIXTEEN

AMNESIA

"I didn't think that boy would ever let you out of his sight!" Maggie said when Eddie drove away and I turned around. She was standing behind me on a small tiled landing. The house was a split level; from where we were standing at the front door, you could either go up or down.

I smiled. "He's sweet."

Maggie laughed. "Sweet is one way to put it. A pit bull is another."

"A pit bull?" I questioned, not quite making the connection.

She nodded sagely. "He's mighty protective over you. I pity anyone who even looks at you funny."

I thought about the person in the hospital garden, in my hospital room, and the haunting figure who loomed over me in every dream.

"Well, how about a tour? I'm sure you want to see the place you're going to be living." Maggie gestured for me to follow her up the stairs.

"I really hope this isn't an imposition," I said, feeling shy.

"Oh, hush. I'm enjoying the company. Truly."

Up the short flight of stairs, the house opened into a large space. A living room, kitchen, and eating space made up almost the entire floor. It was clean and uncluttered, something I realized I rather liked. The walls were painted a soft yellow, and there was a fireplace against the far wall that was white-painted brick. She had framed photos on the mantel and a few unlit candles.

On either side of the fireplace were bookcases built into the wall. They were crammed with books, all neatly lined up by size. In front of the fireplace was a large oval-shaped rug that was thick and multicolored. It looked handmade, because surely something that beautiful couldn't be bought in a store. There were two large fabric chairs upholstered in deep-green velvet and a leather couch all facing each other with a wooden coffee table in the center.

Toward the front of the house were large windows that overlooked the street. They were draped in sheer curtains, and a large wooden piano sat in front of them.

"Do you play?" I asked.

She nodded. "Yes, for many years. My husband actually was the one who taught me."

"Eddie told me he passed away. I'm very sorry."

Maggie smiled sadly. "I miss him every day. But when it gets to be too much, I just sit down and play, and I can feel him in the room with me."

How heartbreakingly romantic.

"Where's Elmo?" I asked, gazing around.

She made a tsking nose. "I put him in the bedroom. I didn't want him running around and scaring you. He's a mischievous thing."

I could tell just by the way her eyes lit up she loved the dog more than anything else. "I'd love to meet him," I said.

"I'll let him out, but be prepared!" She went past the kitchen and disappeared down a hallway that I guessed led to the bedrooms.

When she was gone, I glanced around at the paintings on the walls (mostly landscapes), smiled at the huge basket of dog toys, and nearly tripped over a half-chewed bone. Clearly, it was Elmo who ran this place.

The kitchen was open, an L-shape, with an island facing the living room. The countertops were stone, and the cabinets were white, each door with a different-colored knob. On the counter was a coffee pot, a toaster, and a few other things filled with utensils. The appliances were all white, and there was a calendar on the front of the fridge.

Off to the side in the kitchen was a wide archway that led out into what looked like an eating area. I went toward it because it was so bright. The entire room was made up of windows, and a round table sat in the center. The table was brown, but the four chairs were all painted various colors. The windows literally went down to the wooden floor, taking full advantage of the view of a beautiful backyard filled with trees that painted the sky with autumn shades.

The sound of paws scampering across the floor and Maggie laughing made me smile. I spun just as a little white fur ball streaked into the room and circled me. He disappeared under a chair, from where his white face peeked out, and a very large bark filled the room.

"Elmo!" Maggie scolded. "This is Amnesia. She's our friend."

"Hi, Elmo," I said and dropped nearby and held out my hand. He barked twice more, then stopped, watching me carefully as he inched his way closer and closer. He was a cute little thing with long hair, mostly white but with patches of brown and black. His dark eyes stood out among all the white fur and his nose was little but seemed to work overtime.

"Hey," I said when he got close enough to sniff me. "Good boy."

Elmo wagged his tail and let me stroke his head and ears.

"Give him some cheese and he'll be your friend for life," Maggie said, watching us.

I giggled, and Elmo lay down and showed me his belly for rubs. He was warm and soft, his belly round and pink. I totally saw why he ran this house and realized that soon, he would likely own me, too.

"He's adorable," I said, standing. Elmo jumped up and moved to stand at my feet.

"Aww, he likes you." Maggie approved. "Let me show you the rest of the house."

The tour didn't take long, but the house was fairly big, with four bedrooms and a bathroom upstairs. The fourth bedroom was going to be mine. It was downstairs, along with another family room with a TV, laundry room, and entrance to the garage.

"I thought to give you this room down here," Maggie explained as we went down the stairs, "because it has a TV, and I assumed you might enjoy that."

"That was thoughtful," I said, gazing around the lower level, which was just as comfortable as the upstairs.

"The laundry room is through there." She pointed. "And so is the linen closet with a bunch of towels and blankets. Also, through there is a bathroom, the one you can use. It has a shower and everything you'll need."

Just on the other side of the staircase was a doorway Maggie led me through.

"Here it is. I hope it's okay."

The room was large, almost running the width of the basement. The space was shaped like a rectangle with a small window facing the street to my right and, to my left, a set of French doors that led out onto a patio in the backyard. There were more bookshelves in here, filled with books, and a bed against the wall by the door. It was covered in a thick, white comforter, but over that was a colorful quilt that for some reason made my eyes tear up. Across from the bed was the television on a wooden dresser.

Over by the French doors and the bookcase was another green velvet chair with a blanket draped over the back. Beside it was a small round wooden table. It was a nice chair to sit in and read.

I had no idea if I liked to read, but I wanted to find out.

"This is all for me?" I said, gazing around. It seemed huge and almost too nice. "It's too much."

"Hush now. It is not. It's a good space. You can sit out back and read if you want." She motioned to the doors. "And you have your own bathroom down here."

Swallowing thickly, I turned, catching Maggie's hands. Once again, I felt as if I might cry. "Thank you."

"Don't go making me cry," Maggie said, sniffling.

"I can't help it. You didn't have to do this. You've basically taken in a stranger."

She glanced away, dotting at the corners of her eyes to keep the tears at bay. "You aren't a stranger," she said. "I've been visiting you for weeks."

"I won't let you down." I vowed.

Maggie smiled. "Oh, honey, there isn't anything you could do that would let me down."

I set my bag on the floor near the bed. It was strange being here, but it would likely feel strange everywhere because nothing was familiar.

"How about some tea? Do you like tea?" Maggie asked, moving to the door.

"I have no idea." I laughed.

"Well, c'mon then. Let's find out."

I followed her back up to the kitchen, where she made two cups of hot tea and added honey to both mugs. As she did, she told me this was the best way to drink it. We carried our mugs out into the eating area made of windows and sat down.

"This room is beautiful," I murmured, gazing around. "I feel like I'm in some kind of treehouse. Like we're outside."

"My late husband built this room for me. I love to sit out here, especially in the spring and fall. The scenery in Maine really can't be matched."

"I think you must be right." I agreed and took a sip of the warm liquid. It was a deep flavor and sweet with the honey. I took another sip.

Maggie watched me. "Good?"

"Very."

"I have to ask." She began, sitting forward a little. "Have you remembered anything at all? Did the drive here maybe spark some memories?"

Why would the drive to Maggie's house spark memories?

I must have looked confused because she hurried to say, "You know, just the new scenery. Maybe something brought something back."

My body slouched back in the chair. "Nothing. I still don't remember anything." I didn't mention the flash I had of hair falling to the floor and the sense of despair that came with it. I didn't know if that was real or what it meant. Seemed no point in mentioning something that only lasted a few seconds.

"Perhaps with time," she said, almost sad.

"I'm not sure." I hedged.

A quizzical look came over her face. "Do you want to remember?"

"I'm not sure about that either. I'm sort of afraid to." I admitted.

"Are you still having dreams about the night someone tried to kill you?"

I nodded. "Sometimes. But it's always the same, and I never see a face."

"You know what I think?" Maggie said, a lift to her voice.

"What?"

"I think when you stop trying to remember, you will. Maybe just getting out, seeing the town will distract you."

"Eddie's showing me around tomorrow," I told her. A smile graced my face. "I'm looking forward to it."

"Wonderful. I thought tonight you might like to help me make dinner, and then we can be ill-mannered and eat it in front of the television."

"I didn't watch much TV in the hospital. The nurses took the remote control. I think they were afraid I'd see the news reports about me and the fact no one came forward with any information."

"Well, you're in for a treat. Reality TV is absolutely horrible." She leaned over the table. "I'm totally addicted to it."

I giggled at her confession. "What's reality TV?"

Maggie laughed. "Oh, honey! You think you have problems? Just wait until you see the way people behave for all the world to see. It's downright trashy."

"And that makes it fun to watch?" I asked, sort of intrigued yet sort of horrified.

Maggie beamed. "Exactly!"

Maggie was right. Reality TV was horribly addictive. I'd never seen such a thing before, and I wasn't sure I wanted to again. Yet I knew we would probably watch it again tonight, and I was looking forward to it.

Opening my eyes in my new room for the first time was slightly disorienting. It took a moment to realize where I was, but when I did, I couldn't help but smile. I was going to like it here.

Don't get too comfortable. This isn't where you belong. The thought crashed into my happy mood, threatening to abolish it. Frankly, it was quite rude.

I did my best to ignore the haunting thought and sat up, leaning back against the headboard and all the colorful pillows tossed around the bed. I hadn't had a nightmare last night, which was a welcome reprieve. The bed was comfortable and warm, and I'd felt safe, something I didn't really realize I'd been missing.

Tucking the blankets around me, I yanked a bright-blue pillow into my lap and hugged it to my chest. Maggie said a lot of these pillows were for decoration, but I couldn't bring myself to toss them off the bed. Having this many felt luxurious, and I liked it.

Even though I tried to ignore the previous thought, I couldn't. It was there and it would remain until I acknowledged it. Maybe I didn't belong here, but I didn't know where I did. This seemed like a good place to be while I figured it out.

Anyway, who said I didn't belong? I was invited and I wanted to be here. That counted for something. Right?

A scraping noise caught my attention, and my body stiffened. Fear flooded me so fast it made me dizzy. My first reaction was to dive back under the covers and pull a pillow over my head. The scraping didn't stop, though, and I felt my hands begin to shake. Lifting the pillow just slightly, I glanced across the room to the French doors. Curtains were drawn across them, keeping out the light. I imagined someone standing on the other side, trying to pick the lock, trying to come in.

He's coming for me.

A high-pitched bark made me jump. "Ah!" I gasped, not expecting the sound at all. Then I started to laugh.

"Elmo!" I said, flinging back the covers and pillows to jump out of the bed. The second I opened the door, the little dog rushed inside, circling my legs and jumping up so I would pet him.

I laughed and picked him up, sitting on the bed with him. He rolled around in the blankets and rubbed against the pillows. "I guess I'm not the only one who thinks this bed is comfy," I said and rubbed his belly.

His tail wagged against the sheets, and I smiled.

"Elmo!" Maggie gasped, poking her head into the room. "I'm sorry, Amnesia. Soon as he came in from outside, he ran off to find you."

"It's okay. I like him."

"You're a naughty thing," Maggie told Elmo. He wagged his tail some more, as if it were a compliment. "Come on now. You come with me and leave Amnesia alone."

"Oh, he's fine." I assured her as he poked me with his nose for a pet.

"I'm making breakfast if you'd like some. Just come up when you're ready."

"Thank you," I said sincerely. "I think I may take a shower first, if that's okay."

"You don't have to ask. This is your home now. Do what you want."

Elmo ran after Maggie when she disappeared, and I gathered up some clean clothes to take into the bathroom with me. I thought longingly for a moment of picking out my own things to wear, of shopping and trying on clothes, seeing what I liked. I didn't have any money, though, something I was going to need.

The entire time I showered, I pondered getting a job and wondered if any places in town were hiring. After deciding to ask Eddie about it, I toweled off and slipped on my pair of jeans, the white T-shirt that went with everything, and tugged on a pullover sweater in a color that reminded me of pumpkins. The sweater had a wide neckline and was slightly too big, so it slid down over one shoulder, revealing the T-shirt I had on beneath it.

I stared at my face in the mirror, my freckles, pale skin, and brown eyes. To be honest, I hadn't thought much about the way I looked until now because it seemed there were so many other things to worry about. There still was, but eventually, a girl had to look in the mirror. Eventually, I had to get to know myself.

"Who are you?" I whispered to my reflection.

My face wasn't quite as gaunt as it was when I first woke up. My cheekbones weren't sunken into my face like before. Though I was still pale, I had some color to my skin. As I smoothed on some cream that Maggie gave me, I pondered the way I looked. Sort of natural, like a girl who never bothered much with her appearance before. My eyebrows weren't perfectly shaped like the women on TV. My teeth weren't pearly white, and there was a big chip in one front tooth. I wondered why I never seemed to care what I looked like, because I found myself caring now. The broken tooth bothered me, as if it were a reminder of something terrible. The thick, full brows over my eyes felt too untouched, and my hair... oh, my hair.

The chunks missing out of the long lengths got caught in the comb and seemed to stick out, where the rest would hang straight. I hadn't worried much about it before, but now, knowing I was going to be going around town with Eddie, I felt self-conscious. As if my hair were a walking reminder of where I'd been. A place I couldn't remember.

Sighing, I put down the comb and left the bathroom. Maggie was in the kitchen, making pancakes, and my stomach grumbled the second the scent hit me.

"That smells so good," I crooned, entering the kitchen. "What can I help with?"

Elmo beat his tail against the floor when I stepped in but then went back to attacking the bone between his paws.

"Not a thing!" Maggie said. "Help yourself!"

I made a plate, then sat in the window room and watched a few squirrels gather acorns down in the yard.

"Do you need a ride into town?" Maggie asked, joining me at the table.

"No, thank you," I replied. "Eddie said he would pick me up."

"He's a good boy." Maggie smiled fondly. "And rather handsome, too."

He was handsome. "Why doesn't he have a girlfriend?" I asked abruptly.

Maggie glanced up, then lifted her coffee to take a drink. "Well, I think there's been a few girls in the past."

"But?" I pushed. Eddie seemed too special to be single. Surely all the other girls in town saw it, too.

"Eddie has been pretty focused on the general store. He's going to be taking it over soon. I think he's just had other things on his mind besides dating."

There was more to it than the general store. I knew.

"He seems pretty smitten with you, though," Maggie said, a twinkle in her eyes.

Warmth spread in me and my lips tingled when I thought of the kiss we shared in the truck. My first kiss. My best kiss. I felt so alive when I was with him. So... whole. It was an odd way to feel, I supposed. But for a girl who had so many pieces missing, feeling whole was important. It dawned on me how much Eddie gave me. How much I'd come to rely on him. It was selfish, especially when I couldn't offer anything in return.

"What's the matter?" Maggie asked, sensing the dark turn in my thoughts.

"I don't understand why he spends so much time with me." I admitted.

Maggie swallowed, her eyes widened. "He likes you."

Such a generic answer. "But why?" I pressed.

"He sees something in you, something that maybe no one else does."

"Do you think I'm pretty, Maggie?" I whispered, pushing aside my pancakes.

"Oh my, yes." She nodded, her dark eyes widening. "You actually remind me of someone I used to know... She was beautiful, too, on the outside *and* the inside."

"Really? Who?"

Maggie glanced away, her eyes almost shuttered. "Her name was Ann. She was my best friend. She died many years ago."

"Oh, I'm sorry," I murmured, feeling guilty for asking. Eddie did say Maggie had known a lot of loss in life. I couldn't imagine losing a friend and a husband.

"Don't be sorry." She reached across the table and patted my hand. "Having you here makes me feel close to her again."

I squeezed her hand and smiled. "I'm glad."

"Now," she said, perking up. "Tell me why you would ask such a question. Are you still wondering about Eddie?"

"Yes and no," I said. "It's still a little strange to look in the mirror and not recognize myself."

Maggie nodded. "That would be strange."

"And my hair," I said, reaching up to the damp strands. "Something about it really bothers me."

"Well, I have to say," Maggie agreed, "the cut is rather odd."

My eyes flew to hers, and we both laughed out loud.

After our laughter died down, Maggie asked, "You're going into town today with Eddie?"

I nodded.

"Why don't you call him? Tell him you'll meet him there instead. I have just thing for you," she said, getting up and going out into the kitchen.

"What is it?" I called after her.

"You'll see!" she called back.

Curiosity got the best of me, and I agreed.

CHAPTER SEVENTEEN

EDWARD

At just after noon, I stepped out of Loch General and onto the sidewalk. My father was inside with one of the employees. He came into work this afternoon because I was taking the rest of the day off.

I was anxious to find Amnesia. It was already later than I'd planned to pick her up. But a mysterious phone call from her changed my plans. Apparently, she was going somewhere with Maggie this morning, but she didn't say where. My eyes strayed to the windows of the store more than once this morning as I watched for her on the street. I didn't see her, though, which made me even more curious. There wasn't much to do in this town that wasn't on this main street.

When my phone finally beeped a few moments before, it was a text message from Maggie, asking me to meet her up the street in front of Barb's. I nearly ran out of the place without saying good-bye to anyone.

Barb's was more than halfway up the street, on the right-hand side of Loch Gen. Attached to the front of the shop was a barber pole, but instead of being blue and red, it twirled around with pink and white. Above the door was a sign with the name of the place and a big pair of scissors. All the ladies in town (and some of the men) got their hair done here. And their nails... and all the other stuff women were always doing. I stayed away from the place. Too much gossip and giggling for me. I preferred the actual barber around the corner. Jack's place was tiny, literally a barber's chair in the center of the room. Sports played on the TV, and the only gossiping men did was about each other's boats.

Fall was definitely in full swing here in Maine. The wind was close to being cold; leaves blew across the brick sidewalks and gathered at the doorsteps of all the businesses. Everyone was putting out pumpkins and mums, and the store already had a big load of Halloween candy in the back room, ready to be put on display.

When I got close to Barb's, Maggie stepped out of the shop, the bell on the door jangling behind her. She waved the second she saw me, and I smiled.

"Where's Am?" I asked.

"Inside. She's just finishing up. She'll be right out."

I hitched my thumb at the door. "Barb's?"

Maggie nodded and leaned closer. Her voice was secretive. "I think she's feeling a little insecure about the way she looks. Especially her hair."

I nodded. I'd picked up on that.

"I think she's just trying to feel comfortable in her own skin," Maggie added.

"She got her hair cut?"

Maggie bobbed her head. "She got a new outfit, too. Picked it out herself. I thought it might be good for her to make some decisions regarding herself, even if they are as small as her appearance."

"That's a really good idea," I murmured. I wished I'd thought of it. The lack of control in Am's life had to be disconcerting. She had no power over nearly everything. She was sort of just swept along by life, and it seemed all she could do was hold on and try not to be swept away completely.

"It might really brighten her day if you complimented her when she came out." Maggie elbowed me in the middle.

"Like that's going to be hard to do." My mouth twisted with a smile.

"I thought you might say that." She chuckled.

The bell on the door jingled again, and a young woman stepped out. I glanced at her, then immediately away, turning my attention back to Maggie while I waited.

"There she is." Maggie beamed. "It's just perfect for you." She went on.

My neck snapped back around. It took a moment for my brain to catch up with my eyes.

Holy shit.

"Do you like it?" Amnesia asked, her voice slightly unsure.

All I could do was stare at her. My mouth was dry, and my heart hammered erratically.

"Just beautiful," Maggie said and threw out her arms to hug her.

Amnesia looked to me once Maggie stepped back, offering a tentative smile. I shuffled on my feet, suddenly feeling as if all the charm in my body somehow dried up in seconds and left behind an awkward boy with no vocabulary. Shoving my hands into my pockets, I made a sound kind of like a grunt.

"I've never seen this one speechless before!" Maggie exclaimed and then laughed.

Amnesia's smile faded, her brown eyes drifting downward.

Speak! I commanded my brain. "I love it," I said, low.

Am looked back at me. "Yeah?"

Um, yeah. Her hair was no longer uneven and choppy. It no longer fell past her shoulders. Instead, it had been cut into a style that just grazed over her collarbone. The ends were cut into layers so all the short, uneven pieces blended in. The style itself still looked like her (or at least the way I thought of her), the strands wavy, sort of uncontained. Some of the ends curled out and some flipped under. All of it was shiny beneath the sunlight and looked more golden out here than it ever did in the hospital.

She also had a fringe of bangs now, which I assumed blended a couple of the severely short pieces that had been around her face. The bangs fell slightly to the side, trying to conceal one eye.

The cut made her freckles stand out more, her cheekbones seem wider, and her eyes more of the focus of her face.

"You cut your hair," I said, only realizing after the words came out it was a dumb thing to say. *Way to point out the obvious, Eddie.* Stepping close, I lifted a strand and rubbed it between my fingers.

She nodded, eyes bouncing between mine.

"And you got a new dress." I continued.

Just call me Captain Obvious.

"Well, I'll just leave you two to it. Eddie? You'll make sure Amnesia gets home okay?"

I nodded but didn't look away from Am.

"Amnesia, I'm assuming you won't be home for dinner?"

Amnesia shook her head, her eyes still on mine.

Maggie laughed, reached out, and took the bag I didn't even notice Am was carrying. Then she disappeared. Or maybe she walked away. I didn't know. I wasn't paying attention.

"You really do look beautiful," I whispered. "Even more beautiful than you usually do."

Amnesia smiled, and it felt I'd been given some kind of prize. "I mentioned to Maggie how much I didn't like my hair, and she suggested we come here and get it fixed. On the way, we passed by this little store..." Her brows furrowed.

"The boutique at the end of the block?" I asked.

Her eyes lit up. "Yes! I saw this dress in the window, and I thought it was so beautiful." She glanced down at the fabric, smoothing over it with her hands. The dress fell to about knee length and wasn't tight or fitted, but loose and sort of flowy. It gathered around her waist, which kept it from swallowing her up, and had long sleeves that flared out a little around her wrists. The dress itself was multicolored with mossy green, yellow, and burgundy. Up at the neckline, two long strings tied together to make a bow, and the ends trailed down over her chest and fluttered every time the wind blew. "Maggie insisted," she said, still glancing down at it. "She said I should have something I picked out for myself."

"You should," I said, unable to keep my hands to myself any longer, palming the side of her hip. "Waiting for you this morning was worth it," I told her.

She smiled.

"I'm gonna kiss you now," I murmured, stepping so close my Adidas bumped against hers. "Right here in the street."

Her tongue jutted out to wet her lips. "You are?"

"Unless you tell me not to," I replied, cupping the side of her face. "I should warm you that probably everyone on this street is plastered to the windows, watching us."

"Everyone inside the salon asked me about you," she whispered, then giggled.

I cocked my head to the side and smiled. "And what did you tell them?"

"I told them you were a terrible kisser." She couldn't even say the words without grinning mischievously.

"Did not," I countered. My thumb swept over her lower lip.

Her breath caught. Slowly, she shook her head. "You're right. I didn't."

"Here I come, Am." I warned her.

She didn't pull away.

I touched my lips to hers with gentle pressure. The soft sigh of relief I felt throughout my entire body was most alarming. Instead of pulling back, I shifted closer, wound one arm completely around her waist, and pulled her fully into my chest.

She sighed and clutched the front of my T-shirt, her lips moving beneath mine, so I kissed her a little bit deeper.

I didn't want to pull back. I wanted to get lost in her, but we were standing on the street. My father was going to give me a damn lecture about respecting women and blah, blah, blah. I respected women. Amnesia above them all.

But I also admired her beauty and couldn't help myself.

Pulling back, her eyes fluttered, then focused on mine.

"The entire town is going to be buzzing about this." I mused.

"I'm sure I'm not the only girl you've ever kissed on the street." She scoffed, looking down.

Using my thumb, I lifted her face. "The only one who's ever mattered."

Am reached for my hand, and I gave it wholeheartedly.

"You're mine the rest of the day, Am. You ready to see the town?"

"First stop, Loch General?" she asked, gazing past me down the street.

"How about hot chocolate, then Loch Gen?" I compromised.

"You know the way to a girl's heart." She grinned.

Oh, I hope so, Amnesia. I truly do.

I'd never wanted anything as much as I wanted her heart.

CHAPTER EIGHTEEN

AMNESIA

I learned a few more thing about myself I could add to the so-called Amnesia checklist.

1) Dresses made me feel pretty

2) Hot chocolate was definitely my favorite

3) Kissing Eddie was something I would never get tired of

And

4) Small town life appealed to me. (Or maybe that was just Eddie.)

The people in town were curious about me. I felt their eyes everywhere I went. It wasn't necessarily uncomfortable, though, because there wasn't anything malicious in the way they stared.

Who wouldn't be curious about a girl whose mind was completely wiped clean? Even *I* was curious about me.

The bakery was across the street from the salon where I got my hair cut. I held Eddie's hand when we dashed across the road, the hem of my dress fluttering out behind me. I felt freer today, lighter. Maybe it was because I cut off most of my hair, or maybe it was the dress. I wasn't really sure, I just knew I was enjoying the feeling.

It almost felt like happiness, something that almost seemed bizarre, as if my own body wasn't used to being happy or free. I embraced the sensation instead of marveling at why it was unnatural to me.

Joline and Jeremy were in the bakery, along with a couple other people who lived in town. Eddie introduced me to everyone I'd yet to meet while Jeremy made me a large hot chocolate, piling on so much whipped cream there was no room for a lid.

Laughing, Eddie and I sat at one of the two tables by the front windows. "I think he gave you more whipped cream than actual hot chocolate," Eddie cracked.

I leaned forward and licked off the top, making a sound of appreciation. "Jeremy sure knows how to treat a girl," I called out, and Joline laughed.

"Take him home with you, then. All the laundry he generates will change your mind quick!"

I giggled and licked at more of the topping. Feeling Eddie's eyes, I looked up. One hand was wrapped around the paper coffee cup (his actually had a lid), and his body was gravitating over the tabletop, his sapphire eyes intent on me.

"What?" I said, my stomach feeling a little funny. He had a way of looking at a girl. A way no one else seemed to have.

"You have whipped cream on your nose," he mused, reaching out to wipe it away.

"Thanks," I whispered, still caught by his stare.

"Fresh, hot donuts," Joline said, sliding a large glass plate on the table between us. "On the house."

"Thanks, Jo," Eddie said, not breaking the eye contact we had going on.

Her light laughter faded as she went back around the counter. We were blissfully alone for the first time since we'd met on the street. Jo and Jeremy were in the back, and the other customers had left.

When he didn't say anything, continuing to eat up my face with his eyes, I cleared my throat and lifted the drink. "I'm excited to see your store."

His mouth curved up on one side. "It's not really mine. My dad owns it."

"A family business?" I asked.

He nodded, withdrawing into his seat and running a hand through his loopy, unruly curls. "I'll take over it completely someday."

"Really? Do you know when?"

He sat forward again. Eddie's intensity was something that caught me off guard sometimes. "When I can focus better."

A few people walked by the large front window, stared in, and then their lips began moving.

"You weren't kidding when you said everyone would be watching us."

He shrugged. "Who cares?" His attention went to the donuts. "Mm, chocolate." He picked up the frosted pastry and took a huge bite. When he pulled his hand away, frosting was smeared on his nose.

"Now you're the messy one!" I laughed and leaned over to swipe it away.

The second I did, Eddie caught my hand, gently brought it down, and wrapped his lips around my thumb, sucking off the icing.

My belly flopped so much it made the room spin. The gentle roughness of his tongue against the pad of my thumb was delicious.

If he noticed my reaction (nearly melting out of my chair), he didn't comment. Instead, he released my hand and went back to shoveling the chocolate into his mouth. "Drink your cocoa, Am." He reminded me.

After I drank enough that the lid would fit on the cup and ate a donut covered in sprinkles, Eddie carried the plate into the back for Joline and then stuffed some cash in a tip jar on the counter.

The cool fall air danced around my bare legs when I stepped out the door he held open, and my newly cut hair floated out around me.

"I was thinking," I said as we started down the sidewalk.

"Dangerous," Eddie teased.

"I should probably get a job."

"A job?" he echoed.

"Yeah, I can't just let Maggie and you pay for everything. Besides, I'm sure I'll have a ton of hospital bills coming soon."

He was quiet as we walked. I looked up at him. The muscle in the side of his jaw worked, a small movement I was quite drawn to. It spoke of restrained strength. Maybe of frustration.

"You don't like the idea," I surmised.

"I'm just worried it will be too much, too soon."

"It's been almost a month since I woke up. How much longer is too soon?" I asked, feeling frustrated myself.

Eddie caught my hand, giving it a gentle squeeze. "I'm just protective of you, Am. You have to understand that. If you think you're ready for a job, then I'll help you find one."

"Really?"

He nodded.

As we approached the end of the street, Loch General became more prominent. It was the biggest building on the street, so large it took up the entire end. It sort of sat on the street like a king at the head of a table.

"The store is beautiful," I said, gazing up at it as we approached. "It looks almost like a house."

He nodded. "Yeah, it was built to look that way," he explained. "The man who built it actually lived there when it first opened. My family was part of the group of people who founded this town."

That was a lot of history. Very deep roots. It was fascinating to me because I didn't have any at all.

"But as the years and decades went on, the store got bigger. Things were added on, and of course, no one lives in it."

"Where do your parents live?" I asked, curious.

"One street behind the lake," he said, gesturing behind the store. The lake was there in the distance, not too far away, but not so close that Main Street was on top of it.

"I'm not sure they like me," I said, thinking of the times his parents would come and visit me at the hospital. They were always friendly, but they were also slightly reserved. It was just a feeling I got when they came that they were there more for Eddie than for me.

"They like you. They're just helicopter parents," he murmured.

"What's a helicopter parent?" I wondered.

He laughed. "It means they're all up in my business all the time."

"Oh," I murmured and drank more of the rich, warm drink.

He chuckled and tugged me along, across the street the stretched out in front of the general store. There was a big wooden sign on front with a Loch Ness image on it and the words Loch General Store.

He saw me gazing at it, then nudged me in the side. "That sign was my idea. It's only a few years old."

"I like it. He's kind of like the mascot of the place," I said, still looking at the creature.

"Exactly!"

There was a huge bin of large orange pumpkins on the sidewalk outside. I was drawn to their shiny skin, spicy color, and rough stems. "That's a lot of pumpkins," I said, running my hand over a couple, looking down into the heaping bin.

"It's fall. People around here really get into this time of year."

"Have you ever carved one?" I asked, glancing around.

"Of course." He scoffed. "I'm a brilliant pumpkin carver."

I rolled my eyes.

"Pick one," he said, and my eyes snapped back to him. He laughed. "Go on. Pick one. We'll carve it later."

"Really?" I echoed.

He nodded.

I pointed to one sitting on the ground outside the bin. "That one."

He threw his head back and laughed. "That's the biggest one here!"

I felt myself grinning back at him. "I know."

He made a bunch of sounds as if he might be dying as he lifted it up. "Open the door for me, baby."

My stomach flipped with his words, but I rushed around him to pull open the door. He went in ahead of me, telling everyone to make way for "the great pumpkin." People were chuckling, and I heard them talking to Eddie as he carried the pumpkin off somewhere.

Loch General was beautiful. I'd never seen anything like it. I was barely inside the door, but I couldn't go any further. There was just too much to see. Everything was wooden, but not so dark it was uncomfortable. Even though it was a huge grocery and goods store, it was quaint and charming. I could feel the history here. I could almost picture generation after generation working here side by side.

To be part of something like this, to have somewhere I'd always belong, I thought to myself. It was amazing, almost too good to be true. *Way too good for you.* I physically recoiled from the last thought. A pang of hurt pierced me when the words drifted through my head. What a horrible thought. *What if it's true?*

"Hey," Eddie said, coming up behind me. His voice was soft with concern, the warmth of his palm at the small of my back bringing me out of my head. Without thinking, I turned, stepping incredibly close, and buried my face in his chest.

"Hey now," he murmured, folding me into his embrace. "What's wrong?"

I just shook my head, pressing a little closer.

I felt his hand smooth over the back of my head, over my hair. It soothed me, and I took a breath. "Sorry," I said, moving back.

He tugged me close again. "I'm not ready to let go yet," he whispered against my ear.

My arms slipped back around him, holding him tight. I didn't know why, but I felt as if my time with him was suddenly limited. Like I was just living in a fairy tale and soon I would wake back up to reality... and my reality was nothing at all like this idyllic lake life.

"Me either," I whispered.

Eddie held me firmly, his body swaying a little, rocking me into a sense of calm. "You want me to take you back to Maggie's?" he asked eventually.

"No!" I gasped, ripping away from him and shaking my head adamantly. "No way. Show me around."

Amused, his eyes lit up. "You sure?"

I grabbed his hand and spun around, ready to wander through this amazing place. My feet faltered, though, when I saw we were being watched.

A few shoppers had literally stopped what they were doing to stare. I blinked, feeling like an attraction at the zoo.

"Hello." I finally spoke out because the women were still standing there staring at me in shock.

My voice seemed to shake them, and all at once, everyone started moving around again.

I glanced back at Eddie, and he rolled his eyes. "Gossip hounds," he whispered.

I made him show me every inch of the general store. I loved it. It was my favorite place I'd seen in town so far, and I told him so.

Eddie's dad, Forest, heard me going on about it when we were behind the register, and he came around, chuckling. "Well, son, I guess if you ever decide you don't like the old place, we know who to sell it to!"

Eddie smiled, his eyes turning thoughtful. "She was just saying she wanted to get a job."

Forest raised his eyebrows. "So soon?"

"Why does everyone keep saying that?" I muttered. "I'm perfectly capable of getting a job."

"A woman with work ethic." Forest nodded. "I like it. I'm sure we could find something around here for you to do."

"My thoughts exactly." Eddie agreed.

"A job here?" I exclaimed. "Really?" I looked around again, gazing up at the old wooden beams and looking out the back windows to the lake in the distance.

"Sure. Maybe then Eddie here would want to come to work," Forest said with a laugh.

Eddie made a rude sound. "I work all the time."

I could see him every day. "I'll take the job." I agreed swiftly.

Forest laughed loudly. "You don't even know what the job is!"

"I don't care what it is," I said, gazing at Eddie. "It's here. That's all that matters."

Like two magnets, we sort of shifted, drawn closer to each other. The look in his eyes nearly melted me.

"You two are something else," Forest muttered, then went off to help a customer.

Eddie's hand slid around the back of my neck, my eyes closing just because his touch was like a warm blanket. "Oh, Am," he murmured, pressing his lips to my hairline. "What am I going to do with you?"

After my heart settled back down, I tipped my chin up and squinted at him. "Show me around some more."

"You've seen every inch of this place." He chuckled.

"Out there?" I pointed toward Main Street.

"Let's go," he said, then called out a good-bye to his father.

Instead of going straight to the door, he pulled me along behind him, toward the back where there was a cooler filled with drinks. He reached behind the cold glass doors and pulled out two glass bottles of root beer that he told me was made right here in Maine.

"For the road." He grinned.

"Oh, good, you're still here," Forest said, coming out of the storage room. "Can you give me a hand?"

"Sure." Eddie agreed, handing me the two drinks. "Be right back."

I walked to the next aisle, browsing at all the products, still pretty much in awe of this place. It made me proud there was so much of Eddie here, so much of his own work.

Hushed whispers from the other side of the aisle stopped me in my tracks.

"Looks just like her," exclaimed a woman.

"I know. They said she did, but we all know it's just not possible," someone else answered.

I stepped closer to the shelves, tipping my head so I could hear the rest.

"Poor Eddie. That boy has been through enough. This is only going to set him back."

"Poor Claire and Forest, their only son—"

Suddenly, I lost my balance and fell into the shelf. A few boxes dumped to the floor, making a loud banging sound.

Wincing, I hurried to pick them up, setting them back the way they'd been. When I was done, I listened for more of the women's words, but they had moved on.

Still, the whispered conversation stuck with me. Haunted me even.

They said I looked familiar, implied I might be someone they knew. And Eddie... They acted like I was going to hurt him. That me being here was the last thing he needed.

I knew he said the people here liked to gossip, but this went beyond silly speculation. This seemed as if it were rooted in truth, a truth no one bothered to mention.

And Eddie was right in the center of it.

What wasn't he telling me?

CHAPTER NINETEEN

EDWARD

There were moments of affinity, moments of distance. Our relationship wasn't so much a push and pull because neither of us pushed away, yet sometimes an invisible current swelled between us, carrying us apart.

I treaded the water, fighting against it and swimming up shore to stay next to her. I wouldn't lose her again.

Never again.

Always, though, the current would shift and change, and we would find our way back to each other.

Cross my heart.

Hope to die.

You will be forever mine.

In this moment, we were drifting and I was swimming, trying to get back to her side. When I left her at the cooler, everything was fine, but when I returned just moments later, there was a noticeable partition between us.

"Well, you've seen the entire street," I said, gazing out over the small "business" district of Lake Loch. "What next?"

Amnesia stood silently beside me for a moment. She was looking out over the street we'd just been up and down. I was worried she would say back to Maggie's. If she did, that's where I would take her, but that would mean saying good-bye for today. I wanted more time. I was always going to want more time.

Her body shifted, angled toward me. "How about a tour of your place?"

It was the last thing I thought she would say but the first thing I wanted to hear. "My place is a disaster." I warned. "It's still a construction zone."

"I want to see." She cajoled.

"C'mon, then," I said, holding out my hand, hoping she would take it.

She did, a smile lighting her face.

I'd parked around the back of Loch Gen since I'd worked this morning. We jogged around the back, and then I loaded her giant pumpkin into the bed before driving off. We drove with the windows down. The air was cold, but she seemed not to care. Her fingertips trailed out the window, catching the wind. Golden strands of hair blew around her face, and it was as if she were letting go of whatever seemed to try and drag her down.

The trip to my place was short, and I turned off the road down a driveway that wasn't really. It used to be, but it was overgrown now, the gravel that used to be here pretty much all gone. It was on my list of things to do, but my top priority was the house.

"It's so cute," she said, sitting forward when I drove up.

"That's not the look I was going for," I muttered, shutting off the engine.

"It's like a little cabin," she exclaimed and flung open her door.

I joined her at the front of the truck, looking at my place. "That's what it was used for years ago. A vacation cabin because it's on the lake."

Amnesia followed my gaze past the house, across the yard to where the lake met land. "What a beautiful view."

"The lake calls me," I said simply.

"I can see why," she whispered.

If you only knew.

Sometimes I wanted to blurt out everything they told me not to. There were moments when I was so sure it nearly spilled out of my every pore. I was tempted to just start talking, spill my guts, and see if anything lit up her eyes with recognition.

I didn't. The last thing I wanted to do was hurt her more.

"The wood is beautiful," she murmured, wandering to the house and rubbing her palm along the weathered boards.

"Thanks. Most of it is original, but some of it had to be replaced. I found this old barn about twenty miles from here. They let me salvage some of the wood, so I used that to replace what needed it."

"You did all this yourself?" she asked, gazing up at me in awe.

I loved that look in her eyes. I wanted to see it more.

"Yeah. I had some help. My dad, some of my buddies."

"I haven't met any of your buddies," she said, scowling.

I caught her around the waist. "Because I want you all to myself."

The smile in her eyes slowly drained away.

"Kiss me, Am," I told her.

Her lips pressed together. I saw temptation in her eyes. I waited, still holding her. Slowly, she lifted up on tiptoes, bringing her face close.

My eyes shut, lips tingling with want.

"Eddie," she whispered, still incredibly close.

I opened my eyes. "Kissing doesn't require talking."

She smiled. "I've never kissed anyone before. What if I do it wrong?"

I laughed. "Kiss me wrong?"

She nodded sagely.

"Baby, there is no such thing as a wrong kiss from you."

"You kiss me," she said.

"No."

Her eyes widened with shock, and she drew back slightly. "What?"

"You want these lips, come get 'em," I said.

A stubborn glint came over her expression and so did desire in the depths of her brown eyes. I smiled, and her lips pressed fully against mine.

My heart jackhammered against my ribs and my fingers quaked with need. I held still, though, forcing myself to let her take the lead. Her lips whispered across mine, pulled back, then did it again.

Her hand lay flat against my chest, palm gliding up to curve around the back of my neck, and she pulled me down.

The second her tongue slipped across mine, all bets were off. With a groan, I wrapped her close and kissed her with reckless abandon.

She moaned when my tongue swept deep and my lips slanted across hers.

We kissed until my lungs burned and spots swam before my closed eyes. I ripped away, only because I had to. The sound of our ragged breathing was proof passion burned between us.

"Good Lord, woman," I drawled. "You can kiss me anytime."

She giggled, but I knew she was pleased with herself.

The front of my cabin was pretty boring, all wood and windows and not much else. All the stuff to look at was around to the "back," which was really the front. Houses that faced the lake always looked plainest on the side that faced the road.

The front of my place had a small porch with just enough room for chairs to sit and watch the water. There was a screen door because there wasn't anything quite like a lakeshore breeze. The inside was pretty barebones because I really was working on fixing it up.

"This is beautiful," Am murmured, running a hand along one of the cabinets in the kitchen.

"Woodworking is kind of a hobby," I said.

"You built these cabinets?" she asked, her eyes swinging to mine.

I nodded. "I like to work with my hands."

Her cheeks pinked, a color that looked very good on her. "The kitchen is gorgeous."

"I've done most of the work in here," I explained. "And the bathroom, my bedroom. I'm just now getting to the other rooms."

It was a simple house with a kitchen, a living room, and fireplace. There were only two bedrooms, likely the reason this place stopped renting out and sort of fell in disrepair. Most people wanted larger houses to vacation in because most families were big. But I was just me, and this place was the right price and on the water.

Eventually, I could build onto it if I ever needed more space. The land was the most valuable thing here anyway.

She didn't go down the hallway or ask about my bedroom, and I didn't bring it up. Her standing in my bedroom would test my patience anyway. Hell, just having her wander through my house, seeing her here, watching her admire all the work I'd put into the remodel was enough to do that.

She belonged here. With me. This wasn't just my house. It was ours.

I wanted to tell her that, but I held back.

"Thank you for showing me," she said, moving to the door, gazing out.

Reaching around her, I pushed open the screen and motioned for her to go outside. On the porch, she turned toward the water, gazing out.

"What's that over there?" she asked, pointing toward the island.

"Rumor Island," I answered. "It's a private island about a mile or so from shore."

"Someone lives there?" she asked.

"Yeah, a reclusive woman."

She turned to me. "Why's it called Rumor Island?"

I smiled. "Why else? There's lots of rumors about it."

Her eyes lit up. "Tell me."

"How about I tell you over dinner?" I suggested.

Her stomach growled. "I could eat."

I laughed. "Clearly."

"Maples?" she asked, naming off the place on Main Street she knew. I always brought her burgers and salads from there when she was in the hospital.

I tilted my head, considering. "How about Lobster Shack?"

"What's that?"

"A tiny place near the lake that has the best lobster rolls in the entire state."

"I don't know if I like lobster."

"You have to like lobster, Am. This is Maine."

"Okay, Lobster Shack it is." She agreed.

"You're a cheap date," I teased, hopping down off the porch.

"This is a date?" she echoed, pausing on the steps.

I could have backtracked and told her I was teasing. I should have.

I really didn't want to. Stepping close, her eyes were near level with mine since she was on the stairs and I was at the bottom. "Do you want it to be?" I murmured.

"I-I'm not sure."

I tucked her hair behind her ears, leaned in, and pressed a kiss against her mouth. "It's not a date, then," I said, taking her hand.

When I stepped back, tugging her along, she wouldn't budge. Glancing back around, I lifted a brow.

"Do I get a goodnight kiss if it's a date?"

"Oh yes." I promised.

"Then I want it to be a date."

I smiled. And smiled some more.

"I like your dimples," she confessed.

My heart turned over. "I like everything about you, Am."

"Cross your heart?" she asked.

She had no idea what she did to me.

"Hope to die," I murmured.

The smile that graced her face was enough to charm ten men. But it was entirely directed at me.

"C'mon, then, Eddie." She laughed, rushing down the stairs, pulling me along with her. "We have a date to finish."

Oh, Amnesia. I'll never be finished with you.

CHAPTER TWENTY

AMNESIA

When he said he was taking me to the Lobster Shack, I really didn't think it was going to be an actual shack.

But it was.

Guess I *was* a cheap date.

A date. My first date. I kind of liked having all these firsts again. I had a feeling these firsts were way better than any of my original ones. This had been a good day so far—no, actually the best day I'd had since waking from the coma.

I wasn't about to let some ladies whispering in the general store ruin it for me. So I shoved their hushed words to the back of my mind and got lost in Eddie's dimples, his curly hair, and the tour he gave me of Lake Loch.

The Lobster Shack sat near Main Street, but not on it. It was perched closer to the lake, an actual four-walled shack in the middle of a grassy patch. The sound of the water, the rustle of the wind in the too-tall grass was all that was around, but you could see Main Street from its location.

Outside, there were large pots where they cooked the lobster, a couple big tanks (without fish), and a few other things scattered about. The building was white, weathered, and the roof was pitched. Perched on top of the triangular roof was a giant red lobster, and in its claw was a sign that read: Shack.

The air around us was tinged with the smell of fish, something I wasn't sure I liked.

Grinning, Eddie caught my hand and towed me toward the door. "I'm telling you, Am. Best lobster rolls in the state."

"What's a lobster roll?"

He jerked to a stop and abruptly spun to face me. "Stick with me, kid. You have a lot to learn."

I laughed. "That wasn't an answer."

"You'll see." He wagged his eyebrows and tugged me inside.

"Eddie!" a man yelled the second we stepped in the door.

"Frank!" Eddie yelled back. "We're here for the rolls."

"Ahh, this must be the infamous Amnesia," Frank said, stepping out around the crudely made counter. He was a large man with a big white apron tied around his clothes. He had a hat on with (surprise) a big lobster in the center. Surprising me, Frank grabbed me by the shoulders and looked me over. "Ya look good, kid," he said.

Seemed like an odd thing to say.

"Um, thanks?" I said.

He laughed and pulled me in for a hug. Shocked, my eyes went right to Eddie. He winked.

"A few rolls coming up!" Frank announced, retreating behind the counter.

I slid over to Eddie's side. Casually, he draped an arm around my waist.

Frank worked quickly, pulling out some rolls (that kind of looked like hotdog buns but were squarer) and then stuffed them with some kind of mixture, which I assumed contained lobster. When he was done, he packed them all in a white cardboard box and closed it up.

After placing it in a plastic bag, he added two bags of chips and two bottles of water.

"You're all set," he told us.

Eddie handed over some cash and picked up the sack.

We carried the food away from the shack toward the lake and settled between Main Street and the water in a patch of grass that wasn't overly long. We had a good view of the water from where we sat because we were on a hill that sloped down to the shoreline.

"So," I said, tucking the dress around me and reaching for a bag of chips. "Tell me about the Loch Ness."

"You're so sure there's a legend of the Loch here, aren't you?" Eddie asked, taking out the box filled with lobster rolls.

"Isn't that why you picked the picture for your store logo? And why else would this place be called Lake Loch?"

"Technically, it's Lochlain after the man who founded this town." Eddie corrected. "But we all just call it Lake Loch, and yeah, there's been some sightings of the infamous Loch Ness."

"I knew it!" I squealed, leaning forward, ready for the details. "I need the deets."

Eddie laughed. "It's just stories, just like all the rumors about Rumor Island."

"Most stories are based off a single truth," I rebutted, sticking a chip into my mouth and crunching it.

"How do you know?" he teased.

I shrugged. "Everyone knows that."

The sound of his low laugh drifted on the wind and wrapped around me. I loved being here like this with him, with the sun on my face, the wind in my hair. These chips were pretty tasty, too.

"Back after this town was established, it was mostly known as a fishing town because the lake is so large. A lot of people came here to fish, but eventually, the stock began to dwindle. One night after a long day of fishing, one of the older residents came in from the water, ranting and raving about finally knowing why there was suddenly no fish."

"It was the Loch Ness," I said, my eyes going wide.

He flashed his teeth. "So he says. He got everyone all whipped up in a frenzy over a possible monster living in the lake and stealing their livelihood. So he got together a small hunting party to go find the creature."

"And they never found it?" I said, let down. For some reason, I loved the idea of a giant creature living in the depths of the lake. And why couldn't there be? If I could have my entire mind wiped and no one claim to know me, then why couldn't there be a Loch Ness?

"Actually, no. Well, kind of."

Reaching for another chip, my interest grew. I gestured for him to keep talking, and his eyes gleamed.

"Only one man came back. He was dirty and dehydrated and clearly out of his mind. He ranted about the monster and how they found it, but instead of them killing it, it killed everyone but him."

"Oh, that's terrible!" I said. "They never saw those other men again?"

"Nope. All four men disappeared."

"What happened to the man who did come back?"

"He spent a few years in the hospital. He never could get anyone to believe his ranting and raving. Eventually, he was put on trial for the murder of the men who disappeared."

I covered my mouth with my hand. "And then what?"

He frowned. "You know it's not the happiest of stories," he said. "Maybe we should change the subject."

"Don't you dare, Eddie!" I burst out. "Tell me!"

"He killed himself in jail. Used a bedsheet to hang himself. They found a note in the cell with his body."

Intriguing. "What did it say?"

"It said: Beware the Loch Ness." Right after he spoke, he jumped at me, and I screamed, falling back into the grass.

Eddie leaped on top of me, tickling my sides.

I laughed and squirmed beneath him. "Eddie!" I gasped. "Was that a lie! You were trying to scare me!" I collapsed, giggling, as he wouldn't let up. "Stop." I gasped, wiggling away. "Stop!"

He pulled back, gazing down at me with a smile on his face.

I smacked him in the stomach. "Was that a true story?"

"It's a legend. Did it really happen? Probably not, but everyone tells the tale."

"Is that the only sighting of the monster here?"

"No, but it's the only exciting one. There have been other 'sightings,'" he said, putting air quotes around the word. "A couple pictures that have turned out to be hoaxes. Mostly, we just say Lake Loch because it sounds cooler than Lochlain. Plus, it's good for summer tourism."

He shifted, and I realized he was still straddling my legs. The sun-warmed grass was at my back, and I could hear the water in the distance. The smile faded from my face, and I gazed up at him, the sun glinting off his dark hair and the wind plastering his shirt against his chest.

"Don't look at me like that, Am." He warned.

"Like what?" I murmured.

"Like you like what you see."

"I do."

He groaned.

"Today's been the best day of my life, Eddie," I whispered. "And I can say that because it's the truth."

"Amnesia," he said, coming over me, caging in my head with his elbows. "I think it's been my best day, too."

I shook my head. "You've had a lot of other days to compete."

"No one compares to you."

I sighed. I liked his weight on me and how he blocked the sun and sky. My eyes dipped down his lips, then back up to his eyes.

Without another word, he closed the distance between us. My world tilted on its side as his mouth claimed mine. He kissed me fully, the weight of him over me molding my back into the grass. Without waiting, I slipped my tongue along his lips, then into his mouth, seeking out his. He opened instantly, slanting his head, and our tongues twirled together.

Balancing all his weight on one arm, his hand slid down, grazing my arm from the shoulder to my wrist, his fingers dancing over my palm. Then our fingers linked together.

Eddie kissed a little deeper, his body drooping a little farther against mine. Without thinking, I arched up into him, wanting more, but not sure what.

With a deep groan, Eddie shoved up and off me.

Blinking, I looked up at the blue sky, turning my head to look at him. "Why did you stop?"

"Because I wanted to keep going."

Well, that didn't make any sense.

He held out his hand. I gave mine, and he pulled me up so we were sitting so close our shoulders pressed together.

Reaching for the box, Eddie grabbed another lobster roll and took a big bite. "C'mon." He cajoled. "Try one."

"Are they good?" I asked, wrinkling my nose. "I'm not so sure about it."

"Maine is famous for its lobster," he said and shoved another bite in his mouth.

Well, he sure did seem to like them.

Chuckling, he held out the half-eaten roll he was working on. "Here, I'll share."

Suddenly, that lobster sandwich thing had a lot more appeal because it had been between his lips. "Yeah?" I asked, leaning toward it.

He nodded, holding out the food so I could take a bite. The bread was soft; the flavor of the meat, seasonings, and sauce was savory. I chewed as it all melded together in my mouth in a symphony of taste.

"It's actually really good," I said, swallowing it down.

"That's my girl," Eddie said, wrapping his arm around my waist. He held it out, offering me another bite, and I took it.

Laying my head against his chest as I chewed, we both stared out across the water. "So what about Rumor Island?" I said, staring at the large formation out in the center of the lake. "Tell me some stories about it."

"Maybe another day," he murmured. I could tell he was far less keen to talk about the island than the Loch Ness.

"Are those stories true?"

"Some of them." He hedged, looking down.

I started to speak, but he covered my lips, effectively silencing me. "I could kiss you all fucking day," he murmured against them.

I smiled and leaned into him.

After about a second of kissing, I felt a tickle in my throat. Clearing it, I went right back to his lips, but it happened again.

"Am?" he said, drawing back.

I ducked my head and coughed. "I think there's something in my throat," I croaked.

"I'll get the water," he said, reaching for it.

I coughed again, then tried to swallow, but my throat was incredibly thick feeling. Blindly, I reached out, groping for Eddie's arm.

"I don't—" I started to wheeze. The world tilted, and I felt faint.

"Amnesia?"

I looked up, blinking. "I can't breathe." I gasped, reaching for my throat.

"Holy shit," he said, grabbing my chin and studying my face. "You're breaking out in hives."

"Wha—" I couldn't speak. The need to breathe was too strong; trying to get air in was becoming impossible.

Eddie dropped my chin, and my entire body drooped forward. I caught a glimpse of my arm, and I slid toward the ground. It was full of red welts.

What was happening to me?

"You're having an allergic reaction," he said, his voice completely panicked. It made me panic.

I reached for my throat, wheezing.

"You need medicine. Right now." He surged to his feet, glanced around rapidly. Leaning down, his words were frantic. "I'll be right back, Am. I'll be right back. Stay awake. Breathe."

He disappeared from sight, and it caused me to panic. Where was he going? Why was he leaving me?

Oh my God, I can't breathe!

"Eddie," I wheezed, but the sound didn't carry. I heard him shouting, but his voice was getting farther away.

My vision started to grow dim around the edges; the sky began to grow dark. I felt like I was choking, like I was dying.

For the second time.

A figure backed by the lowering sun appeared above me. My heart leapt thinking it was Eddie, but then I realized the shape was all wrong.

"Help," I gasped, trying to reach for the person.

They grabbed my hand, squeezing so hard I wanted to cry out. A cold, rough palm slapped the side of my face, causing my head to rotate toward the lake. The same hand came back, pressing my cheek into the ground. I felt a pair of lips against my ear.

"You shouldn't have changed your hair," the voice growled. "I hope you die."

I whimpered, struggling to get away.

My vision was going completely dark. I could barely move at all now. My breathing was so shallow I was seriously afraid each breath could be my last.

"This isn't over," the person spat, fingers digging into my cheek, and then the weight was gone.

The sound of pounding feet and the distant blare of a siren cut into my consciousness.

"Amnesia!" Eddie yelled, gently pulling my face up so he could look into my eyes. "It's okay, baby," he said, then moved back, lifting something and plunging it into my body.

CHAPTER TWENTY-ONE

EDWARD

Anaphylactic shock, the last thing on this planet I was expecting. Everything about this girl was a total surprise.

The second she started struggling to breathe, sheer adrenaline surged through my limbs. I barely had time to think. I had to react.

My legs pumped so fast they ached as I surged across the field toward the small shop near the general store. As I ran, I dialed the phone and screamed into it the second I heard someone pick up.

"I need an ambulance. Amnesia is going into anaphylactic shock. I need help. Now! Behind the general store, in the field," I hollered and then shoved my phone in my pants without even ending the call.

People heard me yelling and stopped to stare. "I… need an Epi… Pen!" I yelled, hoping someone would hear. "An EpiPen!"

My heart was near bursting out of my chest. I wanted so badly to turn and look back, but I was afraid if I did, I'd lose my shit.

All I could think about was getting her help as fast as humanly possible.

Please don't die. Please don't leave me again.

One of the pharmacy employees came rushing out of the store, running toward me. My eyes zeroed in on his hand and what he was clutching.

"Throw it!" I yelled.

He did, and I dove at the medicine, snatching it out of the air and hitting the ground on my side. Upon impact, I bounced up and raced back toward her. She was still lying in the same place, not moving at all.

"I'm coming," I yelled, my chest about to explode.

Her lips were turning blue when I dropped down beside her, turning her face to look down. Shit, she looked horrible. Welts covered her arms, neck, and face. Her lips were slightly puffy.

"Hang on, baby." I urged, ripping open the EpiPen and jamming it into her thigh.

The second it was administered, I leaned over her, smoothing the hair away from her face, and I started to pray. Leaning my ear down beside her lips, I listened for the sound of her breath.

Almost instantly, she gasped, and I nearly fell back in relief.

"Thank fucking God." I moaned and gathered her close to my chest.

I could hear the EMTs arriving and knew they'd be here within a minute. She was breathing now, each inhalation sounding like pure pain, but it was better than not breathing at all.

I held her out, looking down into her face.

"Eddie," she wheezed.

"It's okay, baby. You had an allergic reaction. It's okay now. You're going to be fine."

Her body began to tremble, and I hunched closer around her, trying to give her my body heat.

"We need you to move back, Eddie," one of the EMTs said.

I glanced over my shoulder and frowned. "She's having trouble breathing."

"We can help her," the guy said. I'd gone to high school with him.

As they laid her out flat, her hand reached for me. I sat down nearby, holding her hand while the medics worked.

In no time, they had oxygen on her, her body strapped to a stretcher, and they were picking her up off the ground.

Suddenly, she began to struggle and cry. I heard her screaming something, but the mask on her face muffled her words.

"Whoa," one of the guys said, and I rushed to her side.

"Am, I'm here," I told her.

Tears streamed down her face. She blinked up at me, pleading, then struggled against the straps holding her down.

"Unhook her," I said, flat.

"We can't," the man replied.

"Unhook her!" I yelled and started doing it myself.

"You can't do that!" the man demanded, and I nearly busted him in the face.

"She's freaking out about being tied down," I explained. "Just unhook her."

"She'll fall off the board."

I unfastened her anyway. The pressure of me moving around and her struggling tipped the board, and her body began to slide.

Everyone reacted, reaching for her.

I caught her, lifting her against my chest. "Fix the mask," I said, and hands were suddenly there, making sure she was getting the oxygen she needed.

"This is against policy," the man said as I started walking toward the ambulance.

"Sue me," I growled.

At the back of the truck, I climbed in with her still in my arms and sat down. Her head rested against my chest, the brown of her eyes never once leaving my face.

"It's okay." I promised. "I'm coming with you to the hospital."

She started to say something, her body tense. I shook my head. "Shh, it's okay. Calm down."

"Lay her down," the guy said when he was in the back and the ambulance doors were closed.

Amnesia made a sound and clutched onto me. I pinned the EMT with a stare, and he sighed and sat back. "She needs monitoring."

"Hook her up while I hold her," I said.

"Good thing it's a short trip to the ER," he muttered.

I ignored him.

Her body was still trembling, the welts looked like she'd suffered some horrible beating, and my stomach rolled just seeing her in this condition. This was worse than the night I fished her out of the lake.

As the ambulance barreled toward the ER, I leaned against the side and let out a deep breath. Suddenly, I was spent, my body completely drained.

Thank God the pharmacy was that close. Thank God this town was small enough they could get to her in time.

Too many close calls with Amnesia. Too many ways to lose her.

I hadn't been expecting this. Not at all…

It wasn't just an allergic reaction. What just happened changed everything.

CHAPTER TWENTY-TWO

AMNESIA

The official diagnosis: allergic to shellfish.

Unofficially: I was tired of almost dying.

The second Eddie carried me into the ER, a team of people surrounded me, some of them I recognized. I was swept away on a gurney, and Eddie was forcibly told to stay back while they stabilized my condition.

How was I supposed to feel stable when he wasn't right beside me?

I'd been out of it; I still slightly was. My vision was going dark; my lungs refused to expand. My tongue felt as if it had grown about ten sizes, and my skin was on fire.

But someone tried to kill me. And I wasn't talking about the lobster roll.

Actually, okay, they hadn't tried to kill me. They just stood over me and literally wished I would die. Also, they were angry I cut my hair.

Maybe I was delirious, because that seemed outrageous, even for me.

Who cares if I cut my hair? If they couldn't be bothered to tell me my own name, then they certainly had no say in how I styled the hair on *my* head.

I tried to tell everyone in the room with me, but every time I tried to pull the oxygen mask away, they would push it back into place.

Exhaustion grabbed hold of me. The adrenaline and fight inside my limbs started to wane, leaving behind someone more lethargic and slow thinking.

I got another IV, a shot, a breathing treatment, and eventually was wheeled into a private room.

Nurse Ellen bustled in and tsked at me. "Didn't plan on seeing you back this soon," she said, patting me on the hand.

Tears welled in my eyes.

"Oh, hush now. It's all gonna be all right. You'll be out of here in the morning."

I glanced at the door, silently asking for Eddie.

"I'll see if I can find him. The doctors gave him a good talking to and told him to stay out."

I shook my head.

Nurse Ellen laughed. "I know. I'll find him. You're stable now, so the doctors won't complain."

Before she could go anywhere, I grabbed her hand and gave it a squeeze.

She smiled. "You're welcome, honey."

The slow, methodic beeping of the machine beside the bed lulled me into a sort of sleepy trance. I wondered where Eddie was and if he was okay after everything that happened.

There was something I needed to tell him… but I couldn't quite recall what.

My eyes grew heavier and heavier until they drifted closed and I fell asleep.

The feeling of not being alone crept over me, disturbing the sleep I found. Eyes still closed, body still heavy with sleep, awareness washed over me in the form of something or someone hovering over me. Goose bumps broke out along my arms and tingles of awareness flowed down my spine, causing my toes to curl beneath the blankets.

I lay still, fighting the urge to jerk upright out of terror. All my effort went to breathing naturally, something that was made a little easier because the oxygen mask was still over my face.

I knew it wasn't a nurse or doctor. They wouldn't just stand over me so creepily. They wouldn't practically hum with nefarious intent. It wasn't Eddie either. Even though he was at times very intense, he never scared me. He never just lurked over me without saying a word.

Recalling what happened earlier today, the person who'd been there during my allergic reaction, my body involuntarily stiffened.

Immediately, the mask was snatched off my face, yanking some of my hair with it. I cried out, reaching for the spot on my scalp that stung. My eyes flew open, caught a flash of dark fabric, and anger stole over me.

Why couldn't I ever see their face? Why did they keep coming back? What in the hell was going on?

My hand shot out to grab the cloak concealing their identity, but my arm was instantly knocked away. A strong arm held my hand down, and I struggled, bringing my other hand up to shove them away.

"No!" I yelled.

A thick, white cloth appeared in the person's hand, the strong smell of some putrid chemical hitting my nose, and they rammed me back against the pillow.

"Help!" I screamed.

The person brought the rag down to my face, trying to cover my nose and mouth, but I twisted, rolled away, and fell off the bed.

Jumping to my feet, I braced myself, feet wide apart, ready to fight. I felt woozy from everything that happened earlier, my throat still slightly tight, but I shoved it all back.

We stood with the bed between us, effectively creating a barrier. I expected them to leap over the mattress or rush around. But they didn't move. Instead, they just stood there, head down so the cloak concealed their face, the rag clutched in their hand.

I was shocked to realize they weren't much taller than me. Not nearly as big as I'd thought before. I couldn't make out the size or shape of their body because the stupid cloak was gigantic, covering them like a tarp.

"What do you want?" I demanded, my heart pounding relentlessly.

The person lifted their arm, pointing at me with a gloved hand and arm. They said nothing, just stood and pointed.

I think that single act was creepier than them trying to drug me with a chemical-drenched cloth. I jolted into action and started around the bed to run for the door. To get out of there, to get some help!

The person shoved the bed into me, the mattress swinging inward. I fell back, screaming, grappling for something to break my fall, and caught hold of the curtain that hung around the bed. I dragged it down with me. The popping sounds it made coming unhooked from the track in the ceiling were so loud they were like gunshots.

"Help me!" I screamed again, getting tangled in the fabric.

"Amnesia?" someone yelled. "Call security!"

Out in the hall, another voice shouted, "Stop right there!

After fighting off the curtain, I clambered to my feet.

Mary Beth was there helping me up, steadying me. "Oh my gosh, what happened?" she asked.

"Someone tried to drug me," I said, glancing wildly around the room. But the person was gone. The only thing they left behind was the tinge in the air of whatever they were trying to poison me with.

"Chloroform," Mary Beth said, making a face. "I'd know that awful scent anywhere."

"Amnesia!" Ellen exclaimed, rushing into the room. "Are you all right?"

"Did you see them? Did anyone see?" I asked desperately.

"I did," Ellen said sagely. "I saw them run down the hall, all covered in black."

I sagged in relief.

Mary Beth put her arm out to steady me. "Back to bed," she told me, steering me toward the crooked bed.

"I'll call the police," Ellen said, rushing from the room.

Tears fell down my cheeks and trembles overtook my body.

"What can I get for you?" Mary Beth asked, concern in her voice.

"I want Eddie," I wailed.

Where the hell was he?

CHAPTER
TWENTY-THREE

EDWARD

I didn't know how to feel or what to think.

Actually, my brain was filled to the brim with thoughts. Sorting them out was the problem. Focusing on just one seemed near impossible.

I wandered the halls aimlessly, barely paying attention to where I went or how long I walked. The doctors lectured me about not going back with her. They needed time to stabilize her, and I would only make their job harder.

So I walked away. Actually, they shoved me away, but gradually, I went. I knew Am would be okay, but I was a different story.

I felt I was walking through a mixture of the past and present. As if I were outside walking through sunshine and bouts of rain.

I thought I'd known. In fact, I'd been absolutely sure. It felt right.

Amnesia felt right.

But it was wrong. Totally wrong.

The sense of loss I felt plagued me. I didn't know where to turn or even what to think. I thought I had the answers, but instead, I just had more questions.

Who is she? Where did she come from? Who does she belong to?

I stopped walking and flopped back against a hard, cold wall. The back of my head hit the blocks, and my eyes drifted to the stark white ceiling with fluorescent lighting.

After today, I couldn't fool myself anymore. I couldn't convince myself or anyone else. The hope I had was shattered; only mysteries remained.

This wasn't the girl I lost long ago. This wasn't a second chance.

My body skidded down the wall as my legs gave out. I slid until my ass hit the floor, and I rested my elbows on my knees.

Everyone told me. I was warned, cautioned, even pleaded with. Sometimes the only thing your ears hear is the words whispered by your heart. Sometimes the only truth you want to hear is a beautiful lie.

Amnesia wasn't the girl I lost, and I wasn't sure where that left me or how it made me feel.

I was numb, so numb. And so incredibly tired.

I sat there in the quiet corridor for an unknown amount of time, my head in my hands, my heart in my throat. Images of the way she looked as life drained out of her body, gasping for breath as welts disfigured her skin. I recalled how she clutched onto me in the ambulance, how her body relaxed the instant she realized I had no intention of putting her down.

Her kisses.

Her laugh.

Who is she?

Squeaking shoes slapped against the shiny floor, intruding upon my thoughts. They came closer, but I didn't bother looking up. I hoped whoever it was would go the hell away.

"Eddie!" Mary Beth gasped. "I've been looking for you forever!"

The alarm in her voice made me surge up off the floor. "What is it?"

Mary Beth was breathing heavy, as if she actually had been looking for me for a while. How long had I been down here? I blinked, glancing around. Where the hell was I?

"It's Amnesia," she replied, breathless. "She's asking for you."

All the confusion and sorrow blew from my mind with the gust of those words. Rushing forward, I asked, "What's wrong with her?"

"Someone was in her room... Someone tried to hurt her."

"What?" I spat, fear making my chest hurt. I took off running, my shoes now making the terrible sound.

Mary Beth yelled out her room number behind me, and I kept going, suddenly not exhausted anymore.

Amnesia needed me. I'd been gone too long.

The answer to a question that plagued me smacked me so hard in the middle I almost stumbled as I rushed up the stairs.

Who is she?

She is mine.

I burst onto her floor and sprinted down the hall. Ellen was at the door, motioning me with her hand, a frown on her face.

I could hear Am crying from outside the door, and panic spurred me on.

"Amnesia!" I bellowed, sliding around the doorframe and into the room.

"Eddie," she cried. A hiccup caught her breath.

Another nurse was at her side. I barreled past her and climbed right into the bed.

"Be careful," the woman scolded.

"Get out," I growled, and she gasped.

Amnesia climbed into my lap before I was even fully sitting. The long tubing of her IV tangled around us, but I ignored it and wrapped her against my chest.

"I'm here now, baby," I whispered, rubbing down her arm.

"Where were you?" she asked, a catch in her voice.

"I was lost," I whispered. "But I'm not anymore."

"Lost where?" She pressed into my neck.

"It doesn't even matter," I told her, kissing the top of her head. "What happened while I was gone?" I asked.

Amnesia tilted her head back, looking up with swollen, tear-filled eyes. "They came back," she rasped, clutching the front of my shirt. "In this room."

I glanced up at Ellen, who had walked farther into the room. Her face was grim and she nodded. "You saw them, too?" I asked, shocked.

"I saw someone running down the hallway. Security is sweeping the building."

"Do you believe me now?" Am cried, turning toward the nurses who stood around the room.

Dr. Beck rounded the doorway and stepped into the room with a syringe.

Amnesia saw and shrank into me. "No." She shook her head. "No way. The last time I fell asleep in here, someone snuck in my room."

I frowned. "You were sleeping?"

She nodded.

"She needs to calm down. She could go into shock again," Dr. Beck said sternly. Clearly, he didn't approve of me being in her bed.

Too damn bad.

"Just give us a minute," I said. "I'll calm her down."

"She's too dependent on you, Eddie," Dr. Beck practically barked.

"I am not," Amnesia argued.

Maybe she was. Hell, I was dependent on her, too. Knowing it didn't mean I'd change it, though.

"Give us a few minutes." I urged.

"The police are on their way," he said as if it were some kind of warning.

"Send them in when they get here," I told him calmly.

Everyone shuffled out, closing the door behind them.

"Tell me," I said, stroking her hair.

"They were at the lake. They taunted me when I was lying there in the grass."

My body went rigid. "What?"

"They said they hoped I died."

What the actual fuck? "Are you sure?"

She nodded. "Then they came here, but I woke up and started screaming." Am pulled back, wiped at her welted face, and took a breath. "This is the second time they've come for me in this place."

"Who?" I asked not necessarily her, but the universe in general. *Who's doing this?*

"They were mad I cut my hair."

My face twisted. "What?"

"I know it sounds crazy. Please believe me."

"I believe you," I told her, pulling her back into my chest.

"Someone knows who I am. And I'm pretty sure it's the same person from my dreams, the one who tried to drown me."

"Do you have any idea who it is? Who it could be?" I queried. "Think, Amnesia. *Think.*"

"I have!" she said, a sob ripping from her throat. "Every time I try to think of something, it physically hurts me. I'm so tired, Eddie."

"Okay," I soothed, leaning back against the bed with her. "It doesn't matter right now," I told her. "I'm here. I won't let anyone hurt you."

"I want to go home. I don't want to stay here tonight."

"They won't let you go home like this. You're going to have to calm down and breathe."

"You'll stay?" she asked.

"Cross my heart." I vowed. A lump formed in my throat after I said those words. *I'd been so sure... so, so sure.*

Amnesia whispered, "Thank you."

"For what?"

"For saving my life again."

I stared at the wall, thoughts and emotions drifting through me like a boat lost at sea. She was mine.

And I wasn't the only one who saved a life.

She saved mine.

CHAPTER TWENTY-FOUR

AMNESIA

The police had no new leads, and my lack of detail and description gave them nothing to go on.

How could I have seen this person practically five times and not have gotten one look for a description?

I didn't have an answer.

Story of my life. I didn't have an answer for pretty much anything.

But I knew I was allergic to shellfish.

The police said they would investigate. That meant they'd file all this weird shit with the rest of my weird shit and hope something came along that gave them an actual clue.

Dr. Beck told me I couldn't go home. I told him too bad. I wasn't staying in that hospital another night. All the time I spent there before was enough to last me an entire lifetime.

After another breathing treatment, a vitals check, and a bunch of disapproving looks and lots of notes on his clipboard, Dr. Beck let me go. He gave me strict instructions to rest, as if he thought I were going to go run a marathon or swim the lake.

The thought of swimming in the lake gave me chills, and I shuddered.

"Okay?" Eddie asked, tightening his grip on my hand.

I nodded and smiled. Nurse Ellen was driving us to Maggie's house. The people in this town (when they weren't gossiping) were very nice.

Well, almost all of them. Someone was trying to kill me, and it had to be someone in Lake Loch. I could have smiled at them today or passed them on the street. I wouldn't have known. They were probably laughing right now at my stupidity.

Eddie walked me to the door, where Maggie was standing with concern on her face. Ellen was in the still-running car, waiting for Eddie so she could take him to his truck.

On the porch, beneath the harsh overhead light, he cupped my face and shifted close. "You sure you're okay to sleep here tonight?"

"I'm sure," I said. "I'm tired of the hospital."

He kissed me softly on the lips, right in front of Ellen and Maggie, then whispered a good-bye.

"Call me if you need me," he said as he walked away.

I nodded.

At the top of the steps, he turned and stopped. "In the house, Am. Before I leave."

I went inside with Maggie, and she locked the door behind us. She hugged me tight and clucked her tongue at me, looking over the battered, swollen mess I was.

"Lobster doesn't like you," she said.

"The feeling is mutual," I grumped.

She laughed, and something inside me eased. Elmo came racing down the stairs and jumped on my leg. I picked him up and hugged him close, his soft fur brushing against my cheeks and making me smile.

"You should have called," Maggie said.

"There was nothing you could have done," I told her, putting Elmo back down.

"I could have been there."

"You're here now," I murmured. Then a horrible thought overcame me. "I shouldn't be here."

"What? Why on earth would you say that?"

"Whoever is after me will come here. You're in danger."

Maggie waved away my genuine concern. "Honey, there ain't nothing around here that my Colt .45 can't take care of."

"What's a Colt .45?" I yawned.

"A gun. And I'll put a bullet in anyone's ass who comes here," she said, stern. "Now off to bed."

"But…" I began.

"No buts. Go to bed. We'll talk tomorrow."

"Yes, ma'am," I replied and trudged down the stairs.

"Good night, Amnesia," she called.

"Good night," I called back.

Once downstairs, I peeled off my dress and picked up an oversized Lake Loch T-shirt I used to sleep in.

227

After shutting myself in the bathroom, I took a cool shower and cringed at my reflection in the mirror. The welts were still hanging around, making me look lumpy and lopsided.

Stupid allergies.

I avoided getting water in my hair and quickly washed. My limbs were heavy, and my brain was foggy. Once I was finished, I put on the T-shirt, brushed my teeth, and left the bathroom, not bothering with cream on my face. It hurt too much to touch.

The bed with the colorful pillows and homemade quilt called to me. My body practically melted into the sheets, and my sigh of relief filled the room.

It lasted all of two seconds.

The jangle of the French door handle made me spring up and clutch the blankets to my chest. My heart started pounding, and I gazed around for something to use as a weapon.

A soft knock had my head whipping back to the doors. "Amnesia," a muffled familiar voice called. "It's me. Let me in."

Rushing to the door, I pulled back the curtain and peered out. Eddie stared back.

"What are you doing here?" I said when the door was open.

"You really thought I was just going to drop you off on the doorstep and walk away?"

"Yes?" I half asked.

He chuckled as though I were funny, then shut and locked the door. When the curtain was pulled over the windows, he turned to me. "I promised you a goodnight kiss."

I smiled. "Yes, you did."

"I always keep my promises." He stepped close.

I puckered up and tilted my head back, squeezing my eyes closed.

He laughed.

But the kiss he gave me was no laughing matter. The way his large hands supported my head, the soft, warm brush of his lips across mine. My knees went wobbly, and calm washed over me as his tongue swept inside.

Easing back, he dropped a kiss on the tip of my nose. "Someday I'm going to count all those freckles."

"Stay with me tonight," I prompted, taking his hand and tugging him toward the bed. He followed behind me, saying nothing when I slid between the sheets. Scooting way over, I glanced back at him, a question in my eyes.

Eddie reached behind him and tugged his shirt over his head. Next, he kicked off his shoes and socks, then slid into the bed (jeans on).

"Are you going to be comfortable like that?" I worried.

He laughed low. "With you beside me? I'll be just fine." He settled back against the pillows, stretching his arm out behind me. "Come on, Am," he invited.

I lay beside him, and his arm tugged me right up against his side, his hand pressing my head gently down on his bare chest.

"I like this," I whispered, wrapping an arm over his waist, tucking my hand between his side and the mattress.

"Me, too," he rumbled, his voice thick with fatigue.

I fit along him perfectly. It wasn't a shock to realize Eddie's arms was my favorite place to be.

CHAPTER TWENTY-FIVE

EDWARD

She snored.

It was charming as hell.

I was glad she invited me to stay last night because I hadn't planned on leaving, and in her bed with her in my arms was a hell of a lot better than the floor.

After I picked up my truck, going home hadn't been an option, not after the day we had, not after the way she clung to me in the hospital and the reality of almost losing her again.

Although, had I really lost her in the first place?

I woke before her but lay there unmoving with her still plastered against my side and her hair spread over my bare chest. The soft snoring sounds she made literally swelled my heart.

There was nothing I didn't love about her, not one thing so far.

Sure, a couple things might come, but I'd probably be blind to them. She was my second chance. Or perhaps maybe my first.

It scared the shit out of me that someone was out there lurking. They had to be trailing her, watching her every move. How else would they know to show up at all the places she was at the most opportune times?

If the cops didn't do something soon, I was going to have to take matters into my own hands.

Amnesia's breathing changed, her adorable snoring ceasing. Glancing down, I watched her stretch against me, lift her chin, and slowly open her eyes.

A flicker of surprise registered, but then it was instantly replaced by warmth. She was glad I was here. Nothing could warm me better on a cool fall day.

I didn't say anything, instead rubbing her back. She exhaled and snuggled back into my chest, her fingers floating along my side. I wanted her; there was no denying it. No hiding it.

But it wasn't all I wanted. I wanted all of her.

Slowly, I dragged my fingers through her short strands of hair, twirling it around my finger and then smoothing it out to start all over again. Her leg lifted over mine, pushing between them.

I couldn't help but wonder what if.

What if that night hadn't happened all those years ago? Would I still be here today, or would life have taken me down a different path?

It was hard to think of what-ifs when the moment you were living was everything you could ever want.

"I didn't think I was going to be able to sleep," Am murmured, her fingertips outlining my figure. "But I did. All night."

"Me, too." I agreed.

Her head cocked to the side, her brown eyes curious. "Do you ever have trouble sleeping?"

"Sometimes," I rasped, playing with her hair again. "But not last night."

Again, she stretched against me like a cat. I didn't think she understood the lust that shot through me every time she did.

"How are you feeling this morning?" I asked, my hand dropping to her hip.

"Better," she replied. "Do I still look lumpy?"

I chuckled. "Lumpy? No."

She grunted like she didn't believe me. I felt like grabbing her ass and letting her know it was my favorite lump on her body.

I refrained.

Regretfully.

"Do you have to go into work?" she asked.

"Nope. Called in. Dad's watching the store today."

Her brow furrowed. "Because of me?"

I considered fancying up the words but decided against it. "Pretty much."

She laughed as though the answer pleased her. I knew it would.

"Another date day?" she suggested.

I winced. "This time I'll try not to poison you."

"That wasn't your fault,"

I grumbled because she was right, but I felt guilty about it anyway. Poking her in the ribs, I said, "What kind of Maine girl is allergic to lobster?"

She smiled, but then it faded. "Maybe I'm not really a Maine girl."

"It doesn't matter," I said quickly.

"Eddie..." She began, her tone thoughtful and more serious than expected. "I overheard—"

"Breakfast!" Maggie sang from the other side of the doorway, making Amnesia jump.

"Thank you!" she called out after a moment of silence. "I'll be up in a bit."

"I know Eddie's there. Did you two think I was blind and deaf?"

Amnesia covered her mouth with her hand as giggles shook her body. Grinning wide, I slid out from beneath her, strolled over to the door, and pulled it open.

"Morning, Maggie," I drawled.

"Well, at least you have pants on," she said, breezing into the room with a tray of monkey bread muffins, juice, and coffee. "I take it you slept in them, too?"

"Yes, ma'am." This was only mildly embarrassing. A twenty-five-year-old man assuring someone he slept in his jeans and didn't in fact just have sex in their house.

Not awkward. Not at all.

"I hope it's okay Eddie stayed last night," Amnesia said, sitting up in bed. Her hair was mussed, her shirt slightly wrinkled, and her cheeks were still red, partly from the reaction yesterday and partly in embarrassment.

Maggie waved away her words. "Of course. Can't say it didn't make me feel better when I glanced out the window last night and saw your truck."

"Glad to be of service." I saluted her.

She laughed and turned to Am. "Now, I just wanted to let you know I have to go out for a little while, but I'll be back this afternoon. Maybe we can catch up then?"

"Of course." She agreed.

"Good." She nodded once. "Breakfast is there. Eddie, take care of our girl. I'll see you in a bit!"

When she was gone, Am and I looked at each other and laughed.

We ate breakfast in bed, and when she came back from the bathroom, dressed in a pair of jeans and the hoodie I gave her, I figured I should get dressed, too.

"I need to head home. Shower and change. You wanna come with?" I asked, rubbing a hand through my hair.

"Sure."

I put on my shoes as she stuffed an EpiPen into her pocket and returned all the dishes to the kitchen. We met at the door and, after locking up, headed to my place.

The sky was overcast today, foggy and cold. It felt more like winter than fall, and I knew soon all the trees would be bare and snow would cover the ground.

At my place, I started a fire for Am and left her in the living room, where all I pretty much had was a couch and TV.

The shower felt good. I spent more time letting it pelt my tight muscles than anything else. Finally, after I was clean and a little less tense, I shut off the spray.

The house was quiet as I dressed in jeans, a T-shirt, and combed my unmanageable hair. The silence was almost unnerving; it left me with an odd sense of foreboding.

"Amnesia?" I asked, walking down the hall toward the living room.

She didn't answer.

"Am," I said, stepping into the living room. The fire was still crackling, but she wasn't there. Starting to worry, I went into the kitchen and breathed a sigh of relief.

"What are you doing in here?" I murmured, coming up behind her at the window, wrapping my arms around her.

She didn't relax against me; she felt rigid and aloof.

"Did something happen?" I asked, gazing around. Everything was fine. Another thought plagued me. "Did you have a memory?"

Pivoting from the glass, her eyes landed on mine. I wasn't prepared for the accusatory spark in them.

"Is this me?" she demanded, holding out an old photograph.

My stomach plummeted. I didn't even have to glance at the picture to know. "Where did you find that?" I rasped.

"It fell out of the back of a frame on your mantel."

Dammit. I should have been more careful. "Amnesia—"

"How long ago was this taken?" she asked.

I rubbed the back of my neck.

"Look at it!" she insisted, shoving the image under my nose.

It was a photograph of me about twelve years before, and standing beneath my arm was someone I used to know. She had blond hair and freckles. And brown eyes.

Both of us were smiling into the camera. Young. Innocent. Full of life. Neither of us knew how drastically things would change just one year later.

"I've seen the picture, Am," I spoke, miserable.

"Is that even my name?" she asked, upset.

"Yes."

She paced away, practically marching across the kitchen. "How long ago?" she asked again.

Finally, I admitted, "Twelve years."

She gasped. "Where is she now?"

I glanced up, not replying. She practically growled. I exhaled. "She doesn't live here anymore."

"Where did she go, Eddie?" She pressed.

Well, that was an easy answer. "I don't know."

"Is this me?" Her voice was raw, scared.

I went to her, trying to pull her into my arms.

Her hands shot up defensively. "Stay back."

I stopped walking. Pressure built up in my chest, making it hard to breathe. I glanced down at the photograph in her hand, at the past, and felt sorrow and confusion bubble up inside me. "Please, Am." I tried again.

"Do you know me?" she whispered, relentless. "Is the girl in this picture me?"

"No," I said, flat.

Her arms fell to her sides, utter disappointment written on her face. "I don't believe you," she rasped.

"Why else would people whisper about us in the aisles of the store? What other explanation is there for the strange comments some people make or the way they look at me like they've seen a ghost?"

I stepped forward; she stepped back.

"The lake isn't the only thing keeping secrets. This entire town is keeping a secret, and that secret is me!" she burst out. "Don't lie to me!"

"Why is it so easy to suppose I'm lying to you?" I exclaimed.

"Why else...?" She paced away, then back, looked down at the photo and then back up. "Why else would you act like you're obsessed with me?"

"Because I am obsessed with you!" I burst out. The second I heard my own voice, my own words, horror stole over me. My eyes rounded so wide my skin stretched taut over my face.

Reluctantly, I looked up at Amnesia. Her wide-eyed reaction was exactly what I was hoping not to see, but I knew full well it was the only one I would get.

Gentling my voice, I tried to backtrack. "That came out wrong." The husky tone in my voice christened me a liar. "Actually," I confessed, "no, it didn't. It's true. I *am* obsessed with you, Am. I have been since that night I found you floating in the lake."

I knew it was unhealthy. Everyone looked at me with pity, with worry. Poor Eddie the victim who really wasn't. I should have gotten over that night all those years ago. I should have learned to move on, but I couldn't. I was haunted. Haunted by the lake. The memories... the what-ifs.

238

Everyone here in Lake Loch loved me, but I wasn't an idiot. As much as I charmed them, when I walked away, sometimes they would whisper. Sometimes they would speculate.

He's never been right since that night.

He's a ticking time bomb.

Poor Forest and Claire. Their only son unbalanced.

He's trying to assuage his guilt with her. He thinks he has a second chance.

"Why?" Amnesia whispered. The fact she backed away a few steps was something I didn't miss. In fact, the newfound distance cut me like a knife. Not just the physical distance, but the mental barriers I felt her preparing to throw up.

I wouldn't survive this twice.

Maybe the town had it right. Maybe I was unbalanced.

"I wouldn't hurt you," I told her, practically begging her to believe me. "I would hurt myself before I ever hurt you. I'd kill anyone who tried."

Her breath rushed in. "Murder isn't a joke."

"I know that. I'm not joking. Given the choice between you and anyone else, I would choose you. Always."

"You don't even know me." She was bewildered. I guess I understood that. But she didn't know.

"Yes, I do."

"Why, Eddie?" she cried, clutching the picture I wished she hadn't found.

Why was I obsessed with her? Why did I claim to know her? Why had I been there since that night? Why, why, why?

Regret turned my voice into sandpaper. "I can't tell you."

"Can't or won't?" She was angry.

I couldn't even blame her. I was angry, too. So angry it nearly drained me dry.

"Both."

"Please, Eddie," she pleaded, taking a step closer, holding the image out between us.

My entire body groaned as if it were trying to hold up the weight of the world. I felt my muscles straining, my resolve weakening.

How could I deny her anything? Especially when she had every right to know.

"Please tell me."

I took a step forward, bringing us that much closer together. Am reached for my hand, and I surrendered it readily. She gave me a light shake, and the vibration traveled up my arm, tingling my heart.

Solemnly, my eyes searched hers. I felt this was a make-or-break moment for us. I wanted her so badly, so very badly.

"I can't." My head shook once.

Her fingers slipped away, her body floating backward. The picture in her grasp fell to the floor, crumpled from her grip. "Then I can't trust you."

"No, I guess you can't." I agreed, feeling as though my heart were literally being ripped from my chest.

"Good-bye, Eddie," she whispered, turned, and walked out of the house without looking back.

I stood there for long moments, allowing the crushing weight of her rejection to splinter every part of me.

She was long gone. Silence wrapped around me, but I spoke anyway.

"Please, don't go."

CHAPTER TWENTY-SIX

AMNESIA

My life was a beautiful lie. And beneath the beautiful lie lurked an ugly truth. I wanted to ignore it, to start over and let go of whatever brought me here.

People here knew more than they would say. I was in the dark, kept out of my own life.

The look on Eddie's face when I walked away was almost enough to make me stay.

Just like my plea was almost enough to make him talk.

Almost wasn't good enough. Not from him.

I wanted desperately to trust him. But I couldn't, not when he all but admitted he was lying.

If I was going to use my blank memory as a clean slate to start over, it had to remain clean. Eddie's lies were dirty. *I* felt dirty now. Dirty and filled with sorrow.

I wondered if the entire town knew what I didn't. Maggie? Dr. Beck? Even Dr. Kline? They all acted as if they were trying to help, but deceiving me wasn't help.

The entire walk to Maggie's was a blur, my thoughts too loud for me to really pay attention to anything. Her car wasn't in the driveway when I walked up. Relief nearly made me sag. I wasn't up to facing her right now, confronting her about what she might or might not know.

Using the key she gave me, I let myself in. The house was quiet when I walked through the living room. Wherever she was, she must have taken Elmo. In my room, I flopped across the bed belly first. I thought about burying my head in the pillow to cry, but tears didn't come because I didn't know what I would be crying about.

I shoved up away from the bed, rubbing my hands over my dry face. I really did feel dirty. My skin felt taut over my muscles, as if the tension in my body were making me tight. After rummaging around in the dresser for some clean clothes, I went across the hall to shower. Maybe the water would help wash away the worst of how I was feeling.

Just the sound of the falling spray soothed some of the tension away, making me eager to step beneath it. Where did I go from here? I wanted to stay in Lake Loch. Even though I didn't technically have a home here, the place itself still felt like home. Was it because it was all I really knew or something else?

Like Eddie?

I shied away from thoughts of him, turned, and pushed my head beneath the spray. The gentle massage of the jets above made me feel I was melting. Sighing, I propped one hand on the shower wall and let the spray pelt me until my mind began to numb.

I was tired of thinking. Tired of feeling. Tired of being confused.

Not wanting the water to run cold before I washed, I snagged the body wash off the shelf and forced myself to stand up. The glass on the shower door was steamed up, the entire bathroom sort of hazy with humidity. Water dripped off the tip of my nose and clung to my lashes when I gazed down at the plastic bottle gripped in my hand.

Suddenly, it was hard to focus, hard to remember what I was doing. Blinking, I fixated on the body wash again. I was showering… using soap.

I continued to stare down, water rushing across my bare skin, my eyes not really seeing anything. A high-pitched whistling noise filled my ears and everything around me tilted. I grappled for balance, throwing my hand out against the tiles.

Involuntarily, I left the shower, even though my body remained. My brain, my eyes, my ears all abandoned my wet and naked form until it seemed I wasn't even in my body at all.

Thoughts and images were forced upon me; they came in flashes like a movie screen suddenly flickering to life. The quality was grainy and dull like an old horror movie on an old-school projector.

The smell of must assaulted my nose, so strong, so potent my eyes watered. I wondered if I would ever get used to the unnatural scent. I wondered if perhaps I would start to stink of it, too.

My cheek lay against cold, uneven dirt so dry it scraped against my skin. I was thirsty, so thirsty. I didn't dare move, though, for right now I was invisible. Right now, I was forgotten in this corner of dirt and filth.

The sound of chains rattling turned my stomach. I couldn't stop the trembles violently assaulting my body, though I begged and pleaded for them to quit. He would know I was awake. He would come for me.

A door opened and a sliver of bright light stretched across the ground. Unable to stop myself, I moved toward it, my dirty, bloody fingers reaching for the light as if it were heaven come to hell.

When the light was gone, my hand dropped out of the air onto the dirt floor, and tears drenched my face. Heavy footfalls made me cringe. Forgetting to play asleep, I scurried backward, pressing against the cold, rough wall. Its uneven edges cut into my flesh, but I barely noticed. Small pricks of pain like that were nothing.

"S-aaaa-deee," a terrible voice sang.

I started to cry.

He was coming for me.

Even though my fist was dirty and bloody, I shoved it into my mouth, trying to stifle my sobs. Maybe if I was very quiet, he would go away.

"Sssss-aadeee," he sang again.

The tell-tale click of a flashlight broke through the darkness. The beam of light wasn't at all like the one I saw just moments before. This wasn't the rays of heaven.

This was the fires of hell.

I watched the round spotlight it created on the floor, waiting as it swerved around, searching, playing games… as if it didn't know where I sat plastered as far away as possible.

Too soon, the beam found me. I blinked and squinted against the harsh, blinding light, throwing up my forearm to try and block the worst of it.

"There ya are," said the voice.

My knees knocked together.

The light swung away, and something reached through the dark to snatch me by the arm and squeeze. I cried, though I didn't want to. The hand was like a vise, my bones groaning, wanting so badly to break.

My body was dragged across the rough floor. My skin ripped and gashed as I went. I didn't fight, not anymore. It only made it worse.

A large, heavy figure pushed me down, straddling my bare waist. The sound the flashlight made against the floor as it was tossed aside echoed inside my chest. I turned my head, watching it roll away, the light facing the opposite wall.

Rough, calloused hands seized me. I knew what was coming next.

"This is your fault," he told me as he began. "This is all your fault, Sadie."

I gasped loudly; the force of it hurt my ribs, and instantly my body folded in on itself. Awareness was slow to return despite the violence of the awakening. My teeth chattered, the sharp clapping sound loud to my ears. I was freezing, trembling so much I could barely control my movements.

Loud banging broke through whatever haze I was in. I blinked. My vision was blurry, something that scared me at first, but then I realized where I was. I was in the shower, lying on the floor, huddled in a fetal position.

Water sliced over me in icy spikes, causing pain with every contact.

How long had I been lying here? Oh my God, did I faint?

"Amnesia!" a woman's muffled yell filtered into the room. More loud banging. "Amnesia, I'm going to break the door down!"

"Maggie," I called out, but my voice was pathetic. I sounded like a mewling newborn kitten. I pushed up onto my hand, elevating my shoulders off the shower floor. "Maggie!" I yelled out, stronger this time.

It took all my strength, and my arm gave out on me. I collapsed against the wet, cold tile.

"Amnesia, are you okay? I've been calling for you. I'm very worried."

"I'm fine. I just slipped," I yelled, blinking and looking up at the ceiling. The water was icy, but I barely felt it.

I was numb.

The memory assaulted me again, just flashes this time, not a full-on takeover. Realizing what just happened horrified me.

I bit down on my lip so hard the metallic taste of blood spread across my tongue.

"I'm coming in!" Maggie yelled.

"No!" I said, dismayed at the thought of her seeing me in this condition. "I'll be right out. I'm coming out!"

"I'm waiting right here!" she announced, and her insistence brought me back a little more into the moment.

My present and past were warring. It felt like the good and the bad battling it out. Dear God, the past was beyond bad. Just that little glimpse was so very horrifying.

My fingers felt like ice and creaked when I sat up and flexed them. My toes looked blue. I must have been lying there a long time.

I shut off the shower, bringing quiet to the room. The only sound was the slow dripping of water into the drain on the floor. My legs were wobbly, my teeth still chattering. Holding on tight to the shower door, I stepped out and snatched up the fluffy towel waiting for me. Warmth seeped into my limbs, making them tingle with pinpricks of discomfort.

The mirror over the sink was fogged. Using my hand, I wiped away a streak and glanced at myself. I drew back, barely recognizing the woman who stared back.

Tears filled my eyes, and I turned away. If those were the kind of memories waiting for me, if that was what my life was like before I became Amnesia… then I was right.

I was better off not knowing. I didn't want to remember.

A low knock came on the door. "Amnesia, please."

The door cracked open, and I peered out.

Maggie gasped. "Honey! What happened?"

Water droplets fell from the ends of my saturated hair and trailed over my shoulders, between my shoulder blades, and down my back.

"I remembered something," I said, hollow, wishing to God I could forget again.

Her face mirrored the terror I felt. "What did you remember?"

"A name," I told her. My chin wobbled. "My name."

CHAPTER TWENTY-SEVEN

EDWARD

The water was choppy tonight. The waves slapped around, bullying one other and violently crashing against the pebbled shore. The wind matched the water's fierceness, ripping at my hair and clothes, as if warning me to go inside.

I couldn't go inside. Not now, maybe not at all tonight. I felt a bone-deep loss.

Though this loss was similar, it was eerily distinctive, but the difference wasn't one I could put my finger on.

I wished things were different. I wished the past didn't shape our futures. I wished I'd swallowed all my fears and just told Amnesia everything. I made my choice, though. I chose her, even though from the outside looking in, it appeared I'd chosen myself.

I chose to protect her, which cost me everything.

At least the regret I would live with now would be regret of my own making.

The wind blew again, cutting into me fiercely. Autumn had definitely taken hold here. Summer was just a distant memory now.

The grass was long. I needed to mow it, but I didn't see the point. Long blades whipped around, battering against my legs and shoes, as if berating me for being such a crappy landscaper.

Staring out across the churning water, my gaze homed in on Rumor Island. It seemed farther away right now in the fading light of day. It didn't matter the hour; it always seemed slightly ominous, the house up high as if it rose up out of the water and perched there on its throne.

Memories from long ago swirled in my brain, the wind whistling in my ears.

"Eddie!" I thought I heard my name, carried near by the wind. I ignored it, sure it was just more memories haunting me.

But then they called out again.

I twisted around, nearly stumbling while jumping to my feet. Amnesia was running across the yard, the back door of the house flapping in the wind, not latched from where she'd burst through.

"Am!" I yelled and started running.

She came back.

Amnesia tripped and fell, her knees taking the brunt of her tumble. I called out again, surging forward, but she pushed up and kept rushing forward as if she hadn't fallen at all.

When she was close enough, I snatched her out of the wind and pulled her against me. She went lax for only a second before stiffening and pulling away.

"Am, I'm so sorry. I—"

"I remembered something, Eddie," she rushed out over what I was trying to say.

I blinked, her words registering. "You remembered?" I whispered, my stomach free-falling toward my knees.

"It was…" She instantly choked up, her face falling.

Taking a chance, I reached out and tipped her chin up so I could look into her face. She didn't pull away, but I saw she wasn't totally present. Amnesia was lost in whatever memory filled her mind.

"It was horrible," she confided, tears filling her eyes and instantly spilling over. "Maggie wanted me to tell her. She tried to make me stay and talk…" Her breath hitched.

I resisted the urge to pull her into my arms.

Wide, brown eyes met mine. "I wanted you."

"I'm here," I said, giving in and wrapping my arms around her shoulders. Her face burrowed into my shirt, and her shoulders shook. "I'm here."

I didn't say anything more, just turned our bodies so my back was blocking the wind coming off the water, shielding her from the worst of it.

After long moments, she pushed off my chest, wiped her face, and looked up. Her hair was damp.

I frowned. "Let's go inside. It's cold."

She shook her head adamantly. "No. I want to be outside. It's less claustrophobic."

"Am, what did you remember?" I asked, afraid to even know.

"I remembered my name, Eddie."

Like an eagle zeroing in on prey, I felt my gaze sharpen. "What?"

"I told Maggie," she explained. "And she started sobbing."

Without thinking, I snatched her by the shoulders, shaking her a little. "What's your name, Am?"

"Sadie," she whispered. "It was Sadie."

My hands fell away. I stumbled backward. "No." I shook my head. "No, it can't be."

"Yes," Amnesia came forward as if stalking me. "I remember." She shuddered. "It was horrible."

I knew it. Hadn't I known it? Everyone said I was crazy, that it was just wishful thinking. Hell, even I had come to terms with it.

But how else could this be explained? It fit. She fit.

"Sadie," I murmured, my eyes raking over her anew. Emotion so thick welled up inside me it stole my breath. "Holy fuck."

"You look just like Maggie did," Am said suspiciously. "Like you've seen a ghost."

The wind pulled at my clothes, tugged at my hair. I didn't feel it because the weather around me was nothing compared to the tornado inside me.

"Amnesia…" I reached for her.

She pulled back. It damn near killed me.

"You know who I am, don't you? You all know."

I swallowed thickly, still trying to make sense of it all.

"Don't you?" she screamed. A strand of wet hair slapped against her cheek.

"Yes," I rasped, feeling incredibly ashamed and suddenly very drained. "Yes, Sadie… I know her… you."

"You lied to me all these weeks," she accused.

I shook my head. "It wasn't like that… I swear."

If she walked away again, I'd chase her. I'd make her understand.

She didn't walk away this time. Instead, she stood amongst the wind, darkening sky, and tempestuous water, looking like a warrior intent on battle. "Start talking," she demanded.

And so I did.

CHAPTER TWENTY-EIGHT

EDWARD

Eleven Years Ago...

Truth or Dare.

Real men picked dare. Truth was for pussies. It also got me here, sneaking out of my house at two o'clock in the morning.

Creeping around my room like I was a ninja trying to catch a picture of Santa on Christmas Eve, I dressed in the first clothes my hands touched. Once I was done, I stood at my bedroom door for a moment, ear pressed against the wood, making sure no one heard me sneaking around.

I was clear.

Dad snored so loud Mom probably had hearing damage.

On my way to the window, I snatched a baseball cap off my dresser and pulled it over my hair, stuffing it all beneath. The hat was tighter than usual. Maybe Mom was right; maybe I should just get a haircut.

Summer wasn't meant for haircuts. No one cared what you looked like when school was out, and most days were spent at the lake or at Pat's ice cream stand.

Forgetting about my hair, I unlocked the window and pushed it up. I'd already loosened the screen from the outside earlier so all I had to do was give it a nudge, quietly pull it through the window, and prop it against the wall.

I gave a quick glance behind me, making sure I still wasn't caught, then hoisted myself out into the side yard.

The bush broke my fall. If Dad noticed the broken branches, I'd just blame it on the neighbor's cat.

Stealthily, I clung to the shadows near the house as I made my way around front. The evening bugs were out in full force tonight, filling the air with noise. Just before I stepped out into the driveway, something hard clamped down on my shoulder.

"Ah!" I whirled around, ready to punch whoever was there.

"You scream like a girl," the voice remarked.

"I do not," I muttered, then gave her a light shove on the shoulder. "What the hell are you doing out here, Sadie?"

She rolled her eyes so hard I thought they might fall out of her face. She flipped her long golden hair behind her shoulders. "Please. You didn't think I'd actually let you do this."

"You aren't my mother," I snapped.

"No, I'm your best friend."

She was. Sadie had been my best friend since we were five and they'd moved in down the street. I'd thrown a rock at her, and she threw one back. She had better aim than I did. I still had the scar. Since that day, we'd been inseparable. We did everything together, but not this. Not tonight. This was my dare. Not hers.

"This is my dare."

"You can't go out on the lake alone at night," she argued.

"I'll be back before anyone even knows I'm gone."

"This is stupid," she disputed. *"All those rumors are just made-up stories to scare us all. It's why they call it Rumor Island."*

"I know that," I said, stepping into the driveway. I didn't have time to argue with her. Geez, she was going to wake up my parents. *"Which is exactly why it will be an easy dare."*

"Wait and go tomorrow. We can take our dads."

"You don't win a dare by bringing your dad." I scoffed. Was she even for real?

"Eddie." Sadie grabbed my wrist, stopped me. I turned and glanced down to where she gripped my arm. If she slid down just a little bit more, we'd be holding hands.

Sadie was my best friend, but lately, I looked at her with new eyes… grown-up eyes.

"I won't let you go," she said.

"Go home, Sadie. I'll come over tomorrow."

"I'm coming with you."

I sighed loudly. *"You are the biggest pain in the ass, ever."*

She laughed and fell into step beside me. She knew she'd get her way. She always did.

"How'd you get out here anyway?" I grumped as we stepped out onto the street.

"Snuck out the window, just like you."

My bike was hidden in the bushes just down from our house. My dad always complained the neighbor did a terrible job keeping them trimmed. I thought it was pretty handy; the out-of-control branches made a nice hiding spot.

I grabbed it up, climbed on, and glanced over my shoulder at Sadie. Her brown eyes twinkled when she stepped onto the small petals coming out from the wheel and slipped her arms around my torso.

I took off as I had a million times before. We rode like this all the time. In a couple years, I would trade in this bike for a car, and she would ride shotgun instead of behind me.

I'd miss this bike, though. It was a good excuse to get her to put her arms around me.

The ride to the lake was quiet. I steered to the opposite side where the beach was. This side was calmer. It had more houses and less places for people to just spend a day on the water. The docks, the beach, and all the other stuff everyone liked were on the other side.

I drove through someone's yard and right down to Mr. Schroder's small dock. The canoe he used for fishing was tied up and bobbing in the water.

"If we get caught, we are so dead," Sadie said.

"We're not gonna get caught."

Creeping out onto the short dock, I hopped down into the canoe. Holding out my hand, I helped Sadie down into the rocky boat.

She sat on one end, and I untied the boat and shoved us away from the dock. The wooden oar was inside, and I used it to row us away from shore.

"What are we even looking for anyway?" she asked, fear creeping into her voice.

"To see if any of the rumors are true," I said simply.

"You really think a bunch of murderers are hiding from the law out there?" She scoffed. "Or that the island is cursed by some witch who was burned at the stake a hundred years ago?"

I snickered.

"Oh, I know!" she said. "Maybe that's where the Loch Ness Monster lays her eggs!"

"I fully believe the Loch Ness Monster isn't a myth," I replied, serious.

"Yes, I know." She laughed. "You and your imagination."

"Just because you've never seen something doesn't mean it isn't there," I told her.

"Usually not seeing something means exactly that. It's not there."

I flashed her a smile. "Then why'd you come along if you thought nothing would be there?"

"Someone has to make sure you stay out of trouble."

We were away from shore now, the canoe bobbing unsteadily over the water. The wind out here was strong and cold. I glanced out across the water, making out the dark, skulking shape of Rumor Island.

"Shouldn't be too long to get there," I said, tossing her the backpack off my shoulders. "Here, hold the flashlight."

"This is so dumb," she commented.

"You love spending time with me," I teased, my arms already getting tired of rowing.

"Always," she whispered. I glanced up, our eyes connecting for long moments.

A large wave collided into the side of the boat and jostled us both. Sadie fell to the side, and I grunted. "You okay?"

"Fine," she said. "You're a terrible driver."

"Get the flashlight out. Shine it out there. It's too dark."

She did what I asked, and we rowed in silence for a while toward the island. I didn't expect to find anything at all except what everyone knew for sure about the island. Some woman lived out there alone, becoming a recluse after her beloved husband died.

She refused to leave the island because he'd loved it there. She rebuffed everyone's attempts at friendship. Eventually, everyone gave up, pretty much forgot she even lived there, except when she came to town for supplies.

"The water's rough tonight," Sadie said, breaking into my thoughts.

"Yeah." I agreed, rowing again. I thought momentarily to turn around, but the looming shape of the island and the house perched onshore was close. We'd dock and spend five minutes on land, long enough to say we'd been out there, searched around, and found nothing.

Looking back, I knew I should have turned around. I shouldn't have gone at all.

"Wanna go see a movie tomorrow?" Sadie asked.

I groaned. *"You wanna see that new chick flick, don't you?"*

"I saw that stupid action movie with you last week," she argued.

"Fine," I muttered. *"But I'm getting popcorn and candy."*

"Like that's anything new," she rebutted.

I laughed, glancing up at the way the long blond strands of her hair glowed in the dark and waved out behind her like a flag.

She was pretty, the prettiest girl in our class.

A loud thud made us both stiffen. We looked at each other as if to say, *"Did you hear that, too?"* and we both nodded. Another thud sounded, and I shot to my feet, making the boat rock.

"Sit down, Eddie!" Sadie cried, grabbing the sides of the canoe.

"That's coming from underneath us!" I exclaimed. *"The light!"* I demanded.

Sadie shined the beam into the water all around us. There was nothing there. Nothing at all.

"*Again,*" I said, thinking we missed something. Bringing the oar up over my shoulder like a bat, I prepared to swing at whatever it was that made that sound.

"*Maybe it was just a big fish,*" Sadie whispered.

"*Maybe,*" I whispered back.

BOOM! Another loud crack sounded. This time it was accompanied by splintering wood. The boat tipped instantly, and we both screamed.

I fell into the dark, cold water, and it pulled at my clothes, stole my hat, and robbed my breath. In shock, I tried to suck in some air but got a mouthful of water. My lungs and nose burned, and I fought to find the surface.

The water was dark, its tentacles sticky and greedy.

Sadie! I had to find Sadie.

I fought against the current, and eventually my head broke the surface. I coughed and sputtered. Blinking, I searched the area around me. It was so dark, so very dark.

I was alone.

No boat. No Sadie. Nothing.

"*Sadie!*" I screamed, treading water and scanning the surface for any movement. "*Sadie!*" I yelled.

She didn't call out. She didn't answer.

Filling my lungs with a deep breath, I dove beneath the inky surface. Forcing my eyes open, I could barely see a thing, but I searched and searched. Up ahead, I saw a blink of light. I swam toward it, my arms and legs burning with the effort, but I forced my way through.

The light continued to sink, to fade out until there was nothing at all. It disappeared just as my hope was beginning to. Once more, I broke the surface. Sputtering and gulping for breath, I yelled her name again.

And again.

And again.

She didn't answer. Not even once.

I treaded water for what felt like hours. I searched for her. I cried.

She wasn't there. She was just gone.

Eventually, I found the boat. It was still upside down. It took every last bit of energy I had to flip it over and crawl inside.

I woke up in the morning, several yards from shore. People were standing on the beach, yelling and screaming at me. Police lights filled the early morning light with harsh red and blue flashes.

My first thought was of Sadie. I sat up and started screaming her name again. Frantically, I searched the shore, hoping she'd swam there last night.

I didn't see her.

I never saw her again.

CHAPTER TWENTY-NINE

AMNESIA

"Eleven years ago, a girl falls into the lake and is never seen again," I repeated, reeling from the tale Eddie just told me.

I believed him. I believed every word. The horror and regret on his face could never be faked. The way he spoke about that night pulled me in. I felt I was there in that moment, reliving it all with him.

Or maybe I just felt that way because I *had* been there.

"Sadie Gordon, gone," he whispered, gazing out across the lake.

"No one knows what happened? The police found nothing?" I questioned.

He shook his head. "There was a huge search. It lasted weeks. People from other counties, even neighboring states, came, search and rescue. The state police brought in helicopters, search dogs…" His voice roughed. "They even dragged the lake, looking for a body."

The scene he depicted was grisly, and I could imagine how something like this would rock a small lake town. "And nothing?" I pressed.

Eddie laughed, humorless. "They said we hit some kind of rock because it was dark and we couldn't see. The rough current pushed us into it and it upturned the boat."

"You don't think that." I didn't phrase it as a question because I observed the look on his face. Partial disgust, partial confusion. I tried to picture him, a younger, more innocent version of the man who sat in front of me today. A little less controlled, a little more daring.

That night had to have changed him. Forever.

Just as it changed me.

"It makes sense. What else could it have been?" he replied. It sounded like something he'd repeated over and over to himself until it became the truth. "Nothing was out there. I swam around for hours. I lost my voice I yelled so much. The bottom of the boat had some damage from where it hit. The searchers found some rocks below the surface..." He shook his head again, rubbing the back of his neck.

"But?" I pressed.

"But the rocks were so far from where I thought we'd been. It just didn't make sense."

"You said it was dark, that the current was strong."

"Yeah. Yeah. I just lost her."

How horrible that must have been for him. Now I understood the searching looks, how his eyes tracked my every move, why he was so determined to visit me daily at the hospital. He felt responsible for me. For what happened.

"What about her parents?" I asked. "My parents. Why didn't they come for me?" There were so many questions. So many.

Eddie made a sound, stood, and lifted a rock. I watched him turn it on its side and skip it across the lake.

"My mother," I said, getting up and grabbing his elbow. "Is Maggie my mother?"

"No," he replied, hoarse. Eddie spun around, his eyes searching my face, lingering on my eyes and hair. I didn't pull away when he tugged his fingers through the short strands and cupped my cheek. "Maggie was best friends with Ann Gordon."

"Was?" I pressed.

"After the accident…" His hand fell away from me, and he rotated toward the water. "Sadie's father, Clarke, he… ah, he started drinking."

Sadness washed over me. Sadness for everyone involved.

"It went on for years. He drank and drank. He pretty much became the town drunk. He hated me. I couldn't blame him. I was the last one to see his daughter alive. I was the reason she was out on that lake."

I touched his arm lightly. He gazed down at it but kept talking. "Ann stayed with him. She'd already lost her only child; she wasn't about to lose her husband, too. She was faithful and loyal. She always picked him up off the floor and cleaned up any messes he made in town."

"She was a good woman," I said. It was odd to realize we were talking about *my* parents. My mother and my father. I knew I was Sadie. I had the proof now, but even with that one horrible memory, it still seemed I was hearing about someone else's life. I still felt oddly detached.

I didn't fight that feeling anymore, though. I embraced it. That memory scared me to the core. I didn't want to go back there.

"One night, Clarke got drunk and went on a rampage, ranting about Sadie. He got in the car, and Ann followed. He ran into a tree about five miles out of town, head on. They both died instantly."

I covered my mouth with my hand. What a horrible way to die. After long moments, I said, "It's why no one came to claim me."

My parents were dead. Died having no idea what happened to their only child. And I wasn't there to meet them in heaven. So even in death, they didn't have their answers. A single tear slipped from my eye, making a trail down my cheek.

Eddie turned to me, his eyes finally focused on my face. "I wanted to tell you so many times. When I pulled you out of that lake, I thought I was going crazy. But then you looked at me, your brown eyes…"

"I look like her."

"In so many ways," he whispered.

My throat ran dry. I was having a hard time keeping up with it all. I was still shaken from my memory and now with all of this… It was overload.

"You were in a coma for so long, and when you finally woke up, you had no memory. We had no way of knowing for sure who you were, and we couldn't just ask."

"Yes," I said. "You could have."

He shook his head. "No. You wouldn't have known, and it would have confused you more. The doctor told me if I said anything, it could hurt you. It could set you back, and after everything, I just couldn't do it."

"But it's been weeks now, Eddie. I'm stronger. I begged you just hours ago to confide in me."

"I couldn't," he said simply.

"Why?" I demanded, becoming agitated and slightly dizzy.

The warmth of his palm curved around my upper arm. "Easy," he murmured, steadying me. "Let's sit."

Sitting seemed like a good idea. I dropped—not very gracefully I might add—into the too-tall grass. Wind tore my hair back behind me and stung my eyes.

Eddie sat beside me, pulled off his hoodie, and tucked it around my shoulders.

I couldn't let the sweet gesture go unnoticed. "You got a new hoodie."

His dimples appeared. "Yeah, well, someone kinda stole my other one."

I smiled. "You gave it to me."

"You can have this one, too."

I wanted to rest my cheek on his shoulder, to curl my arms around his torso and burrow in. He represented safety to me. Warmth.

Home.

I knew he was with me the night I was lost. I knew everyone blamed him for whatever happened. I probably should, too. But I didn't. I looked into his sincere eyes, heard the anguish in his voice as he told me about that night.

"You loved her," I said. "You were in love with Sadie."

He nodded.

"Did she love you back?" I asked. *Did I love you?*

"I don't know."

I whispered, "I think she probably did."

Without looking down, Eddie reached for my hand. I gave it, and he towed it into his lap. We sat staring out at the lake for a while, not saying a thing. I liked the quiet. My brain was already loud enough.

"What do you think happened to her?" I asked. "Where do you think I've been all these years?"

"I don't know," Eddie replied, gazing down at our hands. When his eyes lifted, I saw something else. Something bleak. It was a look I wasn't used to seeing him wear. He always looked at me with so much hope, so much wonder.

Now I understood why.

"As much as I wish you were her," he began, surprising me, "you aren't."

"What?" I gasped, my hand spasming in his. "You just said I'm Sadie. Everyone in this town thinks I'm

Sadie. I remembered... Someone called me by my name."

"Who?" he demanded, his face going dark.

I shrank away from the memory. "I don't know who it was... It wasn't clear in my memory."

Eddie reached up, tucking a strand of hair behind my ear. "What happened in your memory?"

I shook my head. "I want to know why you suddenly don't think I'm Sadie."

"I thought you were for a long time. But there are things, details that prove you aren't her."

"What details?" I pressed.

"Sadie wasn't allergic to shellfish,"

"Adults can develop allergies," I argued.

"She hated when it rained. She was scared of storms."

"After being missing for eleven years, I have worse things to be afraid of than a little rain."

Eddie frowned. "You aren't her."

"If you're so sure, why didn't you tell me once you decided I wasn't your long-lost love?"

He laughed. "Damned if I do, damned if I don't." His voice was bitter and so was the way he dropped my hand and stood.

"What good would it have done?" He raged. "You were already dealing with enough. You lost everything. You were in a coma, confused, scared. Telling you this horrible story only would have added to it. It would have messed with your mind. Everyone already thought I was crazy for insisting you were Sadie. Then you had the allergic reaction, and someone's trying to kill you.

Seemed like you had enough going on without me putting more on your plate. I was trying to protect you."

"Were you disappointed?" I asked, standing near his back.

"What?" He flew around, his eyes still glimmering with anger.

I stepped closer, tilted my head back. "Were you disappointed when you realized I wasn't Sadie?"

Eddie's eyes softened. "Disappointed I still didn't know what happened to her." His fingertips drifted over my cheek. "But never disappointed in you. You mean so much to me."

I touched his hand, flattening it over the side of my face with mine. "You really don't think I'm her?" His reasons hadn't been enough to convince me.

He took his time, really thinking, really weighing all the moments we had the past few months. I knew he was remembering her as a girl, really trying to understand.

"I don't know anymore," he finally admitted.

My eyes fell. Eddie gently tugged me into his embrace. My arms wound around his middle as he tucked me close. We stood there on the bank of the lake, in the too-tall grass, with the wind whipping around us. He said nothing, and neither did I.

I didn't know what was going to happen next or how to even prove I was the girl who'd disappeared eleven years ago.

Eddie shifted, his chin dropping down beside my ear. With his arms still around me, the low tone of his voice drifted against my hair. "It doesn't matter, Am."

I tilted my head, not lifting it off his chest. "What doesn't?"

"If you're Sadie or not. It doesn't change the way I feel about you."

I pulled back. Using his hands, Eddie pushed the hair out of my face and stared down. "How do you feel about me?"

"I love you."

My lips parted on a tiny gasp. "No one's ever said that to me before."

"That you can remember," he teased.

"No," I said, firm, somehow knowing this to be true. (Yes, I knew it made no sense. I had two parents who loved me.) "You're my first."

"I love you," he said again, the words like music floating in the wind.

I opened my mouth to reply. Eddie put his fingers over my lips and shook his head. "You don't have to say it."

I scowled, trying to speak, but my words were muffled against his hand.

He smirked, his eyes sparkling. "Wait until we figure out who you are, Am. I'll love you, Sadie or not. But you…"

I ripped my mouth free and glared at him. "You think it will matter to me!"

His eyes turned sad, flickering back out to the water. "I think it would be very hard to love the man who lost you out at sea."

"You're also the one who found me," I whispered.

Blue fire ignited in his eyes, nostrils flaring, and then his mouth crashed over mine.

CHAPTER THIRTY

EDWARD

The center of my chest churned the same as the waves on the lake. My heart bobbed along with the swell of emotions, buoyant because she was here. She came back. And because I finally got to tell her the words I'd kept locked away.

I loved her. Since the first night I plucked her from the surf. True, maybe at first I loved her because of Sadie, because of all the moments we had as kids and all the moments I felt we never got to have.

But eventually, Sadie merged into Amnesia in my head and my heart. The love I knew grew and changed; it morphed from a boyish crush turned into agony to something stronger, deeper, and not so dire.

Amnesia didn't represent something I'd lost anymore, but something I'd gained. Something I desperately wanted to keep.

I didn't know if she could ever love me, if even she was capable after everything she'd been through, but her whispered words just now felt like a jolt of lightning right through eye of the storm inside me. Everything lit up, electrified. The determination to take it slow, to let her learn to live again and not put any undue pressure on her, disintegrated.

This wasn't our first kiss, but it was the first of many more. The amount of desire I held for her seeped from my pores and caused my fingers to quake. My fingertips clutched at her waist, anchoring her right up against my torso. Her thin frame fit along mine so well it was as if she melted right into me.

The wind around us picked up, tossing around our hair, grabbing at our clothes. It only spurred me closer because I would never let it rip us apart. Amnesia slipped her arms around my waist, just above my hipbones. At the small of my back, her hands clasped together, her arms tightened, and I felt a sigh brush across my lips. I took advantage of the slight lift off of her lips to cup her face, splaying my fingers wide, cradling as much of her in my palms as I could.

Opening my eyes, I sought out hers. We were still so close our noses bumped, our breaths mingling. Instead of seeing both her eyes, it was like I looked in one, straight into her... past all the unknowns and right to the core where there was nothing but truth.

I meant what I said about it not mattering to me who she was. The girl I lost at sea or a woman with no past—I didn't care. I didn't think I even realized how true it was until I gazed into her face just then.

The wind picked up again, the sound of water slapping against the shore and splashing along the banks carrying through the air. Her eyes closed and her head tilted, offering me more. I surrendered to the invitation.

My tongue slipped between her lips, tangled around hers, and then languidly explored her mouth. Amnesia welcomed me inside, but that wasn't all. Her own tongue sought me out, did some exploring of its own.

Deep in my throat, I moaned, wanting her to know how much I loved it, and then pressed harder, claiming her a little deeper. The pads of her fingers dug into the small of my back, and her body rose up on tiptoes as I assaulted her mouth more fully than ever before.

Thunder rolled overhead, slow and low at first, then drew closer, the sound sort of cracking overhead like a warning. Forcing my mouth away, we both gulped in deep breaths. My lips slipped along her jawline and down her neck.

Am tilted back, my palm supporting her head as she offered up her creamy, delicate skin. I licked over it, then nipped at her flesh before sucking her deeply into my mouth.

Another roar of thunder boomed through the sky. Amnesia jolted a little. Her body went stiff, her hands clutching at me a little more desperately.

Taking her hand, we ran through the yard all the way up to the house where the back door still banged against the side of the house. The air inside was a little warmer, the blustery wind kept out by the sturdy walls.

Almost the second after I latched the door behind us, the sky opened up and sheets of rain plummeted from above, pelted the grass, and stirred up the lake even more. The heavy way it pounded against the roof made my house feel even smaller, as if we were suddenly, amazingly in a world of our own, where nothing else existed and no one else mattered.

"You okay?" I rasped, shoving the hair off my face and going to her.

The lighting in here was dim, and it had grown much darker with the storm, so the light filtering through the window over the kitchen sink wasn't much to go on. This close, though, I could see her eyes, the slightly rounded look, and the swell of her lip.

"Are you?" she whispered.

"Oh, baby. I was okay the minute you came back," I murmured, taking in as much of her as I could.

Am stretched up, wrapped her arms around my neck, and pressed close. Her mouth was tentative at first, and it sent my stomach, heart, and lungs into a nosedive. Once, twice, and then a third time, she grazed the fullness of her lips over mine. I might have thought she was flirting if she were any other girl.

She wasn't any other girl, though. She was the only girl like her. Maybe, just maybe that's why she was so hard to figure out.

Keeping my hands at my sides was sweet torture. The tips of my fingers hummed with desire and jerked with need. I remained steadfast in not moving, allowing her the time she wanted to explore as I knew she never had.

I felt her stare, so I opened mine and then watched her brown eyes watch me as she licked across my lips with one achingly slow pass.

"Mmm," she hummed and then fit her mouth fully against mine.

I kissed her back because there was no way in hell I couldn't. With a moan, I lifted her off her feet, spinning, and sitting her ass on the countertop behind us. Amnesia's knees fell open, and I stepped between them. She didn't stop kissing; her tongue grew bold and stroked along my teeth and wrapped around mine.

Pressing my hips into the lower cabinet, my cock freaking throbbed so hard it hurt. The pressure of pinning it between me and the cabinets was somewhat of a relief because it eased some of the worst throbbing.

Amnesia pulled back. Her lips made a slight sucking sound against mine as she did. I didn't pull away. I was too tangled in her web. I'd stay exactly there until she either claimed me as her prey or let me go.

The tip of her pink tongue darted out, rubbed across her lower lip, and she smiled. I didn't smile back, too heavy with desire.

Her eyes were dark, partly from longing and partly from the lack of light. With the window at her back, she sort of glowed before of me like an angel, sure as hell making me feel divine.

I didn't even try to conceal the fact my eyes ate up her face and that she was literally the only thing in the room to me.

Another boom of thunder made her body tighten. Carefully, I reached out to smooth my palm over the front of her thigh. "It's okay. It's just a little rain."

Amnesia glanced down to where I stroked her bare skin. Neither of us acknowledged the fact she was covered in goose bumps. Her hand lifted off the counter, and my hand paused. She reached past my arm and toward my waist where her fingers found the hem of my shirt.

I swallowed thickly, then tried to swallow again. My body stilled, so inert I didn't even think my blood dared to flow. The second her fingers delved beneath the fabric and stroked over my side and up my back, I nearly slumped forward, unable to hold up my own weight.

Both my palms pressed flat on the countertop on either side of her hips, my head bowed toward my chest. Am's hand explored the bare skin of my back, gliding along, tracing the line of my body.

When her other hand came around to join it, I sucked in a breath and prepared for another assault. But instead of more of what she was already doing, she lifted the shirt, gently tugging it upward.

Lifting my chin, I gazed at her, surprised. Her eyes met mine, hands tugging again. Shifting, I stood back and pulled the shirt over the back of my head and tossed it at my feet. Before I could lean back down, her palms hit my chest and brushed outward toward my biceps. My eyes drifted closed, and I submitted to her completely.

Her fingers discovered my chest and shoulders just as they had my back. When her thumbs brushed over my nipples, they hardened instantly, so much it was almost painful. Shifting, I pressed my lower half even harder against the cabinets as her hands travelled down my stomach.

I didn't know how long she touched me, but it would never be long enough. After a while, she sighed, sat forward, and dropped her forehead onto my chest. Instantly, my arms went around her. The only sound I heard was the thundering of my own heart.

"I'll drive you home," I offered when I thought I might be able to speak normally.

Her back stiffened, and she lifted her head. "I don't want to go."

"What do you want, Am?" I asked, trailing a finger down the side of her face.

"I want to stay here tonight," she said, her eyes sweeping over my naked torso.

Sweet Jesus, she was testing me tonight.

It took me a minute before I could reply. "I don't think you're ready for that."

"Why?"

"Because you just remembered something about yourself. And I know you didn't say it, but I can tell whatever memory led to your name wasn't a good one."

"It was pretty terrible," she admitted, glancing away.

"Sex won't make it any easier, baby," I said gently, barely believing the words coming out of my mouth. God, I was insane. I wanted to have sex with her more than just about anything on this planet, but here I was saying no.

Dude. I must really be in love.

My dick was threatening to leap off my body.

Amnesia laughed. An odd response to basically just being turned down. Of course, maybe that was the shit I heard in my head. Maybe something else had come out of my mouth.

Well, shit.

"Easier?" She scoffed. "Nothing has been easy since I woke up in that hospital with literally nothing."

I tried to really listen. She deserved my undivided attention, but man, I was relieved. I had to give myself a mental high-five for keeping my shit together and doing what was best for her.

With a low groan, I traced a couple freckles over the bridge of her nose. "I know. That's why I don't want to make things any more complicated."

"Sex complicates things?"

Sometimes I forgot just how innocent she was. Waking up with no memory or experiences to fall back on made it so I had to be so incredibly careful with her. And doubly, I had no idea what kind of experience could trigger a memory or flashback.

Some of the burning horniness in my body dwindled when I thought about that. I had a very strong feeling that whatever Amnesia had been though, rape was part of it.

I fucking pray to God I'm wrong.

"Sometimes," I admitted.

"Can I be one hundred percent honest with you?" she asked, her voice a little shy.

"I would one hundred percent fucking love that." I smiled.

She smiled back. She had a beautiful smile.

Thunder still rumbled in the distance. Rain still pattered against the roof and windows. Suddenly, a flash of lightning streaked through the sky and momentarily lit the kitchen with a crack of neon light.

280

I knew she told me she wasn't scared of the rain anymore and there were bigger things to be frightened of now. But the need to shield her was ingrained in me. The loud sounds, the flashing light, and yeah, remembering how much Sadie hated the rain made it near impossible to just ignore the storm outside.

Or maybe I just wanted an excuse to hold her.

Before she could confess whatever it was she wanted to, I lifted her off the counter, and her legs wrapped around me automatically. I carried her across the linoleum floor, through the archway, and into the living room. I sat on the leather couch, keeping her in my lap.

With a heartfelt sigh, Am melted forward, laid her chin against my shoulder, and tucked her face into my neck.

Yanking the blanket off the end of the couch, I spread it out, tucked it around her back, and wrapped my arms around her. After long, quiet moments of me just lightly rubbing her spine, she began to talk.

"Dr. Kline said memories could come like flashes, just kind of taking over my brain and vision. But I really had no idea it would be like that. It was so scary."

I didn't say anything because she didn't want me to. She just wanted me to listen.

"I was in the shower. I was still so upset from what happened between us. I grabbed the soap. Then all of the sudden, I was back there…"

She began to tremble, something I fiercely did not like. Abandoning the backrub, I wrapped both arms around her tight.

"I…" Her voice faltered, and she drew in a shaky breath. "It was worse than I imagined."

"You don't have to tell me," I murmured. Anger lit inside me. I didn't know what happened to her. I didn't even know if there was someone to blame. But if there was, I truly wanted to kill them.

"Honestly, I don't think I can." Abruptly, she sat up, her eyes apologetic.

"Hey," I whispered, pulling the ends of the blanket closed around her chest. "It's okay."

"I've always had this sense of… relief about not being able to remember. I always was kinda ashamed of that. Kinda confused, you know?"

I nodded. I didn't really know. I didn't think anyone could know. But I definitely empathized.

"It's sort of like having something checked off your to-do list. You know, that sense of accomplishment, the feeling of truly being able to relax."

"Yeah, I get that."

She nodded. "That's how I felt. I wanted to remember. I try every single day. Having an empty mind is greater than that sense of relief. Dr. Kline told me my amnesia was my mind's way of protecting me. After today, I know she's right."

Cupping the side of her face, I leaned up, pressing a lingering kiss to her cheek.

She turned into it and smiled.

"I don't want to remember any more, Eddie. I'm terrified of what lives inside my own head."

I had no idea how to protect her from that. From herself. "I wish I knew how to keep the memories out of your head, sweetheart. If I knew, I would do it in a heartbeat."

"I know a way," she said, looking straight into me with her deep eyes.

Grasping the ends of the blanket, I tugged her near. "I'll do it," I vowed quietly, resting my forehead against hers. "Anything that will put your mind at ease."

"Give me a *good* memory, something to combat the dark when it comes. In case it comes back."

Leaning forward, I kissed her swiftly, then pulled back. "You mean our Lobster Shack date that landed you in the ER wasn't good enough?" I scoffed. Then I muttered, "I better up my game."

Amnesia smiled, a smile wide enough it showed her teeth. "Well, that *was* a good day... up until the ER part."

I grunted. I had some making up to do. Majorly. Filling her mind with memories so happy definitely seemed like a good way to fight back the bad.

After all, the only thing strong enough to battle hate was love.

Outside, wind gusted and the rain shifted, splattering harder against the windows and side of the house.

Her voice cut through the peaceful sounds the way a tornado rips through a small town. "I remembered being raped."

My body stiffened and without meaning to, I jolted upright. Am began to tumble backward off my lap, but her arms came out to grasp me.

"Shit," I spat, pulling her back into me, my body still rigid. "I'm sorry," I swore and kissed the side of her head.

"I didn't know how else to say it besides spitting it out," she replied apologetically.

"Don't apologize, Am," I growled. "Not ever."

She fell silent.

"I'm so fucking sorry." I groaned, leaning back, pulling her with me. "I wish I'd been there. I wish my fourteen-year-old self had been quicker, stronger... something."

"I don't actually remember the act... or the way it felt. I don't feel..." She paused, weighing her words. "Damaged from it, if that makes sense."

"Because you can't remember?"

She nodded against me. "I just remember knowing what was coming, like it wasn't the first time... I'd been dreading it. And yeah, I'm horrified, but the memory went away as quick as it began."

I whispered her name, sort of like a prayer.

"I think I might have passed out. When I woke up, I was lying on the shower floor. The water had run cold."

Clutching her against me, I combated the rage and sickness warring inside me. So much emotion welled up, so much hate and sorrow.

"That's why I'm so scared," she confided, tucking her hand between her body and mine. "I'm so afraid the next memory will be of the actual act, and it will change me. If I start remembering the things he did to me, of the way I was abused..." She pushed up, her eyes pleading and damp. "I won't be the same. I won't be like I am now. Yes, I'm damaged… but that girl I was before… I think she might have been destroyed."

What could a man say? What did he say when the woman he loved, the woman he was admittedly obsessed with, told him she could change in the blink of an eye? That a monster once did things so horrendous to her she'd rather live knowing only a few weeks of her life rather than reclaiming all the years she had before.

I couldn't fix this. I couldn't fix her. I wasn't there. I hadn't been strong enough that night to prevent it. I wasn't sure I was strong enough now. What if I wasn't enough? What if nothing was?

So many questions…

Only one answer.

"I'm not going to leave you, Am. No matter what. I love you. No matter what."

"No matter what?" she echoed.

I lifted her hand, wrapped mine around it, and held out our pointer fingers. Making a large X over my heart, I said, "Cross my heart."

"Make love to me, Eddie."

My hand jerked, dropping hers. "What?"

She smiled, partially amused.

"Considering the conversation we just had, you have to realize that right now, I think I'm hearing things."

"That's why we just had this conversation," she replied, stroking her palm down my chest. "I wanted to make you understand. I feel like there's a clock ticking inside me, and every second, every minute, every day that passes us by is a moment lost. Another moment closer to when my brain unleashes hell upon me."

I groaned.

Am grabbed my face, staring into my eyes. "Make love to me before it matters who I am. Before identities and terrible recollections come into play. Show me what it's like to be in love—*to be loved*—before memories shatter the idealistic mind I own right now. Prove to me that there can be so much more between two people than pain."

Give the woman I loved a first time that could overshadow everything else? No pressure or anything.

I couldn't say no to the woman in my lap. I wouldn't.

"C'mere." I reached for her. She came without hesitation, her body malleable beneath my hands. Delving my fingers into the hair at the base of her skull, I directed her down, our lips meeting softly.

I coaxed her open, using gentle strokes and soft pressure. Our lips met again and again. Occasionally, I would draw back enough to nibble at her lower lip and massage her scalp with my fingertips.

Amnesia's body remained relaxed. Not once did she hesitate or grow tense. I kissed her languidly, slowly, for an undocumented amount of time. Eventually, I moved, laid her against the cushions, and wedged myself beside her. Our legs were tangled and my arm was across her chest. I nuzzled her neck, licked over her collarbone, and whispered in her ear.

Her heavy sighs were quite the reward, and her roaming hands only spurred me on. Eventually, I pulled back to gaze down at her.

"Eddie?" she asked, rubbing a hand over my hair. "What is it?"

"You really do want this. Me," I said vulnerably.

Her lips curved up. "I really do. So much. This isn't some experiment or some sick way to try and trigger a memory. I don't want that. Just you. Just Eddie and Am together. Alone. Nothing or no one else."

Her body didn't lie. The languid feel of her limbs and the way her body arched against mine when I kissed her couldn't be faked. Nothing about this was making her upset, scared, or nervous. She was totally in the moment with me, just like she said.

I couldn't prevent the past from coming back to haunt her. But I could give her a present, a present that bled into the coming days and promised something more.

Without another word, I moved over her, past her, my feet hitting the floor. Straightening up, I saw her watching me with a question in her eyes.

I smiled even as desire rolled beneath my skin, then picked her up, cradling her against my chest.

"Where are we going?" she murmured, laying her head against my chest. Clearly, she trusted me.

"I'm taking you to bed."

CHAPTER THIRTY-ONE

AMNESIA

"I have three rules." Eddie's voice brought my head up off his shoulder. His bedroom was at the back of the little house, a room I hadn't yet seen. I barely gazed around because I didn't really care what was in this room. I was more concerned with *who* was.

So much of life was unclear, especially for me. But there was something so sharp I knew it would always be in sight. Eddie. He was the first person I thought of when I lifted my head off the shower floor. The person I wanted to talk to first, despite having Maggie nearly plead with me to stay. It didn't matter we'd had a fight. It didn't matter my head told me not to trust him and that he was lying.

I trusted Eddie anyway. My heart didn't care what my head said. My heart wanted him, and so did my body.

"Let's hear them," I said, tilting my head to seriously consider these rules. Eddie began to speak, but I held up my finger, silencing him. "I'd just like to say that while I know I am very new to this, I have a feeling most men don't care much about rules when they're about to get some."

He arched a very dark brow. "Get some?"

I shrugged. "I've been watching TV."

Eddie chuckled. "Well, you aren't most women, and that makes this a unique situation."

A dark, twisty feeling wormed in my belly. "Have there been many women for you?"

Eddie shook his head. "Not many. I've been waiting for you."

At first the words warmed me, but then my dumb brain got in the way. Did he mean Sadie or me as I am now? I shoved back that thought because I didn't like it.

"Okay, hit me with them," I announced.

"You need to stop watching TV, Am," Eddie muttered fondly as he moved farther into the room and sat me on the edge of what looked like a giant bed.

I glanced around, momentarily distracted by it. The mattress took up half the room.

"One," Eddie said and held up his finger, gliding back just a little so he could pace in front of me. His bare chest was distracting. He was lean and firm, his skin supple.

"If you want to stop, just say so. I'll stop. Two..." He went on. "If anything we do triggers some kind of memory, you'll tell me immediately." His eyes met mine. I nodded so he would continue. "And three..." He finished. "We go slow."

I held out my hand. My heart suddenly felt bruised. Not bruised in a hurtful way, but in a squishy fruit kind of way. Like his words caused it to over ripen, and now I was just a puddle of mush waiting for him to scoop me up.

Eddie came forward, took my hand, and tugged it so I would rise up onto my knees. The mattress dipped slightly beneath me, and I still didn't meet his eye level.

"Can you live with all that, Am?" he murmured.

I nodded, then pulled back from him to peel my T-shirt over my head, tossing it aside.

Eddie's blue eyes widened and darkened all at the same time. The storm that raged outside seemed to match the one he held in. Even though I was pretty much inexperienced (meaning I didn't have any working knowledge in my head of doing this), I still knew how much he wanted me. I could feel it wave off him and wrap around me. It was heady, almost addictive.

"My head keeps telling me we shouldn't do this," Eddie murmured, his palms hovering over my bare shoulders. "But, *my God*, Amnesia, my heart literally beats for this. For you."

"I want you just as much," I confided.

With a shaky exhale, Eddie's palms settled over my shoulders and dragged down over my arms, his fingers circling around my wrists. My eyes slid closed. I tilted my head to the side and gave myself over to him.

I trusted him. I hadn't even tried to. Hell, most days I didn't want to. But I did. Even after today, after his confessions, after the lies and the truths. Even with all the still unknowns. I cast aside all those thoughts and let the trust I felt surround me. The weight of his hands and the warmth of his skin was all I wanted and needed in this moment.

His hands began to wander, careful and slow. Electricity crackled in his fingertips as they caressed my arms, the inner part of my elbow, and stroked over my collarbone. Gradually, he skimmed the sides of my waist, settling his palms above my hips where my body naturally curved in.

I was trembling beneath him, but not because I was scared. I'd never felt this kind of closeness with someone. The intimacy in this dark room was unmatched.

Thunder rolled overhead, rain pattered against the window, and his lips lowered, drifting over the exposed part of my neck. With a soft moan, I grabbed his waist, tilting my head farther, granting him better access. His tongue seared a path over my skin, so hot when the air brushed over it, I shivered.

Drawing back, Eddie gazed down at me. Slowly, I opened my eyes. He was so incredibly handsome. His eyes, the strength in his jaw, his loopy, dark curls that never knew order.

I reached for him, unable to stay away. After brushing my fingers through his hair, I gripped the back of his head to pull it down. Our mouths fused together and a spark ignited in my chest.

I shoved my body against his bare torso, clutching at his shoulders as our mouths met again and again. Eddie's hands slipped up the small of my back, stroked over my spine, and reached for the clasp on my bra. Slowly, he unhooked it, letting the back fall open.

I didn't pull back right away. We kept kissing, and his fingertips explored my bare skin, teasing and stroking until I started to squirm against him for more.

In a surge of desire, I shoved back, our eyes met, and I stripped the bra off my body and tossed it aside. I felt slightly self-conscious, baring myself this way, exposing the scars that told of a past I couldn't recall. But the insecure feeling was banished the second his eyes grazed over my body and then met my stare.

"You really are the most beautiful woman I've ever seen."

I threw my arms around him, hugging him close. My skin against his skin, my bare chest rubbed against his. He didn't do anything but hug me, his lips brushing the top of my shoulder. On impulse, I nipped at his shoulder, sinking my teeth into his skin just lightly.

His indrawn breath made me do it again, and his palms slipped down to cup my ass. Against his chest, my breasts began to ache. My nipples grew hard, and I rubbed against him. The pressure felt good; they ached for more.

Instantly, he picked me up, laid me out in the center of the bed, then joined me on the mattress. His body settled along mine. His mouth dipped to my chest.

The second my hardened pebble was surrounded by his lips, I moaned. Tingles of excitement shot through me as he lightly sucked. I reached for his curls, buried my hands in the softness, and held him to me, silently asking for more.

He obliged, lavishing attention on my breasts until my skin was damp and my body squirmed against the bed. His lips were swollen when he lifted his head. I smiled at him, feeling drunk even though I hadn't had a drop.

Eddie climbed over me, straddling my hips, rising so his chest came above me like a piece of artwork, and the bulge beneath his jeans was too obvious to deny.

Curious and slightly intimidated, I reached out, stroked my hand over the bulge, and watched him swallow thickly. His throat worked compulsively as I rubbed against his cock, then left it to trail my fingers over his lower abs.

"Is this okay, Am?" he whispered, his voice strained. "Is it okay for me to be on top of you."

"Come closer," I beckoned, crooking my finger.

His body folded over mine, and once again we were chest to chest. I wrapped my legs around his waist, his weight pushing me into the blankets. We kissed and stroked each other until my skin was flushed and I felt feverish. Eddie was breathing heavy, and I felt the restrained need pulse beneath his skin.

I pushed at his shoulder, and he lifted, a concerned look crossing his face. I sat up, reaching for the button on his pants.

His hand covered mine. "You sure?"

"I've never been so sure of anything. Ever." I promised.

Eddie rolled off me, practically ripping the pants off his lower half. He was wearing a pair of black boxer briefs, the kind that were tight and hugged his thighs. His legs were thick, wide with strength, and at the center of them, the bulge strained against his boxers. I wrapped my hand around it, giving it a squeeze. He made a sound, and his hips jutted out.

I pushed him down onto his back, and this time I crawled over him. Grabbing my hips, Eddie positioned me so I was straddling his bulge and it hit me right in my center. Surprise widened my eyes when he rotated up against me.

"Oh, that feels so good," I murmured, still feeling the buzz of pleasure in my limbs.

"That's nothing compared to what it will be." He vowed. "Like this, baby," he murmured, grasped my hips, and rocked my body against his.

I sucked in a breath as desire so strong pulsed through me. Liquid heat slicked my panties, and it felt as though my heartbeat moved down into that secret place. I throbbed, I ached, and there were even twinges of pain.

With every twinge, I rocked against him. His eyes closed, head fell back, and I stared down at his bare chest, smooth skin, and locked jaw.

I loved the power in his body. I loved how even though he could overpower me in two seconds flat, he didn't. He used his power to give me pleasure. He used it not against me, but for me.

"Eddie, I want more," I whispered.

His eyes shot open, head lifting off the pillow. He sat up so fast I barely saw him coming. One minute he was lying down, and the next he was sitting up, I was in his lap, and my legs were wound around his torso.

"I love you, Amnesia," he said, cupping my face and pulling it close. "So goddamn much." Our mouths fused.

His tongue stroked mine, and he rolled, pinning me beneath him.

Instinctively, my legs opened, and he settled between them. I pushed at the waistband of his boxers. He rose and pulled them off. Peeking up, I looked at his dick, so rigid it stood out from his body. I reached for it, glancing at him for permission.

He took my hand and brought it to him, cupping my palm around it and encouraging me to stroke him. Oh, he was smooth. Silky soft. It seemed like such a surprise because he was so hard with need. I loved the combination of soft and hard. It intrigued me. It made me hungry.

I pushed up onto my elbows to press my lips to the tip. Eddie groaned and pulled back a little. "You're so fucking sweet," he murmured.

I licked my lips. They tasted surprisingly salty.

Eddie pushed my body back, slipping his fingers into the waistband of my jeans. I helped him push them down, and he yanked them off and tossed them aside.

When he reached for my panties, again he paused to look at me.

I reached between us and shoved them down. The second they were gone, his hand was back, cupping my center, and he made a sound. His free hand gently pushed my thigh, and I spread my legs. A single thick finger slid against my slit, and I moaned.

"You're drenched," he whispered, sliding his finger inside me.

I gasped and glanced down. He paused, unmoving. Our eyes met. "Am?"

"Deeper, Eddie. Go deeper." I urged.

His finger surged deep, stroked against my inner walls, and my hands gripped the sheets beside me. I lifted my hips, and he slid a second finger inside. The next thing I felt were his lips closing around the swollen bud at the center of my body. He sucked and licked it as his fingers pumped inside me.

Need hammered within me, and all I could think about was getting closer to him, for him to hurry.

I grabbed his hair, tugging him closer. His laugh vibrated my clit, and I groaned. My knees were shaking, knocking against his head, and beneath us the mattress shook.

Eddie lifted his head, his lips slick and shiny.

"Kiss me," I demanded.

He crawled up my body, lying over me completely. He tasted like me, and I couldn't get enough.

I felt the tip of his thick head at the center of my body. I opened my legs, inviting him in. His cock slid along my slit, but didn't penetrate. I felt the silky lubricant from my core coat him, and I started to pant.

"I want to be inside you, Am," he said, his voice strained.

"Please." I urged, opening my legs farther.

In one long stroke, he slid inside. My mouth opened, but no sound came out. He felt big, and I was tight. A momentary pinch of pain hit me, but then my body stretched around him, the slick wetness between my legs reducing friction.

Eddie's body was vibrating, his arms shaking as he supported his weight. I felt him struggle to hold himself still, his eyes seeking out mine.

I cupped the side of his face and smiled.

Relief shone in his face, and then he smiled, too.

He started moving, slow at first. Long, easy strokes that felt like a fire was being lit inside me. I marveled at the fact he was closer to me than anyone else. I thought it might be awkward to have someone actually moving in me, but it wasn't at all.

It was powerful. Heady. Something I couldn't get enough of.

I felt my body begin to strain. His slow, easy strokes weren't enough. My fingernails sank into his biceps, and I squeezed him, surging up against his hips. Eddie's eyes flashed, and he began to move. Faster, harder...

I began to pant. I whispered his name.

"Let go," he told me.

I did. Bright lights burst behind my eyelids. Pleasure like I'd never experienced before rolled over me like a tidal wave. Pure bliss was all I felt, and it was amazing.

Eddie made a sound, and I glanced up. His eyes were closed, his jaw locked. I surged my hips up, our bodies grinding together. He shouted and his body began to convulse, and deep inside me, I felt him pulse.

After we both came down off the high, he exhaled and collapsed. Wrapping his arms around me, Eddie rolled so I wasn't pinned beneath him. Instead, I lay draped over his chest, our legs so tangled together I wasn't sure what was his and what was mine. It didn't matter really. Everything I was now belonged to him.

His palm covered the entire side of my head. He stroked my hair and pressed his lips to the center of my forehead. "Are you okay?"

I giggled. "I'm perfect."

"Was that a laugh?" he asked. I could actually hear the way he raised just a single eyebrow when he spoke.

Against his chest, I smiled. "Maybe."

"Are you laughing at my skills in the bedroom?" He poked me in the ribs, and another giggle came out.

"No!" I laughed as he started to tickle me full on. "Stop!" I gasped, wiggling so much I fell off his chest.

He rolled, pinning me beneath him. His eyes were warm when they settled on my face. "So if you aren't mocking my performance…."

I rolled my eyes. "Your performance was pretty damn good and you know it."

He made a surprised face. "Did you just curse? Did my freckled little angel just say a dirty word?"

I gasped, feigning a shocked voice. "What have you done to me? I'm corrupted."

Eddie swooped in and kissed me, laughing as his lips brushed mine. My heart nearly burst with fullness, and there was a pang of something else as all this happiness surrounded me.

Guilt.

He felt the change come over me. Of course he did. We were becoming very in tune with each other, and what we just shared only bonded us further.

"What's wrong?" he asked, drawing back.

"Nothing." I shook my head.

"Amnesia, tell me."

I sighed. "I've never felt like this before. So happy... so carefree."

"And that's a problem?" he asked, trying to follow.

I smiled, brushing my fingertips over his cheekbone. He smiled, his dimple appearing. "No. It's just... I feel kind of guilty."

"Guilty?" he asked, frowning.

I nodded, trying to understand. "Like maybe I shouldn't be happy. It feels sort of wrong, like happiness doesn't belong to me."

I heard him swallow and watched a curl fall into his eyes when he shifted, caging my body beneath his to gaze down. "If there is anyone in this entire world that deserves happiness, it's you. That much I am absolutely sure of."

"I want it. But sometimes..." My voice faded.

He brushed over my jaw with the pads of his fingers. "What?"

"Sometimes it feels like being happy now will only make things harder later."

"Why would things be harder later, sweetheart?" He kissed the top of my shoulder.

"Because they're going to keep coming for me. And when they do, this happiness, *you*, will be ripped away, and I won't have anything left."

CHAPTER THIRTY-TWO

EDWARD

"No one is going to take me away from you." I swore, staring at her intently until her eyes, which had turned worried, finally rose to meet mine.

With her stare still on me, she whispered, "They'll take me."

My stomach plummeted, the "afterglow" from making love to her dimming.

"And we'll be apart. Again." She finished.

The fear in her eyes was unmistakable. It made me sick and angry at the same time at how fast she crashed from bliss to anxiety.

"I won't let that happen," I told her, gut tight. "Not again."

I went from believing Amnesia was Sadie to being convinced she wasn't, and now… now I was stuck somewhere in the middle. There were too many things that pointed to her being my long-lost best friend, but also things that pointed to her not being the girl I lost.

Amnesia smiled softly, almost sadly, and raked her fingers through my hair. "I love you."

Breathing became impossible for long moments. Everything in the universe stopped, maybe—probably even my heart. I hadn't wanted her to say those three words. I'd been afraid they would be too easy for her to take back.

She couldn't have them back. Not ever.

I had to remind myself how to breathe, and the first breath I took after those words sounded more like a gasp.

"It's so easy to love you." She confided, still pulling her hands through my hair. "I never thought it could be so simple for someone to get in here." She pointed to her chest.

I kissed her. Just like that, we slipped back into the cocoon we'd been in before. My chest felt tight, so unbelievably full. I pulled away, dropping my forehead so it rested against hers. "Cross my heart,"

"Hope to die," she added.

"You will be forever mine."

She spoke softly. "Did you used to say that to Sadie?"

I nodded. "All the time. Except the forever mine part. That part is yours."

"Forever is a long time," she said.

"Not long enough."

"Maybe I was wrong," Amnesia said, wiggling a little beneath me. I sat up, so she could lean against the headboard. "Maybe the happiness and the memories I asked for will only make it harder when the truth comes back, when the memories resurface. Maybe it will make me realize what I lost."

"You aren't lost," I told her, firm. "You're found."

"They're coming back for me. You know it. Everywhere I go, the killer shows up."

I shook my head adamantly. My inner lion paced inside me. The need to protect what was mine was stronger than I ever felt before. It was almost blinding, and I reminded myself I couldn't allow this urge to make me stupid. Now more than ever I had to be smart. "I swear to God, Am, I will murder them before anyone gets the chance to harm you."

Her head tilted to the side, a thoughtful glint coming into her chocolatey eyes. "There's something else,"

"Tell me," I demanded. I needed to know exactly what I was working against.

"I'd been so sure the person stalking me wanted me dead, but this last time, the other night in the hospital, it was different."

"Different how?"

"They pulled this rag out of their cape thingy. It smelled so strongly of chloroform it nearly made me gag."

"Yeah, I remember the odd scent in the room." I realized. "They hadn't done that before?"

She shook her head. "No. Up until then, it was more violent, almost urgent. The strangling, luring me into the woods, even in my nightmare from the night I nearly drowned. It felt like physical harm was imminent. But the other night…"

My brow furrowed. Trying to come up with an insane person's motive wasn't easy. "Maybe they planned to knock you out then kill you. Make less noise?"

She shook her head. "I don't think so. I think they wanted to take me."

My eyes widened, and alarm coursed through me. "Kidnap you?"

She nodded. "But why?"

I grabbed her wrist, giving it a gentle tug. "Am, did you tell the police that night when they came to the hospital?"

"Of course."

"And?" I demanded.

"And they said usually, chloroform is used for kidnapping."

"Why didn't you say anything, baby?" I murmured, brushing the hair from her face. I couldn't be mad at her, not when she looked so vulnerable.

"I've been so confused, Eddie. I'd been so sure they were trying to kill me. And now I'm not. No one is still convinced that first attack wasn't a dream. I can't even identify them. I don't even know if it was a man or woman!"

"Okay." I soothed her, wrapping an arm around her shoulders, drawing her into the circle of my body. She was shaking. "It's all right."

"I didn't want to think about it. I still don't. But I can't stop now. The more days that pass, the more hunted I feel... I have so much more to lose now." She lifted her head, looking into my eyes. "So much more to protect."

"You leave the protecting to me," I said, tenacious.

"I can't shake the feeling that maybe they don't just want to kill me. Maybe they want something more."

The sick thoughts parading around in my mind made me nauseous. Amnesia might not have a memory, but she had natural instinct, and there was no doubt at least partially that instinct had kept her alive. If she felt the person had been there to kidnap her the other night, I believed her.

It also opened up a whole new frightening realm of possibility.

What if this was Sadie right here in my arms? That meant she had to have spent the last eleven years somewhere, with someone.

What if that someone wanted her back?

CHAPTER THIRTY-THREE

AMNESIA

I was a light sleeper. It didn't take much to wake me or disturb my slumber. I wasn't sure if that was just a personality trait, something learned in the past, or my mind's way of always being alert for when my attacker/kidnapper/killer came back.

Geez. My life was beginning to resemble the people we watched on those crazy reality television shows.

When a very faint knock rapped against the glass of the French doors my eyes popped open instantly. Fear didn't even flicker into my mind; my body was already humming. With a sleepy smile, I slid from beneath the quilt and raced across the room.

Eddie ducked inside the second I unlocked the door.

"It's freezing!" I exclaimed and leapt at him.

"Whoa." He chuckled low. I liked his voice in the morning. It was always raspier than normal. It gave me tingles over my entire body. The good kind.

Somehow, he caught me, lifting me so my legs could wrap around his waist, without spilling the tall paper cup in his hand. "You're gonna end up wearing this if you aren't careful." His voice was far from scolding. He liked when I climbed all over him, which was something I'd been doing a lot more.

I peppered his face with kisses, and he chuckled some more, holding me tight with his arm. Carrying me over toward the bed, he set down the cup, which I knew had hot chocolate in it, and climbed into the bed with me still in his arms.

"I missed you last night," he said, mouth crashing over mine.

I sighed into his mouth and returned the kiss with just as much need. My insides vibrated and my stomach fluttered wildly. His skin was cooler than I was used to, and I knew it was because it was cold outside this morning. Leaning up, I grabbed the covers and pulled them over us. The bed was still warm from when I'd be sleeping.

Eddie's hand delved below the hem of the T-shirt I slept in, his palm gliding over my stomach. I tugged his shirt until he broke the kiss and let me yank it over his head. Surging up, I kissed his chest and shoulder. His palm cupped the back of my head and held me to him.

"I swear I didn't come over here for this." He groaned, kissing me again. "But I want you so fucking bad."

I unhooked the button on his jeans, sliding down the zipper. My hand brushed over his stiff length, and he groaned. "I want you, too," I whispered.

After that, we were in a frenzy to remove all the barriers between us, and he joined his body with mine. I started to moan, but he caught the sound with his mouth and began pumping his hips. My nails scraped over his back as the familiar feel of an orgasm built within me.

Eddie pushed up on his palms, his body hovering over mine. Our eyes collided, his cock surging deep. "I love you," he rasped.

My heart turned over, and I reached for him, pulling him back down so our bodies were pressed together. I felt his lips brush over my neck, and I arched up.

My climax rolled over me, and my body went limp against the sheets. Wave after wave of pleasure stole all thought from my head. The only thing that brought me back was the soft sound he made into the pillow beside my ear as he exploded.

After we both came down off the high, I snuggled into his chest to listen to the sound of his heart galloping under his ribs.

"Maybe it's better that we haven't been sleeping over at night because I don't think we'd ever get any sleep," he murmured, palming my bare hip then my bare ass.

"I miss you, though." I sighed.

"Yeah, me, too. Not sure I can keep it up any longer." The serious tone made me look up. His fingertip trailed down the bridge of my nose, and he smiled. "I want you beside me all night."

It had been about a week since we first made love. I'd only technically known him for not quite two months since I'd first opened my eyes, but it honestly felt like longer. Maybe because I was Sadie, and Eddie and I had a history that went far beyond a few months' time. I didn't really care about the reason. I didn't need a reason to be so in love with him. I just was. My heart knew what it wanted, and I didn't want to deny it. Life was too short, life was hard, and though I remembered barely anything, I knew I'd seen a lot of bad in my time. I was going to grasp the good, especially since I still felt it was fleeting.

We didn't talk much about that fear of mine, though it was always there between us. Sometimes we acknowledged it in a passing look or the way our hands clung to each other's before we said good-bye for the night.

Eddie was giving me exactly what I asked for, exactly everything I could ever want.

Happiness. Memories drenched in smiles. Kisses. Hugs. Hot chocolate with whipped cream, popcorn at the movies, and pancakes for breakfast at Maple's. We even carved that giant pumpkin.

I could stay like this forever; I didn't want anything more. Except, yeah, maybe to sleep in his arms every single night.

We'd been holding off on that. Maybe it was our way of not moving too fast.

Okay, fine. It was ridiculous. Ridiculous seemed to work for us. It sure as hell made me happy.

But Eddie wanted to "date" me. To pick me up and drop me off, to show up in the morning with hot chocolate before he had to work, and to kiss me good night at my door before I went to bed.

I loved it—the anticipation of him. Of having my world revolve around him, but not just him. I was building a life outside of him, too. Maggie and I were close. We spent a lot of time together, cooking in the kitchen, watching TV, and laughing. I wasn't ready to give up my time with her to move in with Eddie. She'd become important to me.

"Did you really mean it about me having a job at Loch Gen?" I asked.

His hand stroked up my back. "Absolutely. Whenever you're ready. Take your time."

"I think I'm ready," I answered. "I like it here, this town. I want to become a part of it—not just the town mystery, but an actual part."

"You are a part, Am. You always will be."

"Not as Sadie, though," I whispered. "As me, as Amnesia."

Speculation had only grown throughout town. Rumors were flying that I remembered who I was and that I really was Sadie. I never said a word, though. How could I? I wasn't positive who I was, and I wasn't going to say I was her unless I knew for sure. For now, the only people I'd talk to about remembering my name was Eddie, Maggie, and Dr. Kline.

"Not many people would want to stay in this tiny town," Eddie murmured.

"You did," I said. "Why?"

He gazed at me, the blue of his eyes so deep it pulled me in.

"Because of Sadie?" I whispered.

He nodded, then added, "And because this is home, where my parents are. The general store. That place became a refuge of sorts for me after Sadie disappeared. I spent a lot of time there working, and I sort of fell in love with the place."

"I can see why. It really is amazing."

He grinned, both dimples charming me. "It's a good challenge, keeping the old-school charm but also bringing it into the modern world."

I loved his passion for the store. I could see it in his eyes. I even felt it in the air when I walked in.

"She was lucky," I mused.

He tilted his head. "Who?"

"Sadie. For having you as a best friend and as a crush... maybe even a first love."

"Have you had any more memories?" he asked, rubbing his thumb over my lower lip. He always got a little sad when I talked about Sadie. Even though I was Sadie, I didn't think of myself as her. I couldn't. I couldn't be someone I didn't know and couldn't remember.

All I could be was me. Amnesia. For some reason, I felt I was different than Sadie, the girl I was before I nearly drowned. I couldn't explain why or even how I knew; I just did. Dr. Kline said personality changes after something like what happened to me weren't uncommon.

I shook my head. "No."

Eddie leaned down and kissed my forehead, a gesture I'd almost come to rely on. It was probably the most comforting thing I'd ever felt.

"When do you have to be at work?" I asked.

He groaned. "I have to open."

Pushing up into a sitting position, I reached for the hot chocolate he'd brought. The warmth of the cup against my palm made me smile. "Thank you for the cocoa."

"Anything for my girl." He smiled.

I glanced at the clock and frowned, sticking out my lower lip in a pout. "You don't have time for a shower with me."

"Sorry, baby. My dad would be pissed if I was late."

"I know," I said, understanding. "It's okay."

"Lunch?" he asked.

"Definitely."

He smiled, tugging on the ends of my hair. "I'm doing some scheduling this afternoon. How about I put you on starting next week?"

I nodded enthusiastically. "Can we work the same shifts?"

He grinned. "Duh."

I smiled widely, so happy in the moment.

Laughing, Eddie slipped out of bed, kissing me on the cheek on his way past. "Drink your chocolate, baby. I gotta get dressed."

I made a sound of sadness, and he laughed more. I watched him pull on his clothing, a pair of jeans and a Lock Gen hoodie, and slip his feet into his Adidas. He patted the front pocket of his jeans, making sure his keys were still there, and then held out his hand to me.

Slipping mine into his, I let him tug me to my feet and collided with his chest. I felt swallowed whole when he wrapped his arms around me. Burying my face into his hoodie, I tried to soak up as much of him as I could, enough to last me a few hours.

"What are you going to do this morning?" he asked, still holding me.

I shrugged. "I'll go upstairs and see what Maggie's doing. I don't have an appointment with Dr. Kline for a few days."

"Call me if you need me," he said, finally pulling away. He pursed his lips. "We need to get you a phone, Am."

"Once I start working, I'll be able to."

He frowned. "You need one now."

"It's only a couple weeks." I pointed out.

He grunted as if he didn't agree but wasn't going to argue (at least not right now) and leaned down to kiss me softly. "See you at lunch."

"I'll meet you at the store."

I went with him to the door. His lips lingered over mine before he finally groaned and walked away. Inside, I smiled to myself, carried the hot chocolate and some clothes into the bathroom for a shower, and got ready for the day.

The scent of coffee wafted down the steps when I opened the bathroom door a short while later, and I knew Maggie was up. Instead of going straight upstairs, I put away my pajamas and went back into the bathroom, plugging in the blow-dryer Maggie let me borrow.

Since it was cold out, I didn't want to let my hair air-dry, and I wanted to look nice today since I was meeting Eddie for lunch. It didn't take long to dry my short hair using a brush and the high heat setting. When it was done, I smoothed my hands over it and admired the way it shined beneath the light.

It was less wavy today because of the brush, and I found myself pondering a style as I looked it over in the mirror. The idea of a braid popped into my head, and I wondered if I even knew how.

On impulse, I picked up the brush again and sectioned out a piece in the front, not really knowing what I was doing. The feel of the silky, thick strands between my fingers sent me spiraling back into a memory from the past...

Laughter faded out the instant booted, heavy footfalls sounded overhead. Instantly, I shrank back, my stomach coiling into a tight knot. I shouldn't have laughed. I shouldn't have smiled. It was almost a guarantee to summon him, something I never, ever wanted.

Dragging my body back into as much darkness as I could find, I cowered against the cold stone. My body creaked like I was old, my joints protesting in ways I knew they wouldn't if I were able to get up and move around.

Wouldn't it be wonderful to feel the sun on my skin, the breeze in my hair?

He was coming. All wistful thoughts were banished from my mind. Survival kicked in, and my body tensed. The beam of a flashlight hit me in the face, blinding my eyes. I shrank back, throwing up an arm to shield myself.

"What the hell is this?" he roared.

I began to shake. He surged forward, grabbed me by the arm, and towed me forward. I felt some cuts and scrapes on my bottom and legs break open, and I wanted to cry. They'd just been healing.

"What have you done to yourself?" He raged, grabbing my chin and forcing it up. The light blinded me again. "I told you not to mess with your hair!"

"I'm sorry," I whimpered, squeezing my eyes closed.

The force of the blow knocked me sideways. The metallic taste of blood hit my tongue, and I lay there limply, hoping he would go away. The force of the flashlight hitting the side of my face had made it momentarily blink out, but then it came back on.

"This is MY hair." He seethed, grabbing me by the scalp and lifting me. I yelped, feeling as if the strands were going to rip from my head. "You don't do anything to it unless I say so."

His hands and fingernails were rough and painful as he ripped at the braids in my hair. I cried. When all the braids were gone and the long, thick strands hung over my shoulders and around my face, he smoothed them out.

"Look at that," he crooned. "Just perfect."

I turned my face away.

He grabbed my hair and yanked so hard I fell over. His foot connected with my middle, and I doubled over in pain.

"Don't ever touch your hair again. It's the most beautiful part of you, and I won't have your whore fingers tainting it."

I blinked rapidly, grasping for reality as the memory faded away. My hands gripped the edges of the sink, the skin white, and when I glanced up, I saw my cheeks were wet.

My hair was completely braided, even though I had no memory of actually doing it. It was some sort of braid that looked like a crown; it started at one side of my head and swept over to the other. The back fell straight, slightly curling up on the ends.

Wiping the moisture off my cheeks, I grappled with the memory, the pain and fear I felt. Punished, beaten for braiding my hair?

I shuddered.

Reaching up, I tugged some of the braid so it wasn't so tight to my head. When I was done, I couldn't help but admire the way it looked. It was beautiful. I was good at braiding.

Resolve and stubbornness rose inside me. Screw him. Screw whoever that was and his stupid rules. This was *my* hair, and I would wear it the way I wanted.

Turning from the bathroom mirror, I made it to the doorway when another flash of memory assaulted me, causing my body to sag into the frame.

"I hate you!" I raged. "I hate you more than anything in this world!"

"Don't you talk to me like that!" he spat and backhanded me across the face.

I fell across a table. Everything that was scattered on top went flying. Holding a hand to my battered face, I opened my eyes. Anger welled within me. Frustration and desperation.

The scissors were lying there within reach. I snatched them up and surged to my feet, brandishing them like a weapon.

He laughed. The type of laugh that chilled me to the bone. "Put those down, girl. You can't do nothing to me."

"I'll kill you!" I screamed, waving them around.

He laughed some more.

My body slumped forward. He was right. I couldn't kill him. He'd never allow it. I was too weak.

"You're gonna pay for that," he intoned.

CAMBRIA HEBERT

My head snapped up, anger filling me once more. "No," I said. "You will."

Lifting the scissors, I held out a chunk of hair and snipped it off. I watched the blond silk fall to the dirty, cold floor.

"No!" he bellowed and lunged forward. I scrambled back and cut some more. Again and again, I sliced into my long, perfect hair. The hair he coveted so much. Maybe now that it was hacked up and ugly, he'd have no use for me.

A few moments of him yelling and screaming went by, and then I was tackled. The scissors were ripped away. The sound of the metal slapping against the wall was like a shotgun.

"What have you done?" he roared, wrapping his hands around my throat, pushing so hard I thought my windpipe was going to collapse. I stared up at him, my eyes empty, all feeling gone.

I was happy. Happy for the first time in what felt like forever. The pain etched in his face at the loss of my beautiful hair was sweet.

"You should never have done that," he spat, spittle flying into my face. His hands let go of my neck, my lungs automatically gasping for air. "Bad girls get reprimanded."

"No!" I screamed, rolled over onto my belly, and clawed at the floor to get away.

He laughed, grabbed me by the ankle, and dragged me back. I swung my arm out. My fist caught him somewhere in the chest.

A sound of rage erupted all around me, and he dropped me onto the ground. Large, heavy boots stepped on my fingers, crushing them into the floor and pinning my arm out away from my body.

"I'm sorry," I said, fear making me tremble.

He said nothing as he brought up the other booted foot and stomped down onto my arm just by the elbow.

The bone snapped with a sharp cracking sound, and pain made my vision go dark.

Screams echoed off the walls around me… and pain was my entire life…

I gasped, sagged against the wall, and fought to shove back the memory.

"No more," I pleaded with myself. "No more."

I gazed down at my arm, the one Dr. Beck warned had been broken and healed wrong. Now I knew how it had broken… and why.

The mess my hair was in when I woke up in the hospital, I'd done that to myself. I hacked up my own hair as a punishment for someone else.

But in the end, I paid the ultimate price.

Ache echoed through my arm as if it too remembered that day. With another gasp, I spun from the doorway and back to the mirror. I ripped at the braid, the one I'd just thought of as so beautiful. I couldn't look at it anymore. I couldn't take the chance it would remind me of something else.

Once the hair was smooth and tucked behind my ears, the tightness in my chest eased. I sucked in a deep breath, releasing it slowly.

"Whatever that was," I whispered, looking at my reflection, "that was the past. Someone else. You're safe now, and everything is fine."

I repeated it several times, a mantra. Feeling a little steadier, I left the bathroom to go find Maggie. I didn't want to be alone.

Yes, I was safe now… But for how long?

CHAPTER THIRTY-FOUR

EDWARD

Loch Gen was busy, more so than usual. Part of it was because I was the only one working this morning because all our summer help went back to school. Also, because I'd been kind of neglecting the place, not putting in quite as much work as I used to. I was too wrapped up in Am and spending time with her.

And then there was Amnesia. People were curious about her so they were coming into the store, asking about her, looking for her… wanting to know if we knew for sure who she was.

When she actually started working here, business was going to be steady, at least until everyone got used to seeing her around and the memory of how she came to Lake Loch faded.

I worked out front most of the morning because I had to be accessible to customers. So mostly, I worked on stocking shelves and pulling up the schedule on a laptop at the front counter. It was actually good timing for Am to start here. I could use some daytime help.

The staff here was almost a skeleton crew in the winter because it was such a small town. During the summer, we usually hired high school students or college students home for the season. With Dad taking more time away from the business, I needed someone else to be here with me so I could work in the back or up in the loft when I needed to. There was a lot that went into running this place that required me to not be at the register all day.

Ms. Scarlet pushed through the door midmorning with the same canvas sack she always carried.

"Good to see you, Ms. Scarlet," I said, giving her a big smile. "What can I help you with today?"

"You know damn well I don't need any help, young man," she said in her no-nonsense way. "I'm perfectly capable of doing my own shopping."

"I just got in a fresh shipment of apples," I told her. "I'll be sure to put them out before you come in tonight for your snack."

"I think I'll take one now," she said. "No point in coming back in a couple hours."

"Of course," I said, biting back a smile. She just wanted me to run to the back and get them all out now. "I'll go get them and start stocking."

"I'll be in the back. I hope you got some more teas in. The last time I was in, you were low."

"I sure did. Ordered just the kind you like."

She made a sound and went off toward the back.

I snickered a little as she went. I loved her sassy attitude. After making sure none of the other shoppers were at the counter for checkout, I went into the back to get the box of apples that was delivered this morning. I'd yet to have time to stock the produce aisle. Thankfully, I'd just stocked the tea and coffee.

Hoisting the cardboard box in my arms, I headed out of the back, turning the corner for the produce section. Over the top of the rounded apples, I noticed someone standing right in my path. I jolted to a stop so fast an apple fell over the side and smacked on the floor, rolling away. I watched it, mesmerized by the way it wobbled as it went, only to stop at the toe of someone's shoe. Gazing up, I tried to hide my surprise.

It was the widow from Rumor Island. It took me a moment to place her because of the way she was dressed. I barely saw her face. She wore a large hat with a floppy brim. It was the color of wine. Her long, gray hair hung down over her shoulders and back, and she was dressed in a long denim skirt that skimmed the floor. It was cold out, but she was dressed for winter in a turtleneck with a cardigan. She was even wearing a pair of gloves that matched the color of her hat.

"Mrs. West," I said. "I'm sorry. I nearly ran you over."

She bent down at picked up the apple. "I'm afraid this one is bruised now." She didn't make eye contact. She never did.

Shifting the weight into one arm, I took the offered apple. "No problem," I said, still surprised to see her. She only came into town a few times a year, and it seemed a little early in the season for her to be stocking up for winter.

"What brings you by?" I asked.

"Supplies," she answered, gesturing to the shelves.

I smiled. "Of course. Is there anything I can help you find?" She wasn't holding a basket or even pushing a cart. I couldn't imagine she'd come off the island if she only needed one or two items.

I felt her gaze from beneath the brim of her hat. "No, thank you."

"If you need anything, just yell," I said and moved off to unpack the apples. She was an odd woman. Her weirdness was part of the reason there were so many rumors circling her island.

I tried not to listen to them. I stopped after that night, after a dare took Sadie away.

Some people said they could hear screams echoing from her island in the dead of night. They said she was crazy and would go outside and yell for her husband, the one who died years before. Some people said it was Sadie's ghost, that she roamed the lake, doomed to relive the night she drowned.

I'd lived on the lake for a little over a year now, and I never heard any screams... thank God. I didn't think I could take that kind of torment. Always wondering...

The bell on the front door jangled, and I glanced up from the pile of apples I was arranging. Maggie walked in, followed closely by Amnesia. A smile broke out over my face, and all the dark thoughts about islands and screams in the middle of the night dissipated.

"There's my girl," I said, abandoning the fruit to sweep her into a hug. She giggled when I lifted her toes up off the floor and kissed her cheek loudly.

"You two," Maggie said, smiling, "remind me a lot of me and Chris when we were young."

I sat Am back on her feet, slinging an arm across her shoulder. "It's not lunchtime already, is it?" I asked, craning my neck for the clock near the front.

"No," Am said. "Maggie and I needed some groceries. We're making pasta tonight."

"She's becoming quite the cook," Maggie told me.

Am blushed, all her little freckles turned pink. "I never said it was going to taste good."

"I'll eat anything you make," I told her, patting my stomach.

Maggie laughed. "You should come for dinner."

I made a face. "Wish I could, but I'm going to be working late tonight. I have a ton of inventory that has to wait until my afternoon help gets here."

Amnesia's face fell, and I knew instantly something was wrong. When I caught her eye she smiled at me, but she couldn't hide it.

"I'm going to go get some dog food and a few things back here," Maggie called, heading to the back with a small cart. "Come meet me," she told Am, who nodded.

The second she was out of hearing distance, I zeroed in on Am's face. "What's wrong?" I asked quietly.

"I had another memory," she murmured. I knew by looking in her eyes it wasn't a happy one.

I hugged her close, resting my chin on the top of her head. "I'm sorry, baby."

She exhaled, then pulled back.

"Wanna go talk about it now?" I asked.

She shook her head. "No. It wasn't anything major, just a... memory."

"It upset you." My fingers grasped her elbow, and she flinched back automatically.

"I'm sorry." She gasped, covering her mouth with her hand. Her brown eyes were wide and apologetic. "I didn't mean to pull away... I—"

"It's okay. I'm not upset."

Her eyes filled with tears that threatened to spill over. I wanted to hug her, but I was afraid she didn't want to be touched. I didn't know what she remembered, but my stomach turned anyway.

Whatever happened to her, I hated it.

"You know what? Inventory can wait. I'll do it tomorrow," I said, making a decision. I needed to be with her tonight.

"No!" she said instantly.

"Why not?"

"You've already put this place second to me enough. You need to get your work done. I know how much this place means to you."

I shifted closer, dropping my voice. "You mean more."

"I know." She smiled. "How about I come back tonight, bring you some of the dinner I'm making, and keep you company while you work?"

"You'd do that?"

"I want to be with you," she whispered.

"Okay," I said, trying hard not to cave at the vulnerability she displayed. I knew she didn't mean to, and if I reacted, she'd probably only grow more upset. It was hard, though. So fucking hard not to scoop her up and take her out of here. Not to try and kiss away the worst of whatever haunted her mind.

"Can I stay at your place tonight?" she asked, stepping so close she had to tilt her head back to look up at me.

"You don't even have to ask," I murmured, dropping a kiss onto her mouth.

That seemed to relax her, so I took a chance and hugged her close. She clutched at my back, and my chin rested on her shoulder. "I'm going to hold you all night," I whispered.

Her head bobbed against me.

"I'm ready for my apple, young man," Ms. Scarlet said, appearing out of nowhere. That woman was like a ninja. And old, sassy granny ninja.

Amnesia jolted in my arms, but I pulled back casually, more used to Ms. Scarlet's ways. "I'm just about done stocking up. You can take your pick," I told her with a smile.

Her eyes slid to Am. I cleared my throat. "Amnesia, this is Ms. Scarlet. She has lived here—" I started, but Ms. Scarlet cut me off.

"Since the beginning of time."

Amnesia smiled. "Nice to meet you."

"Let me take a look at you, girl," she said, shuffling closer. Ms. Scarlet handed me her bag, and I took it so she could grasp Am by the chin and study her face.

"Hmm," she said, finally releasing her. "I can see why Eddie is so taken with ya."

"Thank you...?" Amnesia replied.

"He's an ornery one, this boy. When he was young, he used to carry frogs in his pockets. Nothing but trouble," she muttered.

Amnesia laughed. "Frogs!"

Looking at Am, I said, "Ribbit."

She laughed even harder.

Scarlet looked at Am again, then at me. "Could be, Eddie. But I don't think it really matters."

I knew exactly what she meant. "You're right," I said softly. "It doesn't."

Ms. Scarlet poked around in the apples a few minutes and selected only one. Afterward, she took her bag from me and put the fruit inside. "Come along," she beckoned, heading toward the register. "It's time for me to be heading home."

I winked at Am. She giggled. "I'll just go help Maggie."

At the counter, I rang up Ms. Scarlet carefully packing her things back into her bag. "Do you need some help outside?" I asked.

She rolled her eyes. "I'm not an invalid."

"Yes, ma'am," I said.

"And you need to fix that display of rice back there. One of the boxes is loose and dented. I was damn near crushed when I walked by!"

"I'll do that right away." I promised.

I bet when she woke up in the morning, down in hell, the devil sighed.

Even though she told me she didn't need help, I walked her to the front entrance anyway and held open the door. "It was nice seeing you. I'll see you again tomorrow."

Just before stepping outside, she stopped beside me and glanced up. Her white hair was short, her face bore wrinkles, but her blue eyes were clear and sharp. "It's good to see you happy again," she said, reaching out and taking my hand. "It's been too many years since I've seen that glint in your eyes."

"Thank you," I said. My heart held a special place for Ms. Scarlet.

"I know I only just met her, but my old eyes don't miss a thing. She's a keeper. Don't you let her go."

I shook my head. "I won't."

She nodded once, satisfied. "Good."

With that, she walked onto the porch, down the steps, and into the sunshine.

CHAPTER THIRTY-FIVE

AMNESIA

The feeling of being watched crawled up my back like a long-legged spider. Each of its eight legs left a trail of discomfort and a stark need to slap at my skin to brush it away.

There was no spider, though, and as I gazed around, I saw no eyes.

The memory I had this morning had been terrible (to put it mildly), but it hadn't necessarily been the kind to leave behind this creep-tastic feeling I couldn't rid myself of. I did my best to ignore it because I had a life to live.

Maggie already had dog food, dog treats, and ice cream in the cart when I found her by the milk. Glancing down, I laughed. "Priorities."

"That's right," she mused. "Treats for Elmo and treats for us."

Reaching into the case, I grabbed some milk and then moved down to grab some cream cheese and other items we'd put on a list. I'd been cooking a lot with Maggie; she was really good in the kitchen and she showed me how to make a lot of things. I was still definitely learning, but it was fun and I enjoyed the time with her.

"Maggie?" I asked, turning from the case and glancing at her.

"Yeah?" She gazed down at the list.

"You were best friends with her," I said. "With Ann."

She paused, glancing up. Her eyes held a note of surprise but also wistfulness. "She was my very best friend, so close we were more like sisters."

"How did you meet?" I asked.

She smiled. "Actually, it was in this store. She and Clarke had just moved to town, and she was trying to find some ingredient in the aisles. I heard her muttering to herself about being lost. I gave her a tour of the place, and we were friends ever since."

"You miss her."

"Oh, honey. Every single day. Her, Clarke, and my Chris."

That was a lot of loss for one person, and I felt bad for her.

"Do I remind you of her?" I whispered.

Maggie's eyes turned sad. She reached for my hand and gave it a squeeze. "You definitely have the same kind heart."

"She was a good person? And so was Sadie?"

"She was the best woman I knew. And Sadie was her pride and joy."

I nodded, digesting the information and wondering what my life might have been like if I never disappeared. Did it really matter, though? Because I had.

A slight noise behind me caused me to turn and scan around, but no one was there. "Can I see the list?" I asked, brushing it off.

"Sure," she said and handed it over.

We wandered up and down a few aisles, selecting some things, and I stood in the pasta aisle for a long time, marveling at the many different kinds and shapes. "How the heck am I supposed to pick something?"

Maggie laughed. "Get a few."

"Really?" My hair swung around my neck when I turned.

"Of course!"

"Maggie!" a woman called from the other end of the aisle. "I was just going to call you this evening."

"Oh Lord," Maggie muttered under her breath. "Run! Save yourself," she whispered dramatically, then turned back, plastering on a giant smile. "Grace!" she called. "So wonderful to see you!"

She walked away, and I couldn't help but feel she was saving me from an inquisition. I went back to picking pasta and gazing at the jars of sauce. Once I had my choices in the cart, I glanced around to see Maggie still talking to her friend. I headed in the other direction to collect the rest of the items on the list.

I noticed a corner of the store dedicated to T-shirts and Lake Loch merchandise, so I wandered over because there was a stuffed Loch Ness monster on the shelf, and it made me smile. Eddie probably had those made for the store. He said it was the legends of the Loch Ness being spotted here that brought in tourists, but I knew better. He liked it.

The toy was small, just a little bigger than my hand, and soft to the touch. The color was a cross between a green and a blue, a shade that somehow seemed mysterious. There was a long neck, of course, a small head, and four feet/flippers on its oval-shaped body. The tag advertised Lake Loch with the same logo that was on the hoodie Eddie gave me.

I smiled and hugged it into my chest. I thought Eddie needed one of these.

"You don't belong here," a voice said from behind.

I gasped and spun around, clutching the toy to my chest. "Excuse me?"

There was a woman a few feet away with a large hat shadowing most of her face. Her clothes were baggy and didn't have much shape, and she was wearing sneakers with her long skirt.

"I know who you are," she said.

"I'm pretty sure you don't," I said. My heart still pounding, I glanced around behind her, looking for Maggie. Or Eddie. Or anyone really. "I don't even know."

"You're remembering things," she said knowingly. "You don't belong here."

I blinked, not sure how to respond. "Who are you?" I asked. I hadn't seen her around before, yet there was something familiar... Something about her made me very uncomfortable.

"Amnesia," Eddie said, appearing around a shelf.

I practically folded to the floor with relief. "Eddie."

"Mrs. West," he said. "Everything okay here?"

"Of course. I was just introducing myself to the most famous girl in town," she replied.

I recoiled. Eddie's eyes narrowed, but then he smiled. "She's also the most beautiful." Brushing past the woman, he came to my side, angling himself just slightly in front of me. I was grateful for it, and I reached out, clutching the side of his shirt.

"I should be going. I need to get back to my boat." She turned away.

"I'll be right there to check you out," he called, and we both watched her walk away.

"Who was that?" I asked.

"The widow of Rumor Island," he replied.

"She's odd." I shuddered.

He rubbed a palm up and down my arm. "Yeah, she definitely is." He looked down. "Did she say something to you?"

"She said I didn't belong here."

His face screwed up. "What?"

I shrugged. "I'm glad you came over when you did."

He kissed the top of my head. "She doesn't come around often. You won't have to see her."

I nodded, and he reached up to finger the toy still clutched into my chest. "This on your grocery list?"

I laughed. "No. But I saw it and couldn't help but come over…"

"You have a thing for the Loch Ness, don't you?" He chuckled.

"It reminds me of you."

His eyes softened, a small smile playing on his lips. "In that case, you should keep it."

"It's not on the list," I teased, moving to set it back on the shelf.

He made a sound and grabbed my wrist. "Keep it. On the house."

Oh, how his eyes beguiled me. I was pretty sure he could convince a nun to sin and the devil to show leniency. "Thank you," I whispered, rose, and kissed his mouth.

"The cost of that is two kisses," he said when I pulled back.

I laughed. "I thought it was on the house."

"Then kiss me 'cause I'm asking."

I kissed him again. This time I slipped him some tongue. He moaned deep in his throat. When I pulled away, he tried to clutch me back.

I shook my head. "We're at work!" I hissed.

"I'm pretty sure the owner won't care." He winked.

Somewhere in the store, a little bell rang. Eddie groaned. "I gotta go check out Mrs. West."

I wrinkled my nose at the mention of her.

"I'll see you up front," he said, then went off to do his job.

Quickly, I gathered up the rest of the items we needed and met Maggie somewhere in the middle. On our way to the register, I saw the widow walking out, pulling a small wagon filled with bags behind her.

Maggie saw me gazing after her and said, "That's the widow who lives out on the island in the lake."

I nodded. "I met her just now."

"Oh?" Maggie said.

"She's very strange."

Maggie laughed. "Oh, yes. Well, I suppose that's to be expected considering she lives alone with no human contact except for a few times a year."

"Yeah, maybe," I confirmed, watching her figure disappear. But there was something about her I couldn't shake. And oddly enough, the second she was out of sight, that spidery, tingly feeling of being watched went away.

Maybe Widow West was just an awkward, sad old woman like Maggie said.

Or maybe there was something more to her. Something a lot less harmless than people thought.

CHAPTER THIRTY-SIX

EDWARD

I was working in the loft when Amnesia arrived back at Loch Gen. The second the bell on the door chimed, I knew it was her, before I even swiveled around to look.

Brian was manning the front counter, and I watched from above as Am looked around for me. "Is Eddie here?" she asked.

Brian's eyes swept over her, and a fuse of jealousy lit inside me. She was beautiful, and of course people (men, more specifically) were going to look, but I didn't like it. I watched Brian smile at her, then point upward to where I was staring down.

Am swung around. When she found me, a smile lit up her features. "There you are."

I leaned on the railing and smiled. "Here I am."

"Brought you some dinner," she said, holding up a plastic container.

"Get up here, woman," I said, motioning with my head. I heard her rushing up the wooden steps, her feet echoing as she ran. When she made it to the top, I practically lifted her off the last one and swept her into my arms. Burying my face in her neck, I growled, "It's been a long day. I missed you."

"I missed you, too," she said.

After a quick kiss, I snatched the container out of her hand and popped open the lid. "What did ya bring me?"

"Homemade alfredo," she said proudly. Then she frowned. "Do you like alfredo?"

"If you made it, I like it," I said, towing her along with me to the chair at my desk. The second I sat down, I pulled her into my lap. "I'm starving."

She handed me a fork wrapped in a napkin, and I dug in. The sauce was creamy and rich and the wide noodles were cooked perfectly. Making a sound of appreciation, I shoved another bite into my mouth. "This is bomb," I told her.

"Bomb," she echoed.

"Really good. Best ever," I explained.

Pride shone in her eyes. "Maggie helped, but I'm glad you like it."

"Did you already eat?" I asked, scooping more into my mouth.

She nodded. "With Maggie."

I propped my feet on the desk, leaning back in the chair. Amnesia's legs hung over the side, but the rest of her cuddled into my chest. "Tell me about your day," she said.

"It was boring," I muttered.

"I just want to hear your voice." She sighed, pressing a little closer.

Far be it from me to deny this woman anything. I told her about my day, about the stock and the boring spreadsheets, how someone spilled milk in the dairy aisle, and how Ms. Scarlet was *allegedly* almost crushed by rice.

She giggled when I talked, and the sound filled me up in a way no food ever could.

After I was finished eating, she stayed in my lap while I finished up some computer work. Then I showed her next week's schedule with her name on it.

"Two hours 'til close," I said. "You sure you want to hang out that long?"

"Definitely."

"Everything okay?" I murmured, stroking her hair.

"It's been a weird day."

"The memory threw you for a loop?"

Am nodded and sat up. "Yeah. And ever since, I've had this weird sense of... foreboding."

I wasn't sure what to say to make her feel better. I wasn't sure anything could. I kissed her temple and asked, "Still want to stay at my place tonight?"

"Of course," she retorted.

"Good! Come help me downstairs in the stock room so we can finish up and get out of here."

I sent Brian home an hour before closing, and it took nearly the entire two hours to finish up the inventory in the back. Of course, some of that time was spent making out between stacks of boxes... but I wasn't really counting.

At five 'til nine, I turned the open sign to closed and locked up the store. Am and I left out the back entrance, where my truck was parked.

"You can see the moon's reflection in the lake." Her voice was hushed as she gazed down at the water.

"When I was in high school, my English teacher was a real romantic." I scoffed. "She said something one time that made all the girls swoon and all the guys roll their eyes. But even so, I still think about it sometimes when the moon is low in the sky."

Amnesia looked away from the water and the moon and up at me. "What did she say?"

"The sun sees your body, but the moon sees your soul."

"That's beautiful." She contemplated the words. "Do you think it's true?"

Thoughtfully, I nodded. "I think darkness is far more revealing than sunlight."

The drive back home was quiet and short. I parked close to the house. The only light when the headlights went off was from the moon. She waited inside the cab for me to come around and lift her down. I knew she didn't need the help, but it was just one more reason for me touch her.

As we walked along to the back door, Am caught my hand. "Let's walk down by the shore."

"Put your hands in your pockets so they don't get cold," I ordered, reversing direction toward the lake.

"You're bossy," she muttered even as she stuffed the hand I wasn't holding into the pocket of her hoodie.

"Just looking out for my girl," I said, lifting our joined hands and tucking them both into the pocket of my hoodie.

She smiled.

"Do you ever go out on the lake? You know, since that night?"

"I have a couple times. Mostly just to fish. It's not my favorite place to be. It brings up a lot of, ah, memories. Guilt."

"Yet you live on the water." She pondered.

I shrugged. It was a paradox. "Yeah, as much as I dislike the lake, I'm drawn to it."

Her voice was soft when she replied. "I can understand that." After a moment, she spoke. "You blame yourself."

"It's hard not to. If I hadn't insisted on doing that stupid dare, Sadie might still be here."

"I might not be."

I stopped walking, turning so we were facing each other. Down here, the water lapping at the shore was the loudest sound in the night. The breeze off the water was strong, and there was a slight bite to the air.

"I didn't mean it that way." I started. "I'm so glad you're here, but that's eleven years she'll never get back. *You'll* never get back."

"Neither will you."

A disgusted sound ripped from my throat. "I don't matter."

"You matter to me." The words carried on the wind, somehow extending their life.

My heart lodged in my throat, making it hard to swallow.

We walked along some more, not quite close enough for the water to touch us, but enough that if a strong wave came in, it would.

"Tell me what you remembered today." I cajoled, knowing it was hard for her but also sensing she wanted to talk.

"I'm the one that made my hair look the way it did before, all uneven and messed up."

That surprised me. It was probably the last thing I expected. "You cut your hair?"

"With scissors," she admitted. "I did it as some sort of revenge or something. He liked my hair... said it was his, and one day I snapped, started hacking it up to spite him."

I swallowed, the lump in my throat only growing thicker. "Maybe that was the only thing you had in the moment to feel in control." I reasoned.

"He broke my arm in punishment." Her voice was flat, almost disconnected.

I stumbled. "He what?"

She stopped beside me, turned, and all the hair blew into her face, concealing it. It was dark out here, but the shadows in her eyes weren't because of the night. "I can still feel the way his boot pinned my fingers to the floor. He stomped on it," she murmured, her voice far away. As she spoke, her hand wrapped around her arm, near her elbow, as if the pain were still there. "I heard the bone snap."

The string of dark curse words I let loose were ripped away with the violence of a sudden wind. "Jesus," I muttered, pulling her into my chest. "I'm so fucking sorry, Am."

"It's not your fault, Eddie."

I would forever feel it was.

"Did you remember anything else?" I asked, my words coming out harsh.

"No. That was enough."

Wrapping an arm around her, we started walking again. She tucked her hand back into my pocket, though she could have used her own. Tenderness swelled inside me; it matched the anger I was consumed with knowing someone had once treated her that way.

If I knew who it was, I'd destroy him. "Did you see a face in the memory, Am? Something that would help you recognize who did this to you."

"No," she answered, forlorn. "Even if I did, I probably wouldn't recognize them."

Still. A face was better than nothing. We could do police sketches, look at criminal profiles... something. Hell, anything to make this bastard pay.

We walked along a few moments more. Amnesia gazed out across the ever-fluent water and the shimmering reflection of the moon.

"Did they search Rumor Island after Sadie disappeared?" Even though she was right here in my arms, her voice seemed far away.

"They searched everywhere," I told her. "Including the island. More than once."

"What was out there?"

"Nothing. Just Widow West alone on the island in her old house. The police interviewed her a few times, wanting to know if she saw or heard anything that night. The island was looked at closely because that's where we'd been going when the boat flipped."

Amnesia glanced at me out of the corner of her eye. "She didn't see anything?"

"No. They searched the entire island. It's pretty wooded with old trees and bushes. There's a small beach on the back side. That's where the dock is and where she keeps her boat."

"And the house?" She pressed.

"They searched that, too. There was nothing." I'd been angry in the weeks following Sadie's disappearance. Angry with the police for not being able to find her, angry with myself for losing her, even angry with my friends who issued the dare. Everyone in town looked at me with pity and accusation. Even though I was in a shit ton of trouble, I searched with everyone. I searched until I was so tired I nearly fell over, until my feet had blisters the size of silver dollars. "I kept searching, even after the investigation was called off. I was obsessed. I couldn't understand how a person just vanished like that."

"I'm sure you did everything humanly possible," Am said softly, pulling her hand out of my pocket and reaching for mine.

It wasn't enough. "One night I fell asleep on the lakeshore. When my parents found me, I was half in the water, half out. My mom was so upset. I still remember the look on her face." A ghost of a smile tugged my lips. It wasn't funny, not at all, but the way her eyes nearly

341

popped out of her head when she demanded I stop searching was something I could look back on eleven years later and find a little humor in.

"She was worried about you."

I nodded, clearing my throat. This wasn't about me. What happened wasn't about me. Gesturing with my chin, I stared out at the looming shape of Rumor Island. "So why all the questions?"

"There was something about her today. When she spoke to me, all the hairs on my body stood on end."

"She normally doesn't talk to anyone," I said, thoughtful. "She just gets what she needs, tolerates me, and leaves."

"I didn't like her," Amnesia said, fully committed to her aversion.

I turned my back on the water, facing her. "She scared you."

Amnesia still stared out at the lake, in the direction of the island. Slowly, she nodded. "Yeah, I guess she did."

I made a mental note to keep Mrs. West away from Am the next time she came in the store. This was the first time I'd seen her react this way to anyone in town. Usually she had a smile for everyone.

It made the already eerie quality of the island even more so.

"C'mon. it's cold," I murmured, tucking her into my side and steering her toward the house. We walked quietly along. Every few moments, the water would come so close it would splash my shoes.

"Amnesia?" I said, still thinking about what she said.

"Yeah?"

"Do you think the widow had something to do with what happened to Sadie?" What the fuck kind of universe would it be if that were true? That the truth to the town's biggest mystery was actually here right in front of us all this time.

She thought for a moment, then shook her head. "No. The few memories I've had, it's always been a man. There's never been a woman with him." She glanced up at me with a rueful look on her face. "Maybe she's just not a likable person. Maybe that's why she lives alone."

"Well, you're pretty likable."

"I am?"

"Mm-hmm." I agreed. "In fact, I'd go as far as to say you're insanely lovable."

"Insanely?" She gasped. "Why, that's the sweetest thing anyone's ever said to me."

I smiled wide.

Giggling, Am peeked up at me. "You're pretty *insanely* lovable yourself."

I arched a brow as we walked up the steps to the door. "Did you just proposition me?"

"Depends. Did it work?"

Scoffing, I asked, "What do you think?"

The sound of her laughter echoed behind us, drifting out toward the moon. "Good thing we have all night."

Amen to that.

CHAPTER THIRTY-SEVEN

AMNESIA

There was a calmness about Eddie's lake house that no other place quite had. The kind of calm that possessed the ability to blanket the worst of a person's worries and make you feel no matter what, everything was going to be okay.

Or maybe it wasn't his house, with the custom handmade woodwork, the faint scent of fresh paint still wafting in the air, and the constant of the shimmering lake beneath the midnight moon right in the back yard. Yes, all those things drew me like a moth to a flame, but there was something else about this house that I knew was the biggest draw.

Him.

He was the one I craved when my world tilted. His touch was the first one I wanted when the past reached out its cold, boney fingers, and it was his voice that drowned out the echoes of pain my body sometimes ached with.

It probably wouldn't matter if he lived in a charming little cottage or a falling-down shack, as long as Eddie was inside, it would be the place I always wanted to be.

After we came inside, he built a fire that made the inside glow with warm embers and chased away the coldest air of the night. We managed to resist the sparks between us for a short while, but they proved to be too strong, so we left the fire to die out on its own and went back into the bedroom where the only light was from the moon shining through the open curtains.

Eddie was a master at speaking without words. His body talked to mine in the most profound way, leaving me languid and breathless but always with the energy for more. I was grateful for him, for the experiences he gave me, and though I wasn't certain, I still knew deep inside me that I'd never known anything like him before.

I drifted off to sleep against his side, tucked close in his arms, our naked bodies tangled beneath the covers. The house was quiet, the only sounds coming from the blowing wind outside. I always slept soundly with him, always felt protected.

The serenity of the night was disturbed cruelly when a loud banging sound caused my eyes to fly open and tension tightened my entire body. Eddie was still asleep beside me, and I sat up, breathing hard as I clutched the covers to my bare chest. Thinking I'd been dreaming, I sat stock still, afraid to move as I listened again.

Just as my body began to relax, the sound erupted again.

Bang! Bang! Bang!

An involuntary whimper ripped from my throat, and I reached for Eddie.

This time, the sounds woke him and he sat up, instantly awake. "What is it?" he asked, focusing on the way I cowered into him.

"I think someone's trying to get in the house!" I whisper-yelled.

Bang! Bang! Bang!

"Stay here," he demanded, leaping out of the bed.

"Wait!" I exclaimed, trying to grab him back.

He picked up the jeans he'd thrown on the floor earlier and tugged them on, covering up the fact he was naked. "I'll be fine, sweetheart. Just stay here. My cell is by the bed if you need it."

If he's so sure he's going to be fine, why would I need his phone?

The second he disappeared out of the room, I shoved the covers off and quickly pulled on some clothes of my own. Actually, it was my jeans and his T-shirt, but it was the first available. The second I was dressed, I rushed down the hallway after him and into the kitchen.

When he saw me there, he frowned. "I told you to stay in bed."

"I decided not to listen."

He muttered something, but it was short lived because there was more banging, which, standing here, I realized was actually someone knocking on the door.

"Do you always get visitors in the middle of the night?" I asked.

"Who is it?" he yelled, not bothering to open it up.

"It's Mrs. West," a muffled voice replied.

Fear shot through me, and I took a step back. "I thought you said she doesn't talk to anyone in town."

"She doesn't," he murmured.

"Don't open it." I urged, scared.

"I need some assistance," she called through the door. "I had an accident trying to get back to my island. My boat is damaged."

He glanced back at me, then the door. I knew the look on his face. He was completely torn. How could he leave an older woman outside in the cold when she needed help?

"Go back in the bedroom, Am. I'll help her and be right back." After unlocking the door, he pulled it open only far enough to look out. "Mrs. West?"

"Eddie, thank you," she said, her voice relieved. "I've been trying to get back to the island for hours."

"You're wet," he said.

"My boat was taking on so much water. It was all I could do to make it back to shore. I recognized your truck outside, and I knew you would help."

His back muscles relaxed, and he sighed. The door was pulled open wide, and he stepped back. "Come in."

"Thank you," she said. "It's freezing out here."

The instant she walked in, she saw me standing in the doorway. I felt her gaze from beneath the brim of that big floppy hat she was still wearing. Her skirt was wet, and so were the shoes on her feet. I couldn't tell if her sweater and turtleneck were also wet because they were dark.

Though, the ends of her long hair appeared damp.

"Oh, you have a guest," she said, but her voice wasn't that surprised.

Eddie gazed at me with some concern because, once again, I refused to go hide in the bedroom. Latching the door, he walked around the woman toward me, angling so he blocked me from her line of sight.

"I'm so sorry to bother you in the middle of the night," she said.

"It's not a bother," he replied, sounding truly sincere. "You said your boat is damaged?"

"Yes, too damaged to make it the mile I need it to go to the island."

Eddie walked to the window and gazed out, down to the water. "Did you use my dock?"

"No, I used one a few houses down. I knocked on your door because, as I said, I recognized your truck. You're really the only person in town I've spoken to in recent years."

"Right." He nodded, digesting the words. "I don't have a boat, and I won't be able to see if I can repair yours for a few hours when it's light out."

"I really wanted to get home. I haven't spent this much time away from my island in years."

"Well, we can walk next door. I'll ask Tom if I can borrow his boat. I can take you out there and then look over your boat tomorrow and bring it to you once it's fixed."

"Oh, would you?" she asked, very relieved. "I'll pay you for the time and for any parts the boat needs."

"Of course," he murmured. At my side, he glanced back at her. "Just let me get a shirt and some shoes. I'll be right back."

Eddie took my hand so I would go down the hall with him.

The second we were in the room, the door pushed around, I glanced at him incredulously. "You're going to take her out onto the lake? Now?" My stomach churned just thinking about it.

His face and voice were grim. "It's better than offering her the couch for the night."

I shuddered. Staying under the same roof as that woman was a horrendous thought. But so was the idea of him out on the lake. At night.

"I don't want you to go." I worried, chewing my lower lip.

With his boots and hoodie on, he crossed the room, cradling my face between his hands. "I won't be long. Lock the door after me."

Panic gripped my chest. It felt like bone-chilling fingers that squeezed so hard my ribs felt they might snap. Gasping for breath, I trembled all over. "Please don't go out on the lake," I begged. "The last time…" My teeth started chattering, making a sharp snapping sound each time they smacked together.

"Oh damn." He groaned, yanking me against his sinfully warm and cozy chest. His hand stroked the back of my head, and I clutched him close. "All right, baby. It's okay."

I pushed back, my eyes pleading. "Please don't go."

He nodded. "I won't go out on the lake. I'll just walk next door, see if Tom will take her. Or let her use his boat."

"Promise me." I urged.

"I promise, Am."

A tear tracked down my cheek. Relief so strong flooded me. I felt momentarily dizzy. Suddenly, my body was drained, as if I'd just sprinted ten miles. Dr. Kline warned me of the possibility of panic attacks, especially as memories began to resurface, but I wasn't sure if how I was feeling just now constituted as such.

"Thank you." I sighed.

"Anything for you, sweetheart." He kissed my forehead. "C'mon. The sooner I take her to the neighbor's, the sooner I'll be back in bed with you."

My eyes scanned the living room as we walked down the hall. The room was still dimly lit because there were a few glowing embers left in the fireplace. Widow West wasn't standing where we left her, though.

"Where is she?" I whispered, worried.

"Kitchen?" Eddie guessed.

Instead of going straight into the living room, Eddie started to move left, through the wide archway leading into the kitchen.

A blur of sudden movement startled me, and a low cry ripped from my throat. Eddie saw it, too, tensed immediately, and reacted.

He shoved me hard to the right, so hard I stumbled and fell back onto my bottom. But I barely noticed because I was too horrified by what was happening.

"Eddie!" I screamed.

The sound of thick wood connecting to the side of his head was sickening and ear splitting. I gasped and my hand flew up to cover my mouth as his body dropped from his upright position to a crumpled heap on the floor.

"Eddie!" I screeched again, scrambling on all fours toward him, dread clawing at the back of my throat.

"Leave him!" the widow demanded, her voice sharp as a nine-inch nail.

Leaning over Eddie, I gazed up at the older woman who was standing fiercely, a crazed look in her eyes, over his prone body, a giant wooden boat oar clutched in both her weathered-looking hands. Behind her and farther into the kitchen, the door leading outside was wide open, the blackness of the night like a void ready to suck us all away. Wind whipped in from the opening and caused her overly long, gray hair to fly around her shoulders as though she were a witch on a broom.

"Oh my God!" I yelled. "What the hell are you doing?"

Without a reply, she lurched forward. Her boney, icy fingers wrapped around my wrist and yanked. I half rolled over Eddie's body as she dragged me forward.

"Let go!" I screamed and twisted until my arm fell out of her hold. Scrambling to my feet, I stood in front of Eddie, trying to block him in case she had any more ideas about swinging that oar. "I'm calling the police!" I threatened, shuffling from foot to foot. I wanted to rush back to the bedroom for the phone, but I was terrified to leave Eddie here unprotected.

He hadn't moved at all, something that scared me more than this woman, so I dropped back onto my knees, pushed him onto his back, and gently cupped his head. Behind his ear was sticky with a thick, warm substance. Pulling my hand away, I saw my fingers were red.

"Eddie," I groaned. "Wake up!" I shook his shoulders and called his name again.

"Leave him!" the woman demanded, grabbing my shoulder again.

"Get off me!" I screamed and shoved her back. She stumbled a little, and I surged up to go get the phone. I needed to call for help. Eddie needed an ambulance.

"You're coming with me," she said, stepping forward. "Let's go."

"I'm not going anywhere with you," I retorted.

Using the end of the oar, she pushed the floppy hat off her head. It rolled down her back and hit the floor. I gasped. Her eyes were blackened and there was a huge knot on her forehead and a cut in her eyebrow. Even her upper lip was swollen, something I hadn't noticed until now.

"Take a look at me!" she roared. "This is nothing compared to what is waiting for you."

Was that supposed to make me want to come? She was insane!

As if to prove my thought, a wild look stole over her eyes. "I will not take another beating for you. I will not be punished because of your selfish, selfish ways."

"What are you talking about?" I whispered, horrified. "Who are you?"

"I'm here to collect you."

"I won't go with you," I vowed.

The glint in her eyes was cold and mean. Instantly, she swung the long oar down and smacked Eddie again.

I made a wailing sound and threw myself on top of him, shielding his body with mine. "Don't touch him!" I screamed. "Leave him alone."

"Come with me or I'll kill him. That stupid boy is always around."

My head snapped up. How did she know we were always together? Had she been watching me? "It was you," I whispered in awe. "You've been watching me."

"Up!" she said, reaching down and taking a fistful of my hair. Stings of pain erupted over my scalp as she yanked me up.

On my feet, I kicked her, and she made a sound of pain but only gripped harder. "Do it again and I'll smash his skull open where he lays."

The graphic image she painted forced my eyes closed for long moments, which gave her a chance to drag me toward the door. I went with her, thinking to lure her away from Eddie as far as possible. I let her haul me out onto the small porch, my eyes not once leaving Eddie, who had yet to move an inch.

I was scared. Terrified. But I couldn't let the fear swallow me whole. I had to protect Eddie.

The second my feet hit the wooden slats on the deck, I surged up, taking control of my body again and shoving away from the woman. I went to shove her backward, hoping she would tumble down the stairs, but she moved quickly, sliding around me so I was the one with my back to the steps.

"Help!" I screamed as loud as I could, then lunged toward her, hoping to rip the weapon out of her hands.

Unfortunately, she seemed to anticipate my move and countered it with one of her own. Bringing up the oar once more, she swung it like a bat, hitting me square in the face. Pain exploded throughout my head, and I fell backward, grappling for something to break my fall.

All I was able to grasp was air. I sprawled backward, flipped over the railing of the porch, and plummeted, smacking into the hard ground. I lay there stunned for long moments, trying to breathe, to realize what happened, and to get up and run.

But I couldn't; my body wouldn't cooperate, and everything radiated with pain.

The hulking shape of the widow came over me. She leered down.

"No," I muttered, trying to sit up.

"I wish you would just die," she spat, then smacked me again with the oar.

After that, a blackness so intense enveloped me. Not even the light of the moon could break through.

CHAPTER THIRTY-EIGHT

EDWARD

Awareness came back in the form of sharp pain blistering across my skull. Lying on a hard surface with cold air swirling above me, I groaned, lifting a hand to my ear, which was ringing in agony.

Instantly, my fingertips met with a thick, sticky liquid, and reality came rushing back to me so fast it made me nauseous. "Amnesia!" I roared, choking back the wave of sickness and leaping to my feet.

"Amnesia!" I roared again when no one answered.

Wildly, I looked around as I swayed on unsteady feet. Blinking furiously, I forced the world around me to right itself as I looked for my blond-haired girl.

She wasn't anywhere in sight, but the door was flapping open against the side of the house. Screaming her name again, I rushed down the hallway, looking in every room, but the house was empty.

Back in the kitchen, I lunged through the door and onto the porch. It was empty, too. Rushing down the steps, I searched frantically in the yard, cupped my hands around my mouth, and screamed her name again.

Nothing.

No answer.

Just like eleven years ago.

What the fuck is happening right now? Bending at the waist, I sucked in deep breaths and tried to understand. That bitch Mrs. West hadn't needed help. She was insane, and she clobbered me with something hard.

Now she had Amnesia.

The conversation I had with Am earlier by the water came back to me in a sudden flash. There was something about the widow she instinctively didn't like. Something that scared her.

"Amnesia!" I roared, running toward the water because I wasn't sure where else to look. "Answer me!" I screamed.

A wave of nausea made me stumble, and I bent frantically, puking up my guts. The entire time I was heaving and the world was spinning, I thought of Am. Of getting to her before it was too late.

The second I was done, I straightened, wiping my mouth with the back of my hand. Just as I was about to yell for her again, a distant sound slapped the shore along with the waves.

A scream. Someone was screaming. A woman.

I thought fleetingly of the people who said they sometimes heard screams around the lake at night. Screams of the past from people who never got saved, people who were eternally sentenced to reliving whatever torture befell them.

Another scream drifted through the bitter wind.

I knew it was Amnesia. And I knew if I didn't get to her soon, her screams of terror would turn into those that would haunt me forever.

CHAPTER THIRTY-NINE

AMNESIA

The credit for the rude awakening I got went to the bitter, angry gale off the churning water. It sliced through me like a knife, leaving splinters of splitting pain throughout my limbs.

As terrible as it was, the pain was welcome. It meant I was alive. Pain this sharp would only keep me alert, because I had to get back to Eddie.

Eddie!

The single thought of him jack-knifed me up. The urgency of the movement caused everything around me to sway and rock. My stomach rolled, and I reached out to steady myself. My hand closed around rough, hard wood. Even after blinking, my surroundings continued to bob and sway.

Looking around, my wobbly gaze finally settled on the widow. "What are you doing?" I demanded, sitting up to take better stock of my surroundings.

Oh my God, we were in a boat in the middle of the lake. Frantically, I looked around for the shoreline, for Eddie's little cabin. All I saw was darkness.

"Help!" I screamed. "Eddie!"

The oar slammed down on the top of my hand where I gripped the side of the boat. I cried out in pain and cradled my fist against my chest.

"Shut up!" the widow ordered in a harsh voice. She was sitting on the other side of the boat, which could be considered little more than a canoe. The oar she used to bust open Eddie's head and smack me in the face was the same one she used to row us across the lake.

I didn't have to ask where we were going. It was obvious. There was only one place we could go. Rumor Island. I shook my head, confused. That didn't make sense. That was the first place people would look. The second Eddie woke up, he would come to the island because it was Widow West who bashed him in the head.

If he woke up at all.

The horrible thought caused my body to quake violently.

"Hold still!" the woman snapped. "You're rocking the boat."

I tossed my weight around, and the boat reacted instantly. Maybe I'd get lucky and she'd fall out and drown. It wasn't a very nice thought, but there had been much worse in the history of thoughts.

The woman screeched and lifted the oar. "I'll knock you out again!" she threatened.

Shielding my head and face with my arms, I shrank away. "No, please," I begged. I couldn't let her knock me out again. I needed to stay alert. I needed to get away and get back home.

Home. That one thought proved to me it didn't matter where I'd come from. That place wasn't home. Not anymore. My home was in Lake Loch, with Eddie and Maggie.

"You have no idea the trouble you've caused," she retorted, going back to rowing us across the water.

I gazed out, noting how black everything was out here. How low fog clung to the surface of the water, giving everything an ominous look. The moon was low in the sky. From out here in the boat, it almost looked as if it were floating in the distance, a part of the lake, of the mystery of this place.

"I don't understand," I murmured.

"How convenient for you." The woman groaned. "Memory loss. It's the only thing that's kept you alive, you know. If you'd woken up and started talking, you'd be dead."

"You know who I am," I said, desperation in my tone. "Why haven't you said anything? Why didn't you come to the hospital?"

She cackled. "Oh, I did. I came and watched you quite often. No one ever pays attention to the hermit widow from across the lake. I can slip around practically unseen because no one ever expects me to be around."

I stared at her, shocked.

She laughed as if my confusion gave her joy. "You don't remember my visits?"

I gasped, sitting upright. "It was you! You're the one who's been stalking me. Trying to kill me!" I stared at her hard, trying to decide if she was the figure beneath the dark clothes, cloak, and oversized hood. She could be. That last time, I noticed the stalker wasn't much taller than I was... *The figure could most definitely have been a woman.*

"Make no mistake; I wish you were dead. But if I'd been there to kill you, I would have." Her voice was ominous and promising. It was also void of the emotion I expected. It was almost as if she were numb, as if she didn't even know what she was doing.

"What happened to your face?" I asked, observing the mottled bruises and cuts on her face. I wondered if her clothes concealed even more injuries.

"You happened!" She raged. "You and that stupid boyfriend of yours. If you hadn't screamed your head off in the hospital and tried to fight me off, I wouldn't look like this right now!"

"What?" I wondered. She looked half crazed, wet and dry, her hair flying out around her face as she furiously paddled.

She was crazy. Purely insane.

"Every time I came back without you, he got angrier and angrier, until this last time. He beat me so much I was in bed for days." The oar started slapping against the water, not really rowing the boat forward, but creating a lot of splashing and sharp cracking sounds every time it hit. "He told me if I didn't come back with you this time, he'd kill me."

"Who?" I pleaded, desperately trying to remember something. Anything. *The man from your memories.*

I didn't want to know, but not knowing might end my life. It seemed as though it were quickly coming down to dying in the dark or living with the knowledge and likely being changed forever.

"He's going to be livid about your hair." She went on. "I didn't tell him, but he'll see and you'll pay."

I shivered. Her words were proof the memory I had was the truth and not some distortion of my mind.

"You've been trying to kidnap me," I said, thinking of the last time at the hospital.

She nodded. "He wants you back. You're his."

A sick feeling washed over me. I glanced around again, looking for something I could use as a weapon. Or some way to escape. I thought about jumping into the water, letting the dark depths conceal me from view.

My limbs locked up at the idea, and memories of the night I almost drowned filled my head. The last time I was in this lake, I nearly died. Someone tried to drown me. But it wasn't her... The looming figure had been bigger, stronger.

My voice was shaky when I spoke. "If he wants me back so bad, why did he try and kill me in the first place?"

"Kill you?" She scoffed, incredulous. "He didn't try to kill you."

"Yes, he did!" I cried, lurching toward her. She waved the oar near me, clipping me on the shoulder. I grunted and fell back. "I remember! I'd been drowning in the lake, and he was looming above the surface, waiting for me..." I swallowed, pushing the fear that arose in me back down. "The second I came up for air, he hit me with something hard, and I blacked out, nearly drowned."

"Is that what you think?" she mused, once again calmly rowing like this was some Sunday afternoon activity.

"I know," I spat, unnerved by her erratic mood swings.

She chuckled. "You have it all wrong. He never tried to kill you that night. We haven't tried to kill you since."

"But I remember," I argued, starting to doubt myself. An uncomfortable, dark feeling arose within me. I stared at the widow as she rowed.

"Someone did try to kill you that night." She went on, adding fuel to the sick fire within me.

"Who?" I commanded.

Her eyes, which were dark and sort of vacant looking, swung to mine, and though she was looking right at me, it was as if she didn't see me at all.

"You," she answered simply. "You're the one who tried to kill yourself."

The reply was like a current of supercharged electricity slamming into my chest and electrocuting my entire body. I fell back against the boat. The wood on the bottom dug into my scalp and shoulder blades the second I collapsed. I stared up at the endless sky, inky black without the presence of stars. It served as a backdrop for the memory that overtook my brain, flickering to life like a B-rated horror film.

The terror of the present fell away, and I was transported back to the past.

The night I tried to kill myself.

CHAPTER FORTY

AMNESIA

I couldn't hear anything but the sound of my own frantic breathing. My lungs wheezed and burned, but I begged them not to fail. If they did, a fate worse than death would befall me.

I was so out of practice in running, but I did it anyway. It was hard and I was scared, but part of my brain flickered with freedom and the rush my limbs got from being able to move the way they were meant to.

My bare feet were cold and numb. I could feel the flesh ripping with every step I took. The rocky, uneven ground tore into my soles like a hungry wolf after the first scent of fresh blood. I kept going, trying not to stumble as I glanced behind me every few seconds.

I heard him yelling, the sound of breaking branches and rustling trees as he lunged after me. He was angry, so, so angry.

I didn't care. This was my chance, the only one I'd ever had and probably ever would again.

Long-fingered trees reached out to me, my hair tangled in the branches, and I felt it torn from my scalp as I continued to rush.

The smell of earth and water was all around, the air tinged with something sweet... something like honeysuckle.

He hollered again, and I tripped and fell. My hands and knees smacked into the ground, the palm of my hand slicing open on a jagged rock. Shoving up off the ground, I continued running, looking for somewhere to hide.

Not far ahead, there was an old hunting stand. I remembered it from the one time I was allowed on this side of the island. I remembered staring up at it, wondering what the view would be like that high above the ground and wondering if I would be able to signal for help.

Glancing behind me once more, I saw he was out of sight. Hope sparked inside me, an emotion I genuinely thought had drained away completely. I surged forward and leapt onto the tree. The ladder leading up was broken, so I had to climb partially up the tree to get to it.

My fingers and toes shredded on the bark, but I clawed my way up until my hands closed around the ladder and I was able to scramble the rest of the way. Once atop the hunting stand, I didn't admire the view or scream for help. I squished myself as far into the corner, as close to the rotted railing, as I could, rocking back and forth, praying he would forget this place even existed.

The sound of him crashing around below made my body tremble so violently I had to scoot forward so I didn't fall off the edge of the stand. The view caught my eye, and I noticed the endless stretch of lake just beyond the platform. The sun had nearly set; the hour was twilight, quickly fading into night.

Below, the water was moving rapidly, smacking against itself. The color was ominous and turned up a putrid brown shade.

"Got ya!" he growled, his voice nearby.

A small whimper escaped my throat, and I went to the other side of the platform to stare down below the tree. Our eyes met and held.

He smiled.

I wondered if I would see a pleasant smile ever again. I probably wouldn't even recognize what it looked like.

"Nowhere to go now," he intoned and started his climb up the tree.

Frantic, I looked around, trying to figure a way out. But there was none. I was trapped. He was coming for me, and the spark of hope I'd felt only moments ago extinguished.

A tear tracked down my cheek, and I wished for death as I had a thousand times before. Death would be far better than the existence I was sentenced to.

I was young, though, something he loved to taunt me with. As if my age were a weapon. He liked to remind me I still had decades before my body even thought about giving up on me. Decades to be nothing but a prisoner, a slave to be used and abused.

No more. If my body refused to give up on me, then I would give up on it.

He crested the ladder and hoisted himself onto the platform. His dark hair and eyes made him look like Satan. He was practically salivating, and I swallowed back the urge to vomit.

"Stay back," I warned, throwing out a palm to shield myself.

He laughed. "You're mine. Mine to do with what I will."

"No," I said, rallying from my bone-deep exhaustion to put up a final display of defiance. "Never again."

He must have seen the look in my eye, or maybe he smelled the death already clinging to my bare skin. He gasped and started forward, but it was too late.

I took a running leap off the high stand, plummeting into the rocky coastline of the lake. Cold water slammed into me, enveloping me. It slid down my throat and into my nose. My body wanted to rise back up, but I forced myself down and found a moment of pure peace, something I hadn't known in so very long.

Maybe drowning was a peaceful way to die. It was quiet down here. The water didn't hurt me, but sort of cushioned my body as I waited to die.

I'd daydreamed about killing myself, about dying, so many times. I lived in fear, though. Fear of everything around me, of everything done to me. I had even been afraid of dying.

But now I knew. I knew death wasn't scary. It was freedom.

My lungs seized, breaking into the peace I reached for. My body began to fight what was happening, and I surged toward the surface. Even as my brain shouted, No! my body took control.

The closer I got to the surface, the clearer the dark figure became. He was here. Of course he was. He couldn't even let me die in peace.

I hated him.

My head broke the surface, my lungs gulping in giant drafts of oxygen.

"You're mine," he yelled, reaching for me.

I kicked and fought, slapping away his hands.

"No!" I went back under, but he grabbed a handful of my hair and yanked.

I fought him again. My wet body made it easy to slip away. I started to tread backward, though my limbs were sluggish and heavy.

I watched him pick up the oar he used to row out to where I'd been. "When you wake up, your punishment will be waiting," he growled, swinging the wood down.

My body sank with the force of the hit, the dark, cold water claiming my body as unconsciousness claimed my mind.

In the end, it hadn't been a bad way to die. Life had been far, far worse.

I didn't die.

I'd merely fallen unconscious, carried away by the overzealous current, then floated to the surface where I bobbed and drifted to where Eddie had been walking.

He'd been trying to knock me out so he could tow me back to shore. He hadn't tried to kill me.

I did. *I tried to kill myself. I actually prayed for death.*

All this time, I'd been running from a killer, terrified they'd come back to finish the job.

I was running from myself. Scared of myself.

Oh, I was so much more fucked up than I ever could have imagined.

"Amnesia!" a familiar voice yelled in the distance. "Amnesia!"

I perked up, forgetting momentarily about the memory swamping my brain. "Eddie!" I screamed.

"Shut up!" Widow West shrieked and swung the oar at me again.

I was ready for it this time, though, and caught the end before it could smack me. The force of the blow rattled my body and made my arms ache, but I held firm, stopping the hit and throwing all my bodyweight into shoving her and the oar back.

She stumbled and tripped over the side of the canoe, her body making a splash when she hit.

"Eddie!" I screamed again before turning back to where she fell in the water.

"Am!" he roared. "Where are you?"

The widow was sputtering and splashing around. Her angry yells barely registered as I scouted around the bottom of the boat, feeling through the darkness for anything I could use to signal where I was.

The low hum of what sounded like a motor sounded in the distance, and hope spread through my chest that it was him and he was coming for me as fast as he could.

Hope. Not a feeling that was gone forever after all. Maybe all I needed was to forget how it felt to have none at all.

My hand closed around something slim and cold. A sound of triumph slipped from my lips as I found the button and clicked on the flashlight.

"Here!" I yelled, waving the light around madly, trying to signal where I was.

The boat rocked, and I fell backward. The light slipped from my hands, dropping into the bottom of the boat. Widow West was attempting to pull herself over the side. Grappling for the flashlight, I used it to smash down over her hands.

She cried out in pain and dropped back into the water. Clicking the light, I glanced around for the second oar so I could use it to get away from her. But there wasn't one; the one and only oar had gone overboard.

Using the light to create a spotlight on the dark, murky water, I sought out the paddle. It wasn't hard to find. The widow was using it as a floatation device as she stared daggers at me.

"Give me the oar," I ground out.

She laughed.

I reached for it, trying to pull it from beneath her, but she swam backward, out of arm's reach. Frustration welled in me, but the sound of a boat drawing closer made me forget about it. I surged around and began waving the light again.

A shape appeared in the dark. It was a light spot against all the black, and my heart leapt. I screamed his name and waved my arms wildly, ignoring the dizziness in my head and the pain in my crushed fingers.

The canoe began rocking as the boat approached, made a wide turn, and the engine cut. Silence settled over the night, with the exception of the moving water.

"Am," Eddie called across the short distance. "Thank Christ. Are you hurt?"

"I'm fine. What about you?"

"Fine now that I have eyes on you," he said. "I can't get much closer," he explained. "I need you to swim over to me."

I nodded, tossed down the flashlight, and prepared to jump in.

The widow emerged from the depths, somehow throwing herself into the canoe. I stumbled and fell under the unsteady movements of the boat. Mrs. West leapt on top of me, her hands going to my throat.

"I don't care what he says!" She raged. "I'll kill you!"

Her eyes were nearly popping out of her head, the wet strands of her hair in clumps around her face and shoulders. Her icy fingers wrapped around my neck. It was as if she were coming apart right before my eyes.

I felt sorry for her. She was evil and nasty, but I knew she was a victim. Just like me.

Clawing at her hands, I tried to buck her off. The boat rocked madly, and Eddie called my name. There was a splash off to the side, and I knew he abandoned his boat and leapt in to come to my aid.

Fear she would hurt him again provided me a surge of adrenaline, and I rolled, knocking her sideways, sliding out from beneath her. I jumped up, ran to the end of the boat, and searched for Eddie in the dark.

"Here!" he said. "C'mon!"

He was only a few feet from where I stood, motioning for me to jump. I did, but an arm snaked around my waist and yanked me back.

Frustrated, I yelled, swung around, and grabbed handfuls of the widow's hair, shaking her violently. Our struggles were no match for the unsteady boat, and the entire vessel flipped over, plunging us both into the murky waves.

Water tugged at my clothes and hair, wrapping around my limbs in a caress, as if it were trying to convince me to stay.

Maybe once upon a time... back when I was a different girl. Back when I had nothing to live for.

That was then. An entire lifetime ago.

I had so much to live for now.

Kicking my feet, I surged upward, feeling a little out of sorts as I searched for the surface. Everything looked the same down here; the surface was just as dark as the depths.

Panic assailed me. I was lost, unable to find my way to the top.

Just as I realized how badly I wanted to live, death was reaching out its greedy fingers as if it decided it was finally my time to die.

CHAPTER FORTY-ONE

EDWARD

It was eleven years ago all over again.

I watched the boat pitch and rock until she was flung backward into the deep. I screamed her name, watched the surface frantically…

But she never appeared.

Not again. Not fucking again.

Wild, I dove into the water, slicing my arms through the current, searching for a sign of her. In the back of my mind, a clock was ticking. It was the loudest sound I ever heard. It was counting down the seconds I had to find her until I lost her a second time.

My lungs were stinging, begging for air. Angry, I started to kick for the surface, when a flash of color in the dirty depths caught the corner of my eye. Pushing back the urge to breathe, I changed direction and shouted into the water when I saw her struggling not too far away.

I could see the weariness in her body, the way her limbs were trying to give out.

Hang on, baby, I urged silently and gave a great kick to propel myself forward.

My arm wrapped around her waist, and I towed her up toward the surface as black spots began to swim before my eyes. The second air touched my lips, I breathed greedily, hefting her body against my chest.

"It's okay, Am. I got you now," I told her between great gulps.

She didn't reply, and I realized her body was limp against mine.

Adrenaline surged in me again. I snatched her chin and peered down at her face. Her eyes were closed, her skin pale. I swam like a madman toward the boat, begging her to hold on just a little bit longer.

It felt like forever swimming to the boat, but I got there and hoisted her torso over the side, allowing her legs to dangle into the water. Careful not to knock her off, I pulled myself into the boat, instantly towing her the rest of the way in and laying her flat.

"C'mon, baby," I murmured, tilting her chin up and checking for air. My heart stopped when I realized she wasn't breathing, and just like the night I first found her, I began CPR.

It was endless minutes of breathing and pumping. The entire time, I begged her to open her eyes.

Finally, there was a gurgle in the back of her throat. I pushed her onto her side as water emptied out onto the boat floor. When she was done, I sat down, pulled her partially into my lap, and rocked her back and forth.

"Eddie," she whispered, reaching for my hand. I gave it readily, my heart damn near collapsing in my chest.

"It's okay now," I told her, kissing the back of her hand.

"You came for me," she said, her voice hoarse.

"Always," I whispered.

"Cross your heart?"

"Hope to die," I murmured, fighting the emotion trying to choke me up.

Her lips pulled into a smile. "You will be forever mine."

"I love you." I groaned, pulling her a little farther into my lap.

Her teeth began to chatter, and I remembered we were in the middle of the lake, it was cold as shit out here, and someone just tried to kill my girl.

"No time for romance now, baby. We gotta go."

She laughed, but it turned into a wheeze. Concern darkened the relief I felt at finding her, and I flipped a cushion off one of the seats. Thankfully, there was a blanket, and I quickly wrapped it around her shoulders.

"The widow," she murmured, teeth still chattering.

"I hope the bitch drowns," I growled.

Am snatched my arm as I pulled away. "Wait," she implored. "She knows who I am."

"Fuck!" I spat. Truth was I didn't care anymore. Sadie or not, I loved her. But I knew that answer might not be good enough for her. Especially not after tonight. She needed answers. We wouldn't be able to move on until we had them.

If the widow of Rumor Island had them, then I couldn't let her drown.

"I'll find her." I promised, briskly rubbing my palms up and down Am's arms. "You sit right there. Don't move."

She nodded, and I spun around, scanning the darkness for the woman. The sound of splashing drew my attention, and I moved to the end of the boat, closer to the sound. Squinting into the dark and wind, I thought I could make out a shape moving away from the boat, not too far away.

With a curse, I picked up the flashlight I had onboard and shone it in her direction. Sure enough, it was her trying to get away.

I fired up the engine (saying a little prayer of thanks it actually started, because wouldn't that be some shit if it didn't) and made a U-turn, pointing it directly toward her. She saw me, attempting to swim faster, but she was no match for the boat.

I drove up right alongside her, not worried in the least I might hit her. If I did, we'd get our answers some other way. Fortunately for her, I didn't run her down. She was sputtering and coughing when I reached over the side and grabbed a handful of her hair.

"Let's go, psycho," I ground out and yanked her aboard.

I'd been ready for a fight, hell, even primed for one. But she collapsed against the floor almost instantly. Exhaustion clung to her like a newborn kitten to its mother. I grabbed some five-fifty cord out of the same cubby I'd gotten the blanket and quickly tied her hands and ankles together.

She didn't say anything at all. It was almost as if she'd gone catatonic. It was creepy as hell. When she was tied up, I snapped my fingers in front of her face, but she didn't even react. Thinking she could be faking, I stood over her and watched her chest, finally seeing it rise and fall with her breathing.

"Don't move," I growled, but again, she gave no reaction.

Keeping myself on high alert, I picked up Amnesia and brought her to the wheel. Keeping my body anchored around hers, myself positioned between her and Mrs. West the entire time, we flew over the water back to shore.

Glowing blue and red lights served as a guide as I barreled toward shore. Hopefully, Tom wouldn't be too pissed I hijacked his boat without asking.

Not that it mattered. He could be pissed all he wanted. I didn't care. All that mattered was Amnesia was here and she was safe. Although, I did make a mental note that maybe it was time for me to get a boat of my own.

When I drifted to the dock, the police were already there waiting.

"I tied her up," I said, motioning toward the widow. She had yet to move. I was beginning to think she wasn't even blinking.

Everyone was shocked silent, strange for the people in this town, but this was something no one expected.

"What the hell happened?" one of the officers asked as I practically lifted Amnesia off the boat and onto the dock.

Before I raced onto Tom's boat, I'd called 9-1-1 and gave a very basic rundown of what was transpiring—no details, just enough to get them the hell out here.

"She was trying to kidnap me," Am answered, drawing everyone's stare. "She knows who I am and where I've been all these years."

Her teeth started chattering again and her legs gave out. I scooped her up the second she started to sink, holding her close against my chest.

"Let's get you guys to the hospital," the officer said, abandoning his inquiries. "Ambulance is right over there." He pointed.

I left the cops to deal with the old woman as I trudged through the grass toward the waiting EMTs.

I knew this was likely the only reprieve we were going to get from the questions. There were going to be so many. I just hoped, for Amnesia's sake, there were some answers, too.

CHAPTER FORTY-TWO

AMNESIA

We both had a concussion and were admitted for the night. Thankfully, the staff here knew us well enough they didn't even bother putting us in separate rooms. There were two beds in the one they put us in, but only one was going to be used.

Eddie had stitches in his head behind his ear. They had to shave off a patch of his dark curls to stitch the gash the witch had put there. The fact he was able to get up off the floor, with a split head and a concussion, steal a boat, and find in me in the center of the lake was a marvel to the police and the hospital staff.

He saved my life... I'd lost count how many times it was now. After tonight, there were more questions than answers, but I knew something that would never change. I would always be able to count on Eddie. And maybe the circumstances in which we met and fell in love were totally odd and a little unbelievable, but the love was real.

I didn't have any stitches, but I had a knot on my head, various cuts and bruises, and my hand in a cast. One of the bones cracked when the widow crushed my hand with the oar.

The second we arrived at the hospital, everything was a blur. The doctors and nurses bustled around, took us both for CT scans, and made it a priority to get us warm. By the time we were moved into the private room, I was so tired I was dizzy. Or maybe that was just the head injury. Either way, I wanted to sleep.

We weren't allowed of course. So instead, I lay in the bed with Eddie, beneath itchy hospital blankets, and relived the horrors that just occurred over and over again.

We hadn't talked about it yet; there hadn't been any time, and I felt so raw I wasn't sure I was ready. Or if I ever would be.

"You remembered more, didn't you?" Eddie murmured, holding me tight against his chest.

I nodded, tears instantly flooding my eyes. "Something she said triggered it," I whispered. "It was horrible," I rasped, hugging him more fiercely.

"I can't believe old Widow West was behind this all these years," he said, his voice flat and lifeless. "All this time... you were right here."

"It wasn't just her." I began, pulling back to look into his face. There was a bruise on the side of his head where I figured she'd hit him the second time. On impulse, I leaned up, brushing my lips over the area.

He made a soft sound, covering my lips with his. I let myself sink right into his warmth and the softness of his kiss.

The door opened. Eddie drew back first, glancing up to see who was coming in. I was still watching him, his full lips, strong jaw...

"We have a lot of questions," a man said, drawing my attention away. Glancing around, I saw several police officers, Dr. Beck, and Dr. Kline.

"Do we really need to do this now?" Eddie asked, surly. "She's been through enough."

"I'm afraid so," the officer said, stepping forward. "We need all the information you can recall. The sooner the better."

I sat up, still keeping my body against Eddie's, and looked at the people in the room. "I remembered my name," I announced. "It's Sadie. I'm the girl who went missing eleven years ago. I didn't drown. I was kidnapped."

There were low gasps in the room, the ruffling of papers, and a concerned look on Dr. Kline's face.

"Are you absolutely certain about this?" the officer asked.

I frowned. "Not absolutely, but it all makes sense."

"And it was Mrs. West who kidnapped you all those years ago, and she's been holding you hostage against your will ever since?" He went on.

"Yes," I said. Then I faltered. "Well, I can't remember."

"Which is it, miss?" the officer asked, his pen pausing over the pad of paper.

"Watch your tone," Eddie growled from beside me. "She's been through enough."

I patted his leg. "It's fine," I murmured over my shoulder.

"Like hell it is," he muttered back.

"Please continue." Another officer urged.

I nodded and went back to what I was saying. "Earlier tonight, Eddie and I were in bed sleeping when there was a loud knock at the door."

"You and Eddie are in a relationship?" The officer cut in.

"Oh, for fuck's sake, Doug! You know we are!" Eddie snapped.

I winced. "He hit his head. They had to shave his hair. He's had a bad night."

A few people in the room snickered. Eddie growled.

"Anyway…" I went on before anyone else could make him angrier. "Eddie answered the door, and it was Mrs. West. She claimed she needed help, that she'd been trying for hours to get back out to her island."

"We have witnesses that she was in town today at the general store."

Eddie nodded.

"She came inside, and Eddie offered to help her. We left the room for a minute, and when we came back, she attacked us."

"Knocked me out and kidnapped Am," Eddie corroborated.

I nodded. "She knocked me out, too. Next thing I knew, I was on her not-damaged boat in the middle of the lake."

"Where was she taking you?" the officer asked.

"She said back to where I belong. She hates me." My voice fell as I remembered the venom that spewed from her eyes. "She blames me for the injuries on her body and says someone forced her to come and get me. She said he wanted me back."

The room fell silent as my words sank in. The entire situation was sick and twisted. "She was the one who attacked me at the hospital. She's been watching me."

"So you're saying the people who kidnapped you and held you prisoner for eleven years wanted you back?"

I nodded.

"Why?"

"I don't know," I said. "I don't remember."

The officer shifted, glancing up at me. "What do you remember?"

I told them about the first memory I had when I fell in the shower, how I was certain I'd been physically assaulted and abused. I talked about my hair and what I'd done to it, and then finally, I told them about the night I'd somehow gotten away and ran into the hunter's stand.

My voice trembled, my body shook, and horror made me want to vomit.

"And..." I said, stopping to take a deep breath, groping behind me for Eddie's hand.

"We can be done," he whispered, rubbing my back. "I'll tell them to go."

"No," I said, shaking my head. "It's been nearly twelve years of mystery. I don't know much, but I can at least tell what I do."

I felt the attention of every single person in the room. Everyone hung onto every horrendous word.

Taking a deep, shuddering breath, I said it out loud. "That night Eddie found me, no one tried to drown me. I jumped off that platform. I tried to kill myself."

Fat tears slid over my cheeks, and my shoulders shook as I began to cry. Eddie wrapped himself around me from behind, whispering in my ear it was going to be okay.

I felt everyone's eyes avert, an uncomfortable wave going through the room. Everyone pitied me in that moment; no one knew what to say.

After a moment, the officer Eddie called Doug cleared his throat. "So you are claiming to be Sadie Gordon, the girl who went missing at the age of fourteen, over eleven years ago. You were kidnapped by Mrs. West, the widow of Rumor Island, and she held you hostage all those years there on her island. You were regularly abused, raped, and ultimately, in an attempt to get free, you tried to commit suicide. After being found here onshore by Mr. Donovan, you were in a coma for over two months, woke with amnesia, and have since been stalked by the widow until tonight. You were both attacked, and you were kidnapped again."

It was unreal. If I hadn't lived it, I wouldn't even believe it myself.

"Yes," I said. Then I faltered. "But I don't know if she's the one who kidnapped me all those years ago. I know she's involved, but there is a man, someone she seems afraid of... but oddly loyal to."

"You're sure you were held on Rumor Island?" The officer pressed.

I nodded. Then realized I couldn't be sure. I couldn't be sure about anything. "I can't be sure," I said miserably. My eyes found Dr. Kline, who had been listening intently to this entire conversation. "You said my memories could be distorted, but these felt so real. Is it possible everything that's come back to me is true?"

"It's very possible. But as a professional, I can't rule out the fact that not everything you remember should be taken as absolute. There are still large gaps in your memory, still a lot of information unknown."

"So everything we know is basically speculation," an officer said unhappily.

"Not everything," Eddie said. "That witch attacked us, tried to kidnap her tonight. That alone proves a lot of the other stuff."

"It's definitely a lead." The officer agreed pragmatically.

"Are you fucking kidding me?" Eddie said. "Have you even questioned the widow?"

I perked up. I'd forgotten about her. I gasped. "Where is she?"

Doug was quick to tell me, "She's been admitted as well, but not to worry. We have an officer posted at her door."

Dr. Beck stepped forward. "She's in rough shape as well. It's still very early yet, but I can already say she's suffered a lot of abuse."

"But you questioned her, right?" I worried. "She told you who I was? She told you I'm Sadie."

Dr. Beck frowned. "I'm afraid not."

"What?" I gasped, trying to scramble off the bed. Eddie clutched me, trying to keep me from leaping forward. "Let me go!" I demanded.

He didn't; instead, his arms wrapped a little tighter. "Calm down, Am. You have a concussion. Don't make it worse."

"She needs to tell everyone!" I wailed. "She's known all this time!"

Dr. Beck came forward, as did Dr. Kline. "I think that's enough for this evening," he said.

The officer closed his notebook, a concerned look on his features.

"No! Wait!" I exclaimed and stopped trying to struggle against Eddie. "I'm sorry. I'm fine. This is all just very frustrating."

"Memory loss can be, especially when you're remembering things and trying to make sense of what is real and what's a distortion," Dr. Kline said in her schmucky head-shrinker voice.

I wanted to poke her in the eye. How dare she be so calm and nonchalant? Hell, she was acting as if half the stuff I was saying wasn't even real.

I knew real!

"You don't think I'm Sadie?" I said, my voice low.

Everyone glanced at the head shrink. "I think it's very likely you are. Frankly, I'm more concerned with you and your mental health."

What a crock.

"Just ask her," I pleaded with the police. "Just go in her room and ask."

They all shifted uncomfortably.

"What aren't you saying?" Eddie demanded.

Dr. Beck sighed. "Mrs. West is currently in a catatonic state. She is unresponsive to stimuli, her body is unmoving and rigid, and she is not currently able to speak."

I fell back against Eddie, disappointment swelling within me. "What?" I cried. "Why?"

"I think it has a lot to do with what has happened. As I said, she shows signs of long-term abuse, and after hearing about the events of this evening, I'm prepared to say this has been brought on by a psychological illness."

"So she's insane." Eddie deadpanned. "Shocker."

"We won't know more until she begins to respond," Dr. Kline put in.

"But I need to know," I said, desperation clinging to my words. "I need to know who I am. What they did to me all those years ago."

"And you will, remember." Dr. Kline reminded me. "But not all at once. And that's okay."

"I don't want to remember." My voice scraped out of my throat. "I don't want to re-feel all those horrible things done to me. What I do remember is more than enough. I don't want to be changed forever—damaged— over the past. I just want to live in the present, with a clean slate."

Everyone stared at me; no one quite knew what to say.

"All I want is for her to admit that I'm Sadie, for her to tell everyone what they did. I want to *know*... but I don't want to remember."

"It doesn't matter if you're Sadie, Am," Eddie said, brushing my hair over my shoulder and kissing the side of my ear. "I love you no matter what."

My chest squeezed. Turning, my lips brushed his cheek. "I know, and I love you, too."

Facing everyone else, I said, "But I need to know. For me." *For Sadie, the girl whose entire life was ripped away.*

"As soon as we can, we'll question her." Officer Doug assured me.

"How long?" I asked, glancing at Dr. Beck.

He shook his head. "There is really just no telling. Could be hours. Could be days."

"Weeks?" I pressed, feeling dread collecting inside me.

"In some cases." He hedged.

More tears fell. I shoved them away and sat up. "I want to see her."

"No, that's not a good idea," Dr. Kline said.

"Why?" I asked. "It's not like she can do anything more than what's already been done."

"She really shouldn't have any visitors," Dr. Beck said.

I laughed. "Are you kidding me? She tortured me, kidnapped me, stole eleven years of my life! Eddie has stitches in his head, and I know nothing about who I used to be! She owes me!"

"Five minutes." Dr. Beck said.

"The officer will remain at the door," Doug added. "I think that's all for tonight." He continued. "If you think of anything else, call me immediately. Otherwise, we'll be in touch."

The officers left the room, leaving behind both doctors. "Are you sure you want to do this?" Dr. Kline said. "Facing someone who's hurt you so much isn't easy."

"I'm sure." I said, slipping out of the bed.

She nodded. "I'll stay for a while. If you want to talk after, I'll be here."

"Thank you," I said, feeling some of the frustration I held against her soften.

"I'll be just outside," Dr. Beck said. "I'll take you to her room."

When both doctors were gone, I turned and looked at Eddie. He was standing just behind me, his azure irises bouncing between mine.

"So now you know," I told him, my stomach knotting.

His forehead wrinkled. "Know what?"

"That I tried to kill myself." I glanced down at the floor, feeling oddly ashamed, even though I remembered how I felt in that moment. How ready I'd been to die. I whispered, "Does that change how you feel about me?"

Eddie was silent for long moments, longer than I expected.

Nervously, I found the courage to lift my chin, meet his eyes. "Does it?" I echoed.

He swallowed thickly, nodding once. "Yes."

CHAPTER FORTY-THREE

EDWARD

"Yes," I told her. Her face fell, but I lifted it back up with the back of my hand. "It makes me love you even more, something I seriously had no idea was possible."

Amnesia's lips parted with a small intake of breath. "What?"

I smiled, a lopsided grin, making sure my dimples were on full display. "C'mon, Am. What kind of guy did you take me for? I ain't no pansy that can't handle my girl's drama."

I sputtered. "Suicide is not drama."

I chuckled. The pink blooming on her cheeks was a welcome sight. She'd been too pale for too long. "I know," I replied, sincere. "I just wanted to see your face."

Her eyes grew round, shock registering on her face, but then it gave way to a beautiful smile.

"There it is," I murmured, swiping at the corner of her mouth with my thumb.

"That was a serious question," she scolded.

I felt my eyes soften. "And I gave you a serious answer. I love you even more. Remembering that you tried to kill yourself doesn't make me think of you as anything but the strongest girl I've ever known. You're a survivor. You prove it over and over again. I'm so goddamn lucky to have you, and I'm never, not ever, going to give you up."

Her voice was watery, and she sniffled. "Really?"

I made an X over my heart. "Cross my heart."

Am flung herself into my arms and cried all over the stupid gown they made me put on. I didn't mind, though. Anytime she was in my arms was perfect.

"I love you," she said, pulling back. Her eyes found the mess she made of my "clothes," and she winced.

I chuckled. "Don't worry about it," I said, tugging on the ends of her still-damp hair. "Hey, you sure you want to go see her?"

Am nodded sagely. "I have to see her. I have to be sure she's not just faking to avoid being thrown in jail."

"She's going to jail no matter what," I intoned. I didn't care if I had to drag the old hag there myself.

"I feel kind of sorry for her," Amnesia confessed, low.

Shock rippled through me. My body jerked backward, and I glanced down at her as if I hadn't heard correctly. "What?"

She shrugged. "I know I shouldn't. But the way she was acting... almost like she was brainwashed. And she was scared of him, too. He beat her because she hadn't been able to bring me back."

I tried to find a shred of sympathy in my body. There wasn't any. Maybe it all leaked out in the hole she put in my head. "She hurt you," I growled, wrapping my arms around her waist, pulling her close. "I'll never forgive her for that."

Amnesia laid her head on my chest, and I hugged her close for long minutes.

"I should go," she said, pulling back.

"I'm coming with you."

"No," Amnesia said, firm. "This is something I need to do alone. For me. For Sadie."

I didn't like it, but I understood. "How about I stand in the hall?" I compromised.

She smiled. "I'd like that."

We held hands as Dr. Beck led us to Mrs. West's room. Just like Doug said, there was a uniformed officer right outside her door. I had no doubt everything that happened tonight was spreading through town like wildfire.

"Five minutes," Dr. Beck said. "No more."

"Thank you," Amnesia replied, staring at the door with an apprehensive expression.

"I'll be right here if you need me." I assured her, leaning in to kiss her gently.

"I know."

Resting my head against hers, I spoke low so only she could hear. "Whatever you find out in there, it won't matter. You're forever mine."

I held her hand until she was far enough away, and we pulled apart naturally. The officer opened the door, admitting her inside.

I took a deep breath and waited, not caring if the woman ever woke up, but hoping just the same, Am got the answers she needed.

CHAPTER FORTY-FOUR

AMNESIA

Her eyes were open. Unblinking and sort of glassy. She looked like a doll from a horror film, the kind with the round glass eyes that followed you when you weren't looking.

I shivered. Ever since I first saw her at Loch Gen, something about her creeped me out. Of course, now I knew why.

This woman with her long grey hair, pointy nose, and seemingly sad, lonely life took everything from me. I estimated her to be in her sixties, which one would think would make her old enough to know better.

She lay in the hospital bed, the head slightly propped up. Her gray hair was tangled around her shoulders, so long it covered her chest. Her skin was pale, making all the bruises and injuries on her face stand out. Her knuckles were scraped and raw, and she looked thin beneath the hospital gown.

Her body was unmoving, her eyes unfocused, and her mouth in a rigid line. It was almost as if someone hit pause on her controls and she was frozen exactly how she'd been.

Creeping closer to the bed, I watched the monitors record her vitals, listened to the beeping of the machines. She didn't seem to know I was here, and if she did, she was an expert at pretending.

"I know you're faking," I said, stepping close to the side of the bed. "Pretend all you want, but eventually, you'll have to come out of it. Eventually, you'll have to tell them what you've done."

I waited for a reaction, but none came. She still sat prone, her spine-chilling eyes staring into space.

I reached up, snapping my fingers over her face. Nothing. I poked her arm then pulled her hair. She didn't react at all.

"You took everything from me," I whispered. "You and that man who I can barely remember." Leaning closer, I whispered in her ear. "But in the end, you didn't win. I did. I have a second chance, a clean mind, undisturbed by the awful things you did to me. And you're going to be locked away forever."

Maybe it was wrong to taunt her, but it felt good to do so. It gave me some sense of justice.

Leaning back, I stared down at her. "You took me away from Eddie once before. But not again. Not ever again. I love him, and he loves me."

The only response I got was more beeping from the monitors.

Even though she didn't acknowledge what I said, I knew deep down she heard me. I knew my words taunted her, and that small victory made me feel better.

Now all that was left was exhaustion. My head hurt, my body hurt, and I wanted to be in Eddie's arms.

Without a single glance back, I walked away from the bed, leaving her there in solitude.

The second my hand hit the handle on the door, her voice, gravelly and low, echoed through the room. "He doesn't love you."

I spun around, not even sure if what I heard was real.

She was still lying in the exact same position, her eyes still staring blankly at nothing at all.

I was imagining things. With a small shake, I turned back to leave.

"He loves Sadie. Not you."

I whirled around when she spoke again, rushed to the bed, leaned over her, and pressed my face close to hers. No reaction at all.

An eerie feeling stole over me, and my stomach began to tremble. "He does love me," I whisper-yelled at her. "I am Sadie. Why don't you wake up and tell everyone that!"

Maintaining her rigid position, her eyes still wide and doll-like, her hand shot out and grabbed my wrist. Nothing else about her moved.

"You aren't Sadie," she said, her voice sort of like a moan. The stiff position of her mouth barely changed. "Not her."

Shuddering, I snatched my arm out of her grasp and stumbled back, falling onto my butt. Instantly, I surged up and stared at her, chest heaving. "I am!" I yelled. "I am Sadie."

She didn't move or reply; she just lay there like a wax figure, as if she hadn't spoken at all.

I whirled around and rushed from the room. She was faking! I knew it! And I'd felt sorry for her. How dare she try and play me—play us all this way?

"She's awake!" I shrieked, rushing into the hall. "She's faking!"

Dr. Beck came from around the counter, followed closely by a few nurses. Eddie rushed to my side.

"She's awake!" I demanded again, pointing at the door.

Doctors and nurses ran into the room. Even the officer stationed at the door went inside.

"What happened?" Eddie implored, looking me over for injury.

"She grabbed me," I said. "And she…" My voice trailed away. Eddie was watching me, encouraging me to finish.

He loves Sadie. Not you. You aren't Sadie.

Her words suddenly hit me like a ton of bricks. I stumbled back, my knees suddenly weak.

"Amnesia…" Eddie worried, catching me by the arms, supporting all my weight. "What happened in there?" he asked again, lifting me into his arms.

I pressed my face into his chest. Tears squeezed out from the corners and ran crookedly down my face. Why would she say something so horrible to me? Hadn't she already taken enough?

Now she wanted to take my identity. My future.

Dr. Beck came back out into the hall, a frown darkening his features.

"Well?" I demanded.

"I'm sorry, but her condition is unchanged. Are you sure she became responsive?"

"She grabbed me!" I insisted. "She spoke!"

"What did she say?" Eddie asked, concerned.

I looked up into his blue eyes, his patient, caring face. I knew he told me it didn't matter who I was… but what if it did? What if I told him what Widow West said and it changed everything?

Worse yet, what if she was lying, trying one last time to hurt me, and I really was Sadie, just like I remembered?

So many unknowns.

"I…" I glanced at Dr. Beck. He too was waiting for an answer. "I couldn't understand what she said. It was more like moaning."

Yes, I lied. But hadn't I earned the right to lie if it meant protecting myself?

"I see," Dr. Beck remarked. "Perhaps she did move, but she is still catatonic. I'm afraid she won't be able to answer any questions at this time."

I nodded.

"You should go back to your room. Rest." Dr. Beck gazed at me with concern. I guess I'd earned the look. "I think it's best you stay away from her from now on."

"I think you're right," I told him.

"I'll let you know if her condition changes." He promised.

"Thank you," Eddie said and carried me back to our room.

Once inside, he laid me on the bed, climbed in behind me, and fitted his body along mine.

"What did she really say to you in there?" he whispered, brushing his fingertips down my arm.

I paused, lifting my head to glance over my shoulder at him.

He smiled, kissing my shoulder. "I know my girl."

"So you do," I muttered, laying my head back down.

"She upset you."

"Yeah, she did." I admitted. "She just keeps trying to take things away."

"I won't let her, sweetheart." He promised, settling closer against me. I tugged his arm so it was tighter around my waist. I couldn't lose this. Him.

"I'm not ready to talk about it," I told him.

His reply was simple and accepting. "Then we won't."

A few moments later, my voice filled the room. "I love you, Eddie. So much."

"I love you, too, baby," he replied.

"This isn't over yet." I tried in my own way to warn him. I wasn't even quite sure what I was warning him about.

"I know."

"I'm scared," I acknowledged, the words that I might not be the girl he lost after all on the very tip of my tongue.

Eddie rose, my back flattened on the bed. Our eyes met and held. I searched for something in his stare that might prove the deep-rooted fear the widow somehow planted. I didn't see anything but love there.

"Don't be scared," he murmured, rubbing my cheekbone with his knuckles. "We're together, and as long as we are, everything is going to be just fine."

"Promise me." I urged, grabbing his hand and squeezing.

"Cross my heart," he said seriously. He mouthed the words *I love you.*

I believed him. I knew he loved me. I felt it. Hope, the emotion I remembered after I'd forgotten it all, welled up inside me, growing in strength with the look of love in Eddie's gaze.

Maybe he was right. Maybe as long as we were together, everything would turn out just fine.

I smiled. He lay down, and I snuggled into his chest.

Even though he'd made me feel more at ease, the widow's words still haunted my thoughts.

You aren't Sadie.

I couldn't help but wonder if she was right. If I would ever know the truth. And if I wasn't Sadie...

Who was I really?

THE END

FOR NOW...

Look for the conclusion to Amnesia and Eddie's story in the upcoming novel **AMNESTY** *by Cambria Hebert.*

Coming Summer 2017

More books by Cambria Hebert

The #Hashtag Series

#Nerd

#Hater

#Player

#Selfie

#Poser

#Heart

#Holiday

#Bae

The GearShark Series

#Junkie

#Rev

#Swag

#Blur

#FinishLine

Standalone Titles

Distant Desires

Maneater

Whiteout

Blank

The Take It Off Series

Torch

Tease

Tempt

Text

Tipsy

Tattoo

Tricks

Tryst

Taste

Trashy

Taxi

The Heven and Hell Series

Before

Masquerade

Between

Charade

Bewitched

Tirade

Beneath

Renegade

The Death Escorts Series

Recalled

Charmed

AUTHOR'S NOTE

This book feels like a triumph. After spending nearly three years with the *#Hashtag* and *GearShark* series, the hangover was real. And so was the doubt I would ever be able to write anything again. Well, maybe not write anything; I knew I could write something. The question was if I would ever be able to write something I loved as much or even connected with.

The doubt was compounded when I started a different book, and it was like pulling teeth (with rusty, dirty plyers) to get any words written. The inspiration just wasn't there, and for someone who has spent a whole lot of time writing over the past six years, it was kind of scary.

The idea for *Amnesia* was one I kind of had on the backburner. I loved the idea of writing about someone who forgot everything, how it seemed her very existence was a mystery. I kept the idea in mind, and one night, I was talking to my daughter about it while we watched Lifetime movies (hello, guilty pleasure!). She gave me the idea of the protagonist being the one responsible for her own memory loss through suicide. I was so intrigued with the twist. It lit a little fire of passion inside me, and I thought a lot about that girl. About what would drive her to kill herself, and if she woke up in the hospital with her mind wiped clean, would her personality be different? Would whatever made her want to die be gone and the will to live return?

I was scrolling through Facebook (as I often do) one day, and I happened to run across a premade cover in a cover group I belong to. The second I saw it, I was immediately haunted by the image. Some images just have that ability, you know? To pull you in, to linger in your mind even after you look away. They haunt you. This one haunted me. The second I saw it, I was first struck by the beauty and mystery in the image. And then I was double struck when I realized it was absolutely perfect for the story swirling around in my head. The idea of a mysterious lake, a small, almost old-fashioned town with gossipy people but a tight-knit community beckoned me. I saw lobster rolls, a lake, brick streets, and a charming town boy with blue eyes.

I wanted that story instantly. I bought the cover on the spot. Then I went back to writing the other book I was supposed to be working on. But this one wouldn't go away. I couldn't get it out of my head. The characters called to me in a way that excited me.

Just to see what would happen, I put aside the other book and started this one. And now we're here. A finished book, a passion, and me sitting here with butterflies because I managed to write a book I love, proving to myself that the magic didn't die with the *#Hashtag* crew.

I know it's different than what I've written in the past, and maybe it's not what you expected, but I do hope you love it anyway. I hope the mystery of the island, the beckoning of the lake, and the intense (almost obsessive) way Eddie loves Amnesia climbed into your heart the way it did mine. More than that, I hope you're looking forward to *Amnesty*, the final installment of Eddie and Am. And who knows? Maybe if we all fall in love with Lake Loch, there will be more stories about this little lake town in the future.

Special thanks to my editor, Cassie, for getting this one done lickety-split and Marisa-Rose Shor at Cover Me Darling for providing the perfect cover that lit a fire in my heart and inspired this book. And my daughter, Kaydence, who watches cheesy Lifetime movies and plots morbid yet intriguing stories with me.

As always, thank you for reading. Thank you for reviewing. It's very appreciated.

See you next book!

XOXO,

Cambria

ABOUT CAMBRIA HEBERT

Cambria Hebert is an award winning, bestselling novelist of more than thirty books. She went to college for a bachelor's, couldn't pick a major, and ended up with a degree in cosmetology. So rest assured her characters will always have good hair.

Besides writing, Cambria loves a caramel latte, staying up late, sleeping in, and watching movies. She considers math human torture and has an irrational fear of birds (including chickens). You can often find her painting her toenails (because she bites her fingernails) or walking her Chihuahuas (the real rulers of the house).

Cambria has written within the young adult and new adult genres, penning many paranormal and contemporary titles. She has also written romantic suspense, science fiction, and, most recently, male/male romance. Her favorite genre to read and write is contemporary romance. A few of her most recognized titles are: *The Hashtag Series, GearShark Series, Text, Torch,* and *Tattoo.*

Recent awards include: Author of the Year, Best Contemporary Series (The Hashtag Series), Best Contemporary Book of the Year, Best Book Trailer of the Year, Best Contemporary Lead, Best Contemporary Book Cover of the Year. In addition, her most recognized title *#Nerd* was listed at Buzzfeed.com as a Top Fifty Summer Romance Read.

Cambria Hebert owns and operates Cambria Hebert Books, LLC.

You can find out more about Cambria and her titles by visiting her website: http://www.cambriahebert.com.

Made in the USA
Columbia, SC
20 August 2017